Yours,
Q^3

Yours,

**A Novel by
Richard Davis**

ALLIANCE HOUSE

Published by Alliance House
220 Ferris Street, White Plains, NY 10603

Manufactured in the United States of America
ISBN 0-9665234-0-7

0 9 8 7 6 5 4 3 2 1

For Patricia, Anne, Geoffrey, Jon,
Christopher, Timothy, and Nicholas

. . . and at approximately 1530 hours on September 194—, the battalion commander led elements of C Company in poorly fitted boats across 400 yards of the Draas River and attacked strongly defended enemy positions. During the subsequent engagement, his combat team of Parachute Infantry destroyed fortifications and captured the northern approaches to the railroad and auto bridges intact. For conspicuous leadership and disregard for his personal safety . . .

—From the citation for the
Distinguished Service Cross, awarded
to Lieutenant Colonel Alexander C. Dunham,
October 194—, Beek, Holland.

R E S T R I C T E D

Contents

Yours,

D^3

One
Destination

An empty bottle smashing against the floor interrupted her irascible shouting.

"Dammit, Alex, you've hidden my wine again. Where the hell is it? I've looked in the laundry basket and through all of the closets. If you've poured it out, I'll smack your silly face."

A tall blond boy about fourteen stood at the kitchen door listening to his mother's drunken outburst. A frown and pinched lips emphasized the sadness in his solemn green eyes.

"Come on, Mother, let me help you to bed. If you don't, you'll hurt yourself again. No more falls." He raised his voice. "You're so drunk you can't walk."

"Alex, why do I need your help?" She jabbered on. "You're a self-righteous goody two-shoes like that father of yours. Always trying to be perfect. Now listen to me; I've got my own friends who will take care of me. The best ones are in a drink filled with ice."

She stumbled toward her bedroom, where Alex propped her head on a pillow, slipped off her stained blouse and shoes, then covered her. She had fine black hair that framed a high forehead. Her bright red lipstick was smeared. He loathed her pungent alcoholic breath and the odor of cigarette smoke clinging to her hair and clothes.

"Mom, what got into you? Why don't you play tennis and golf anymore, the way you did with Dad? I remember how you both laughed and joked about scores. A few years ago I was your caddy, remember?"

"Alex, go away and leave me alone. Baseball...don't you have a game or something to do tomorrow? Get your own breakfast. Don't wake me up."

"I'm going to kiss you goodnight now," Alex whispered. Her flailing arm swung at his face. He pushed her hand away. Chipped, red fingernail polish.

"If you kiss your friend Roy Sorrels, why can't you kiss me? You know I never understood why you would kiss a man with a mustache. It must rub your nose and really tickle something awful."

He touched her cheek, brushed back her hair, then held her hands. They were soft, like his flowers. She was snoring and seemed to struggle for each breath. He turned off the light and quietly shut her door.

Later that night she telephoned long distance to Chicago and taunted his father.

Alex cringed when she yelled, "Brian, we live like gypsies out here in California. You're such a big professor now and make all of that money, but you still don't send us a dime. You'll always be the same strutting peacock who thinks he knows it all. We never counted; you weren't ever home. You married me because you needed a maid. It's your fault; you've made me what I am. You'll hear from my lawyer this week, and by the way, don't dare ask to speak with Alex."

The following day, as the cool autumn afternoon deepened, Alex sat on the lawn fidgeting uneasily when dew began to dampen the seat of his pants. He shifted to the sidewalk leading to the front door of his house, where warmth seemed to lessen his discomfort. Taut arms held his bent legs. He looked down at the scuffed toes of his shoes and one folded pant leg, held by a metal clip that kept the cuff from being shredded by his bicycle sprocket.

Occasionally he glanced across the street at the Japanese gardener who edged a neighbor's lawn to perfection. The new, shiny 1933 Ford "tin lizzie" truck with wooden door panels was parked in the driveway, and from time to time Alex scanned each piece of equipment in its chosen place. As the gardener finished the day's work, his precise movements suggested that it was time for Alex to find a way into his house. Friday nights were habitually late ones for his mother and her various companions. Alex had been locked out again, and there was no key under the door mat or two large flowerpots in the patio.

The modest one-story Spanish bungalow was like others on the block, with rounded red roof tiling and brightly colored shutters. His somber mood was temporarily buoyed as he slowly walked through the small backyard enjoying the variety of sweet peas he had proudly planted and nurtured. He gently touched their pastel petals.

He hesitated after several steps, then turned and ripped down the neat rows of his prized flowers, tucked some blue ones in his pocket, stuffed the rest in a paper bag, and threw it in a garbage can. He had planted them to please his mother, but there had been too many men, then those friends in the bottles who made her feel best of all.

After failing to open the arched wooden front door, he shook the knob of the glass-paneled back door. It wouldn't budge. He sat down on the back stairs, squeezing his hands, frustrated, angry.

Someone in the neighborhood was burning eucalyptus leaves, and the scent reminded Alex of many early evenings when he ate dinner alone in small, nameless diners or drugstores. He seldom went to the same restaurant. No one would know he never had dinner at home. He studied in the school library, then returned to his mother and another new boyfriend. They ignored him.

He pulled out his father's weekly letter, crumpled from being pushed in and out of his jacket pocket. As usual, it was typed in blue print, with more significant words in red. The importance of the letter was punctuated by the large red air-mail–special delivery stamp with a menacing eagle. There were the usual indulgent reminders, to study and compete with his classmates. Had he finished *Jeb Stuart*? *Yes, Dad. Read it three times. His bold cavalry charge around the Yankee army in Virginia. Youthful leader, victorious. His panache, his plumed hat. His daring tells me I can succeed.*

He jumped up, escaping his momentary reverie. It would be now, he thought. He must run away to his father and his new wife, Lucky, where he would have a home. There would be no turning back. He repeated aloud, "Dear Son," and, "Love from your Dad."

He shattered the glass of the kitchen door with a fist wrapped in a dirty cloth from the garage. Turning the knob, he felt sharp pain in his wrist and noticed several glistening tan bands gliding in unison. Blood ran down his hand. He showered, wrapped the cut tightly with a roll of gauze, put on his only starched white shirt, tie, and school blazer, and tried to double-knot the laces of the new shoes that Lucky had bought for him last summer. Before leaving, he snatched his orange toothbrush with black stripes and smirked with perverse pleasure, confident it would never be next to the one "Snortzy" Sorrels had put in the holder above the bathroom sink. His favorite books, *The Grey Knight* and *Jeb Stuart*, were secured with his school belt and thrown in the rear basket of his maroon Greyhound racer.

Tonight, the handlebars were down for more speed, and during the next hour he deftly navigated the evening traffic to the Santa Fe railroad station in Los Angeles. One final look at his two-wheeled friend, then he walked through the station, with its echoes of arrivals, departures, and the hum of an impatient crowd.

During several weeks of his summer vacation that had been spent with "Poppie" and "Nanna," he had learned some of the important details of railroads, trains, conductors, porters, and the complexities of Pullman cars. His grandfather, A. C. Dunham, was a retired locomotive engineer who entertained him with countless stories, took him on visits to engine roundhouses, and glorified his lifelong work. Poppie would ask Alex to bring lemonade from the icebox; then, taking another route to the kitchen, his grandfather hid under the stove and, as Alex passed, would leap out with a terrifying roar. If he stood and faced his imaginary opponent, he was given a loving hug. Alex could still remember the smell of his grandfather's pipe and his insistence that Nanna not call Alex her "sugar doll baby."

Alex entered the station, decorated with brightly colored Spanish murals that extended to an arched blue ceiling. Then he skirted the main entrance gate to the "Chief," turned back to the platform, and mingled with the fashionably dressed passengers and their friends. There were men sporting tweed suits with highly polished shoes and spats, and their ladies wore short pleated dresses with low waistlines and long strings of pearls. Some of the passengers carried dark wool coats with velvet collars, and there was a scattering of feathered, broad-brimmed hats worn by women waiting to board the train.

The fierce profile and headgear of the Indian emblazoned on the electric sign fixed to the rear railing of the observation car seemed to be sternly warning him about running away. He looked at his challenger with equal defiance.

He greeted the porter with assurance, then stepped on the small stool and confidently walked up several steps through the open door. He looked at the flawless black uniform and shined buttons and shoes and saw the familiar brass plate on the front of his peaked cap that read, "Pullman." It shone in the fading light of the open station.

"Mighty pleased you're with us, sir, and let me know if I can be of service." The porter's voice was accommodating and seemed friendly.

"I'm Alex, and my parents are in the next car forward. I have an upper berth, and for now I shall sit out on the platform of the observation car. They know where I am."

"How far are you going, Mr. Alex?"

"Chicago. It's cold there now, always is at Thanksgiving."

"I'll come back and let you know when the dining car opens. 'Bout an hour or so after we pull out."

Alex would have to give this suggestion some thought but had an answer ready.

According to Poppie, the engineer knew his business, because there was no perceptible lurch as the train first moved, then gradually increased its speed. As the rhythm of the wheels striking the evenly separated rails quickened, the station, a colored variety of boxcars and passenger cars, switch engines, and then the skyline all became a purple blur. Alex sat in one of four canvas chairs on the observation platform and now suspected he could reach his new home.

Suddenly he had a feeling of being drawn inside when the porter opened the door and announced with formality, "Mr. Alex, this is the last call for dinner."

Three harmonious tones on the miniature xylophone, carried with pride by a dining car waiter, emphasized the point, and other passengers in the observation car began to walk forward to the diner.

Alex wondered, "Thank you, Mr. . . . . ?"

"Tyler Green, sir." The porter smiled.

"Mr. Green, my parents are discussing business with a friend, and asked me to have a sandwich back here before I go to bed. I'm in upper berth C, and I'll manage. Thank you very much."

Each week, his father had enclosed a crisp one-dollar bill with his letter, and sometimes there was a small felt pennant of a different college. Alex had saved five dollars and had several quarters in his jacket. He pushed open the large glass door to the observation car, walked up to the bar, and ordered a chicken sandwich and chocolate ice cream. Ostentatious lamps were secured to each small table with an ashtray and magazine in a leather-bound cover. His chair was large, luxurious. He relaxed, watching the dull brass spittoons as they tilted back and forth, occasionally disgorging their ugly contents on the carpet. The car gradually emptied as cigar-smoking gentlemen with gold watch chains and glittering tie pins unceremoniously swayed, trying to overcome the abrupt side-to-side motions of the train. Alex was formally served by the barman wearing a trim white jacket and bow tie. He carefully arranged a small tray on a side table. After paying his bill, Alex had four dollars and judged he was still quite rich. It was enough money to buy one or two more meals before reaching Chicago.

Returning to the observation platform, he slouched in a chair so his head wasn't visible. The penetrating coolness of the night air whistling around the end of the train prompted him to roll up the collar of his jacket and sit arms crossed, hands buried inside his blazer pockets. He must have dozed several hours. When the Chief made its first stop, he slipped forward in his chair, then woke.

The two orange signal arms turned a vivid green, their brilliance blinding. The train quickly gained speed. A station clock read three-thirty. He had been aboard almost eight hours. Alex pushed open the door, brushed fine cinders from his jacket, and groped through the darkened coach that Poppie condescendingly called the booze car. He had to hide another four hours before daylight. Locking himself in the toilet, he sat down, leaned back, and closed his eyes. The heat, smell of the small compartment, and motion of the train were a suffocating combination that forced him to open the door every few minutes.

Later, there was a resounding knock on the bathroom door, and when he tried to push the latch, he felt a deep, searing pain in his hand and arm. He pulled the door open, tumbled forward, and sat on the long leather bench of the adjoining men's room. Several passengers were shaving and brushing their teeth with a violence that Alex thought his hand could never endure.

Tyler Green asked, "What's that blood doin' on your hand and shirt? Mr. Alex, you don't look right this mornin'. You is pale in the face."

Alex went to the nearest of three metal basins and vomited. Tyler gently wiped the boy's face with a cold towel and helped him back to the bench, where he sat with his head between his knees. His plight was unnoticed by other passengers, and when they left Tyler sat next to him. He wore red suspenders over his gray undershirt with long sleeves.

"Mr. Alex, things ain't right, are they?"

Last summer his grandfather had introduced him to the small-town undertaker. Formidable, black suit, black hat. Alex could feel his clammy, spongy hand. He must never be afraid. He tried but failed to move his arm and fingers. Sweat ran down his face and neck. His shirt collar choked him. Warm, hot, then cold.

"Look here, son, I know you is here alone and there ain't no folks of yours on this train. That's our secret, but we got to tell the conductor before Kansas City. Understand?"

Alex looked up into the man's large, stubbled face. He had soft black eyes, and tufts of gray hair rimmed his hat. The boy nodded but said nothing. Kansas City wasn't far. The timetable read for arrival about five in the afternoon.

The porter led Alex to an empty compartment and covered him with a blanket brought down from the upper berth. Alex guessed he had slept several hours when Green opened the door and gently pressed his shoulder. The squat, red-faced conductor stood in the frame of the door, and his importance was emphasized by a large, powerful ticket punch tucked in a vest pocket. His pants were speckled with tiny dots of paper debris from hundreds of tickets.

The large man's voice was gruff and intimidating: "Look here, sonny boy, you have no business on this train and it beats the hell out of me how you made it this far. You musta set some sort of damn world's record sneakin' 'round the two crews before I come on. Show me your ticket, if ya got one."

"First of all, sir, my grandfather, A. C. Dunham, is the greatest engineer this railroad ever had and ran your trains for thirty years. He's retired now and lives near Chicago. Next, my father is a famous surgeon. If you send him a telegram from Saint Louis, he will pay for my ticket and come to the station to meet me. After all this time, you can't put me off the train now and if you . . ."

Alex tried to hold the conductor's pen for the telegram but

couldn't move his arm. He felt a strange numbness and tingling in his fingers.

The conductor's orders were emphasized by a nasal midwestern accent, and he spoke with a contemptuous grin revealing stained teeth and a foul tobacco breath. "All right, all right, sonny boy. Green here says you're an OK kid, and we'll telegraph your old man. Gimme the name, address, and phone and we'll get you straightened out one way or another in Saint Louie. If you're not on the up and up, it's good night, Jackson, sonny boy."

"My name is Alex, not 'sonny boy.' Thank you for your help, Conductor. I'll stay with Mr. Green for the next few hours."

Alex watched the conductor saunter through the aisle and remembered how Poppie had once told him that an unpleasant and rude person was a "rummy." He thought the massive-looking conductor qualified for his grandfather's distasteful sobriquet.

No longer threatened by discovery or having to hide, Alex lay down, rested his arm on a pillow, and slept restlessly. After the Chief left Saint Louis, Tyler Green brought in a large bowl of soup and announced that Alex's father, "the doctor," would be waiting for him in Chicago. Both smiled wryly and the porter began to rumble with deep laughter.

Alex turned off the light, lifted the shade, and stared into the night with his nose pressed against the cold window. The edges were framed with gently curved frost. The lights of a passing car and an occasional station interrupted the darkness, and he could see flurries of snow swirling up from the wheels of the train. He remembered his mother's constant hacking cough, frequent confinements to bed, and contempt for the doctor, who was unable to control her outbursts of abrasive temper and unpredictable behavior. She had warned Alex if he left and lived with his father, it would either make or break him. Alex was never quite certain what she meant. But he knew he must go to his new home. There was the memory of his father's warm but restrained friendship and love, his encouragement to study, read, and be a good student. There would be Lucky's laughter, gaiety, and understanding, and parents who would always be home at dinnertime. He saw his room with its dresser and mirror, a bookcase, and the six colored prints of Civil War battles. One of Jeb Stuart's gallant cavalry charges hung in a place of honor above his desk. He thought about the warmth of his bed with its green-and-red tartan blanket and was thankful for more sleep.

He was roused by the sound of plaintive engine whistles and the high-pitched screech of train wheels as the Chief moved across switches that were kept from freezing by small, well-placed fire boxes on the rails. He sat up facing Tyler Green, who had brought a metal carafe engraved with the Indian Chief logo.

"Have some of this, Alex. It'll make you feel better."

"Mr. Green, my grandfather always said coffee stunts your growth, but I'll take my chances. Thank you very much." He swallowed some, then drank the rest.

He waited patiently in the vestibule between the Pullman and observation car watching Tyler help ladies with their coats and luggage, guiding passengers down the steps, sending them on to the redcaps.

Tyler reminded Alex, "You got to comb your hair and straighten your tie. Now put on your jacket and come with me. It's time to find your father; how's that?"

The cold air struck Alex's face and he began to shiver when he reached the platform. The throbbing pain in his arm and the snowy wind made his hand feel strangely alien, phantomlike.

Tyler wrapped him in a gray blanket with a sterile smell; then they walked toward the station with the porter's arm around the boy's shoulder.

"Dad, Dad, I've come home." Alex leaped out of the cocoon-like blanket and ran toward a handsome man whose camel hair coat, dark scarf, and coconut-colored felt hat distinguished him from others in the crowd.

Dr. Brian Dunham reached for Alex, holding his disheveled son, whose sooty face was now streaked with tears. In the emotion of the greeting, his hat tumbled off onto the snowy platform. He leaned over, meticulously brushed the brim, and began speaking to the porter.

Alex interrupted, "Dad, this is my friend Mr. Tyler Green.

He saved me from the conductor and helped me come home."

"Mr. Green, you have been extraordinarily kind to my son. I hope he behaved himself. Sometimes he does foolish, reckless things."

"Sir, you can be proud of Alex. He wants to be with you. I wish I had a boy like him."

Doctor Dunham spoke with Tyler for several minutes. Alex saw his father reach in his pocket; then the two men shook hands.

"Alex, you are back home now, so it's good-bye. Be a good boy and always do what the doctor says. He has the right medicine for you, understand?"

Alex tugged at Tyler's sleeve and looked into his kind face. They quietly said good-bye.

The stale, warm air of the Union Station was of some comfort, but Alex was chilled and from time to time his tall frame shook uncontrollably. He studied his father's fine features, blue eyes, and dark hair parted in the center. As Dunham asked some pointed questions about his son's journey, he saw streaks of blood on the sleeve of Alex's blazer. He picked up Alex's bluish hand and asked him to move his fingers.

"Dad, they don't work now. Please get me home and I'll show you."

Alex watched his father's graceful hands as he rolled up his sleeve, gently took off the red-stained bandage, and asked what had happened.

"I hurt myself trying to get in the house, but it will be all right. Please take me home right now. I need something to eat—you know, those good pancakes, bacon, and orange juice. Let's go, Dad; come on." Alex was insistent.

"Son, how long ago did you cut yourself?"

"It was before I left California." Alex looked into the deep wound, then closed his eyes and tasted coffee as it came back into his mouth.

Brian Dunham took off his coat and draped it around his son. They walked to the cab stand and within ten minutes were at the west door of the University Hospital.

Alex automatically turned into the doctors' lounge, lay down on the large sofa, and listened to the firm, authoritarian instructions.

"Lumsden, this is Dr. Dunham. Have George Ekert and his staff meet me in the emergency room, now, and that means now. Don't keep me waiting; I want him to examine my son, who has injured his hand."

Alex thought the young doctor must have understood, because soon he was on a stretcher and a nurse, with a slight scent of perfume, had snatched off his coat and quickly split open the sleeve of his shirt.

"Miss, please don't do that," Alex implored. "My father gave it to me for Christmas last year and it's the only good one I have." She put a hand reassuringly behind his head. He fell backward.

Alex looked up at Dr. George Ekert's smooth, pale face and closely cropped white hair. "Good morning, sir."

"I haven't seen you in a couple of years, Alex, and your father says you're grown up now. Why don't my staff and I have a look at the arm. All right, 'professor,' steady-on and this won't bother a bit."

After Ekert examined Alex's hand, he said, "Brian, he has several severed tendons and part of the nerve has been damaged. How long ago, Alex, my fine-feathered friend?"

"Sir, a couple of days ago, I guess."

"Don't guess, Alex, how long ago, and have you had anything to eat?"

"Maybe a day or so, Dr. Ekert, but I haven't eaten anything for a long while, honest." Alex wondered what all this timetable talk meant.

Ekert nodded at Dunham. "Brian, we'd better take the 'professor' upstairs now."

There seemed to be so many doctors in white jackets and gray coats that Alex couldn't find his father. Confused, he tried to sit up. "Where's my dad?" he shouted.

His father leaned over and explained that he couldn't move his fingers because some cables and a wire had been cut. "Dr.

Ekert will sew the ends together. Son, there's no need to be afraid."

"Dad, I'm not afraid, but Poppie and Nanna would be angry if you weren't there."

"Of course I'll be with you, Alex. Now the young doctors and nurses will do some things before you go upstairs and then will fix up your hand and arm so they work again."

Alex thought "upstairs" probably meant the operating room. He looked at the walls lined with pale green tiles neatly separated by gray grout and judged each was about four square inches. There were glass cabinets in the walls with strange bundles and what must have been instruments. He heard soft voices, sensed far-off movements, and was startled by a bright light shining on his arm. He felt warm water, a strange-smelling soap, then a cold rubber mask over his face. Someone stroked his forehead as the ceiling quickly narrowed into an endless tunnel. He tried to cry out that he was being smothered, but his voice was only a hollow echo as he took deep breaths.

"Give me more 'fluffy duffy,' and if you would only cut the tape and not tear it. Tearing tape makes such a dreadful sound," Ekert complained. "As usual, I'm surrounded by ineptitude. Please help the doctor."

Alex moved about as he woke up. "I don't care about your tape, Dr. Ekert. Where's my father?"

He glanced at his hand and arm wrapped in a cumbersome bandage that looked like an oversize boxing glove. His wrist was bent and he thought it hurt more now than before his operation. He dropped back on the pillow of the stretcher and was wheeled to his room. For several days an overpowering smell of ether would permeate his clothing, the air of his room, and the taste of his food.

Brian Dunham waited for his son and then propped him up in bed with the help of nurses. Alex was still drowsy as he looked up at his father and again became aware of the iridescent quality of his eyes. They were blue, speckled with brown dots. He decided they were a bluish-gray. When his father spoke, Alex watched and listened. His thoughts drifted to the past. Fatigue broke his concentration.

His father explained how Dr. Ekert had carefully repaired the cables and wire to his hand. He was reassured, happy to be home. "When can I leave the hospital?"

"You must be here at least a week, perhaps longer. Lucky will bring some turkey dinner for Thanksgiving, and we can have a long talk about going back to school as soon as you feel better. Son, you'll like the Academy."

That night, Alex roamed the hospital halls. He felt the simple elegance of trim linoleum floors, green walls, and warm mahogany paneling that extended to the ceiling. Casual, friendly conversations with the nurses assured him the week would pass quickly. Dr. Ekert and his staff changed his dressing each day. The unwieldy boxing glove became smaller.

"Thank you very much, Dr. Ekert. I know I would be paralyzed without your help. Will it be long before I can move my fingers again?"

Dr. George Ekert was humorless, made no commitments, and seemed strangely indifferent, as if Alex were only one of many patients to be seen during a busy day.

"Alex, don't speak while I take out your stitches. Every time you open your mouth you spray millions of germs into the air, and they could infect your wound. Why do you think I have this mask on?"

Alex had no idea about masks or infections; he only wished to speak with Dr. Ekert, who once had seemed to be his friend. Perhaps one of the other three or four assistants would answer his questions. He wanted to know if he could play baseball and football and try out for the Academy basketball team this coming winter. Instead they followed their surgical chief from his room as if they were automatons. Alex had the absolute conviction, a gift endowed by youth, that his father was a different sort of doctor. He would be kinder and answer the questions of his frightened patients and their families. Alex thought he would be more personable, sympathetic with their fears, generous with his time. He also knew his father was a rock-hard disciplinarian.

Lucky came to the hospital to visit her "new" son each day. This afternoon she wore a tan knit suit with pleated skirt and matching soft hat. A gold seashell with a centered pearl completed her wardrobe. Hands reveal age. Her skin was slack, with shallow valleys, and translucent with fine veins. An emerald engagement ring and gold wedding band were on tapered, delicate fingers. Small wrists and hands complemented her slight, attractively groomed figure. Lucky's speech and captivating smile expressed wit, an infectious contentment.

She sat at his bedside and held his bandaged hand. Her accomplished Russian accent was flavored with a southern drawl. "Alexi, Alexi, my secret lover, I have brought you a feast fit for the czars."

"Lucky, please hurry up with your treats, Russian or not. I'm so hungry my stomach thinks my throat's been cut."

She unpacked a warm turkey dinner while Alex sat in his pajamas eating so much and so fast that he was embarrassed to finish first. She told him hilarious jokes and stories about her childhood and imitated Dr. Ekert to perfection.

"Lucky, I've always thought you were secretly an actress. Would Dad let you go to Hollywood? I bet you could probably make Dr. Ekert laugh when he comes to see me."

"How would I know? He's so afraid of germs that he wears a mask all the time. Right, Alexi? You know, your father and I can barely hear him, although there's nothing wrong with his voice. George was good enough to take me downtown one day, and you can imagine he's an awfully careful driver. We were in front of a streetcar and the conductor got annoyed because George held up traffic. It had rained and he was afraid of skidding on the wet, muddy street. The streetcar bell rang and rang and finally George turned around and said in his loudest voice, and believe me, Alex, it was nothing more than a whisper, 'Oh, mister, just be quiet'."

The three laughed joyfully about George Ekert's peculiarities and habits. After turkey and desserts, Alex began to nap. He could barely hear Lucky pack up the dishes and silverware. Sleep, he needed sleep. She kissed him. They would come back tomorrow and take him home after Dr. "Don't Make So Much Noise" Ekert had finished Alex's final dressings and given him his instructions.

He was awakened by shocks of pain in his fingers. Other than a small wall light, his room was dark. He walked to the window, fascinated by the snowfall that cloaked the outside world. Flakes were being driven by the lake wind. He picked up his bathrobe, and after he drew it over his shoulders, a piece of paper fell out of the breast pocket. He switched on the light and read the note:

From the desk of Dr. Brian Dunham:

Dear Alex,

Listen carefully to Dr. Ekert tomorrow morning. He is a fine surgeon and will tell you what to do and when to come back and see him. Don't forget to thank him again. Ask questions if you have any. You are grown up now; pay strict attention; obey his orders. Never be late for your appointments. Sleep well. Jeb Stuart is waiting to see you.

> *Yours,*
> *D3*

Alex wondered what "D3" meant and puzzled over some of the possibilities during the next few minutes. Perhaps it was a short way of saying "Dad" or a lucky number, had something to do with Poppie, maybe was an important date in medical school many years ago, or was it simply his laundry number that was stamped on the collar of his shirts? It occurred to Alex his father might have a special way of saying he was happy to have his son home at last. The "3" could be an abbreviation of the words *I love you.*

It must have been a miracle, repairing the wire and cables in his arm and hand. They would move again. He sat down, stretched his long legs, and looked into the falling curtain of snow, drowsily wondering if he could be a doctor someday.

Two
Beginnings

There had been a heavy snow. The sidewalks were cleared, allowing people to pass. Some bumped shoulders as they hurried through the piercing cold air. Soot, small bits of blowing paper, and an ugly collection of trash had gathered on the shoveled mounds. Alex waited at the corner for Buzz Smith to blow his high-pitched whistle directing endless streams of traffic and the flow of pedestrians. Precariously tilted double-decker buses, assorted trucks followed by trails of fumes, and every type and shape of automobile obeyed his commands. He moved energetically, holding one arm high, waving frantically with the other, admonishing indolent drivers with insulting sharp blasts of his whistle.

"How are things today, Alex?" Buzz always found time to greet his young friend.

"Not bad, thanks, Buzz. The cold makes my arm and hand

17

ache like the devil, though. Those good-looking girls at the hospital say I'm a lot better." Alex smiled confidently; however, he had lingering doubts.

Buzz walked with him across the wet, slick street. "See you tomorrow, big fella."

People said this was *the* place to live. The tall apartment buildings cast long shadows over the snowy park bordering Lake Front Drive. Near the entrance of his parents' building, an elegantly dressed woman in a fur coat lifted her small dog, outfitted in a Scotch plaid vest, onto the snowbank. Alex turned as she carefully wiped its backside with several pieces of toilet paper, which were then casually tossed into the snow. This ceremony of the city was finalized as she kissed her dog's frosty nose, whispering words of endearment: "What a divine poo-poo, angel puss."

Alex looked out over the frozen lake. There was a hard, steely fascination to his new city home—no palm trees or delicious smell of orange blossoms. Still, it was friendly in a different, strangely vitalizing way.

Colleen, the Irish maid, answered the doorbell. She was spotless, with chaste white shoes matching her starched uniform. Her cuffs were rolled, revealing large red hands roughened by hard work. She was friendly, with no-nonsense directness.

He asked Colleen, "Are the folks home?"

"Laddie, you always ask the same question and I always give you the same answer. Of course. They're in the library this time every afternoon. Don't fret. Let me help you take off your heavy coat. How's that banged-up arm?"

"Thanks, it's much better now. What smells so good in the kitchen?"

"Just finished a batch of brownies. Come on out and have one before dinner. How 'bout a glass of milk?"

"I'm right behind you, Colleen." She laughed as he stuffed the whole square of chocolate in his mouth, trying to swallow some milk at the same time.

"You seem like a happy young fellow since you've been with us. I hear you whistling, playing that noisy Victrola, and singing in the shower. It must be my cooking, correct, Alex?"

"You hit the nail on the head. I've never had such good meals in all my life and don't miss the California sunshine."

"Now that you've spoiled your dinner, run upstairs, say hello to the doctor and missus, and show them that big broad smile. Be my jolly lad."

Alex chatted with his father early each morning before he went to the hospital. He was intrigued by the skillful honing of his straight razor and large puffs of lathered soap, never a blemish on his face. Alex waited in the library while his father showered, then watched with delight as his tousled hair was transformed from that of an unruly aborigine to fatherly handsomeness. He vigorously applied his hair tonic, "Lucky Tiger," which was the magic potion allowing him to comb his thick black hair profiling a strong face, with a prominent jaw and a large nose. The two had breakfast together and read the sports page, after perusing the funny papers. They agreed "Dick Tracy" and "Little Orphan Annie" were their favorites. Brian Dunham routinely walked to the hospital. His operations began promptly at eight o'clock. Each afternoon at one, he met Lucky for lunch at the nearby Parkside tea room, then returned to the hospital or office to see patients and attend necessary meetings. They were home at five, read in the library, and dinner was always served at six-thirty.

During the weeks before Christmas, Alex happily kicked his way through snow and skidded along icy sidewalks to the hospital, where his hand and arm were exercised in a room like a gymnasium. At times he was embarrassed; however, he enjoyed the young women who were his therapists. They joked about his height and would tease, "Dr. Dunham has the brains, but Alex has the looks."

Dr. Ekert tested the strength of Alex's hand each Saturday morning. Six weeks after his operation he could make a fist and write. The doctor showed a faint compassionate smile. "Good work, Alex. I know you're giving it the old college try. Take this ball and squeeze it as often as you can. Don't overdo it, because the tendons haven't completely healed."

George Ekert would turn and abruptly leave, followed by his

staff, who had hovered over Alex's hand as if it were some phenomenon, a never-before-seen appendage.

Alex regularly had lunch at Walgreen's drugstore and became a familiar figure at the soda fountain. In the afternoon, he was tutored in French and Latin in preparation for admission to the Academy in mid-January. Walking home, he passed the neighborhood skating pond with a small hut where youngsters warmed themselves and changed clothes. He blinked from the low sun that glanced off the ice and savored the laughter and carefree shouting of teenagers who would probably be his classmates. Sometimes he had a longing for old friends in California ... the tree houses, afternoon baseball games. Dancing school hadn't been as wretched as he remembered. He often thought the dull ache in his hand and arm was punishment for the upheaval in his life, leaving his mother, being a runaway and outsider. He remembered the old Saturday escapades when he and his friends would "crash" the exclusive Del Mar Beach Club to swim away the afternoon. Their parents were not members, and their pranks had never been discovered. This mischief would be restrained now.

A friendly, attractive nurse who treated his arm and hand always asked about school, sports, and family. She gently stretched his fingers, opening and closing them on his palm. "Right now you're sort of in limbo, worried about classes at a new school, getting strength back in your hand, but who knows, Alex? One of these days you may have a girlfriend."

He wasn't quite certain about being "in limbo;" however, he knew the tingling disappeared when she held his hand longer than necessary, then looked into his greenish eyes. *Girlfriend, appealing idea. Consider it*, he mused.

Harried passengers shoved and pushed in the bus designated "Madison Street—The Loop." Alex and Lucky sat wedged together. She had a quality that made him feel wanted, a mother's care, a mother's concern. It was time to shop for school clothes.

Lucky was attentive. "Alex, you are absolutely my wonderful vagabond. You should have gray flannels, Academy blazer, ties, and, of course, saddle shoes. We'll find pajamas, a bathrobe, slippers, and socks in another department where they have shirts with button-down collars."

Alex felt sartorial. "Lucky, you're changing me into the well-dressed man for *Esquire*. It could actually be better than going to school."

Next he placed his feet under an X-ray gadget that measured shoe size. He wiggled his toes, which were strange misshapen green objects.

"Young man," the salesman announced solemnly, "you are extremely fortunate, because your shoes fit perfectly and you will never have bunions. If you take care of these saddle shoes, they'll last a lifetime."

Lucky looked over his shoulder, smiling. "A year will be fine; then we can come back for the black-and-white ones and we'll find out if you're right."

Alex, overwhelmed with his plunder, kissed her several times and proudly carried a treasure of attractively wrapped boxes to the taxi stand.

"Chasing rainbows, Alex?"

Lucky had arranged two crystal fish between candles in the center of the dining room table. She would smile when he moved his head from side to side, fascinated by the changing spectrum of colors.

"Lucky, you have made a beautiful home for us. At times I like to daydream about it. I've never seen a dinner table like this before. Sometimes I went to a restaurant, a diner, but now each night it's a treat being with you. After today, I feel spoiled. You know I'm your lucky kid." He winked impishly. "Get the pun? 'Lucky kid'."

As dessert was being served, Alex questioned his father. "Dad, please tell me about the hospital and your operations."

There was cool firmness. "Alex, why don't you tell me and Lucky what you think about President Roosevelt and our depression? Is the country making a recovery and are people going back to work?"

Alex hesitated. "Well, everyone has more confidence than two years ago. I've read about the banks being closed, special work camps for young men, and jobs being started by the government. The president's fireside chats have helped. But I wanted to know about what a doctor does every day and if the studies at medical school are difficult. I can always read the newspapers and magazines about the president."

"Alex, I'm afraid FDR is leading us down the path to socialism and big government, more taxes, and welfare programs. That's probably what you meant to say. Incidentally, Son, at dinner Lucky and I enjoy interesting conversation other than medicine."

"Well, our country's problems are important," Alex continued. "But from what I have heard on the radio and read, I'm worried about Hitler. Is he really a dictator like the newspapers say?"

"Think about it, Alex. Could anyone be elected president of this country with only thirty-seven percent of the vote? Of course not. Hitler is a tyrant, and freedom in Germany is a luxury of the past. Keep reading the papers and news magazines, and you'll learn more about foreign affairs at the Academy."

Alex's father paused, then winked at Lucky.

"This Saturday morning we're going to the old skating pond around the corner. You will meet a young lady who always says good morning to me on her way to school. She's quite European, you know, a slight curtsey when she speaks."

Alex objected. "But, Dad, I can't ice-skate, and if it involves any girls I am not interested."

"Son, you and Lucky discuss it. I shall be there at ten o'clock, and if I know Lucky, so will you."

Her persuasive southern accent and exaggeration convinced Alex that Stephanie Pfeiffer was not only "the belle of the ball," but the world's greatest ice-skater.

"Come on, Lucky, what sort of a girl would have a name like that? Who can spell *Pfeiffer,* anyhow?"

"Alex, do exactly as your father says and you'll have a good time. You can rent skates from Oscar at the hut, and your new orange-and-black sweater and knit cap will keep you warm. Perhaps Miss Pfeiffer might look twice? She should."

Saturday morning Oscar was sweeping snow off the pond as fast as it fell. Dr. Dunham continued to insist that it was a good morning to skate.

"Now, Dad, I'm a California swimmer. Don't expect too much."

Alex wobbled along the ice, promptly fell, and continued to fall. He braced his hands on his knees, stood, and managed to skate haphazardly for several minutes before sliding on the seat of his pants. His father looked amused, yet encouraged him in what was becoming a tortuous process of survival. At the end of an hour, he seemed to enjoy his progress and found a remote part of the pond where he could practice unnoticed.

He was covered with snow from the last tumble, and when he began to skate again a confident girl in a white wool turtleneck sweater and pale blue skirt flashed by and stopped suddenly in a spray of ice. Her blond hair was tucked under a matching blue beret, and her smile had an attractive poignancy. "You can do better than that, can't you?"

Alex stubbornly continued his attempts, then finally sat down, brushed himself off, and rested his twisted ankles. His father was enjoying the warmth of the hut and having a casual conversation with Oscar.

"You've got a fine-looking son there, Doctor. How old is he now?"

"Almost fifteen, Oscar, but tall for his age. Needs a little more weight, don't you think?"

"He'll grow up right in front of your eyes. He doesn't seem to give up on learning how to skate. It'll only take a few weeks for a young fellow like him."

Alex rubbed his mittens for warmth and stood when Stephanie skated toward him.

She sat down and adjusted her laces and beret, looking at

him with warm blue eyes. Snowflakes clung to her eyebrows and beret.

"You must be Alex Dunham. I talked to your father in the hut a few minutes ago. It looks like you're a beginner. Keep trying; it can be fun."

Although his face was cold, he blushed. His mouth was dry. "Yes, I'm Alex. Moved here a couple of months ago. People in California don't ice-skate."

"Why not come out again next Saturday?" she trifled. "Guess what? Maybe I'll be here."

Alex slid backward on his clumsy-looking skates. A tantalizing feeling. He would see her next week.

Lucky thought the holiday season was an ideal opportunity for him to meet new friends at the Girls' and Boys' Academy. She arranged for invitations to several dances, although Alex seemed disinterested.

His father sensed his son's irritability. "It's Christmastime, Alex, why so moody? Nothing to say tonight? Son, stop bouncing your heel and tapping your foot, right now. Can't you see you're shaking the whole table?"

"Dad, do you realize I have to meet the headmaster at the Academy for my interview? It's this week; what will I say?"

Brian Dunham smiled benignly. "Alex, listen carefully, and answer his questions honestly. T. O. White is a fine gentleman whom I've known for a number of years. His son, 'Tombo,' will be a freshman with you. His younger sister was a patient of mine and, fortunately, recovered from a serious accident."

Alex looked at him admiringly. "Gosh, Dad, you sure must know everybody. Thanks a lot. I really appreciate it."

That night Alex laid out his clothes for the morning meeting with Mr. White. Everything was in order. Alex tried to continue the arduous task of learning French verbs but fell asleep at his desk. Several hours later he pulled off his sweater and crawled under the bedspread. It seemed only minutes before he was awakened by his shrill alarm clock. He quickly showered and, when he put on his blazer, found a note in one of his pockets.

From the desk of Dr. Brian Dunham:

Dear Alex,

Be yourself; speak up; tell him what you're interested in. He knows about the French and Latin tutoring. Say that you will do your best in your studies and you want to play football and other sports. Remember, his word is law with the boys. You must always obey and follow the rules. He'll ask about colleges. Good luck.

Yours,
D3

Alex felt more settled with his father's encouragement.

T. O. White's office had the smell of fresh tobacco. Several large racks of pipes were arranged on his desk, cluttered with family pictures, reports, papers, books, and a large folder with a pen attached. An ornately carved seal of the Academy hung on the wall behind the headmaster's comfortable-looking old leather chair. There were two severe straight-backed chairs without elbow rests facing T.O.'s desk. These were for the boys who were to navigate the rocky shoals of secondary school academia and whose questionable futures lay in his hands. Editions of old books crowded the ceiling-high shelves. The green curtains were floor-length, well worn, and partially darkened the room, brightened only by streaks of morning sunlight. A faded Oriental rug lay in front of the desk, bordered by an oak floor and dark furniture. A shabby charm emphasized the room's importance and dignity.

They shook hands. Mr. White, short and rather stocky, commented that Alex would be tall enough to play basketball and mentioned that the school also needed an end for the football team. The topic of athletics put Alex at ease. White indicated he should be seated.

The new pupil perched rigidly on the end of his chair and listened as T.O. outlined the Academy's program for languages, history, science, mathematics, and English. History would start

Alex's second year. As the monologue on the virtues of a private day school continued, Alex relaxed and loosened his grip on the chair.

Then T.O. cautioned, "All of my boys whose fathers are doctors seem to set their sights on that profession. Keep an open mind. It's far too soon to make any future decision. Do you understand?"

"Yes, sir. I'll be interested in every subject as it comes along. I particularly enjoy languages and history."

T.O. smiled and lit his pipe. A cloud of fragrant smoke hovered over his head as he tucked a small box of matches back in the vest pocket of his blue pinstriped suit.

"Good man. Jim Hodges and Georges Clement are two of my best language teachers, who will stimulate your interest. They've been here since I took over almost twenty years ago. We want hardworking, reliable students who are inquisitive and have intellectual curiosity. Persistence will get you further than brilliance, and don't forget it. Classes begin in the middle of January, and I want you to meet my son, Tombo, who will be in your form."

Alex guessed that *form* meant "grade."

T.O. closed his folder. Alex thanked the headmaster for his time and encouragement.

"Finally, Alex, we have a set of rules and regulations for all of our boys, and I know I can rely on you."

"Yes, Mr. White, I completely understand." He quietly closed the door to the office.

His interview with T.O. had seemed to consume hours. With a sense of unrestrained relief, Alex made several large snowballs and threw them wildly into the air on his way home. There had been a slight thaw and his shoes and socks were soaked as he tried to sidestep puddles of melting snow and ice. Tomorrow was Saturday, and he hoped for a sharp, cold wind that would freeze the pond in time for ice skating. This would be his next chance to see Stephanie Pfeiffer.

Oscar pulled out his skates while Alex slipped on his Academy wool sweater with 1937 over the seal. Oscar gave the novice skater some hints about self-preservation and how to stay on his feet. His skating had improved.

"That's not bad at all, Alex; you're only falling half as much as last week." Stephanie stood behind him with a disingenuous smile, lightly touching his shoulder, then skated away gracefully. He crossed a desert of bumps and valleys that brought him to an oasis, a bench caked with frozen snow.

"It's about time you came in." Oscar's voice was a cheerful welcome. "Have some of my special hot chocolate. Guaranteed to warm you from head to toe. No charge for my two favorite skaters."

"Thanks, Oscar, we'd be icicles without you." Stephanie took off her beret. "I guess we're both freshmen; is that right, Alex?"

"Right you are, Stephanie. I had a long talk with T. O. White the other day, and it sounds like fun. He's really a nice guy, you know. Someone in his office took me around school. It seems like a neat place. He said the Girls' Academy is a couple of blocks away. Are there any classes together?"

"No, but we take trips to the Art Institute with the boys' school each month, and it's amazing to hear everyone's different opinions."

"I bet you like art, don't you, Stephanie?"

"I like to sketch in my spare time. Unfortunately, there's never enough of that. Some Friday afternoons I take the bus downtown after school and wander around looking at the old Italian paintings, but the impressionist collection has more appeal."

"Who do you like best of the modern painters?"

"You mean, 'Whom do I prefer,' don't you, Alex?"

"Of course, Miss Pfeiffer. What's your answer?"

"I think Monet; have you heard of him?"

"Yes, just now. You've confused me, though. Isn't there a Manet?"

"Of course, Mr. Dunham, but his colors are too splashy." Stephanie smiled, leaning over his shoulder. She was coy. "Alex, will you be at the Girls' Academy Christmas dance?"

Their faces were close. "Sure, Stephanie, or is it, 'surely,' Stephanie?"

He stood, put on his heavy sweater, and looked at her intently, staring at her glowing cheeks and heart-shaped face. Her blue eyes met his gaze.

"Stephanie, will you save a dance or two for an Olympic ice-skater?" There was an acquiescent nod. She left the hut.

That night at dinner he was embarrassed by his bogus invitation to the dance, uncertain before asking.

"Lucky, is there any way I can possibly get myself invited to the Girls' Academy Christmas dance next week? I sort of promised Steffi, you know."

"So, 'Mr. Esquire,' you've changed your mind. Your father and I feel you should have new friends. Consider it arranged."

He hugged her and she smiled warmly as they sat together after dinner. "Honest, Lucky, you're the 'bestest' of all."

The next afternoon, when he returned from tutoring, Alex sat at the kitchen table while Colleen prepared a snack. His mouth was ringed with white as he finished a tall glass of milk. "Colleen, where did that bouquet of flowers come from?"

"The doctor usually brings your mother one every week, especially on nights they go out for dinner."

Alex always slept in his easy chair with the lights off until they came home. He would peek through his partially opened door and know they were in bed.

He could hear Lucky say, "Brian, I had a wonderful evening. Do hold my hand before we go to sleep."

Lucky and Alex were arranging place cards for a holiday dinner party.

"Christmas was lonely in California, but after looking at these names, you must have some interesting guests coming tonight."

"Alex, you will meet some of our friends during Christmas. All of them have different lives and professions, and I want you to learn and enjoy their experiences. Take Ralph Bagshaw's card and put it next to your father's place setting. He's a fascinating man, works as a *Daily News* reporter and recently returned from an assignment in London. I know that you're interested in history, and one of these nights you can discuss European politics."

Before dinner, an inquisitive Alex sat at the top of the stairs, eavesdropping on animated conversation.

Bagshaw had wavy, unruly hair and a beard. His pants and coat were invariably wrinkled, and as a journalist he lived from a suitcase in his pursuit of the news. His perceptive mind and speech were a contradiction to his unkempt appearance.

"The British simply don't have the will anymore, Brian." Bagshaw was emphatic. "The cream of the crop was wiped out in 1916 at the Somme. They're frightened by the thought of another war. We know the Germans are building their army and air force, flaunting Versailles."

Alex heard his father chatting with another guest. "Erich, did you and Katherine enjoy your auto trip abroad this summer?"

A cultivated voice with only a suggestion of an accent replied, "Katzie and I visited my Pfeiffer relations in Papenburg, drove down to Salzburg for the music festival, and had the pleasure of meeting the conductor of the Leipzig Gewandhaus. Gifted, young, charming chap. We should have brought him over as the conductor of our symphony, but he has Nazi friends. Obviously, he knows his future isn't with us."

Alex was impressed because Steffi's parents were guests in his home. There was a pause and then he heard Katherine Pfeiffer speaking of changes in Germany.

"The government has reduced unemployment, there are the autobahns, industry has been rebuilt, and the people think they have a leader. Believe me, Brian, our depression was nothing like the situation there after the war."

Lucky asked Alex to come downstairs, then gave him instructions to help Colleen with the party.

"Alex, you are my trusted houseboy for tonight. Answer the telephone and say Dr. Dunham is not available unless it's an emergency. Take care of any interruptions, understand, my dear?"

Colleen was unnerved. "Alex, get the rear door; it's a delivery. I'm busy, gotta get these dishes out of the oven, 'range the food on the platters, and take the whole lot to the dining room."

Hermie was swaying, frantically trying to balance an armful of ice-cream cartons.

"Colleen, what do I do? Hermie is here and where's the dough?"

"Go speak to your mother. Mind you, they're in the middle of dinner and plenty of fancy people are out there."

Alex put on his blazer, straightened his tie, brushed off his pants, and with as little noise as possible entered the candlelit dining room. Lucky was seated at the head of the table near the kitchen, and he knelt down at her side hoping not to be noticed. Everyone seemed to stop speaking at once. Katherine Pfeiffer sat near Lucky.

He said with an unintentionally loud whisper, "Lucky, the guy from Walgreen's is here, and needs a buck and a half for the ice cream."

She gently placed her hand over the side of his face. "Sweetheart, tell Hermie we'll charge it tonight. Please don't worry, Alex."

As he left, the guests laughed, enjoying his predicament and urgent request. Katherine looked at him closely, then turned toward Lucky.

"You're fortunate to have such a handsome son. Where did that wonderful blond hair and those striking green eyes come from?"

Lucky playfully joked, "Stephanie is teaching him how to ice-skate, and Brian and I hope he will concentrate as much on his studies at the Academy as he does on her. Katzie, we think she's poised and perfectly lovely."

The guests reminisced about their childhood days, and after "Alex's ice cream" with Colleen's chocolate sauce had been served they gathered for coffee in the living room.

On Saturday morning, Alex polished his shoes, carefully arranged what his father called "the midnight blue suit," a white shirt, and a tie, and placed them on the bed. When he returned from his tutoring session, he showered and scrubbed his fingers and hands, then bounded downstairs to have dinner with his parents.

"But, Lucky, who will know I've been invited to the dance?"

"Here's your invitation, Alex. Introduce yourself and give it to Mrs. Natalie Henderson."

"I don't know her; will she be greeting everyone?"

"She's the head of the Women's Committee for the Boys' and Girls' Academy and is expecting you."

He was satisfied and asked to be excused. His father looked at Alex's trimmed fingernails, straightened his tie, and reminded him to take his topcoat and gloves. He waved a kiss to Lucky, then returned to his father's side.

"Dad, may I have a buck or two, because Steffi might want a soda or something after the dance?"

He reached for his wallet. "Have fun, Son, nothing drastic, and don't take Steffi to South America.

As Alex left, he pulled a note from his coat pocket.

From the desk of Dr. Brian Dunham:

Dear Alex,

This is your first party. Remember to be a gentleman at all times. Perfect manners, polite conversation. Be certain Stephanie is home by eleven.

Yours,
D3

Alex thought he would try to follow his father's advice, but was happily preoccupied. He wondered what it would be like to dance with Stephanie. After a fifteen-minute walk, his flirtatious fantasies were chilled by cold air stinging his cheeks. He was relieved to reach Clairmont House, where he introduced himself to Mrs. Henderson. His hostess was formal and charming.

"Alex, we're pleased to have you with us for our Christmas

dance. I understand you are a new student, and this is an exciting opportunity to meet classmates. Best wishes for your start at the Academy. Merry Christmas and please remember Mr. Henderson and me to your parents."

Alex bowed slightly, then disappeared among the milling students.

A dark-haired, tall boy with broad shoulders, whose blazer was a size too small, approached Alex with an enthusiastic welcome.

"Hi, I'm Tombo White, and you must be Alex Dunham."

The two shook hands and found a quiet corner.

"Really glad to know you, Tombo. I met your dad at school the other day, and he seems like a terrific headmaster."

"Alex, don't let the old man bother you; all the boys seem to like him, and he's fair. What I wanted to talk about was the basketball team. We need a tall guy like you for center who's tough and has played before. We start practice the week between Christmas and New Year's, and the first game is in the middle of January. Be at the gym about ten every morning and Saturdays, too. I'll introduce you to Coach Bill Hanbury."

"That sounds great, Tombo. Tell me more about him."

"Well, he was the captain of the Dartmouth football team in '32, and has been head of athletics at the Academy for a couple of years now. Super coach, and we've had good teams since he came. See you Monday morning. Let's get a glass of that soapy, bathwater punch. I've got to find 'Shoo-Shoo' Browning; she's my date tonight."

Alex saw Stephanie on the opposite side of the dance floor. Jack Smiley and his "Thundering Herd" combo had begun the next tune as Alex edged his way to her side through the zealous crowd of dancers. She stood with her hands behind her back, wearing a dark green dress with a narrow gold belt and a matching velvet headband. It complemented her blond hair and fair complexion.

"Stephanie, may I please have the next dance?"

"Alex, where have you been? I thought you'd never rescue me from these little fellows."

"Met Tombo White. He's really a swell guy. We talked about the basketball team; the first game is in a couple of weeks. You and your cheerleaders better be there, or I'll never give you another ice-skating lesson."

Stephanie smiled, amused by his self-deprecating humor. They sidled toward the edge of the moving crowd, where they could talk and dance. She spoke with enthusiasm of Christmas, school classes, teachers, field hockey, and her interest in music and art. She regaled him with stories of her family: devoted parents, a younger sister, and the dogs, who always created playful mischief. Steffi took his hand and they sat at the top of the long, winding carpeted staircase after he found glasses of the "dreaded punch."

Before the last dance, she stepped back and gave him a teasing look.

"If you're such a great athlete, why do you smoke? People our age shouldn't do that sort of thing, you know."

"Really, Stephanie, I've never smoked in my life. I hate the smell of tobacco."

"Then why does it feel like you have a briar pipe in your pocket when we dance?"

"Who knows, Stephanie, there may or may not be, but boys are boys. You must know about that sort of thing. Anyway, it's a long, complicated story, isn't it? Time for 'Good Night, Ladies.' Then we can go someplace for a hamburger and a Coke."

"Touché, Alex. I like that cagey story of yours about boys, and if boys will be boys, I wish we could dance longer."

Both laughed as all couples made a final "courbez" nearly in unison. As the music ended with this final dip, she was slightly off balance and moved into him. He felt her nearness. She trembled.

He held her coat while they waited in line to thank their hostess. After Steffi made a quick curtsey, Alex shook Mrs. Henderson's hand covered with a fashionable elbow-length white kid glove. They walked down the staircase into the brisk night air. Their feet sank in new fallen snow as they hurried to the nearest B and G restaurant.

"You're taking me to a 'Bugs and Germs,' aren't you, Alex?

Hope it's not true, because they certainly have delicious hamburgers."

When they reached the elevator door, he brushed the snow off her long, straight hair, which almost reached her shoulders, and dried the flakes from her face with his handkerchief. He took off her headband and put it in his pocket. She stood motionless, gently touching his ruddy cheeks with her warm hands. "Please, not so formal, Mr. Briar Pipe; I really want you to call me Steffi. Night, Alex."

"Good night, Steffi. I'll see you Saturday at the pond."

"Thank you for the fun evening. By the way, I like your haircut, long on the top, short all the way around, sort of like the barber put a bowl on your head."

Alex didn't answer, then self-consciously brushed a shock of wet blond hair off his forehead. He waved one more goodnight as the rattling door of the cagelike elevator closed.

Alex had frosty hands and biting toes after romping through deep snow during the first Christmas at his new home. He joined Lucky when she began to decorate the tree. It graced a corner of their spacious living room overlooking the frozen lakefront. A poinsettia was placed on the piano. He thought its off-white petals looked more fragile than those of the deep red plants that grew wild in California. Red candles in silver candelabras decorated the end tables. Evergreen boughs and dried apple garlands were strung around the stressed oaken mantle. The room had the scent of pine and cinnamon.

"Alex, be certain the tree is absolutely straight." Brian surveyed the tree as if he were aligning a putt. "You'd better crawl under the branches and move the base around. It has to be perfect. When you've finished, go out to the kitchen and ask Colleen for a piece of felt or a coaster and put it under the plant to protect the lacquered finish of the piano."

Alex happily wiped the artificial snow dust from his face, eyes, and hair, climbed the ladder, and adjusted a golden winged angel that crowned the tree. "Dad, what about the lights? Are they the way you and Lucky want them?"

Alex looked down at his parents sitting together, content that their son had shared and enjoyed the festive preparations.

Lucky complimented her youthful Santa Claus, "Alex, they are strung with consummate skill; the tinsel is hung in perfect proportions. Now come down from the ladder. Enjoy some eggnog."

During Christmas Eve dinner, Alex heard his parents converse, yet their voices seemed distant. He was pensive and felt inept.

"This is the first Christmas I've had with my family, and knowing that you are here makes me appreciate the holidays in ways I can't completely explain. You must understand how fortunate I feel being with both of you."

Dr. Brian Dunham lifted his napkin and adjusted a new dental bridge that burned his gums. "Of course we understand, Alex. Lucky and I have always wanted you here. Now, Son, don't you have some reading that we can discuss in the morning before guests arrive for luncheon?"

"Dad, there's a nine o'clock service at St. Mark's tonight. May I please go? It lasts about an hour."

"The weather is terrible. Put on your heavy coat, scarf, and snow boots."

Doctor Dunham pushed back his chair after he had finished his coffee and looked off in the distance.

"You know, Son, I should have gone to church more often, but when I was an altar boy younger than you, the rector held a competition. The boy who learned and recited more psalms perfectly would win a Bible. I won the prize, but he gave it to someone else. I was gypped out of what I had won and didn't forget it. From then on I never returned to church and have always felt I could be of more help by seeing my patients on Sundays. Don't you agree, Lucky?"

Alex knew she attended Sunday services regularly and was a leader in church activities, helping provide food, clothing, and shelter for the poor not only at Christmas but throughout the year.

Lucky replied, "Brian, I am in agreement and respect your

religious attitudes, although I have hoped you would join me in church and prayer."

Alex was hardly surprised by her comments, which consistently supported her husband's opinions on almost all subjects.

He was captured by the familiar feeling of St. Mark's. The candle glow, incense, and subdued sounds were the fabric of his own altar boy days at the Episcopal parish church in his California neighborhood. As he walked toward the altar, he turned, searching for an empty seat. He was surprised to see her. He recognized her soft profile, head slightly bowed. Alex moved across the empty bench and sat next to her.

It was a happy, "Merry Christmas, Steffi."

"I'm glad you're here, Alex."

They knelt together and were cheered by the Bishop's voice, carols, and the soft light and shadows of the cathedral. An occasional cough interrupted his Christmas message.

Bishop Evans' multicolored vestments reflected the spirit of Christmas as he greeted his congregation. Alex and Stephanie looked about the stony grandeur, lingering at the end of the line of parishioners. They wandered to small side chapels, touched the smooth, worn wood of the pews, and felt a voiceless brilliance from the stained glass.

Steffi reached for the Bishop's hand. "Merry Christmas, Bishop Evans. We are pleased to be with you celebrating this holy time."

They sensed his charisma. He was tall, with a majestic air and deliberate movements. "I am happy that you are together on this glorious night."

"Bishop Evans, may I introduce Alex Dunham?"

"Alex Dunham? Do you happen to be Brian and Lucky Dunham's son?"

"Yes, I am, Bishop Evans."

"Well, well, I married your mother and father four or five years ago. We are proud of your father. He's a splendid man and surgeon, Alex. Are you a student at the Academy?"

"I begin in two weeks."

"I expect you'll meet my boys, Geoffrey and Percy. They're freshmen now, and Stephanie has known them for years. I see Stephanie each week, and hope you will join us, Alex. A joyous holiday to both of you and your parents. May God bless you."

As they left, Alex asked Stephanie, "May I walk back with you?"

She stood close to him, shivering in the coldness. "Alex, I haven't felt well today and my father will be along soon to drive me home, but you were kind to ask." She smiled faintly as he buttoned the top of her coat. "Bishop Evans has been a good friend since my confirmation, and I would like you to know him better. Alex, perhaps we can go to church together."

"Steffi, we'll meet for the eleven o'clock service each week." His voice conveyed a measured excitement as he held her hands. "I hope you feel better, and I'll be thinking about you. May I bring a gift tomorrow?"

"Please do; I want to see you Christmas Day."

After he left Steffi, Alex ran through the snow and reached Walgreen's several minutes before it closed. He hurriedly rummaged through the toys, cards, and stuffed animals. There it was: a stuffed doll, a boy ice-skater, balanced perilously on one leg with its arms outstretched. A familiar face at the counter quickly wrapped it, and Alex found a small card with an oversize Santa.

Christmas dinner at noon included Brian and Lucky's friends from their apartment building and younger doctors who were associates at the hospital.

A guest complimented Lucky, "My, what a lovely Christmas tree, Mrs. Dunham. The one in the hospital lobby can't match your artistic touch. What creative decorations."

Small, elaborately wrapped boxes of candy, Christmas wreaths, and flowers were brought by some of the guests, who were grateful for the Dunhams' hospitality and a reprieve from hospital food.

Her kitchen was the backdrop where Colleen always carved a massive turkey. She had been instructed several years before that kitchen knives were far too dangerous to a surgeon's hands. Alex thought carving a turkey would be simpler than performing the type of complicated operations his father did. Lucky's word was final.

One of the young doctors asked for a second helping. "What marvelous gravy. I've never tasted such mincemeat pie, Mrs. Dunham. What a cook you must be."

Her guests dutifully agreed, although Lucky distinguished herself more by ordering food than culinary skills.

After dinner, the living room was crowded with talkative guests drinking coffee from maroon, gold-rimmed demitasses.

Alex stood near the piano, listened, and watched. He stared wistfully at large ice floes on the lake and the winding stream of car lights on Lake Front Drive. Last year he had Christmas dinner alone in a diner and then went to the movies.

"Brian, this fellow Hitler has a systematic program to persecute us in Germany." Dr. Theodore Rosenthal was distressed. "For example, the other night the students burned books in Berlin and Jews are being forced off the faculties of universities. The Catholic bishops are timid and don't say a word in fear of being sent away to who knows where."

Alex had heard his father talk about Dr. Teddy Rosenthal, who was generally considered to be the most brilliant doctor at the University Hospital. He spoke with a high-pitched, heavy accent and seemed older, more earnest than his youthful-looking host. He took off his strange, thick, steel-rimmed glasses and cleaned them repeatedly. His small, wizened wife clung to his arm.

"Teddy, you and I have been friends for years, and this is another crazy politician who promises everything." Brian spoke with assurance. "You know the Nazis' answers: more jobs, autobahns, homes, and nothing will cost a red cent. Besides, Britain and France are strong. Won't let him go too far. You mustn't worry; it will all work out the right way. It could never happen here. By the way, Teddy, why don't we play squash one of these days? Both of us need more relaxation."

Alex thought his father's colleague, with the harried look

and deep concern, was an unlikely athlete. When "B.D.," as Teddy called his devoted friend, turned away, the Rosenthals saw Alex, who had been standing behind his father. As the older Dunham stepped aside, it was as if one image had been superimposed upon the other.

Teddy squinted. "You are Alex. Please meet Mrs. Rosenthal."

Rosenthal studied Alex's sensitive features. During a discussion of his curriculum, Alex's attention was diverted to the man's watch chain, strung with various gold academic keys. Alex thought his high, stiff collar with small tightly knotted tie must be unimaginably uncomfortable.

"Sir, I heard what my father said to you and your wife, and in a certain way he may be right, but perhaps Hitler is a dictator. His politics make that belief possible. Europe is in disorder now, and I think someday all of this must change." He reached for Teddy Rosenthal's hand. "And, you know, I hope and plan..."

"Son, I understand. We live only several blocks away; come along and have dinner with us one night. You must know I'm a wonderful chef, and Rosie here will treat you like a king."

Alex beamed and put his arms around her when she kissed him.

As the guests began to thank their hostess, Alex pressed Lucky's hand. "Is it OK if I take Stephanie a Christmas present? I'll only be a few minutes."

Lucky reminded him, "Call Mrs. Pfeiffer first. And, Alex, comb your hair, dear."

He scrambled through her elaborate telephone book with myriads of crossed-out numbers and addresses that seemed like hieroglyphics. The Pfeiffer maid with a marked German accent asked without elaboration who was calling.

"It's Alex Dunham, and I'm a friend of Stephanie. May I please speak with Mrs. Pfeiffer?" There was a long pause, as a dog whined in the background. He heard the staccato sound of heels on a marble floor.

"Merry Christmas, Mrs. Pfeiffer; this is Alex Dunham. I

hope I haven't disturbed you. Would it be possible to drop by for a moment and give Steffi . . . you know, sort of a Christmas present?"

"Alex Dunham, you're the famous ice-skater, aren't you? Our guests have left, and Erich and I would love a visit."

Alex pulled the price tag out of his new polo coat, thinking what a luxury it was to have such a gift. He introduced himself to the imposing-looking doorman and asked for the Pfeiffers' apartment.

The doorman was aloof. "Are you expected, young man?"

Alex had seen the elevator once before. It was an incredible cage. He could watch the cables, hear the grinding motor, and see a montage of cement and bricks through the vertical latticed pieces of steel. It stopped with a lazy bounce. He stepped out, wiped his shoes, and stuffed his mittens in a pocket.

An austere maid opened the door. She was dressed in black, with a white apron, ruffled shoulder straps, starched cuffs, and a dainty cap. She was slightly more hospitable; nevertheless, her instructions were imperious.

"Come in, Mr. Dunham, give me your coat, take your galoshes off in the foyer, and warm yourself by the fire."

He ruminated, *This is where Steffi actually lives.* It was a luxury to be here. The living room was compact, with furniture that seemed delicate. There were small tables adorned with colorful china objects, and a three-cornered window overlooked the lake. The window seats were covered with inviting-looking cushions. Two ornately framed paintings hung on either side of the fireplace. One portrayed water lilies, the other a medley of fruit.

Alex stood quickly. "Merry Christmas, Mr. and Mrs. Pfeiffer. I hope I'm not interrupting your holiday."

Mr. Pfeiffer was slightly shorter than his wife and had a dark complexion, brown eyes, and thinning silver hair. His benevolent informality attracted Alex. Steffi resembled her mother. The same soft voice, the same arresting smile.

Mr. Pfeiffer held Alex's arm as they shook hands. "Alex, how nice of you to think of us. You know how fond we are of Lucky and Brian. A snowy Christmas in Chicago must be different from balmy California."

"It's an exciting holiday, Mr. Pfeiffer, and Steffi is teaching me to become a winter person." He laughed. "The bruises from ice-skating remind me of her coaching."

Katzie Pfeiffer kissed him on the cheek. "Alex, that should make the bruises feel better, but will hardly help your poor ankles."

Alex held the floppy doll behind his back. It was wrapped in red Christmas paper that was soggy and beginning to stain his hands.

"I wanted to wish Steffi Merry Christmas and give her this little, ah, you know. . . . "

The tone of Katzie's voice changed. "Alex, my dear, Steffi has been in bed since last night, and is terribly under the weather with a cold and high fever. The sweet doctor from the hospital came by this morning."

His cheery expression became one of glumness. He stared at the floor. There was a long pause before he smiled.

"Please say hello for me. . . . I guess there won't be a skating lesson this Saturday." He moved toward her. "Would you please give her this gift?"

A slight rustle, and a young girl stood at Mrs. Pfeiffer's side, gently tugging at her dress. "Alex, this is Tina, Steffi's younger sister."

He thought Tina was probably ten years old. She had blond pigtails and wore a dark blue velvet dress, a red belt, and white knee stockings with black patent-leather shoes.

"Hello, Alex." She curtseyed quickly.

"It's nice to see you, Tina. Do you go to the Girls' Academy?"

"I'm in the fifth grade. My sister goes there, too. She's very sick now, and the doctor told us this morning she might have pneumonia. I really don't know what that means."

Alex forced a casual answer. "Well, that's not so bad after all, is it, Tina?"

Mrs. Pfeiffer put her finger on Tina's lips.

Tina looked down, turning the toes of her shoes inward, and pulled up her knee stockings.

"Honest, Alex, I heard Steffi tell Mommy the other morning she liked you and hoped you would be her boyfriend."

He was elated by her confession. "Tina, I know you'll do a little favor for me, especially because it's Christmastime and your sister doesn't feel well. Would you give her this present for me?"

He handed her the skating doll in crinkled red paper with a limp green bow and card.

"Wish Steffi a Merry Christmas; I know she'll be better soon. Don't forget to tell her I look forward to my next ice-skating lesson; she'll understand."

"I'll do that, just for you, Alex Dunham. It's not wrapped very well, is it? What's in here anyway?" She gave the present an inquisitive squeeze.

Mrs. Pfeiffer took Tina's hand. She promptly vanished.

"Mrs. Pfeiffer, you were very kind to let me visit," Alex stammered. "I must leave now, and please . . . please, tell Steffi that I want her to be well. Thank you."

Katzie was reassuring. "Steffi will be fine, Alex. You mustn't worry, dear. One of your parents' friends, Dr. Greer, has been exceptionally kind, and your father told us he was the best physician for this sort of illness."

He put on his coat and mittens. "Again, Merry Christmas to all of you."

Alex lay down and buried his head in a pillow. Eventually, weariness led to sleep. Later, Lucky tapped on his door and he was awakened by her hand gently ruffling his hair.

"Come along now; we're having leftover turkey in the kitchen. Don't keep your father waiting."

Alex washed his face and tucked his tie into his sweater. Having no interest in food, he sipped some milk and said nothing. His father and Lucky had a lively discussion about a recent Broadway play.

Brian looked at Alex. "All right, 'Jeb Stuart,' be frank with me. What's wrong?"

"Dad, how serious is pneumonia? Who is Dr. Greer, anyway?"

His father's explanation was brief. "Pneumonia is a serious cold, and my friend Dr. Greer takes care of patients who have this sort of trouble."

Alex realized his father knew Steffi Pfeiffer was ill, yet he only spoke vaguely of new treatments and how patients recovered. Alex remained silent. There was no answer as to when she might be well. He finished dinner without looking up from his plate, kissed Lucky, then barely nodded goodnight. "Thank you both for Christmas. It's our first one together."

When Alex left, Lucky gently scolded, "Brian, you really should have told Alex that his friend Steffi will be allright and there is no reason to worry. You know he's so serious, sensitive."

Alex overslept the next morning. It would be breakfast in the kitchen with Colleen. After a shower, he entered his bedroom and saw a note on his desk:

From the desk of Dr. Brian Dunham:

Alex,

My friend Johnny Greer played quarterback at Princeton; he's a fine doctor and will take good care of Stephanie Pfeiffer. Pneumonia means the little sacs in the lungs are collapsed and the patient can't breathe well. She'll recover quickly and won't have to go to the hospital. Don't miss basketball practice, and be home on time for dinner.

Yours,
D3

After he read this last note, he dropped it in his desk drawer with the others, but wondered what playing quarterback at Princeton had to do with pneumonia.

The oak basketball court was embellished with a large "CA"

in orange letters on a blue circle and was waxed to a high sheen. Alex arrived early for practice, and Tombo greeted him as an old friend.

"Alex, come over and meet Coach Hanbury. Coach, here's Alex Dunham. He begins school in ten days with our class, and he's about as big and tall as any upperclassman we've got."

"Dunham, good to meet you. Now go downstairs and get a locker, uniform, shoes, and a towel. See you in ten minutes sharp."

Ten minutes later, on entering the gym Alex heard: "Where's the new guy? Dunham, get your butt over there with Andy; he's our senior captain."

Barkley taunted, "Come on, what's your name, try to beat me, but watch your chin. Don't bite your tongue off when I give you the works."

As the whistle blew for the last center jump, Alex tipped the ball away to Tombo and then came the tooth-rattling smash to his chin. Alex said nothing, but Andy Barkley knew he would probably have a rougher practice tomorrow.

Hanbury yelled, "Dunham, get the lead out. Take the ball away and show me something."

Alex picked a split second, slapped the ball away from Barkley, and dribbled downcourt. There was a swishing sound as the ball went through the net. Barkley put his hand on his shoulder.

"You know you're OK for a freshman, quick and tough; I like those kind of guys. How's that chin feel, Dunham? From now on, I officially dub you 'Alex the Great'."

When scrimmage ended, Coach Hanbury announced there would be practice every afternoon before the first game.

"Listen up, men: no excuses, nobody late. Stay in shape. Get the girls out of the backseats of your cars before ten."

After a Draconian shower, Alex ordered a monstrous sandwich in the cafeteria. Tombo's tone was questioning, even though he was an "old boy."

"Alex, do you think we're going to make the varsity this year as freshmen? I've been here since day one, and not that many are picked."

YOURS, D3 | 45

Alex put down his half-finished sandwich. "We're going to make the team. With some luck, we'll play in every game. Pal, let's count on it and try not to worry."

After his tutoring session, Alex picked up his books and small sports bag, left the Academy library, and walked home along a frozen path by the lake. It was dark and snow was blowing in his face when he reached the open circular driveway of Steffi's apartment building. He guessed Mr. Pfeiffer would be home between five-thirty and six, so he decided to wait at the archway. Alex hoped the doorman would ask him to come inside, but he only showed a formal indifference when he asked, "Young man, what are you doing out there, loitering about on a night like this?"

Alex ignored him. Snowflakes covered his coat and knit cap. He rewrapped his wool scarf. After what seemed an interminable wait, a cab plowed through the snow, stopped, and Erich Pfeiffer stepped out.

"Good evening, Mr. Pfeiffer." The doorman was ingratiating. "Nice to see you home this blustery evening, sir."

"Pardon me, Mr. Pfeiffer." Alex removed his woolen cap. "I'm Alex Dunham."

"Alex, how good to see you. Didn't expect you to be out on a night like this. This weather is dreadful. Come in the lobby and warm up a bit. You look like the abominable snowman."

The exasperated doorman watched as snow from Alex's boots puddled on the highly buffed black-and-white-striped linoleum floor.

Alex was apologetic. "Mr. Pfeiffer, I won't keep you long, sir. One quick question, please. Is Steffi better today?"

"This afternoon I spoke with Mrs. Pfeiffer, and the doctor reported that she has passed the fever crisis. You know she's been strong and healthy all of her life."

"That's good news, sir. Please do say hello for me." He turned to leave.

"Alex, I would hazard a guess another week will see her through and she'll be ready for school on the fifteenth."

"Thanks so much, Mr. Pfeiffer. Good night, sir."

At dinner there was an envelope propped against his napkin ring that read: "Mr. Alex Dunham." He knew from the tasteful printing it could only be from Steffi. He would wait, although he was impatient, anxious to read her note. He thought the weather, basketball practice, school, almost every subject in the *Britannica*, was discussed beyond reason.

After dessert, Lucky smiled. "Come on, Alex; why not open it? It's probably from Steffi."

"Later, Lucky, later. Thanks but no thanks."

It was his and would be his secret to enjoy. After casually leaving the dining room, he rushed upstairs, carefully opened the envelope, and read from the deep blue stationery:

Dear Ice-Skating Wizard,

I am almost well now and will be at school in a couple of weeks. Hope to see you soon.

Steffi . . . SU-7504

He scrambled across the hall to the library, locked the door, and dialed the "SU" number.

"Alex, you got my card, and thanks for calling." Steffi's voice was hoarse.

"How do you feel? Are you strong enough to get up? Seems like a lot of people have a bad cold this winter."

"I'm better now, but staying in bed is boring. Believe me, there's nothing worse. What have you been doing, anyway, snowman? You shouldn't have waited in that storm to speak with my dad."

"Basketball practice, getting ready for school, but, worse luck, no ice-skating lessons. Tombo White and I have become good friends, and we've skated at the pond a couple of times. By the way, you like the movies, don't you?"

"OK, big man on campus, if you win the first game, take me to that new picture show we've talked about, all right?"

"No chance of winning without you and your cheerleaders. You sound a little tired. Time to hang up. Will talk to you again before school starts. Is this a good time to call?"

"Any time is a good time, better sooner than later."

During the next two weeks Alex studied each night, refined the rough edges of his Latin and French, and practiced with the team.

Saturday afternoons Alex skated with Oscar, learning some intricacies of the sport.

Oscar was encouraging. "That's it, Alex—take advantage of the strength in your legs; use your arms for balance. With all of your stick-to-itiveness, someday you'll be as good as Steffi. You'll see her more after school begins. Bet you're excited 'bout the Academy, all your new friends."

Sunday evening before school started, he laughed with his father and Lucky at cartoons in the *New Yorker*. His parents singled out one in which an effete young boy was seated in the grandeur of a large dining room with a butler at his side. The youngster held a spoon and was saying, "Fishwick, this is a good soup, but not a great soup." During lighter moments at home, Alex became affectionately known as "Fishwick."

He was out of bed early on Monday morning and, after dressing, found what he had begun to expect:

From the desk of Dr. Brian Dunham:

Alex,

Remember this is the time of your life to excel in preparation for what lies ahead. There is no substitute for hard work, persistence, studying, and playing every game to the best of your ability. I know you have what it takes to be the best at whatever you do.

Yours,
D3

Alex, alias "Fishwick" and "Alex the Great," hoped he could please his father and make it all come true.

Three
Armae, Virumque, Cano, Troiae Que . . .

Fidelitas was chiseled in large letters around the Academy's seal on a stone arch over two large entrance doors, where boys had walked, pushed, and run for more than fifty years. The upper school was a four-story building that occupied a city block. For Alex, his journey to school was a twenty-minute walk that would become a friendly and familiar passage over the next four years. As he pulled open one of the large oak doors on the first morning of class, he was aware of a strange mousy odor that seemed to pervade the entire building. He imagined it was a combination of the gymnasium, old wooden desks, dusty books, and the boys themselves.

The poorly heated study hall was painted a pea green and seemed vast, with twenty rows of old-fashioned, lidded desks and attached chairs. A card with each student's name and grade printed in calligraphy was placed in a metal frame in the right-hand upper corner of the desk. Alex thought it was ample for his books, notepads, pencils, and erasers, and a sports picture could be taped to the bottom surface of the lid.

The unruly crowd of boys was suddenly galvanized into order when the headmaster, T. O. White, appeared at the lectern with an air of sovereign authority.

The senior prefect's greeting followed: "Good morning, Mr. White," and the entire group was asked to be seated.

A smaller bespectacled student who sat in front of Alex peremptorily belched as Mr. White began to speak. Its echo drifted as he slumped laconically in his chair, legs and feet sprawled across the aisle.

Someone in a nearby row joked, "Good old Barney's done it again. Ya know, he doesn't really give shit for 'Shinola'," and several of the boys began to whistle.

The senior prefect jumped to his feet. "Mr. Wilson, you are dismissed from study hall and you will appear before council at two-thirty this afternoon. You are also to complete your unfinished offensive business elsewhere."

Wilson was defiant as he left the assembled student body, however dropped his head in mock remorse when he passed T.O., into what Alex thought was an outcast's oblivion. He watched the headmaster intently as his expression changed from one of annoyance to controlled amusement as he spoke.

"Gentlemen, I've known your distinguished classmate for a number of years, and once more he has proved to all of us that he is, indeed, a creature lighter than air."

They laughed uproariously, cheered, and clapped for their headmaster. T.O. paused, then adjusted his polka-dot bow tie, proceeding with aplomb. "First, December honor roll cards for boys in all forms." Several students received midyear awards.

"I expect the usual splendid results for the practice college entrance tests that will be given in the middle of next month for juniors. Midterm examinations for all other forms will be in three weeks. The faculty anticipates more honor roll cards. On another subject, the first basketball game will be Friday afternoon at three here in the gym. Attend; show your Academy spirit."

He was interrupted by the clamor of desk lids being lifted and closed, with the chant of, "Beat Oak Hill." The senior prefect lifted his arm, and the demonstration stopped.

The headmaster concluded, "Good luck for the remainder of the academic year, and remember, the door to my office is always open to each and every one of you."

When Mr. White left, two hundred students stood and the prefect spoke: "Thank you for your time and encouragement, sir."

T.O. turned, waved to all of his boys, and disappeared into the long corridor. Alex had the printed schedule for his classes and hurried off to the bookstore, several floors below study hall. He rushed upstairs, precariously steadying an unwieldy stack of textbooks, then arranged them in his desk. The freshmen were discussing Shelley's poetry as he quietly searched for a chair near the door.

Pete Starke, who had come to the Academy several years after graduate studies at Princeton, nodded. "Have a seat... your name?"

"Dunham, sir, sorry but I had to get my books."

Starke spoke enthusiastically. "At first poetry will be an abstraction for most of you, but work at your individual interpretations and let unbridled imagination carry you through the lines. Remember I want more than a gentleman's 'C' from this class."

Alex volunteered nothing, listening, absorbing witticisms, novel explanations, and esoteric ideas.

When class ended, Starke eased back in his swivel chair. "Embryo scholars, you will memorize 'Ozymandias' for tomorrow morning as we wander wide-eyed through Poet's Corner at Westminster. I want your recitation of the fourteen lines without error and explain the structure and meaning of this sonnet, which is one of Shelley's best. Oh, yes, gentlemen, exceptional literary giants, it's Keats and Shelley, not Sheets and Kelly. Dismissed and until tomorrow."

He smiled with satisfaction as groans of discontent filled the classroom. One student complained and the others agreed: "Sir, how can you do this to us so early in the year?"

Alex thought it was an impossible chore. His first day as an Academy student passed quickly, and after practice Coach Hanbury selected players for Friday's game. He and Tombo celebrated by banging their locker doors and snapping each other with wet towels.

At dinner that evening, his father's question distracted him from the novelty and excitement of the first day at the Academy. "Well, Alex, how did it go today?"

He hesitated. "Not bad, sir, not bad at all, sir, I mean Dad, regular routine. Not exactly, though. Of all things, we have to memorize Shelley's 'Ozymandias' by tomorrow. You know it's a sonnet and I've got so much other work, how can I possibly do it tonight?"

While dessert was being served, Alex rolled his napkin into a ball and bounced his foot in frustration.

It was a sharp request. "Go upstairs and bring down your English book. You'll see that we can master this in half an hour."

Alex hurried back, doubtful he was equal to his father's challenge. He opened the new book with incredible fresh-smelling pages.

"All right, we'll take two lines at a time, and repeat them after me." Brian Dunham's directions were exacting.

> "'I met a traveller from an antique land,
> Who said . . . : Two vast and trunkless legs of stone
> Stand in the desert. . . .'"

"That's it, Alex; now you've got it." His father moved his chair next to Lucky. "Now, stand and pretend you're the young Shelley, himself."

Alex recited the sonnet with confidence.

"Now, Son, shift gears and get on with the rest of your studies. When you go to bed, on the way to school, and in study hall before class, think about the meaning of Shelley's poetic wisdom.

Memorizing it was incidental; what was his message?"

His father's smile was one of approval. Alex put his arms around him.

"Thank you for the help, Dad. I'll do my best tomorrow."

Dennis Black Harvey III sat near the window in the back row of Pete Starke's class, tilted against the wall in his wooden desk chair. Denny was slight and had an aristocratic manner, if not appearance. Alex heard from his classmates that he thought if they couldn't match his grades, they would all be truck drivers. The freshmen envied his intelligence, otherwise thought he was a snob. Several boys had stumbled through the sonnet without finishing when Pete Starke called on Harvey. He sat cross-legged, with a pencil tucked behind his ear, smiling with confidence as he effortlessly recited the sonnet. He showed overbearing satisfaction with his performance.

"Good work. Shelley wrote it more than a hundred years ago. Now, Harvey, tell me exactly what all of this means." Starke peered expectantly over his half-glasses.

Denny Harvey timidly begged off. "But, sir, that wasn't part of the assignment."

The young teacher, irritated, looked at the ceiling in dismay. "Mr. Harvey, you've memorized the sonnet, but what's the point if you haven't given any thought to what Shelley was trying to tell us?" There was silence as Starke looked around his class, then called on several more students. Vacuous explanations were not acceptable.

"Isn't there a new boy here somewhere? I thought I got his name yesterday."

After he glanced over the roster of students, Alex couldn't escape Starke's piercing stare. "All right, Dunham, surprise me; say something that makes sense, if you can."

Alex repeated the sonnet, looking directly at his teacher, then tentatively began his interpretation.

"Ozymandias expected his monument would be a permanent reminder of his power and greatness for ages to come, but it was destroyed, that is, eroded, worn away by time and weather.

The sculptor was, you know, sir, kind of a common guy, I mean a man, who made a statue that showed the king's arrogance and evil as well as his strength and pride. Shelley told us it's sort of a contradiction that this unknown sculptor himself won out over the king's wish for immortality. I guess that about sums it up, Mr. Starke."

The class was dismissed after awkward commentaries on the Romantic school of English poets. "Romantic" was mortifying, embarrassing. As the students hurriedly filed out, Starke gestured to Alex. He walked to the chalked blackboard.

"Dunham, it's only the first week of school. Continue your good start in English. I'll be seeing lots of you before college, and I want you to shoot for the best."

Alex stood in front of his desk and looked at the brass buttons and patch on his blazer. It was an orange-and-black crest crossed by two oars. He knew his English teacher had rowed for Princeton.

"I tried to say what Shelley meant, sir, and I hope it was satisfactory. I'm interested in English literature, history, and will do my best, Mr. Starke."

"That's the right idea, Alex, and perhaps, well, we'll see . . ." The class bell interrupted their brief conversation.

The Academy gym was crowded with students from both schools, and scattered groups of parents also enjoyed the anticipation of the season's first basketball game. Periodic frenzied cheering erupted as the teams methodically warmed up.

Tombo nervously passed the ball back and forth with Alex. "Shit, you got the shakes as bad as me?"

"With that first elbow in your ribs, it'll be over." Alex slapped him on the shoulder.

The team gathered around a spirited, red-faced Hanbury. "Remember the plays, feed shots to the seniors, and give 'em the full court press all the way. Got it?"

Alex looked at the polished, evenly spaced floorboards. *Watch your opponents' eyes,* he thought. *Ignore the world. Play hard; play tough. Always think of winning, never losing.* Alex tipped the ball off to Andy Barkley and his first Academy game began. Tombo and Alex pressed the two guards and successfully stymied their opponent's offense. Alex was relentless in the pursuit of his man, forcing errors leading to Academy scores.

An Oak Hill player swung his elbow into Alex's shoulder. "You son of a bitch, stay off my back, wise guy," which only made Alex crowd and bump harder. He drew several fouls and Hanbury had him sit out the remainder of the first half.

"Dunham, what are you doing out there? For God's sake, guard the guy; don't try to kill him. Play it fair and square and don't make your own rules."

Alex sat down, wiped his head, and scrubbed the sweat off his face with a cold, rough towel. He blew his nose, rinsed his mouth with ice water, then spit it out. The team returned to the locker room. On the way, he saw Steffi among the cheerleaders, a maze of gray skirts, saddle shoes, and blue sweaters with large orange "A"s.

"Hey, Steff, we got 'em now; it's the movies tonight."

She smiled and gave him the thumbs-up sign.

With several minutes left, the score evened.

"Dunham, get over here." Coach was loud and rough. "Go in there, and cover number ten; only this time don't try to mug the guy."

The whistle blew and substitutions were made. He and Tombo were working close court coverage again. Alex blocked, then intercepted two passes. He bounced the ball off to Tombo, who made the winning scores as the deafening buzzer sounded.

The two joined their teammates when they left the court. "Good grief." Tombo asked, "Alex, you could have made both of those last two baskets; why me, pal?"

"Your old man is headmaster. I have to graduate, don't I?" Laughing, happy students crowded around the winning team.

After the game, Pete Starke and T.O. were chatting in the stands. "It looks like a good team this year, Mr. White, and by the way, who's Alex Dunham?"

"He's Dr. Brian Dunham's son. His father is a surgeon over at the University Hospital. Alex moved here last fall from California. Has a new stepmother, something like that. Why do you ask?"

"Let's keep an eye on him. Take it from me; he's a good boy, gives it everything out here and in class. You know, there's something special about him. More depth than I usually see in students his age."

The headmaster nodded. "Peter, you have a remarkable gift for reading my mind."

Steffi waited for Alex at the entrance to the gym. She reached inside his jacket, running her fingers up and down his ribs.

"Well, the team finally won a game, and you could have taken those last two shots yourself."

"All sorts of ways to win, Steff. The important thing is, you're stuck with me for the flicks. Ready? The show begins at seven-thirty, so let's start home. You look great, no hoarse voice, but take my scarf and put on this knit cap."

As they walked home, he occasionally brushed her arm and shoulder and reached for her hand. "See you at seven, Steffi. The Cedar isn't that far."

She playfully took off his cap, reached up, and pulled it over his eyes. "Now you can't get away from me," she said, which made Alex grin as she put her nose against his, through the wet wool. She tucked the scarf in his coat, running for the elevator as he pulled up his cap.

They climbed the steep flight of stairs to the last row in the balcony before the cartoons started. The usual newsreel followed while they opened a gargantuan bag of popcorn. A dire commentator spoke of the newly organized Hitler Youth movement. They watched and heard hundreds of uniformed youngsters with bands and banners march and sing in huge military formations. The popcorn was quickly devoured, followed by boxes of Crackerjack. Both chuckled and grimaced during love scenes of the main attraction. Later they enjoyed chocolate sodas garishly decorated with whipped cream and cherries. They walked home in the stillness of falling snow. When they said goodnight, he brushed back her blond hair and she rested her head against his damp coat. His face touched her cheek. He drew her close, then kissed her.

"Please close your eyes and hold out your hand." His Crackerjack prize was an imitation gold ring. He placed it in her palm. "Good night, Steffi. See you next weekend, and no more colds. Take good care of yourself, and stay well."

Alex crawled out of bed realizing he had less than an hour before he was to meet his father at the west entrance of the hospital. They were going to a lecture on Alaskan wildlife. He tried to scrub the rouge and lipstick off his nose and face that had been his disguise as a scarecrow at a costume party the previous night. Soap with hot and cold water made no difference. He asked for Lucky, but she was shopping. Colleen, with her variety of cleaning potions and brushes, had no ideas how to solve his problem. It was past noon. Alex thought he looked like a made-up "fairy" whom the boys maliciously joked about at school. Embarrassed, self-conscious. Guests at the lecture would stare and ridicule him.

Suddenly his door opened. Alex saw his father hadn't bothered to take off his coat or gloves. His face and mouth were twisted grotesquely, and white specks of dried saliva dotted his lips.

"You were supposed to meet me at twelve o'clock sharp. Where the hell have you been? I've told you more than once, always be on time, and worst of all, you have kept me waiting, haven't you? You didn't call, and there's no explanation. Listen to me; you will not grow up in this house to be like your mother."

Alex stood behind his desk when his father reached and slapped him across the face with the front and back of his hand.

He closed his eyes. "But, Dad, my face, I couldn't. . . ."

"Dammit, Alex, don't give me any lame excuses; always do what I say, and exactly when I say it."

He covered his face, then heard Brian slam the door. Alex felt his cheeks burn more from humiliation and sadness than from the gloved blow. He remembered his mother's warning. A home with his father would either make or break him. Bewildered, he thought something dreadful, beyond his comprehension, could have happened at the hospital prompting his father's unexpected outburst.

After several hours, Alex splashed his face with cold water, mumbling that there would be no tears. He would never show his deep disappointment. He sat before the drawings of his gallant soldier heroes from the past trying to imagine their sorrow and disbelief in defeat. He swung open the glass fire escape door to his bathroom and sat on a step watching the afternoon fade into dusk. Lights began to brighten the city skyline, contoured by occasional clusters of trees. He alternately scanned the horizon and ground below. There was the golden cross on the spire of St. Mark's. The height gave him a feeling of detachment. He sought strength to control his rapidly shifting emotions.

A knock on the bedroom door interrupted his meandering thoughts; then came Lucky's voice. "Time for dinner. We're waiting for you, Alex."

"Lucky, not so hungry tonight, thanks anyway. I'm off to bed. See you tomorrow."

The next morning the note was next to his orange juice glass:

From the desk of Dr. Brian Dunham:

Alex,

It's another day. Son, let's forget our disagreement. Sometimes we all say and do things we don't mean. Tonight, we'll talk about summer vacation.

Yours,
D3

Alex read it over several times. He knew there would be no further discussion. He would volunteer nothing and wait until his father spoke.

After collecting his books, Alex left for school, trying to understand his father's clumsy attempt to apologize.

Steffi's voice was a cheerful surprise. "Good morning, scare-crow. Did you ever get the lipstick off your face?"

He tried to joke. "Verily, Your Royal Highness, Queen of Dia-monds, ruler of vast countries and far-off domains, it took the better part of the weekend to get that lipstick and rouge off my cheeks and nose. One thing is certain: no more costume parties for a while. Steffi, since it's such a great time of year and there are only a few weeks left before vacation, let's meet at the corner and walk to school together."

"You're the smartest living scarecrow in the world. I had no idea they could speak. The Queen of Diamonds agrees."

He took her books, pretended to drop them, then swung them over his shoulder. "You won't need these in a few weeks anyway. Has your family made plans for the summer?"

"Alex, I won't see you for a couple of months. We usually spend July and August at the ranch in Colorado."

"We'll write, Miss Pfeiffer. Your letters will make me a happy guy. Seems strange that my organized father hasn't men-tioned any definite vacation plans yet."

She stopped, smiled, and gently pulled his tie.

"Steffi, sometimes my parents are a real pain in the neck. What about yours?"

"They can be totally impossible over absolutely nothing. What do you do when they're unreasonable?"

"Stay calm; agree; try not to get mad inside—most of the time it works. When I lived in California, my real mother had her share of tantrums. She would shout at Dad over the telephone, and I always took his side. Now I wonder who was right. He can really be tough, and I can't seem to please him."

"Do you ever hear from your mother?"

"A short letter once in a while. I send her cards, but she's not well. It's a closed chapter."

Alex stepped into the library, where his father was carefully rearranging magazines. The finely grained mahogany table was circular and highly polished. No fingerprints. No dust. Alex was amused. *Wonder if I should take my shoes off and put on gloves?*

After all, it's the sanctuary. One *National Geographic* was misplaced by date.

"Come in, Alex." His tone was friendly. "As I remember, you were quite a horseman when you lived in California. Am I correct?"

Alex casually agreed.

"Lucky and I know the Hall family quite well. They're looking for help this summer. As the want ads say, 'Riding experience needed.' You could help the guides take dudes on pack trips, do stable and barn work and other odd chores. Their ranch is in the Grand Teton country of Wyoming. You will leave after the school year and be home before Labor Day. How's that sound?"

He hadn't expected a summer vacation. "Really great, Dad, and along with the fun, I hope to earn some money. Is that possible?"

"Jimmy Hall mentioned something about ten dollars a week. You could probably save a hundred dollars for the summer. You will be given room and board and live with the cowboys, which should be worth the money itself."

"Would that include my train ticket?"

"Alex, you're more of a businessman than I thought, and of course Lucky and I will buy your coach seat. No posh Pullman cars for cowhands. It's a beautiful trip, with lots of scenery, and why don't you take my camera? I think this is a healthy way to spend your summer. Jim and Julie Hall will be glad to have you. Anything else on your mind?"

"No, except I'd like to be in the mountains, riding and doing some heavy work to get in shape for football season. I'm off in a cloud of dust in several weeks, and maybe at the end of the summer I'll be able to speak the king's English. 'Howdy pardner, wahoo, yippie-o-kiay'."

After the doorman hailed a cab, Alex lifted his suitcase into the trunk, then sat next to Lucky. She held his hand. His parents would be abroad in July. He tried but couldn't listen. He gave a furtive glance as they passed Steffi's apartment. Several days before leaving, she had given him her address near Denver. He hoped for an invitation after working in Wyoming, perhaps an unrealistic expectation. He kissed Lucky good-bye, found a seat in the coach, and threw his small bag with Levi's, checked shirts, sweaters, and a pair of tooled brown leather boots onto the luggage rack.

The Half Circle T-Bar Ranch sprawled over several hundred acres in the rolling foothills at the base of the Teton range. Alex wiped the dusty sweat from his face and neck after his long bus ride, then surveyed the vista of snowcapped peaks and cloudless sky before he climbed the porch steps to the main ranch house.

Jimmy Hall ambled through a large metal-staved oak door crowned by a set of antlers. "Where you been, cowboy? Julie here and me been waitin' most of two days for you."

"Nice to meet you, Mr. and Mrs. Hall. A great train ride and I'm excited to be here with you. I've never seen mountain ranges like this and hadn't imagined they would still be covered with snow in June." Lucky told him the Halls were "old shoes," with no pretense or formality.

"C'mon in here and have a bite before you head off to the bunk house to meet my hands. You'd better not be one of them fancy 'Chkawgo' city fellers, 'cause we're tougher 'n horse nails out here." And Alex believed it.

The guest cottages were scattered on either side of the main house; stables and barns were down the road. Alex found the bunk house on a small winding path lined with aspens that led to a rushing mountain stream. He turned toward the weathered log cabin, where he would live during the summer. A giant of a man leaned against a hitching post. His Levi's were covered with straw and manure, and he wore a faded denim shirt whose armpits were tan-stained. Dark, scuffed boots were caked with dried mud. His massive belly was set off by a silver belt buckle, looking more decorative than useful.

"I'm Doc Pardee, and I run this here spread. Mr. Hall up there said you was comin' one of these days, and I 'spect you're the Dunham he was talkin' about. Throw that bag on the last bunk and get on out here with me."

"I'm pleased to meet you, Mr. Pardee."

"Call me Doc, none a that 'mister' stuff."

After the other hands taught him how to wash, curry, and brush a horse, Alex spent the rest of the day pitching hay and cleaning stables, thinking he looked and smelled worse than Doc. A week later Doc assigned him and several of the more experienced hands to ride on the first pack trip up to Turquoise Lake. Doc would lead the column of twenty dudes.

"Darling cowboy, do help me on my gorgeous 'horsie'."

Alex listened with incredulity.

The guest was about forty, with bleached blond hair, fashionably outfitted in new, expensive western clothes with a cowboy hat that dangled over her shoulders. Alex had her stand on a small box rather than give her a boost into the broad-seated western saddle. She clutched the reins and saddle horn with both hands while he adjusted the stirrups. He told her to keep her heels down and lean forward when the horse trotted or galloped.

Doc led the group up a winding trail with overhanging branches that narrowed into a rocky path. The morning's clear sky darkened menacingly. In late afternoon, a summer cloudburst of rain and snow forced the horses to strain as they climbed a scarred, rutted slope. Alex was the last rider on the trail and dismounted to help his elaborately dressed charge into a warm poncho strapped to the back of her saddle. She twisted suddenly, dropped her reins, and shifted her weight to the side, causing her horse to lose its footing on the mud-soaked trail. The horse rolled over her lower body, and Alex instinctively booted its hindquarters.

She was frantic. "Oh my God, I'll be killed by this damned animal. Get him off me before he breaks my arms and legs."

"Calm down, ma'am; stop your screaming." His voice was firm as he pulled the reins, put his shoulder into the horse's withers, and struck its croup, forcing it to stumble forward without rearing.

Doc rode back, felt her arms and legs, and made her walk. "Honey, everything's jim-dandy. Maybe a couple of bruises."

That night when the guests had been fed, Doc found Alex cleaning tin plates and cups. The weather had cleared and a group of dudes was singing, led by the rapidly recovered Florence Peterson, who vividly recounted "my close call" and a miraculous rescue from her rolling horse.

Doc put his arm around Alex. "Well, pardner, you done good out there today. When we git back, you and me is doin' some shootin'. How's that sound?"

"Really swell, Doc; teach me all you know."

Doc placed the tin cans neatly on a fence in a deserted pasture several miles from the main ranch house.

"All right, General Custer, do it slick. Aim that twenty-two and shoot them cans. Keep yer elbow straight, squeeze on her easy, and before you go back to the city you should knock 'em all down, like ducks in a row. Go ahead, cowboy."

"Wow, Doc, look at that. I hit four of the six, and it's about fifty yards, right?"

For the rest of the summer, Alex spent his free time in the late afternoons shooting, standing, sitting, and on his belly. He relished a strange excitement as each can crumpled and blew into the air with a metallic ring. The weeks passed. Doc thought Alex was becoming a good marksman.

It was cooler during the last weeks of August. Alex rode over to Kelly and picked up the ranch mail. His suntanned face and neck were peppered by small grains of sand as he trotted along one of the few roads near the Half Circle T-Bar. He was warmed by a heavy wool sweater covering bronzed arms, and leather gloves protected his calloused hands. After sorting letters and an occasional package, he arranged them in a large saddle bag, then opened one addressed to him:

Dear Alex,

You must have had a simply marvelous summer being a real Wyoming cowboy. We are looking forward to hearing about your adventures. Please come along to the ranch before you return to Chicago. Steffi, Erich, and I look forward to your visit.

Fondly,
Katherine Pfeiffer

That night he used the pay telephone, and after dropping innumerable quarters, each followed by a melodic sound, he spoke to Lucky. His father was at a meeting, which suggested that he should use persuasion. She would be his advocate for a visit with the Pfeiffer family.

"Lucky, I've gotten the letters from you and Dad. I hope mine have told you about the fun I've had out here this summer. It's really been great. I've put on weight, ready for football, finished my summer reading, and with the money I've earned I would like to take the bus down to Running Springs. Mrs. Pfeiffer has invited me to spend a couple of days before coming home. Please, Lucky, I want to see Steffi in the worst sort of way. Do you think it's OK?"

"Sweetie pie, you know I'll do my best, but your father's word is final. I'll discuss it with him and he'll drop you a letter. Good night, cowboy; see you soon."

Several days later he received the blue typewritten note. He expectantly tore it open.

From the desk of Dr. Brian Dunham:

Dear Alex,

Try and forget the invitation. You have too many other things to do that are important for your future. At your age I never was able to traipse around the countryside like a lovesick puppy. You're expected home on the date stamped on the return ticket, because I have arranged for a course in penmanship and typing before school starts. Be patient, Alex; you'll be asked again. Lucky will meet you at the station.

Yours,
D3

He dropped the mail bags, went to the rear of the post office, reread the letter, tore it, and threw it in an old knotted pine barrel. He sat on the rough steps of the rickety post office and stared at his pinto pony tied to the rail. He drew comfort from stroking its soft muzzle. Dejected, he threw his arms around its neck. His vivid imagination conjured various devious but vague plans to visit Steffi. At least for now, he had no other choice but to obey his father.

The initial formalities of beginning another school year had passed. A stiff October cross wind swirled around Alex during practice, and he became more irritable when each kick became shorter, although his effort and concentration were greater.

"Dunham," Coach Hanbury's loud voice was insistent. "That's enough for this afternoon; get over here and run your pass patterns and hold onto the ball for a change. Anything you can touch, you can catch. You shouldn't have dropped that ball in the end zone last week, it could have cost us the game, so get sticky fingers."

The midseason practice ended with a wind sprint. Tombo, Ace, Percy Evans, and Alex walked back to the field house together.

Percy was a complainer. "Coach drives us too hard. Then there's all that homework each night. I gotta get over to Squirms for a smoke and a Coke before I go home, and maybe Liz'll be there. We got a big date Friday night after the game."

Ace made a fist and tapped Percy Evans's chin. "Get the drift. If you aren't blocking for us Friday because you've been sucking on those weeds again, the three of us plan to throw you headfirst into the river."

"Understand, old buddy?" Tombo added to the warning with a playful jab at Percy's shoulder.

The boys thought Monsieur Georges Clement was the perfect gentleman among their group of teachers. He was invariably dressed in vested dark suits, wore orange-brown shoes, and displayed flawless manners with an elegant unmistakable French rapport. They agreed if he had a single blemish, it was his oversize toupee that would occasionally slide forward when he leaned over for chalk or an eraser. There were monthly wagers among his students that it was only a matter of time before his hairpiece would ignobly fall and reveal the extent of his baldness.

Alex sat across from Clement's desk and watched his classmates file in through the door with a glass panel above the lower wooden frame. Barney Wilson was always the last to stroll in and inevitably let the door slam.

Alex joined in the friendly laughter as his French teacher greeted Wilson. "Ah, bonjour, Monsieur Moufette. Late again today, eh? It is necessary to open the window *n'est-ce pas?*" Barney had become known, even to the formal Clement, as "the Academy Skunk."

Alex watched and listened as his teacher scratched over the blackboard and simultaneously reviewed idioms and unusual phrases. He tried to pronounce them to himself. Clement's fluency was often beyond his grasp.

"Now, gentlemen, *vocabulaire* with closed books. Of course I expect the correct gender."

Ace and Tombo had done their homework. Alex waited to be called on; however, Clement turned to the indolent Wilson.

"Monsieur Wilson, imagine yourself a stranger in a small Norman village and ask a passerby directions to a *brasserie.*"

Wilson was muddled. There was a lengthy silence. "But, sir, I thought *brasserie* was one of those things that held up tits."

The boys howled wildly and Clement's formality melted into convulsive laughter. The teacher clutched his sides. Suddenly the delicately balanced toupee slid to the back of his head. With joyful tears running down his face, Clement seized his headpiece and without concern pulled it forward, almost covering his eyebrows. The chaos continued.

Tombo shouted above the clamor, "Alex, you owe me two bits."

Several minutes later, Clement regained his composure, opened his desk drawer, and pulled out a small mirror. The class clapped with approval as he gingerly adjusted his headpiece.

Football season ended with a Friday afternoon win over South Shore Country Day that occasioned a noisy locker room celebration at the Academy field house.

Steffi ran to Alex as the team lifted its helmets and cheered for Coach Hanbury. "Did you get my card?"

"Sure did, Steffi. See you as planned. Movies, too."

In the locker room, players were throwing buckets of ice and cold water on one another. Alex and his teammates sat wrapped in towels as each relived in detail his particular part during the exciting minutes of the season's last game.

Alex impetuously showered Ace with another bucket of ice, telling him, "Ace, you're something else. No one laid a hand on you. Great touchdown."

Ace Cooke was brawny, a self-effacing athlete. When they confided, Alex knew it was like putting a prized marble in his old California cigar box.

"Listen, buddy, it was your blocking, not my running, that set up the last score."

"Ace, have it your way. Let's get going. Books, more books tonight. . . . Have some plans for tomorrow after lunch. We'll meet you and Cindy later for the seven o'clock show at the Cedar, right?"

Although his arms and legs were bruised, he managed to stay awake after dinner. All Gaul was divided into three parts. When tempted to doze, he turned to the page where Steffi's card covered a picture of the Appian Way. It showed a confused knight on horseback with a broken lance, furiously chased by a rabbit charging with a floppy carrot, and read:

Alex,

You are my night for tomorrow afternoon and knight. Have a good knight's sleep; don't study all Friday knight. I'll meet my fair night at the noon balloon. Bus stop at usual corner. Good knight, handsome night.

Steffi

He slipped her card in the one desk drawer with a lock.

The following afternoon, dark clouds raced overhead, turning the cityscape into a gray silhouette. Nothing green, nothing bright. They stood together chilled by cold autumn gusts, impatiently waiting for a bus. Both stomped their feet and pounded mittens, climbing steps to the welcome warmth of the Art Institute.

"Please come here, Alex. Look at the grain stacks. It's absolutely incredible how Monet uses color. All are unique because each was painted during a different season or time of day."

Her voice was intimate, as if she were revealing a secret. The stained teak floor creaked softly as they moved from painting to painting—a warm, friendly sound.

He looked at a canvas in the soft light of the gallery. "Steffi, explain the composition of this shore scene. I imagine it's Normandy, as you said. The shades of blue in the sky and water make one color seem like several."

"Alex, I wonder what sort of person could have such talent? Guess I'll just keep trying to improve with my watercolors."

They strolled casually in the late-afternoon quiet of the empty gallery. He slowly guided her to another canvas. It was a serene houseboat on the Seine.

"What do you think, Steffi?"

"I daydream. It says where I would like to be. You're the fisherman. The noisy world is somewhere else. Can you feel the calmness?"

His green eyes scanned the canvas with an expression that intrigued her. Then he drifted to a nearby sculpture. It was Degas.

"Recognize the 'Arabesque'? Although it's a ballerina, I see you skating." He moved toward her, brushing through the back of her fine hair. His face burned.

"Alex, please bring me back soon. We can escape into these pictures, be together. The mystery of knowing, understanding, enjoying each other."

"What are you two still doing here?" The guard's voice was

gruff, impatient. "Come on, right now. I'll show you out this way."

Alex was obstinate. "We've paid for admission. Don't spoil our afternoon. There are five more minutes."

Alex sat at the dinner table enamored with the silent brightness of his crystal fish and their glittering colors. His thoughts were random: on classes, grades, approaching examinations, and sports. Lost in the solitude of the art gallery, sitting on a bench with Steffi, recalling striking scenes of distant places, he dreamily mused. His escape was brief.

He knew by his father's brusque tone a dreary subject would follow. "How was the game this afternoon, Alex?"

"Regular routine, Dad, not bad, not bad."

Brian Dunham carefully put down his knife and fork, as if pausing during an operation. "Alex, you've finished about half your time at the Academy, and we haven't discussed what you have in mind for the future. Remember, it is my belief that each generation should accomplish more than the previous. Give this serious thought. Any ideas?"

Alex hesitated. "Well, I've been preoccupied with school. Maybe I should have spoken more often with Mr. White and my friend Pete Starke. There's one thing I have decided. I want to apply to Princeton. Mr. Starke has offered to help me. How's that sound?"

"It's a start. What about later?"

"Dad, I have several more years before a decision. Perhaps a career in the army or State Department. Is it urgent?"

"The army is absolutely out of the question, because there'll always be somebody telling you what to do and when to do it. You don't ever want that. No, that shouldn't be one of your choices. Someone has complete control over your future. The State Department is interesting. Have you given serious thought to law or medicine?"

"Not serious thought, although I've considered being a doctor for a long time."

"Don't forget, Alex, you'll have to earn a living someday, stand on your own two feet. You can't rely on Lucky or me."

"Don't worry, Dad; you can trust me. I'll always be my own

man, earn a living, and make decisions. When you and Lucky gave me a home, you told me to take one day at a time. . . . Please, Dad, you know I'll always do my best. Speaking of doing my best, I have a ton of homework tonight." Alex turned to Lucky, excused himself, and walked back and folded his napkin.

When he opened his bedroom door the next morning, the note skidded along the carpet.

From the desk of Dr. Brian Dunham:

Dear Son,

I have told you all of the stories of how poor Poppie and Nanna were. He earned sixteen dollars a week managing my tuition for medical school. I want you to do more with your life than stand on a corner selling ribbons. What's the saying, "shirtsleeves to shirtsleeves in three generations"? Think seriously about what I said last night.

Yours,
D3

"Sir, pardon me for interrupting before class. Would there be a few minutes after lunch to talk?"

"Sit down, Alex; the next class doesn't start for a bit. What's on your mind?" Pete Starke brushed his hand over a prematurely graying crew cut.

Alex pulled over a small folding chair whose legs grated along the floor, then sat at his mentor's side. "Well, sir, it's like this. I haven't thought much about what I should do when I finish college; you know my future. It hasn't concerned me, and I don't have any good answers for my mother and father right now."

Alex frowned, twisting a pencil eraser into his hand. "I hate the continual nagging. You've heard the expression, 'I could throw the living room piano'? I don't seem to be able to please my father. He criticizes my best efforts, and, sir, I cringe when he asks me about my plans for the future. I won't graduate from the

Academy for another year. It's discouraging trying to be perfect when there's never a pat on the back. Perhaps you could help me solve some of these problems. Would you do that, Mr. Starke?"

"Alex"—he sat on the edge of his desk, legs crossed—"you're being pushed by your father. There's resentment. You are one of the better students in your class, a good athlete and leader. Move ahead at your own pace. The future is the next few months, not years. Your college dean of admissions will be looking for a man with a wide range of interests, who hasn't decided on a career and is more than a 'bookworm.' You know, the young fellow with an open mind, anxious to learn and work hard. They're the ones who do well. Don't try to please everyone. You and I can discuss all of this again before you're off to college. I know you're really happy inside; have more fun, laugh, enjoy your friends, and before you know it you'll be rowing and rowing down the stream at 'the best old place of all'."

A narrow column of midmorning sun gradually brightened the lackluster room. "Thanks, Mr. Starke. I appreciate your kindness, sir. Now I feel better about myself. I knew you would understand. By the way, sir, where's 'the best old place of all'? It must mean Princeton. Am I correct?"

"Yes, Alex, my friend, now you're loaded for bear when the old man comes down on you. Pop on out of here, and don't let your father make you worry about things that haven't happened. Off with you, and have a good summer vacation."

The full moon was high, bright enough for Alex to watch Doc hold his reins with one hand, a thin piece of cigarette paper in the other. A pouch of tobacco dangled from his teeth. He pinched some into the paper, rolled it, and then licked the edge, forming a perfect cigarette. With his "smoke" stuck in the corner of his mouth, he returned the pouch to his shirt pocket, then pulled out a match that flared after he struck it on his Levi's. He drew a deep breath and blew off a small cloud of smoke while scanning a nearby butte for coyotes. He and Doc tethered their horses at the edge of a clearing with a perfect view of the ridge across a small stream.

"All right, cowpoke, down on your belly. This here is a Winchester thirty-thirty. You never point this goddamned thing anywhere 'cept out there, got it?"

He wound the leather strap around Alex's left forearm, showing him how to steady the rifle by planting his elbow in the dirt. Doc slipped a shell in the chamber, and the two adjusted the sights for thirty yards. Fifteen minutes or so passed.

"Doc, do you see what I see?"

"It's all yours, Dan'l Boone."

The rifle recoiled against his shoulder. He saw his first prey dash into the scrub. They hunted over the next several hours, and with each miss he became more impatient.

"Better luck next time, Alex. We're doin' this every night 'til you git one a them critters."

By the end of the summer, Doc announced his greenhorn cowhand was a heck of a shot, and later Jimmy Hall was heard telling guests, his youngest cowboy was decimating the local coyote population.

The night before he left, Alex had dinner with the ranch hands. Steak, potatoes, corn, and pie with a tin cup of steaming black coffee were served up. Doc said more than two cups would kill a rattlesnake. Familiar stories and anecdotes were passed around the campfire that gradually died out at midnight. He packed up early in the morning, carefully placing his letters from Steffi in the side of his suitcase. Doc drove him to the bus and, before he left, complimented him for working at the ranch several extra weeks to earn more money. No trip to Running Springs this year.

Alex watched leaves tumbling past the window during a mid-morning Latin class. James Hodges rocked back and forth in his splendid antique chair, which he had when he joined the faculty almost thirty-five years ago. He wore baggy gray pants, a frayed tweed jacket with leather elbow patches, and a loosely knotted tie. A well-sharpened pencil protruded above his coat pocket. When he blew his nose into a less than clean handkerchief, it was like a trumpet announcing introductory remarks to Virgil. While he lectured on the Trojan War, its heroes and villains, he tapped out the cadence of the *Aeneid* with his ruler. The more important function of this exercise was to keep the class awake.

Alex sat in the front row near his venerable teacher and wasn't surprised he was called on first: "Armae, virumque, cano, Troiae que primus ab oris Italium, fato profagus, Laviniaque venit litora, multum ille et terris inactatus et alto...," Alex began his recitation. "I sing of arms and the man who, exiled by fate from Troy's shores, first came to Italy and the Lavinian coast. Long was he driven over land and sea..."

From the back of the class Alex heard whispers and snickering while he struggled through his translation. Everyone had been warned to get a good start for the warrior's endless journey. After a late football practice, Alex used an English translation that the boys called a "pony."

"Now, Mr. Dunham, your interpretation of the introduction to this magnificent epic poem is quite superb." His teacher mused. "It's flowing, descriptive, and shows you have a scholarly insight into Virgil. Unfortunately, it's too perfect for your knowledge. With this in mind, drop the reins, dismount, and proceed on foot. Also, make matters simpler, Dunham; remove everything you've written in the margins.

Small fragments of red eraser collected across the page. From the benefit of his late-night venture with the English version he hurriedly changed a few words, managing to finish what Mr. Hodges judged a flurry of nonsense.

"You gentlemen must realize I've heard every possible rendition of Virgil known to a Latin teacher, especially those written by secondary school boys. Believe me, my finely tuned ear knows who has translated and who has taken a pony ride. Do you distinguished group of Latin scholars understand me?"

There was a chorus of, "Yes, sir." Alex agreed more enthusiastically than the rest but kept his "pony in the stall" to help late at night for those once-in-a-while times when he studied after D3's lights-out order. Hodges's sharp humor urged them to excel. None failed to notice that he was always a zealous rooter at Academy games.

"But, Lucky, I've never been to a tea party before. I'm supposed to be at the Pfeiffers' at three tomorrow afternoon. Come on now; what do I do?"

He sat at her feet, confused, as she explained the intricacies of tea time. "Katzie Pfeiffer is terribly nice, Alex. She likes you, enjoys young people, and will put you at ease. She probably will tell a well-known story about one of her guests; however, I won't spoil it for you. Their maid will bring a large tea service. The cups and saucers are fine china, and balance the cup on your lap. She will ask if you prefer sugar, lemon, or milk. Dear, it's that simple, and don't worry."

"This is absolutely for ladies and girls. Why is a guy like me having tea? Steffi's a terrific athlete. She could be a track star. You know, a sprinter. Some of us watched her play field hockey last week. There wasn't anyone who was a better player. She was the whole Academy team. Lucky, would she enjoy this sort of thing?"

"Of course, Alex. Steffi may be a good athlete, but she is also learning to entertain—you know, Emily Post's rules of etiquette. By the way, don't stick your little finger up in the air, keep it tucked in."

"Fingernails and hands perfectly clean, like a doctor, the way they should be, Dad? Is my hair combed right, Lucky?"

"You look fine, Son; have a good time, but remember, don't talk too much, and don't wear out your welcome by staying after four."

"Not a chance; you know I'm not that interested in tea parties."

The Pfeiffer maid greeted him with a modicum of cordiality, taking his coat before he met his hostess.

"Good afternoon, Mrs. Pfeiffer. Thank you for inviting me. It's my first . . ."

He sensed her kindness. "Steffi and I have been alone several weeks now, and you can be the man of the house this afternoon."

Steffi waited in the living room. One arm rested on the

back of a chair, the other at her side. Her hair was accented by blushed cheeks, umber-colored eyebrows, and a broad forehead. She wore a charcoal gray dress softened by the afternoon light. They moved toward one another. Closeness made a handshake clumsy, but they touched gently. A desire to hold longer.

"Alex, it's pleasant to have you with us. We have been busy. Let's talk about our vacations. Happy summer days."

They sat opposite her mother, who reigned over an elegant tea service. Katzie Pfeiffer conversed gaily as she poured.

"You must know about our friend who had tea with Erich and me one afternoon. Erich warned me several times about his large nose and, above all, not to stare. I really had to concentrate, Alex; it simply rolled out: 'Would you like sugar or lemon in your nose, Mr. Schaeffer'?"

Alex laughed roguishly. "My dear Mrs. Pfeiffer, I would actually prefer milk in my nose."

Maxie, one of the dachshunds, snuggled at Steffi's feet, wagged his tail, and licked Alex's hand.

"Is Mr. Pfeiffer traveling?"

"Yes, Alex. You know he's an engineer and has been with a government group to evaluate German industry. It has something to do with a high-level report, airplanes, manufacturing, that sort of thing."

"Do you think I could speak with him when he returns home, if he has the time? These sorts of things interest me."

"Of course, my dear. The four of us can have dinner one night. I know you two would enjoy his stories."

Katzie entertained him; however, it was Steffi's responsiveness that unlocked his imagination and desire. Between anecdotes, her mother offered another scone and more tea. She asked casual questions about his life in California.

"Do you miss the balmy California weather and outdoor living, Alex? We have some dear friends in Los Angeles. Helen and Paul Overton have a daughter Steffi's age who must have been your classmate at Loma Vista. Dori spent part of a summer with us in Colorado several years ago."

A wary Alex put down his cup and slowly pushed himself into the back of the chair. He had an intense expression in his green eyes.

"It's been quite different living in the Midwest, Mrs. Pfeiffer. It seems unbelievable, but I'd never seen it snow before. School was easier, not as much homework, and the teachers, well... About Dori Overton, she might have been a year or two behind me. Loma Vista is a rather large country day school."

"They must have known your mother through the League, school functions, and the hectic social scene out there."

He knew Dori Overton, yet had no intention of revealing any details of his previous life, although he felt a prickly uneasiness by evading her questions.

"Mother always traveled, Mrs. Pfeiffer. She never seemed to be home, and that's why I came east to live with Lucky and Dad. You know, several weeks ago Steffi and I spent an afternoon at the Art Institute. She seems to be an expert on the French impressionists."

"Alex, how awfully thoughtful of you. Steffi has always had a flair for art, and you know she paints. I would imagine it's her real love. She absolutely must spend a year in Florence and develop her considerable talent."

Steffi seemed nonchalant after her mother's compliment, and Alex thought perhaps she was also being pushed by her parents.

"I'm anxious to hear about Wyoming and your wonderful adventures." Steffi was animated. "You must be an experienced cowboy. We want you to visit Running Springs next summer."

"Well, I helped on the high mountain pack trips. The ones up to Yellowstone were really beautiful—wandering trails, dense forests, and small steel blue lakes tucked away hundreds of feet below. Occasional bear, elk, moose, and those soaring bald eagles. Incredible sights. Cold nights after scorching days. It all made summers far too short. I have a great friend who has the intriguing name of Doc Pardee. He's taught me all sorts of things about ranching, handling horses, and hunting. Steffi, you would like it there."

When Mrs. Pfeiffer put her cup on the tray, Alex knew tea time was over. Initially he had had misgivings about the afternoon, but now he was reluctant to leave their engaging hospitality. She turned to ring for the maid.

"Please stay longer, Alex," Steffi whispered.

He managed inconsequential conversation for several minutes before thanking his hostess and asking to be remembered to Mr. Pfeiffer. Steffi procrastinated, then took his coat from the maid. At the apartment door, she stepped in front of him and held his arm. She put her hand over the elevator button.

"Fresh air and a walk along the lakefront would be perfect, but it's late and your mother might not approve. Remember the hayride?"

"Yes, and a week goes by in a hurry, doesn't it, Alex?"

He looked toward the apartment door, slightly ajar. The dimly lit hall was invitingly quiet. He put his arms around her and she sighed when he kissed her cheeks, forehead, and closed eyes.

He spoke softly. "These are special hugs for you, better than those grizzlies in Yellowstone." His lips touched her ear. "See you next week. I'll miss you, Steffi; will call tonight."

Several mornings later he found it on his dresser mirror:

From the desk of Dr. Brian Dunham:

Dear Alex,

After your fancy tea party you seem to be wandering around with your heart on your sleeve. Keep to yourself more; stay on the ball with your studies and sports. Honor roll cards now, moon over Miami later.

Yours,
D3

Alex struck his desk, mumbling. "Thought I had hidden my feelings for Steffi, probably not. I swear he'll never tell me how to feel. I'm waiting for the day, another year."

During the season's last game, Brian Dunham stood on the sidelines. Ace and Alex helped Tombo off the field. "Coach, please have my dad come over here, right now," Alex said.

The headmaster was bent over his son and watched as Dr. Dunham cut off his shoe.

Tombo squeezed his hand. "Alex, I can't move my foot."

"All right, pal, take it easy; you'll be fine. My dad's here. There are still five minutes left to pull off the win, and we'll do it, Tommy boy."

Ace and Alex splashed their faces as the time-out ended. There were blotches of blood on Alex's tan pants and orange jersey. He rolled up his sleeves, wiping red dribbles from his nose and mouth with the back of his hand. After the two ran back on the field, he put his hands on Ace's shoulders.

"Coach says they're bound to run the double reverse about now. I'll get the runner low, and you hit him belt high. Got it, Ace? Blast the son of a bitch hard. Make him feel it."

There was a sound of cracking leather when Alex ferociously smashed the running back above the knees. The solid, crushing blow of his tackle forced a loud groan from the downed player. Alex slammed his fist into the ball. Rolling, he saw Ace catch it in midair. Grass stains, pungent mud, tape, oil of winter-green . . . victory's smell.

That night, Tombo's teammates and friends gathered in his hospital room. His leg was suspended by a set of pulleys and a weight. He playfully greeted his visitors by wiggling pink toes protruding from the bottom of a fresh plaster cast.

"Well, you two birds did it again, but it took three of those guys in their pretty lavender pants to do this to me. Wait until next year. Everybody look at this wild Rube Goldberg contraption that's got me tied in knots. They've got this thing rigged so when I drink some water, push the call button, and sneeze hard, my cast will play 'The Star-spangled Banner.' "

After Alex and Ace signed Tombo's cast with a list of the season's scores, Steffi and Cindy drew colored pictures of football players passing, running, and kicking. When a post mortem of the game ended, everyone offered to bring hamburgers and a shake.

Tombo beamed. "Sounds great; I could use some real food. They're starving me here. Just my luck, I'll miss tonight's hay-ride. Shoo-Shoo will be here looking after my best interests. Know what I mean, guys? Got to get all the mileage I can from being an invalid." Tombo hugged his pillow. Most of the team left.

Alex was facetious. "Thomas O. White Jr., according to Academy rules, we faithfully promise to bring homework twice a day for an extraordinary scholar excused because of a self-inflicted injury."

Before closing the door, Alex added, "Take it from me, Tombo, you'll get a charge out of the nurse's bed bath." He imitated the headmaster: " 'Remember that you are gentlemen at all times, and the Academy always has its eyes on you.' That means you, Tombo. Keep your hands to yourself. Necking with Shoo-Shoo is forbidden on the premises. You were great today. Hope the ankle doesn't hurt too much. Get a good night's sleep. See you tomorrow, and don't forget: winning was worth it."

The Academy players and their dates huddled in the large hay wagon drawn by two ponderous horses. Wet ground muffled the sound of their hooves. The ride was jerky and everyone cheered when it hit a bump. The shouting, joking, and victory celebration had settled down when the players vowed next year they would be undefeated.

Steffi and Alex found a secluded corner among the bales. When they were comfortably settled, the wagon suddenly turned and she fell against his shoulder.

"Steffi, what a break. That's called 'benefit corner'." He pulled his sweater over her head, wrapping the baggy ends tightly around her. Her hair smelled of fresh hay. "Now it's your turn to look like a scarecrow, remember?"

As the wagon rolled away from the lakeshore, they were aware of burning leaves blended with the earthy scent of har-vested corn. Near the end of the evening, Alex sat with his head cushioned against a soft mound of hay. When her lips met his mouth, she tasted and swallowed blood from a cut on his tongue. A part of him.

"Alex, please, for me, don't get hurt the way Tombo did this afternoon. I know you always want to be first in line. There's a price, though, because I'm looking at your swollen face, nose, and eyes. You could be the one in the hospital. Is it really worth it?"

"Don't worry, Steffi." His tone was cajoling. "All these games are a challenge for us. The boys and the teams are terrific. You know about wanting to win. Ask your father; he understands. I can tell."

It was Fifth Form, Junior Class Day. Honor students, team captains, and next year's senior prefect, known affectionately as "the defect," were introduced to the students in the Academy's auditorium. Alex thought T.O. was getting long-winded, and he knew the two hundred faces were bored. Ace recited the prefect's duties and school rules, while Tombo predicted a good season for the basketball team.

A broad smile spread across T.O.'s ruddy face as he congratulated students with stiff, square honor roll cards embossed with the Academy's colorful seal. "Now Dunham will speak to the freshmen."

Alex looked at the restless group, and, when he stepped down from the stage approaching the lower classmen, one snapped, "Here comes Mr. Perfect; wonder what 'rah, rah' crap he'll throw at us now? You don't play to lose. Dammit, win, or I'll kick your butt, that sort of junk. Everybody says he's got a mean temper, too."

Alex walked among the younger students. "You should know there are opportunities to study hard and participate in sports at the Academy. It takes determination, and I want to see as many of you as possible out for football next fall. It's a good way to compete and have fun." He continued, "Find out about yourselves in close games, when the margin between winning and losing is narrow. You will have to concentrate and be physically tough. Have a great summer, and good luck for the coming school year."

He smiled, then left the stage.

The freshman class stood and gave three quick claps, the Academy's traditional signature of approval.

It was a sunset sieved by trees. Alex and Doc rode back from the stables after a long pack trip through the lower Tetons.

"Alex, heads up." Doc reined in his horse as he cautiously rode up next to him. "All right, Dunham, show me how good you are when the chips are down. You've been here three years. What do you see and hear five yards in front of your right leg?"

Alex barely whispered, "Doc, I don't quite understand."

"Boy, you damn well better, or that rattler will be sittin' in the saddle with you in a couple of seconds. Stay quiet, hold your horse still, and take that lasso there off the saddle horn real slow-like. Do jist what I tell you."

Alex lifted the coil of rope into a horizontal position, then threw it on target. The snake struck at the rope, missing his leg by several feet. In one quick motion, he dismounted, picked up a rock, and crushed its head.

"Pick up that SOB, Alex, and be sure it's a goner."

Alex obeyed, then pulled his striped tan six-foot-long trophy into his saddle pouch.

The next morning they were riding in a pickup truck for the bus stop to Denver.

"Doc, I'll miss you, old cowboy. The last three summers have been better than *Gang Busters*. You've taught me everything. Do you think I would be a good soldier?"

"Alex, you can be anything you put your mind to, son."

"Thanks a heap, Doc. I'm off to spend a few days with my girl and her family near Denver. I'll write once in a while."

Doc ran his broad hand through his hair and gave him a cuff across the face.

That summer Alex packed his blazer, a pair of gray flannels, one good shirt, and saddle shoes for his visit to the Pfeiffer ranch. He had saved his ranch pay to make the trip. As the bus hummed down the two-lane highway, he pulled out a letter from his father that had arrived earlier:

From the desk of Dr. Brian Dunham:

Dear Alex,

I expect you to be on your best behavior at the Pfeiffers'. You have waited three years for this visit. Remember the manners we have taught you; dress with coat and tie for dinner. Have a good time. Don't forget, Steffi is a young, lovely girl whom you must always treat with respect. Another matter: don't be late for football camp up at the lake, since you are this year's captain and should report early to meet Coach Hanbury and the team. Not many young men have the chance to end the summer like this. Don't forget to give our best regards to Katzie and Erich.

Yours,
D3

Alex realized it wasn't Doc's black coffee giving him stomach cramps but the letters that always arrived when he was feeling good about himself. With each note, he thought less about the meaning of his father's enigmatic signature: "D3." No sentiment. It was as dull as a stamp on a piece of machinery. He crumpled it in a ball and opened the window.

He knotted his tie and brushed off his blazer as the front door of the Greyhound swung open with a gust of air. Alex walked toward Steffi with his suitcase, threw it aside, then dashed the last few yards. The memory of her smile was now reality. He saw her run from the side of a wood-paneled convertible and picked her up by the waist, whirling her around.

"I thought time would never pass. I've missed you, Alex. Do I write as well as Elizabeth Browning? Welcome to Running Springs, cowhand."

They stood, holding each other's outstretched arms. He had never seen her dressed in western clothes. The tops of her boots were covered by Levi's, and heels made her taller. She wore a cotton shirt open at the collar. Her neck muscles were prominent when she turned her head. A tanned face, hands, and arms made her sun-bleached hair, which had turned a wheat color, more striking.

"Steffi, it's hard to believe I'm actually here. I looked forward to your letters each day. They weren't from Florence or Tuscany, but made me feel close to you."

Lottie took Alex to his room on the ground floor of a two-story ranch house that overlooked a pasture where horses lazily grazed. The furniture was roughly hewn pine and his bunk wasn't different from that at the Teton ranch, but there was a small, welcome bathroom.

"Any laundry, Mr. Dunham?"

"Lottie, thanks all the same. I washed and ironed my clothes at the ranch up in Wyoming before I left."

She seemed relieved. "Dinner's at six on the porch. It's informal, you know, ranch style."

Mr. Pfeiffer was gracious. "Alex, no need for coat and tie at dinner out here in the mountains. We relax over the summer."

"Thanks, sir. Lucky and Dad mentioned I should at all times, you know, wear—"

Steffi and Alex sat facing her parents. There was an incongruous informality about the ranch. The tasteful oak dinner table was set with candles, delicate linen place mats, and a spray of mountain flowers. His preferences were the tin plates, cups, knife, and fork atmosphere of the real West. The Pfeiffers were masked by the flowers, and he felt awkward moving his head back and forth when he spoke.

"Alex, you must have had another grand summer in the Teton country." Katzie Pfeiffer had wonderful skill at opening a conversation. He remembered Lucky referring to these amiable remarks as "ice breakers."

"Yes, I thoroughly enjoyed the people and working outside, but at times I felt isolated. This year I brought my shortwave radio set and listened to news broadcasts from New York at night, and in spare moments I practiced French and German.

You've heard all of my stories about the unfortunate dudes who kept me busy when they fell off their horses."

"Oh, boo, Alex." Katzie was playful. "You're far too modest about rescuing those hapless would-be cowboys plummeting to an ignominious death without your equestrian skills."

To see Mr. Pfeiffer, Alex moved toward Steffi, putting his hand on the back of her chair. She wore a loose V-necked deep blue sweater, and as she reached for her glass, he glanced down at her breasts. He wanted to touch them. He looked up, wondering if the Pfeiffers had seen his salacious peek. He felt a yearning ache; the summer had been long without her. He shifted in his chair, strategically arranging the napkin over his lap, and lowered his voice.

"Sir, Mrs. Pfeiffer mentioned you returned from *Breastlau*, you know—I mean Breslau, sir. Your university town, it's actually Breslau, yes, Breslau. Several years ago, or it must have been weeks, is that correct? Did you visit relatives or have an opportunity to make any other judgments about the German situation?"

Erich Pfeiffer lifted his glass of favorite Mosel. "Alex, my dear boy, congratulations on your amusing pronunciation of German geography. However, to answer your question, my colleagues and I constantly consult with the State Department. Initially, we had good reason to believe Hitler and the Nazis were on the right course, more jobs, better services for the people, and an economic recovery following the Great War. I'm afraid we were mistaken. After a recent journey, I have little doubt the Germans are re-arming with a superbly organized industrial system geared for future war."

"Mr. Pfeiffer, I thought the Versailles Treaty limited arms production and the size of the military."

"Alex, that's naive," Erich emphasized. "We know it was one of Hitler's early intentions to disregard the Allied restrictions. The German occupation of the Rhineland this last spring was obvious proof of his intentions."

Steffi questioned, "Daddy, don't the British and French have the largest armies in the world? Why didn't they stop Hitler?"

"Dear, democracies are a marvelous form of government. Sometimes there's too much talk, pacifism and no action."

"Do you think our country would ever become involved in another European war?" Alex asked.

"I have frequently spoken to congressional delegations warning them about the situation in Germany." Pfeiffer frowned. "Our government is unable or unwilling to accept this reality. The 'America First' movement is politically powerful, supported by influential midwestern senators who are isolationists."

"From what I have read," Alex said, "we have no standing army or air force, which eliminates our role in the equation of containing Germany. Wouldn't you agree, Mr. Pfeiffer?"

"Alex, even if we had a strong military, I believe at this time isolationism is such firm public opinion that we are left with a weak, ineffective foreign policy."

"What happens next?" Steffi and Alex asked at the same time.

Pfeiffer seemed frustrated. "Although it is too soon to judge, I would guess Hitler will attempt to annex German-speaking territories, such as Austria and Czechoslovakia, to what he calls 'Greater Germany.' I can only hope I am mistaken about the future."

After dessert, Steffi and Alex joined Erich Pfeiffer in the living room around a large open fire. The dry wood burned with a smoky odor reminiscent of nights in the Tetons. The couple lounged at Mr. Pfeiffer's side while Mrs. Pfeiffer continued her needlepoint. Alex was never certain about the difference between stitching and knitting. Lottie brought in brandy and a box of cigars for the host, and they continued their discussion.

"Alex, have you made plans for a career after you graduate from the Academy? I understand you are a first-rate student, and Steffi tells me you are one of their better athletes."

"I hope to go to Princeton next fall and might like to work at a military school during summer vacation."

"Are you serious about this, or has Brian convinced you to become a doctor?"

"First, I wish to learn more about military life, and I have no plans or commitment to medicine."

"Good. Then come to my office this spring, and during the next few months I'll look into the matter and see what's available. No guarantees, yet there might be some sort of opening to teach at Harper Military School in Indiana during the summers. They have an outstanding summer camp for high school students from all over the country. How does that sound?"

"I can't thank you enough, sir, and hope to visit with you more before I graduate from the Academy next June. I would like to speak with you again about the rapid changes in European politics."

"Of course, Alex. 'Vielleicht wirst du eines Tages ein Soldat'."

"You may be right, sir. There are demanding challenges and excitement in military life. I would imagine it's a long, hard road."

The next morning, Alex leaped out of bed after Steffi tossed several pillows at his head. That hadn't changed; she still enjoyed teasing him.

"We don't take baths out here, Mr. Alex Dunham. Get some clothes on for a run and an early-morning swim. By the way, you don't sleep with your tie on, do you? Mom and Dad will kill you if you come to dinner tonight dressed for the Waldorf. Last one in gets fifty lashes."

She disappeared as he pulled on a pair of hot-weather football shorts. He chased her through a lush pasture where several horses grazed, then jumped a creek, feeling relief underfoot from a blanket of pine needles where the woods opened on a crystal-clear lake.

The bright morning sun filtered through the water as they both dived, splitting the silver ripples on its surface. The shock of the cold water was numbing, but they were warmed by swimming along the shoreline, uncontrollably splashing one another and having a mock "who can pull me over" battle with an imaginary enemy.

Steffi's hair hung in strands on a white cotton shirt clinging to her breasts and flat belly. Alex tugged at her feet and ankles when he swam between her thighs. After they cavorted underwater, their blond heads surfaced in a rush of bubbles and Alex lifted her by the waist to his shoulders. He lowered her slowly, and she wrapped her legs tightly around him. They kissed and swallowed streams of water running off their faces and necks.

She looked into the sun and closed her eyes. "Alex, I, I . . . you know what I mean. Please don't ever forget about me, promise?"

"Steffi, I think about you every day, and I'm happiest when I'm with you." He squeezed water from long hair behind her neck. "You're full of joy, and I have a feeling that's hard to explain . . . You seem to trust in the goodness of life." He searched her blue eyes. "Please be my girl."

"I have been hoping and waiting for you to ask. Yes, Alex, I am your girl."

He carried her to the shore and found a flat boulder where they dried off in the warm morning sun.

"Three days pass quickly, Mrs. Pfeiffer, and I hope I have been a good guest. My father and Lucky wish to be remembered to you and Mr. Pfeiffer. Thank you both for asking me to visit. I really don't want to . . . "

Katzie put her arm around him.

Erich was cheerful. "Remember, *Generalfeldmarschall*, we'll have dinner one night this fall when I return home, and can make some tentative plans for the next few summers."

"Again, thank you. See you at home in a few weeks."

The Denver bus slowed to a stop, followed by a rush of dust, and Alex threw his bag inside. When the driver honked mindlessly, Alex leaned down and drew a heart in the sandy dirt. He looked back at Steffi once more and smiled. The door closed.

Alex emptied his laundry in the mudroom.

"You'll need them for the next couple of weeks." Colleen was persistent. "Give me those blue football shorts. My goodness, young man, they're still wet."

"There's plenty for you to do, Colleen. Please forget it."

He carefully tucked the shorts away in a corner of his baggage and wore them every day at practice.

During dinner, Alex talked about his hunting adventures with Doc and embellished his encounter with the rattler. He briefly mentioned the several days spent with the Pfeiffers.

"My friend Doc Pardee would call their ranch 'pretty fancy.' By the way, we meet at the Academy about nine in the morning. Should be a short trip up to Eagle Lake. Coach Hanbury has everything set up for the next two weeks of practice. Nice to be home, Lucky. Good night, all."

She kissed him. "Sleep tight, Alex; don't let the bed bugs bite."

He expected a lengthy litany, but this time it was a handwritten note taped to his baggage:

From the desk of Dr. Brian Dunham:

Dear Alex,

You have done an admirable job at the Academy, and this year must go well. Be a team player and leader. Set a good example at football camp, study hard for your college entrance exams this fall, and talk more to Mr. Starke about your interview coming up in several months. Each year becomes more important for you. Make us proud. I know you will, Alex.

Yours,
D3

Alex thought he had won his spurs by being chosen team captain.

The morning sprints, calisthenics, blocking and tackling stationary dummies, and afternoon scrimmages exhausted the players. At the end of the day, they swam around the pier, where they grappled, pushed, and pulled during endless dunking and water fights. At the final dinner Coach Hanbury was unmistakably direct.

"Be athletes ... scholars. Discipline yourselves. You will

win. This year is special for the seniors. You've got the talent, will, and brains to win all nine games. We've kept strict training rules up here, and when you get home, keep up the routine. Smoking or beer after a dance puts you on the bench. Does everyone understand? The buses leave for home after a morning workout. Good luck."

Alex, Ace, and Percy Evans rode in the first bus with half of the team, and there was the usual chorus of bravado, griping, wondering, and bragging during the trip back to the Academy gym. Hanbury was lost in traffic behind the second bus. Bags, helmets, pads, shoes, and the team's accoutrements were unloaded from the buses, and in the midst of hasty unpacking Alex saw Percy sitting on the bus fender, smoking with a nonchalant arrogance.

"OK, Percy, toss the pack of cigarettes." Alex kicked the fender. "You heard Coach last night, didn't you?"

Percy was defiant. "Yeah, I heard the big bag of wind blow off. What's one or two smokes here or there? Dunham, you think you're the big-shot captain telling me what to do, don't you?"

Alex turned his shoulder into Percy Evans's chest, knocked him backward, then hit him across the chin as he fell. He dragged him to his feet, and struck him squarely in the nose. Blood spurted. The players watched in silence as he staggered, then slumped slowly by the door of the bus.

Alex was shouting. "Never again in front of my team. Now get your stupid ass off the ground. If I ever catch you breaking the rules again, it will be worse for you, believe me."

After several players helped Evans to his feet, Ace held Alex by the collar of his sweater. "Alex, let's go to the gym. Shit, pal, you hit him too hard. What gets into you, anyway? Don't be so tough all the time. You're a mean bastard when you lose your temper. You seem to be completely different when you're angry and think you're right. Nobody's perfect, including you. Some of the younger fellows won't understand, although Coach has spelled out the rules."

Alex continued unloading the equipment, throwing ball

bags, helmets, and shoes onto the luggage carts.

Several days later he stood in front of T.O.'s desk and was not asked to be seated. Alex knew he would be addressed as 'Mister' Dunham.

"The school year has not begun well for you, Mr. Dunham. Did it occur to you there was another way to manage a recalcitrant?"

"No, sir. It was my responsibility."

"You're too intelligent for that answer. Explain yourself and be quick about it."

"Sir, Evans broke the rules. You reminded me four years ago when I came to the Academy: obey the rules. I was elected captain. Mr. White, I couldn't allow Evans to flaunt discipline in front of the younger players."

T. O. White was firm. "You should have let Coach Hanbury or me reprimand Evans. Do you have any idea what your teammates think? They say you're an acrimonious bully, trying to be the perfect captain. Are you listening to me, Mr. Dunham?"

"Coach Hanbury spoke to me each day during camp, sir. I respect his standards. He expects me to be a leader. He has always thought a team can be no better than its weakest players." His tone was anxious. "Sir, it's my last year. We must, we absolutely have to, win every game."

Alex remembered the humiliation, lingering depression. The degradation of defeat. Curtains pulled down. Restless in darkness. D3 carping: "Did you try hard enough?" How could his headmaster understand?

"Mr. Dunham, you are the number-one boy in your class. After this unfortunate episode, control your anger and temper. Now, Mr. Dunham, you shall visit Bishop and Mrs. Evans and apologize. I never wish to discuss matters such as this again."

"Mr. White, I'm sorry—"

T.O. interrupted, thumbs in his vest pockets. "Never tell me you're sorry about anything. Next time, think; consider consequences before you act. Don't be so intolerant of someone else's mistakes."

Alex didn't look up from his dinner plate. He waited for his father's barrage, knowing Lucky couldn't help. Nevertheless, Alex looked toward her hoping for a nod of recognition.

Dr. Brian Dunham folded his napkin and slowly finished his coffee. "Well, Alex?"

"I have spoken with Mr. White. I have been excused from English tomorrow and will apologize to the Bishop and his wife."

"Do you think you have done anything wrong by beating the hell out of his son?"

"I probably shouldn't have given him such a pounding, but now he'll respect the rules."

His father asked, "What do Coach Hanbury and the team think of you?"

"Some of the players, including my best friends, have criticized me and said I was malicious. One thing is certain: my team won't fail because one player doesn't care." Alex expected a tedious lecture.

"You have a point, Alex, but you are older now. Give some thought to the impression you convey to people. You have a good share of anger, hostility. Learn restraint, patience. Do follow my advice, Son."

"You have homework tonight." Lucky finished her dessert. "Now dash along to your room, dear."

Pete Starke was engrossed. Some listened; to others it was consummate ennui.

> " 'When April with his showers hath pierced the drought
> Of March with sweetness to the very root,
> And flooded every vein . . . ' "

Alex asked to be excused.

Stark stepped away from a desk cluttered with books and papers. They walked into the hall. "Alex, keep your sense of humor. A good captain takes his responsibilities seriously and remembers he has some warts and bumps on his nose."

"Sir, what do you imagine most of the students think?"

"Most of them don't care about trying to be the best. Pay the price if you are certain you have done the correct thing. Don't worry about public opinion. Get on with your studies and win some games. Tell me what the Bishop says. By the way, our old friend Dickens would certainly have written a story about you for the *Atlantic Monthly*. The same problem: what's right or wrong and what one should do about it. I'll think about you, Alex."

The study was cold and forbidding, with inhospitable stone walls and the humbling sorrow of a miniature Pietà on a small table. Bishop Evans wore a somber suit and thin white collar. He gazed through the lead-framed windows, then looked down and continued writing, seeming unaware of either his wife or the visitor. They sat on a firm, straight-backed sofa. Alex thought of Christmas mass several years ago when his hand ached. Deep pain in his fingers. Kindness to a young stranger.

The Bishop looked up, surprised by their presence. "Mr. White tells me you and my son, Percy, have had a difference of opinion."

"Yes, Bishop Evans, we have."

"You thought he broke the team's rules?"

"Yes, sir, he definitely broke the rules."

"You're probably right about that, Alex. Football has never been of interest to me or Percy. I wonder if he should play such a violent game. Mrs. Evans and I are pleased to see you, son."

"Sir, I apologize to both of you for my ungentlemanly behavior. Percy and I have been friends during our Academy years, and I hope this continues."

"Alex, we understand what the Academy and trying to be the best means to a young man like you, but think of God's words: 'He that is without fault, let him cast the first stone'."

"Yes, Bishop Evans, I understand. Sometimes I expect too much of myself and my friends."

The Bishop sorted more papers, arranged books, then turned to Alex. "By the way, best of luck to you and the team this fall."

"I appreciate your patience with me, Bishop Evans."

It was on top of his schoolbooks.

From the desk of Dr. Brian Dunham:

Dear Alex,

Perhaps I am responsible for some of your desire to excel and seek approval. You have set your sights so high you can't see your own faults. Be more tolerant and less critical of your friends. Your anger with Percy Evans is an example. When you think you are right about things, your temper makes you go off like a Fourth of July firecracker. Learn to control your emotions.

Yours,
D3

He met Steffi in front of her apartment.

"Where are we going this afternoon? Come on, Alex; surprise me."

"It wouldn't be a surprise if I told you, now would it?"

When they reached Walgreen's, he led her into a booth with curtains at its entrance and dropped a dime in the slot. "Steffi, please go in and smile."

There was a flash, strange clanking noises. The small picture dropped in a tray.

"Alex, it's horrid; look at me. Not exactly Miss America 1936. Now, Clarke Gable, it's your turn."

He had one more coin, and they sat beaming at one another.

They found a bench along an obscure stretch of the lakefront. He shuffled through piles of raked leaves. "If we could go anywhere this afternoon, Steffi, where would it be?"

"It's your choice, Alex."

"I think we should ride through the foothills of Wyoming, miraculously become birds, land in Running Springs, fly to the lake, and swim until we become fish. Have you ever seen two fish kiss, Steffi?"

"No, Alex, show me; please, right now."

He pulled her close and kissed her warm, moist lips. He scrutinized every detail of her vivacious face. "Tell me honestly, Steffi, if I did something not everyone approved of, what would you think?"

She hesitated. "Obviously it depends on what you did. . . . How serious was it?"

"I walloped Percy Evans because he smoked in front of the team after camp up at the lake. Some of the younger players are afraid of me now. They think I'm a bully and should have let Coach or Mr. White solve the problem."

"Maybe you're asking too much of yourself, when being Alex Dunham is enough. Believe me, your team will win because you set a good example and always give your best. I'm with you all the way. . . . That's that."

She posed dramatically and made a sophisticated face, head turned upward and to the side, with a theatrical smirk. "Now, dahling, put one of your cigarettes in this fancy holder of mine." Both laughed as she struck an imaginary match. Her cheeks were puckered, pretending to take a deep breath, and then she rounded her lips as if to blow smoke rings.

"Thanks, Steffi; now I've got it straight."

"We have a picture of each other. Who gets the one with both of us?" she wondered, "After all, it was your ten cents."

"Then, Miss America, it's my early Christmas present. Call you in a day or so. Hope your folks don't mind."

"They don't care, but Dad whistles for me after fifteen minutes."

The students had christened the Friday morning class "the Hour of Charm." Chairs in the senior history precept were circled around Mr. James "Buzzer" O'Brien. He wore a hearing aid that made screechy sounds, repeatedly forcing him to adjust its volume.

"Gentlemen, put aside your books, no crib notes, pencils away. . . . I want logic and imagination from you intellectual midgets. Each one of you is in the State Department. Think of the amount of information coming across your desk each day.

What I want is a scenario for the course of American diplomacy over the next several years."

He stood expectantly. "Where's the secretary of state? Speak to me, Mr. Manning."

"Well, sir, I'm concerned about the Italians and their aggression in Ethiopia. A modern nation suppressing a country living in the Middle Ages. All they have are spears, no modern weapons to protect themselves. I think we should put trade sanctions on Italy. The president and State Department must make some noise about their invasion."

"That's a start, Manning. I doubt if you could convince Congress to slap Mussolini's wrist. The Italians seem to be loyal fascists and are reasonably strong under Mussolini, however have lost their warlike character over the centuries. They're basically agrarian, without much industrial sophistication. Do you think trade sanctions would be effective?"

"Possibly not, sir. Their industrial strength is unable to compete with other European countries, and their farm produce, leather, marble, and glass exports are simply luxury items. Furthermore, our hands are tied because we aren't a member of the League of Nations to enforce sanctions."

O'Brien turned down the whistling noise of his earpiece, while other students offered plausible theories and conjectures from neutrality to the vague possibility of another war. As the hour ended, Buzzer put a foot on an empty chair, rested his elbow on his knee, and turned to Alex.

Alex incorporated parts of his conversations with Erich Pfeiffer. "If I were secretary of state, sir, I would keep my eyes on the Germans. They are Europe's most disciplined and well organized animals. Their occupation of the Rhineland last spring speaks volumes and might be the first of several moves in the political, military chess game that will be played during the next several years. Congress has insisted upon strict neutrality, which will limit the flexibility of the State Department and the president. It's probably a good policy for the present. We should use our influence to arrange an accommodation between the

Allies and Germany, although their current approach of appeasement should succeed."

"All right, any other ideas? If not, off to your weekend. Don't forget the last game. I'm bringing the wife and kids, but I'm afraid when they come, we always lose."

O'Brien and Alex sat together several minutes in the wake of students glad to be on their way.

"Alex, what will we do in the last exciting act of your Broadway play?"

"We have great potential industrial strength and an enormous pool of manpower, but isolationism is a political fact of life. It seems to me neutrality and diplomacy are the best solutions, at least for now."

"I know you graduate this June. What's next?"

"I have my college interview in January."

"What schools have you thought about?"

"I'll try for Princeton."

"If you need any letters, recommendations, let me know."

"Thanks very much, Mr. O'Brien, I will. Incidentally, when you come out for the last game tomorrow, we'll use you as a twelfth man. You and Mr. Hodges are two of our best rooters."

The rain had been drenching. The next morning, leaves were stuck to the sidewalk in small puddles. A fresh breeze blew off the lake. It could affect the game's strategy. He wanted the wind at his team's back during the second and final quarters.

Late in the game, Alex stood in front of Hanbury, wiping sweat and dirt from his face. His sleeves were rolled to the elbows. Shoulder and hip pads exaggerated his size, particularly the depth and width of his chest. His legs seemed longer and larger because of knee-length grass-stained white socks. After gulping stale water during the time-out, he tossed up blades of grass that floated straight toward the University School punter. The coach held the front of his splattered jersey.

"You and Warren are the ends. Rush the kicker the way

you've done hundreds of times in practice. Tell Billy Warren what you want from him. Don't draw him pictures; understand, Alex?"

The team surrounded him and waited. Alex spoke to his players, hands on hips, poised, as small billows of breath condensed in the afternoon coldness. As a sophomore, Billy started each game. He was known as "Dunham's shadow." Their teamwork had been pivotal, because they were tall, formidable blockers and receivers.

Billy's warm breath struck his face. "Can we pull it out, Alex?"

"Concentrate; do everything you've been taught. Brush by their end; take out the blocking back. Stay on your feet. They're weaker on my side. I go for the punter. Hammer them, dammit, Billy, hammer them. Watch for the free ball. Shit, you know where the goal line is, don't you?"

There was a chorus of repeated taunts from University School students and cheerleaders. "Little red rover, little red rover, please send Alex over."

"Alex, Alex, thinks he's a big shot, 'cause he beats up his own players a lot," another shouted gleefully.

A pimple-faced student with a megaphone was bitingly obnoxious. "Dunham, look at your panties, Mommy's going to have to wash your undies tonight, little fella."

It was an indelible memory for Alex, the kicker's shoes slipping on the wet field. An extra step made the difference. Alex's six-foot frame was stretched in midair, with arms and legs in full extension when the punted ball hit him on the hand and side of his face. It made a dull, thumping sound as Billy recovered it on the bounce. Alex stood when the sharp whistle sounded. There was sudden, searing pain and the fresh smell of grass and pungent mud. After the score, the exultant sophomore ran back and handed him the ball like a hunting trophy.

Alex looked at his hands, then dropped to one knee when he saw two fingers twisted at an odd angle. Steffi and Dr. Dunham reached the bench after pushing through the confusion of Academy students and rooters.

Steffi held Dr. Dunham's coat sleeve. "His hand and face. Dr.

Brian, something's awfully wrong."

"Son, do exactly as I say. Now bite down and turn your head."

He gave a sharp jerk on each dislocated finger and then quickly taped them together. He painted the side of his face with a foul-smelling, sticky, brown liquid. Alex's eye was swollen closed by the time the last series of plays ended. The players carried Hanbury back to the field house on their shoulders, tossing him up in the air, shouting and singing.

Alex and Steffi ran toward one another. She reached out, brushed back his wet hair, and touched his reddened face.

He put his mud-caked arms around her and held up his helmet to the team.

There was exuberance and pride. "Steffi, it was the game we wanted and needed. We've won it all. We played better when it counted."

"Your sweater was good luck, Alex. What a way to win; I thought the last few minutes would never end. I really like your one-eyed smile. How about your hand, Alex? Dr. Dunham told me your fingers weren't broken."

"They feel better now. Bundle up; stay warm over in the lobby of the field house. Give me a few minutes. We'll take the bus home."

Steffi and some of the parents listened to the shouting and cheers from the showers and locker rooms. She looked for Dr. Dunham, but he had left early to take one of the players to the hospital. She hid her face, grateful Alex only had some bumps and bruises.

His oversize white sweater with four bright orange rings on the arm and a large "A" on its front hung below her waist. A long raincoat, covering a gray skirt, almost reached her ankles. They settled in the back of the bus, bedraggled and happy while she held his bandaged hand. He got up and pulled the cord for the next stop.

"Alex, don't we have farther to go?"

They walked down a small side street near the Academy. Mid-November snowflakes had wet their faces when they

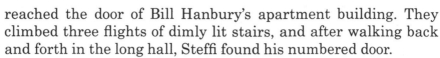

reached the door of Bill Hanbury's apartment building. They climbed three flights of dimly lit stairs, and after walking back and forth in the long hall, Steffi found his numbered door.

Alex knocked. "Good evening, Coach, a short visit. I would like to introduce Steffi Pfeiffer."

"Pleased to make your acquaintance, Steffi. Come right in and meet the family. Molly, we're in the living room; Alex and his girl are here."

Molly's face was plump and her housedress revealed a stocky figure. Three curious children followed her, with remnants of jam and peanut butter around their mouths.

"So nice to see you. Please sit down. It's a cold evening; how about a glass of hot apple cider?"

"Sounds fine, Mrs. Hanbury," Steffi answered for both of them.

Their apartment had a friendly quality, old and hospitable. Alex and Steffi sat on a sofa opposite a tilted print of flowers. A picture of Hanbury's Dartmouth football team hung above his comfortable rocker with an unsteady armrest weakened by time and use. Alex and Steffi sat close, warming their hands on the cider glasses.

"Coach, I . . . we wanted to stop by a minute, and I hope you understand." Alex hesitated. "It's difficult to know how to thank you for everything over the last four years. You've done so much for me, and all of the other players. Hard work, some tough losses. I think our team played its best for you this afternoon. It finally came together."

Bill Hanbury leaned back, hands behind his head, with a satisfied smile. His slipper-covered feet rested on a large stool. "You had a winning team. Today was a fine game. You hit hard, played smart football, and came from behind to win. It's not over yet. Now we have basketball and the baseball season to look forward to before you leave for that New Jersey state school for young ladies."

The children joined the adults in laughter. Alex stood and shook his broad hand; then they slapped each other on the shoulders.

"Thanks for dropping by." Hanbury smiled. "I bet you wear the captain's sweater all the time, don't you, Steffi?"

"Never without it, Coach. It will always mean good luck. Thanks for the delicious cider, Mrs. Hanbury. Hope we see you soon."

Steffi and Alex introduced each member of the team and their dates to the Pfeiffers. Lottie passed among the guests with trays of refreshments. Alex watched his friends file into the dining room, where they were seated at the elaborately set table. Their faces were scrubbed, hair slicked down with liberal doses of tonic. Some had bruised knuckles and cut lips, and there was an occasional taped nose. All wore white shirts, variously knotted school ties, and blazers. They sat stiffly in their chairs.

Dennis Black Harvey III was accustomed to the formality of candelabra, bone china, and delicate crystal. There was an uncomfortable pause in the conversation as the guests admired the elegant setting when Denny confidently flipped open his napkin, then watched helplessly as a hard roll bounced and meandered along the linen tablecloth.

Katzie gave Alex a whimsical glance. "I'm curious, Alex dear. How far is the team's field house from the Academy?"

"Oh, I guess about a roll's throw away, Mrs. Pfeiffer."

The stiff formality was broken as the room rollicked with laughter. Katzie reached for his hand and gave a warm squeeze. Steffi and some of the guests quietly applauded.

A friendly drone of conversation ensued—summer vacations, movies, colleges. Then Mr. Pfeiffer began questioning the players. "Well, gentlemen, this afternoon's game?"

Billy Warren pushed his plate back, wrinkling the delicate tablecloth and almost toppling his crystal goblet. His large dinner fork was dangerously poised on the edge of his plate and bounced along the plush carpet. He leaned over, picked it up, and wiped it with his napkin. He rubbed his taped, bruised nose.

"I tell you, Mr. Pfeiffer, you can't imagine how the game ended. They played us even for four quarters, then got a score. We got one back. Now listen to this. . . .I made the winning touchdown after Alex blocked their kick. I bet he's jealous tonight because I can see Steffi and he can only see half of her with that swollen eye." Billy sat back in his chair, basking in the details of his heroics.

Erich Pfeiffer looked toward Alex. "Is there anything more?"

"Every man played well, Mr. Pfeiffer. All of us are pleased to be your guests tonight, and my friends and I thank you and Mrs. Pfeiffer for your invitation. It's our victory celebration with your family, sir."

Lottie brought a large silver tray of coconut ice-cream balls arranged in a pyramid with a server of chocolate sauce. Alex reached for the ladle when she cautioned, "Your finger bowl first, Alex."

"Thanks, Lottie, you just saved my social reputation."

With one hand, he moved the lace doily and small bowl with a crystal fish and lemon slice to the side. The boys watched, trying to remember each step of dessert etiquette. He managed to place the coconut ball on a large spoon. The ice cream skidded along his dessert plate, followed by a long, dripping trail of sauce.

Billy was visibly relieved. "There you are, everybody, another great job, and he did it with one hand."

After dinner, groups conversed while Katzie Pfeiffer entertained a circle of guests standing before a painting. They listened attentively as she gave her interpretation of the still life. Oranges, pears, and apples appeared to tumble from a slanted table. Alex pressed his shoulder against Steffi as they held hands behind their backs, fingers entwined.

When Alex arrived home, he threw his clothes on a chair and fell in bed. The note was against his bedside lamp:

From the desk of Dr. Brian Dunham:

Dear Alex,

Go to the hospital first thing tomorrow morning for X rays of your hand and face. My congratulations on your successful football season. Perhaps you can be a leader after all of my suggestions during

the last four years. Next, start thinking about your college inter-
view. Use simple common sense. Ask yourself: if you were a horse
and got lost, how would you get home?

Yours,
D3

Alex was weary and thought lost horses didn't have anything to do with common sense. He refused to worry and only
wanted to remember Steffi's graceful body and soft skin and the
scent of perfume she had borrowed from her mother.

The following day, he read Steffi's good-luck note before he
entered a small study leading from T.O.'s office. Her enthusiasm
was like the warmth from the late-afternoon sun beaming
through the room's snow-edged windows. His spirits were lifted
and his apprehension relieved.

Peter van Hagen sat in a tall, cushioned chair unconcerned
with occasional convulsive sounds made by steam registers. He
was a large, thick-chested man with a handlebar mustache contentedly smoking a curved pipe. His speech was direct.

"So . . . Mr. Alex Dunham, prospective Princetonian?"

Van Hagen inquired about Alex's academic interests, athletics, and participation in school activities. What did he think
about the Spanish Civil War, the New Deal, the Depression, and
whether Roosevelt would keep the country out of war? The subjects were diverse, as if Alex were having a discussion with his
parents during dinner.

"Alex, tell me how you spent your last several summers."

"Well, I was fortunate enough to work on a ranch in the
Teton country, where I enjoyed the outdoors and made good
friends with the cowboys. They taught me about the beauty of
living and ranching in the West."

"What a pleasant coincidence. When I was a boy in the
Netherlands, my father took me on summer hiking trips in the
Oetztaler Alpen and around the Dachstein-Schladming in Austria. That was an exciting time of my life. Several years after
coming to this country, I was fortunate to make one of the early

climbs of the Grand Teton. In many ways its grandeur seemed more majestic and expansive than the mountain ranges in Europe. During the late twenties, Jackson Hole was a small village with climbing and ranching supplies. One old hotel, a restaurant, and cars were rare. Has there been any change?"

"Not that much. There are several more stores, a bus from Idaho comes in every day, and if change means more hotels, now there are two. I didn't have an opportunity to climb, but we rode through the foothills every year. Mountaineering is still one of my interests. Sir, to reach the crest of a peak and experience the height must be intoxicating."

"The best you can do at Princeton is climb some of the towers, but I don't recommend it," van Hagen advised. "I'm having dinner with the Whites this evening and would enjoy talking more; however, my train leaves about ten. One more thought: what would you like to do at Princeton, Alex?"

"The Academy has given me a good start, and I plan to continue my interests in history and languages. I need more fluency in French and German, and I'm prepared for new challenges. Sports are important to me, and your friend Pete Starke has spoken about crew. Competition is exciting. It's still early to decide about life after college. Mr. van Hagen, a motor is running inside, driving me to learn and perhaps, in the future, be involved in some type of government service."

"Very well, Alex, finish the next few months as if you were a hardworking cowhand or, better yet, a mountain climber. You and Mr. White will hear from me one of these days. We've had a pleasant talk. Best of luck for the future."

"My sincere thanks, Mr. van Hagen and I hope to see you this fall."

The letter of acceptance arrived in a large envelope on the first of April. There was a multitude of instructions, on sending baggage and a tour for freshmen by the Orange Key, and a copy of the Honor Code reading: "I pledge on my honor as a gentleman..."

From the desk of Dr. Brian Dunham:

Dear Alex,

Good work. You were accepted and have the chance that never came my way, for a number of different reasons. You've done something worthwhile, and see to it you always continue that way. Never make excuses, be on time, don't miss any opportunity, and study hard. You'll be on your own. Stay on the ball, keep your own counsel, and remember, chapel is mandatory.

> *Yours,*
> *D3*

He smiled to himself and thought his father was beginning to sound like a twentieth-century Shakespeare. He tried but was unable to remember the name of the pompous character from *Hamlet* who sent his son off to college with similar advice.

Alex felt pensive, then elated, as he retraced the same walk to the Academy, one he had followed the last four years. He watched T.O. step up on a small stool in the middle of his eighty milling graduates, trying to command their attention.

"Good luck in whatever you do, gentlemen, and make the Academy proud of you. You have my best personal wishes for the future. It's hard to believe I have known many of you since you began here in kindergarten. Mrs. White and I will miss each of you, and don't forget to come back for visits. All right, you're seated alphabetically, awards first, diplomas, and then Cooke and Dunham give their 'Gettysburg Addresses.' Remember now, don't bump into the furniture, don't forget your lines, and smile."

The June morning was humid. Alex's white flannel pants itched unmercifully. Before reaching the auditorium, he compulsively felt the buttons of his fly, straightened his tie, and pulled the collar of his blazer. Each graduate wore a small white garde-

nia pinned to his lapel. The auditorium was crowded with relatives and friends...a flowered collage of summer dresses,
brimmed hats, and cool linen and seersucker suits. Steffi sat
between the Dunhams and her parents, looking for Alex as the
class filed on stage.

As "first boy," Alex elected to speak last and was initially
uneasy, but he had decided to discuss what he considered important current ideas, not offer a dense essay of customary plati-
tudes.

"There will always be puzzling uncertainties in our lives,"
Alex began. "It would seem we face critical decisions and choices
now, that may reveal our national character. The economic
strength and social order of Western democracies are being challenged by dictatorial governments. The German occupation of
the Rhineland was a good example of the pacifist attitude of
France and England. If they had used their military strength,
the Germans might have been deterred. It is not beyond our
imagination that, eventually, the Old World will reach to the
New for protection of its heritage, religion, economy, and perhaps its freedom."

He briefly paused. "Opportunities will arise for the class to
contribute as leaders to our society and participate in a larger
panorama of events we are unable to foresee today. A leader is a
man who is able to overcome his personal fears and inspire others to reach beyond themselves when circumstances appear
hopeless. Gratitude, a sense of larger responsibility, and sacrifice
motivate leadership, which may be the lot of this generation. All
of these demands may translate into some form of service to our
country, and we cannot fail. This graduating class will work and
thrive in a peaceful world, yet must be prepared for other duties
the future may bring. We shall need your help and prayers for
success in the coming journey."

He turned to his headmaster, faculty, then his parents. "I
wish to express for each of my classmates our deep thanks for the
opportunity of a superb education, and the sincere hope you will
be proud of our future achievements. It is not good-bye, because
we have shared many experiences, fond memories, and lasting

friendships. They will be an unforgettable bond as the years pass."

There was the usual polite applause from guests and families; then graduates, friends, and students gathered in congenial groups while parents enjoyed coffee with the headmaster and his wife.

Brian Dunham was piqued as he stood with T. O. White and Erich Pfeiffer. The coffee was dreadful, lukewarm, and definitely needed more cream and sugar.

"Frankly, I was surprised Alex would venture into the dangerous depths of foreign affairs. By the way, T.O., could the outside help bring me another cup of coffee, fresh cream and sugar? I would be the last one to know what he planned to say; however, it's the risk of being a father. Furthermore, I had no idea, but he seems to be reasonably well informed on international affairs. Was he suggesting America might be involved in another war? My, the young people can be idealistic. Gratitude? Gratitude? What is he grateful for, if it isn't for his family? They haven't had any hard knocks yet."

T.O. came to the rescue. "Dr. Dunham, we have encouraged the seniors to be more imaginative and create scenarios in their history precepts. I'm certain 'Buzzer' O'Brien impressed upon him the importance of diplomatic skills and foreign policy stratagems in his classes. You know, Doctor, Alex was one of his favorites."

"Here's your fresh coffee, brewed to your taste, Brian." Erich Pfeiffer reached for a cup, annoyed. "I've had some interesting talks with Alex over the last several years. I would imagine you should be aware of his sincerity and idealism. As you know, he's spending this summer at Harper. He has a good command of history, is interested in military training. I'm not surprised by the latitude of his talk. I'll assume some of the responsibility for what he said, because, in a peripheral way, it reflects what my reports to the State Department and recent travels in Europe, and particularly Germany, have confirmed."

"Well, gentlemen, it's been an interesting morning," Brian said. "I'm off to New York to be honored with the Distinguished

Surgeon's Award from the International College. Hope to see you all soon. Almost forgot; have to write a memo before I leave." He sat at a corner desk, jotting on his ever-present notepad:

From the desk of Dr. Brian Dunham:

Dear Alex,

Your little speech created more problems than it solved. Regardless of my protestations, Mr. White and Erich Pfeiffer thought your ideas weren't all that bad. Why didn't you choose a topic that was more pertinent to the parents and your classmates? What's all this business about gratitude, service, and leadership? You should think more about "winning friends and influencing people." I would grade it as a C, certainly not your best effort.

Yours,
D3

The Pfeiffers and Dunhams found Alex and Steffi laughing and reminiscing with their friends about the last four years.

Brian turned to Alex. "Not bad this morning. Lucky and I must leave for the East now. You know, my award from the International College." As he left, he handed Alex his copy of the graduation program with the note folded inside.

After the traditional luncheon for graduates, Alex and Steffi walked several blocks to the lake and sat on the steps of their favorite fountain, refreshed by a cool breeze. They spoke quietly and watched water splashing from three arched dolphins.

"Isn't there a piece of paper in your program, Alex?"

He read it and without comment handed it to her. "Well, Steffi, what do you think?"

"You know, Alex, I can't believe it. Did your father actually write this, and what's 'D3' mean anyway?"

Alex leaned forward, staring at the sand, then at the splashing fountains. "It's been this way from the beginning. He wrote one during the first week after I came from California. Once I asked what D3 meant, but he didn't explain—he probably expected me to know. Your guess is as good as mine. I hope it's something like 'Dad,' 'I love you,' 'Nice work, Son' . . . who knows? It could be his way of signing letters, memoranda, notes. Perhaps my judgment is too severe, yet it's impersonal, with no emotion."

"Did he ever say that you've done well, tried your best, or met his expectations?"

Alex shook his head.

"Is this why you have always wanted to win and be the best, Alex?"

"No, absolutely not. If I have done anything worthwhile, it's because of my desire, determination. Fathers can't force sons." He stood and took her hands, their faces touching.

"You will build your life, follow your goals, without anyone pushing or shoving. It begins now, Alex."

"I probably shouldn't have shown you the note, although it had to happen sometime. Now you know, and I hope you don't think less of me."

As they turned to leave, he pinned the gardenia to the waist of her pink organdy dress, held her firmly, and kissed her. The words had been there, came easily, although he had never spoken them. "Steffi, I have loved you from the beginning. I love you; please let this be a memory of today."

"I love you, too, Alex. I want to be with you." Her flower had a heavy fragrance. The petals were curled and the stark whiteness had begun to fade.

Early the next morning, Alex traveled by bus to the Harper Military School, on a picturesque lake in northern Indiana. It was known as the "Little West Point" of preparatory schools. The spacious campus was ideal for a ten-week summer camp with military routines and schedules. Alex was a cavalry instructor, trained the jumping team, and, as a bonus, he was given a course in German.

Four
Decision

It was a resplendent late-summer morning at Princeton, and Alex felt there would be more warm, humid days. A still haze gave the imposing buildings a friendly hue. He sat on his suitcase at the edge of Cannon Green, savoring the smell of newly cut, wet grass. The tilted head of the buried cannon led him to the cocoa brown square stones, tall white framed windows, and bell tower of Nassau Hall. He had arrived for early registration, and other than the occasional sound of crunching footsteps on the gravel walks, there was a reassuring calmness, rather than the bustling activity of other students. He moved into the shade of weathered oaks and tall maples, enamored by the greenness of manicured lawns that created a content, pastoral setting. Strolling to the nearby entrance of Stanhope Hall, he was startled by an uncomfortable cloud of steam engulfing his shoes and legs. It billowed from a grate in front of the university bookstore and prompted him to avoid the next two, set between slabs of stone forming the rough walkway.

He introduced himself to the registrar, an older man with a brownish linen jacket, rumpled shirt, and tie, who sat behind a humming fan that partially relieved the oppressive heat of his small office. A green shade was pulled down over his pince-nez. He hastily pushed the required papers toward Alex without conversation; then his room key was snapped on the desk. He found his dormitory entry at the far end of the campus and was greeted by groans from the worn wooden stairs that led to his third-floor room. The rough oak door was numbered "622" and had a metal mail slit. The previous student had affixed an enduring maxim on a cardboard strip: "Stay loose in the notch."

There was a southwest window, small closet, several electrical outlets, and a floor in need of a good scrubbing. Lucky had shipped his desk, single bed, dresser, and small easy chair. That afternoon, he bought a rug and two lamps, then arranged his furniture. At home he was unwilling to place Steffi's picture on his desk, but now he could touch her smile. "S.D.P." was engraved in script at the bottom of the silver frame. The "D" was for Durhing, Katzie's maiden name. She was standing, her blond hair parted on the right falling almost to her left shoulder. She leaned slightly forward, her right hand becomingly clasped in her left. He picked up the frame and held it. She was with him.

After a shower on the basement level, he took a long nap, treated himself to a two-dollar steak, then settled into what would be his university retreat for several years. Later in the evening, after arranging his books, he found the note in his desk drawer, placed there before the furniture was shipped:

From the desk of Dr. Brian Dunham:

Dear Alex,

You are beginning a new life. Take advantage of every opportunity to learn and improve your mind. You have great intellectual curiosity, which is an invaluable asset, and I know you are capable of continuing your good work. Give more thought to your plans for the future. Stay in touch. Lucky and I miss you.

Yours,
D3

He slipped it under his large desk blotter. It was encouraging, so he read it again, with a brief feeling of nostalgia.

Alexander Hall was a grandiloquent monument to Victorian architecture, whose furnishings were a series of semicircular dark wooden benches with straight backs. Ornately framed doors and multicolored windows allowed minimal light to reach its occupants. Illuminated crystal fixtures did little to brighten its cheerless ambience in late afternoon.

The dean of men, "Smiley" Sommerville, was an imposing, feared administrator whose responsibilities included freshmen. He had a large, florid face with deep-set, quickly moving eyes whose scrutiny never overlooked details. Broad, full shoulders filled a rust-colored tweed jacket whose three buttons were tautly stretched. He wore slightly short unpressed trousers and argyle socks. An orange-and-black bow tie bobbed over a prominent Adam's apple as he spoke with unmistakable authority.

"Gentlemen of forty-one, this is not a playpen, from which many of you have come. No doting mothers and fathers to plead with headmasters. You are on your own. No immature behavior. No cars. All women out of your rooms by six—that's six in the evening, gentlemen. We have four proctors on campus, and they will have an uncanny knowledge of your activities, whereabouts, and habits, good and bad." These last admonitions were followed by a sadistic smile, Howard Sommerville's trademark when he expelled a student for a minor infraction.

"What you get from this university is exactly what you put in it. You have your schedules for lectures and precepts. You are expected to be punctual and regular in attendance. Spend your time wisely. Challenge this university with imagination and curiosity. I only want to see you in my office for academic advice, not to order train tickets home. You are probably not aware of the wooden balustrade between the lower and upper levels. It's shaped like a horseshoe. As a matter of fact, some of you are sleeping on it now. Tradition stipulates that all men within the horseshoe will succeed here. In closing, we wish you well. Good afternoon." Smiley turned and swaggered off the stage.

Alex was relieved to see he was in about the fourth row.

After roaming through the university bookstore, whose entrance was marked by an orange-and-black placard: "Welcome Class of 1941," Alex proudly clipped his bright brass identification plate: *"Everything the College Man Needs" 8691* to his key chain. He bought the required books for advanced French, German, a Shakespeare course, and calculus. The "U" store was stocked with novels, calendars, pamphlets, and notes on campus activities and was administered by helpful salesladies. A small tailor shop in one corner displayed neatly stacked, black crew neck sweaters with orange freshmen numerals: "1941." He was determined to win one. It would be for crew.

Alex usually slept longer Sunday mornings. He was late again for chapel. Running up from the showers two steps at a time wrapped in a bath towel, he unexpectedly faced a chubby classmate and his two elegantly dressed roommates. Alex's previous greetings had been ignored by the reticent and aloof trio. Now he extended his hand to Schuyler Holt, who led the group.

"I'm Alex Dunham from Chicago. I've seen you all for several weeks and wanted to say hello."

"Really now, Dunham, how very nice," Schuyler replied disdainfully. "I thought everyone from Chicago carried a violin case."

Alex parried with a wry smile. "Quite true. Believe me, Schuyler, as we say in far-off Chicago, there's a definite chance you could be rubbed out. Now, gentlemen, if you will excuse me."

Students called it the Armory, a name that suggested a massive stone structure adorned with imposing towers and fearsome gargoyles on its facade, yet it was the only group of temporary buildings on campus. Three two-story wooden structures resembling barracks comprised the training center for future infantry officers. Its current director was a West Point graduate, Lieutenant Colonel Alvin Osborne. He was not pleased with his present duty.

Alex was prepared for Osborne's introduction.

"Gentlemen," Osborne's voice was raspy, "you are here at the Armory by choice, and before I'm finished with you, you may regret that choice. One hour, three days a week, four years, and, of course, six weeks for two summers at Fort Benning." He methodically droned on. "You shall drill, there will be forced marches, hikes, and you shall master the manual of arms so it can be done in your sleep. We shall have firing on the range each week, and the eager beavers will be picking off smaller targets Saturday mornings. You shall learn infantry tactics, strategy, and the history of modern warfare. It's still not too late to change your minds." There was silence. The following week fifty, rather than seventy, potential second lieutenants reported for training.

After several classes Alex spoke with his instructor. "Sir, I'm interested in the history of warfare. I guess we'll study that later?"

"Dunham, you are going to learn a lesson in this man's army you shall not forget. Never volunteer. Exactly one month from today I expect an essay on the origins and military details of the Peloponnesian Wars and their consequences on Greek history. It shall be typewritten and you will have fifteen minutes to summarize your conclusions."

"I look forward to it, sir."

Alex was climbing the last flight of stairs to his room after a late night at the library when a voice with a southern dialect boomed, "Yo, Dunham, come on in for a beer. It's ten-thirty, and you-all must be a thirsty hirsty."

Douglas "Red Dog" Harding relaxed on a dilapidated sofa wiping suds on the sleeve of his beer jacket. Alex entered the large living room replete with a fireplace and screen. The room looked as though it had been permanently lived in, fully furnished, with an icebox and a "1941" banner covering one of the walls. There were two bedrooms, one with a double-decker bed.

"Sit down, Dunham; I'm Doug Harding." He ran a hand through thick red hair, then passed Alex an uncapped bottle.

"Good to meet you, Doug. I've been busy getting settled into the new routine, no chance to come down and shoot the bull."

As Alex sat down, he glanced toward the large framed window and saw another roommate peer over a fully outfitted bar with an awning of orange-and-black tigers.

Harding pointed. "Meet Nicholas Dunsmore, the second member of our Tiger Trinity."

Dunsmore emerged from behind the bar carrying a bottle of Wild Turkey. His New York accent was impeccable, as though he were entertaining at his Long Island yacht club. "Awfully good to have you aboard, Dunham. I like the cut of your jib. Actually, what will it be, scotch, a beer, or both?"

Alex enjoyed several bottles of beer and the amicable conversation but knew drinking would not become one of his social pursuits.

Russell Hawkins was the owl of the Trinity, sleeping through afternoons and missing lectures. He made an entrance in his shorts and a silk bathrobe, squinting and fumbling for his glasses.

Doug chuckled. "Come on, Russ, get your ass over to the bar. They're where you left them last night."

Russ unfolded a perfectly ironed handkerchief, moistened the lenses with a puff of breath, then carefully polished them. This precise exercise, a daily ritual, was completed when he blew off the remaining specks of lint. He looked about the room, startled, as if seeing everything for the first time. He settled on the couch with his drink. "Who belongs to this foreign voice speaking to the Trinity?"

Alex got his attention by waving. "I'm over here, Russ . . . live on the floor above you."

Russ bumped a chair. "Oh, you must be that undesirable who carries a violin case and lives alone up there in the loft. We've heard about you."

Doug reprimanded his sleepy colleague, "Dunham, here,

treated them right. Kicked 'em in the butt. You did what I would have done, Alex. Now that's enough out of you, Hawk; you know damn well Schuyler and his friends are a bunch of grinds, absolutely boring crowd. Always in the books, worming around. Never learned how to have fun." He had his own distinctive way of saying "grinds." It emphasized a social distaste.

Doug was restive. "Alex, I guess we are all different. Right about this time every Thursday night I get horny as hell. Dammit, I sure need a date, but it does me good to lift these weights. Always jump in the shower afterward." He began pressing a barbell stacked with two fifty-pound circular discs.

While lifting weights, he continued to speak. "Alex, do you-all have a girl for the game this weekend?"

"As a matter of fact, I do," Alex said. "She's coming down from New York."

"Then we're having a special coming-out party for her. Get her here by eleven Saturday morning, and we'll have a few toddies before the game. By the way, Russ, what's the name of that gorgeous dish from Washington who always wants to spend the weekend in our room?"

"It's actually Mary Jane Wellington from Philadelphia, Mr. Douglas Harding," Russ answered, "and her telephone number is five-three-three-two."

Doug dropped the weights. "I knew you were a smart SOB, Russ. How can you remember my girl's name and telephone number, too?"

"A matter of intense concentration, sir, only made possible by sleeping during daylight hours."

Alex guessed it was late for his self-imposed routine. "This has been great, guys. We'll plan to be here at eleven Saturday, and before the weekend's over the Hawk will probably remember Steffi's place, date of birth, and chest, waist, and hip measurements."

Alex slept well enough, but the friendly beers caused several treks up and down the three flights of stairs to the "Francis X. Hobarty Memorial Latrine," dedicated by students to one of their more intractable proctors.

He finally saw her blond head among a group of girls who arrived at the junction about noon. He jostled his way through the crowd. She was carrying a small suitcase.

"Steffi, Steffi, over here." When she saw him, she dropped her luggage and they ran to each other.

"Alex, it's good to be with you. We've waited ages for this weekend. Tell me everything. Is it all you expected? It must be a change from the Academy—the freedom, you know what I mean. Do you think about me when you're busy?"

"You're on my mind all the time." He spoke softly. "I miss you more than you realize. Let's go to my room, where we can be alone. We have a lot to catch up on, talk about everything, especially you, you blossoming artist."

Walking to the open end of the station, he took off his raincoat and draped it over their heads. Now they could kiss in their own private world. She wrapped her arms around his shoulders. He pulled her close.

When they reached his room, she put her hands on her hips, walking back and forth as if on an inspection tour. "Alex, I've imagined many times where you live and made little drawings of what it might be like here. Everything fits. The old wood and stone sills are attractive, and those three-cornered windows are almost like home. It's terrific but could use a woman's touch here and there. You're wonderfully organized; it's a quiet place to study. Most important, my picture on your desk makes it seem like I'm here with you."

"Does it have your official stamp of approval, without floor-length curtains, chandelier, and a Monet here and a Cezanne there?"

"Absolutely. It's perfect for you. Now I know where you are, especially at night. Sometimes I get a hollow feeling right here in my tummy."

He reached behind her and gave the door a slight push. When it closed, he held her hands and kissed her, pressing her body against the door.

Alex was tentative as they walked downstairs to the party.

"Steffi, maybe you'll find these guys a bit different, and I hope you don't think I spend too much time with them."

The shrill voices of the Trinity and their dates, accompanied by the Victrola, resounded through the entry while they attempted to introduce themselves. Dunsmore frenetically shook martinis behind the bar, while Doug was draped over the couch, beer in hand, charming the girls. Russ had slept through the arrival of his date and peered through the door behind Alex and Steffi. His glasses were steamed from the shower room, as he tried to find his bunk and clothes. He was a compulsive shoe shiner, delaying his formal appearance as one of the hosts.

Steffi raised her voice over the blare of music. "Alex, it's quite amazing. I don't think I've ever been to a party quite like this. Only one beer, then let's leave."

Doug straightened his tie, adjusted his orange-and-black suspenders, and slipped on his jacket. He slurred, "My gawd, Dunham, where did you find that perfectly beautiful blond?"

"Doug Harding, I'd like you to meet Stephanie Pfeiffer. Steffi, this is Doug."

She politely shook hands. "Doug, it is nice of you to invite us, but does this really happen every Saturday?"

A yawning Hawkins explained, "You see, Miss Pfeiffer, we use most any excuse for a good party. Have to escape the books, the grind, these boring lectures and classes. It's quite logical; we choose to close the curtain on reality."

Steffi and Alex were settled in the student section of the stadium when Doug and his friends entered the long row, climbing over their classmates, bumping, shoving, and stepping on feet.

"You Tigers are late," the cry went up. "Down in front. Can't see a thing. Make 'em crawl to their seats."

"They can't win without me here." Doug shouted. "Knock it off." He sat down. "Oh, my gawd," he cried out in mock agony. "I've been bitten by a rattlesnake. I could die for all you care."

Someone in the crowd hollered, "Red Dog, that's no rattlesnake; it's all that Wild Turkey."

His classmates applauded and cheered his humor, and he continued to be the brunt of jokes the rest of the afternoon. Douglas Harding beamed with a witless smile.

Alex and Stephanie lingered after chapel, lulled by its dignity and beauty. The autumn sun had begun to filter through the ornamental stained glass at the west end. They turned and watched the colored rays warm the gray stone. Both were entranced by the magnificence of the place and day. After a Bach concert, they strolled across the campus toward the station and were reminded by the unusual high-pitched train whistle that for now their time together had ended. He picked up a scarlet maple leaf and tucked it in her purse. Soon there would be snow and Christmas.

From the desk of Dr. Brian Dunham:

Dear Alex,

As you probably know, Gen. Paul Gibson has been a good friend of ours over the years. It's a small world and don't forget, sometimes words travel faster than the speed of light. Lieutenant Colonel Alvin Osborne, the director of the infantry officers' training at Princeton, served in his command out in Kansas. Apparently, he wrote a letter about you because of our long friendship with Paul. He said that he saw some leadership qualities and toughness on forced marches. I guess old Doc Pardee taught you something about marksmanship. Keep up the Saturday morning firing, but don't let anyone or anything distract you from your studies. I'm not quite sure why you are in this army program anyway. Lucky and I enjoyed having you here over the holidays.

Yours,
D3

Alex thought B.D. must have been busier than usual or out of town at a medical meeting. His secretary had signed the letter.

Near the end of the sprint, sweat covered Alex's body, running down his forehead into his eyes. As starboard stroke, he had increased the cadence called by the coxswain and no longer could clearly see his oar slice through or lift out of the water. Now it was all timing and feel. With each stroke he became hungrier for air. He thought of cool March mornings after the ice had broken. At the finish he sagged forward, winded, but exulted in their final win of the season. The defeated crew rowed alongside, took off their soaked shirts, and, as tradition dictated, gave them to the victors. After showering, he found his opposing stroke from the Naval Academy and handed him a folded towel. Alex had returned his crew shirt.

Peter Connor, the popular history professor, was known to his students as "Saint Peter." He was tall and slightly stooped, with tortoiseshell half-glasses perched on the bridge of his large nose. He invariably wore a charcoal gray flannel suit with a regimental striped tie and cordovan shoes. His leather heels clicked authoritatively, one of the hallmarks of his popular academic persona. Alex and the Trinity agreed that Saint Peter's wife probably had money. The two were well-known figures in Washington, and his scholarly papers and books had won official government approval and praise from the press.

Steffi arrived in early afternoon, and they hurried for good seats in the lecture hall. Alex scrambled to find one, then sat next to her on the floor in the aisle of McCosh 50.

"Alex, do this many students come every Friday to hear Saint Peter? It's hard to believe. The place is packed, everyone in the aisles, like you down there, Tiger. They're sitting along the edge of the stage, on windowsills, and there is hardly enough space to stand."

Other students had brought their dates for a long weekend, creating a crescendo of animated conversation. He flushed when Steffi sat with her legs crossed and he gently squeezed her thigh. They smiled. She bent down and rubbed the back of his neck.

"Steffi, today he is scheduled to lecture on 'Hitler's Germany: Present and Future.' He's a provocative speaker, thinks logically, and has the ability to reduce international politics to hard facts. I'll be interested in your impressions after the lecture. He makes me think about our responsibilities . . . "

When Connor entered McCosh Hall, there was a gradual silence, as if the volume of a radio had been turned down.

"Good morning, gentlemen, and may I also welcome your weekend guests. There will be an opportunity for questions later. Now let's look at the meteoric career of Adolf Hitler and the changes in Germany between nineteen thirty-two and this spring of nineteen thirty-nine. Inflation, staggering unemployment, failure of the Weimar democracy, and what the Germans thought were the harsh dictates of Versailles are among the more important causes of Hitler's emergence as a political leader. Nazi theories have relegated Jews and other non-Aryan groups to *Untermenschen*, as witnessed by the civil disorder of *Kristallnacht*. Hitler was elected by far less than a majority of the popular vote, and after the Reichstag fire the Communists were blamed and the party outlawed. Since that time, Germany has been governed under a state of emergency. The power of the state became complete, and free elections have never been held since."

Professor Connor spoke without moving or gesturing, and important issues were stressed by inflection and occasional humor. He related anecdotes and his personal observations made during frequent visits to Germany.

"After the diplomatic promises made to Chamberlain and Daladier at Munich, I believe there is still hope for 'peace in our time.' However, the great Western democracies must show a firm resolve to prevent further aggression. Because of isolationism, America has been a nonentity in ongoing international diplomacy. Lastly, I leave you with a daunting unknown. Will it, in fact, be a course of continued appeasement or will this country rescue the Old World in the second great crisis of the twentieth century?"

The audience enthusiastically applauded, then stood. As the lecture hall slowly emptied, Connor remained to answer questions and greet students.

Alex approached his professor. "Sir, may I introduce Miss Stephanie Pfeiffer?"

She smiled and bowed her head slightly. "Herr Professor, darf ich sagen dass ihr Vortrag sehr gut und bedenkenswert war," Steffi complimented him on his lecture.

"Fräulein Pfeiffer, es freut mich dass Sie der Vortrag interessiert hat." He was pleased that the discussion interested her. "Of course, Stephanie, I know your father from Chicago. We often travel to Europe together for the government. Dunham and his precept have been invited for dinner this evening, and Mrs. Connor also expects you and the other young ladies who are visiting for the weekend. I look forward to more conversation then."

Although Alex knew the Pfeiffers spoke German at home, he was delighted with Stephanie's fluency and sophistication.

The Connor home was more elegantly furnished than the salary of a university professor could provide. The after-dinner group crossed worn Oriental rugs to a large sofa with a faded chintz slipcover. A Cluny tapestry covered a wall bracketed by two tables with Ming vases. On the coffee table there was an oblong silver cigarette case engraved with the German eagle and a greeting: "*Mit hoher Achtung für Professor Peter Connor und Dank für seine Beiträge zum Frieden. Aussenminister Hans Stephan.*" His friend from the Foreign Ministry had presented this gift for his contributions to a better understanding between the two countries.

The three were warmed by a smoldering fire. Connor reached for his demitasse on the mantel. "Well, my young friends, it's been a strong dose of medicine today, but, Dunham, we haven't discussed your plans. You know, Stephanie, he's one of my better students. What about it, Alex?"

"Sir, I've been interested in public and international affairs, history and languages, which makes a career in diplomacy inviting. For now, I have elected not to study law or medicine, although my family has encouraged these choices. There is still time to make final decisions, and I hope to discuss my future plans with you."

"That sounds reasonable. Give the whole matter careful thought, use good judgment based on your abilities, and please write or call me after graduation. The State Department and armed forces are looking for men of your caliber and background. Our future depends on critical selection of talented young people."

A lazy stream of water spilled from a coiled serpent's mouth into a large pool located in front of their hotel on Central Park West. It was an uncomfortably warm evening, and Steffi sat with Alex dangling her feet from the edge of the pond. There was animated chatter and laughter.

"Alex, we had an incredible day. There's no time like late May, even though it's New York. I always wanted to see the Egyptian gallery at the Metropolitan. From now on you're King Tut and call me Nefertiti. How's that sound?"

"King Tut is starving and has a hole in his royal stomach, so on with your sandals and let's find something to eat. There must be a late-night restaurant in the hotel."

During their snack, both agreed the Mozart program at Carnegie Hall that evening had been exciting, particularly the Prague symphony.

"Steffi, I would guess the final piano concerto isn't played that often. Doesn't the last movement remind you of an exciting hunting scene?"

"It's always been one of my favorites. I think it was played well, but some of the subtleties were lost because the tempo seemed rushed."

Other than a waiter moving about, folding napkins and arranging dishes and glasses, the small hotel café was empty, partially darkened. They looked blankly at the table, and Alex aimlessly pushed a fork, then a spoon.

He held her hand and pressed between her thighs. "I want to be with you, Steffi, right now. Let's . . . your room, why not vanish, leave the door open a crack, and give me fifteen minutes. Don't King Tut and Nefertiti want to be together tonight?"

"Yes, please, Alex, let's not wait any longer."

Steffi showed the key to the rotund, sleepy elevator operator, found her room, and waited by the open door.

Alex stepped off the elevator a floor below. After finding the fire stairwell, he stood before a tall fence with a locked gate blocking each flight of stairs. This hurdle did not reach the ceiling. He imagined the Tetons would be an easier climb. He scaled the wire enclosure with agility, careful not to snag his pants and coat. After clearing the two barricades, which he reasoned violated the city fire code yet were intended to separate men from women, he reached her floor. And, most important, he had not been discovered by the roaming house detective.

He peered around her door. "Tut, Tut, Nefertiti, the king has arrived."

The early-morning laughter and merrymaking were the revelry of other students, but the rowdiness ebbed to welcome quiet. Scattered lights in Central Park were fading in the dawn. He carried her to bed. She was wide-eyed and smiling as she took off her suit jacket and he threw his coat on a chair. They spoke almost at the same time.

"You're the only one for me, Steffi."

"I'm yours, Alex. Start kissing me now and don't stop until I have to come up for air. Please, Alex, although I want to, don't go too far."

He was clumsy at first, as he unbuttoned her blouse and, rather than remove her brassiere, lifted it up over her breasts, gently grazing her nipples.

"When you do that, it sends shocks all through me. Please don't stop; no, don't stop."

He stroked the inside of her thighs and continued to slide his hand between her legs with increasing pressure.

"Now, please, touch me." Steffi tossed her head from side to side, pulling his face toward her. "I'm so wet, it's beginning, it's happening; now, now, Alex hold me; don't let me go; hold me tight." She was supple, then limp, her arms around his neck.

She slowly released him. He lay back on a pillow, watching her fingers move over his chest for what seemed an interminable time. He felt her hair and lips on his skin; then she held his penis. As she delicately stroked, she felt its firmness, yet petal soft. He drew her face toward him, pulling her tongue in his mouth, when there was a rush of warm liquid between her legs. Their partially clothed bodies slowly stopped moving. He touched her cheeks lightly, brushed her ruffled hair.

She ran her fingers over her thighs and tasted his liquid. She smiled.

"I love you, Steffi."

"Yes, Alex. This is the beginning and I long for a life with you."

They fell asleep in an embrace. She occasionally sighed; he held her tighter. He remembered the word *chiaroscuro* from somewhere and thought her face, blondness, and well-proportioned nose were more compelling in the night's soft light. He kissed her lips. The taste of her mouth, her breath, had a sweetness for him.

In the morning, a grinning Alex stood in his wrinkled shirt and shorts holding a small tray. "Steffi, may I proudly present you with three buttons you ripped in a moment of maddened passion. Right now, I'm flying by the seat of my pants, because the fourth one is only hanging by a thread, and my chances of taking you back to school are definitely slim."

Her smile was seductive.

"You're a lucky guy in more ways than one. I happen to have a tiny safety pin in my purse, and it's for you, big man, and I do mean big."

Alex and several other visitors had been invited for lunch by Steffi and her friends at the New York School of Art in Westchester County. They walked about the campus dotted with various-sized contemporary sculptures and modern buildings.

"How do those two steel triangles impress you, Alex? One is obviously in the conventional position, while the other is balanced on its peak."

"Well, it's different, original, yet I can't be certain what it means."

They found a small clearing in the woods that bordered the

campus and sat under a tree enjoying the succulence of spring.

"Beauty, of course, means something different to everyone," Steffi reflected. "Some people never experience it, yet it stimulates the imagination, provides an outlet to express visual images in a unique, different style. You know, Alex, when I paint, sometimes I dream, am absentminded. Some of those canvases are perhaps my best. This approach is the feeling part of art. Probably the emotional and intellectual combination is what the truly great painters have in common."

Both walked down a grassy country lane to a small brick church. Its interior was painted an antique white, rendering an uplifting, reverent mood. They sat in one of the shiny pews darkened with age.

"Do you think about the beauty of movement in painting or do you concentrate only on still life, you know, objects and scenes?"

Steffi studied the beamed ceiling, then the simple altar. "If I painted or sketched this little chapel, I would recall my childhood, the choir, Sundays and holy days, and the faith I have gained through belief and trust. Perhaps you can also find peace and solace in a refuge like this."

She looked into his eyes, which were almost emerald. "I will remember you here today. You and I can find beauty we are unable to see."

Alex sat with his elbows on his knees, face in his hands. "Steffi, I have always felt your sense of goodness, that everything will be all right, a security. It's your gift. As an altar boy, I was in awe of church ceremony, unable to understand its doctrine. Perhaps my attitude is the same today."

She slowly drew his face to hers. "Where has the afternoon gone? You mustn't miss your train. When we're together again, come to church with me."

Alex had become more fluent in German than French because he could hear and pronounce individual words rather than groups of sounds. At the end of each week, Professor Hans Neumann conducted an exacting review session for his six students in advanced German. He was a tall, austere man who wore knickers with a European-style sport coat and bow tie. A dissonant, clipped voice conveyed authority. He demanded perfection and was cordially known to his special students as "Herr Geheimrat." Questions were asked rapidly, and if answers did not follow quickly, he proceeded to the next unfortunate would-be scholar. As the session ended, he pointed with his chalk.

"Das war ganz gut, meine Herren." Then, with his pronounced German accent, he added, "Memorize; practice; practice; work. That's the formula of learning a language. Auf Wiedersehen, bis Montag."

Steffi left her suitcase at Tower Club, where she and Alex had a hurried sandwich at the weekend buffet before attending Colonel Osborne's lecture on leadership qualities. They reached the Armory as he began his spirited, bombastic discourse, which Alex had heard on previous occasions. He stood in front of an infantry organization chart.

"Gentlemen," he boomed. "You must always attack, attack; never dig in and wait to be captured or killed. Be out in front of your men, because if you as officers move forward, they will follow."

Steffi and some of the other young women, invited to the Armory on special weekends, fidgeted uncomfortably in their chairs. After the lecture, the students marched to the firing range, followed by their dates. Steffi stood behind Alex as the Colonel checked his first target.

Osborne lifted a small pair of field glasses. "Not bad, Dunham. Eight out of ten in the bull's-eye. Now proceed to the moving targets."

Alex was prone and barely tilted his left elbow while aiming, firing and reloading his Winchester 30-30.

"Cease fire, men," the Colonel ordered. "Stack your rifles, and we'll move to the maneuver boards. We'll see if any of these young ladies are better thinking soldiers than you are."

There was a large fifteen-by-fifteen-foot green plywood

board with painted roads, forests, a river, bridges, and elevated areas that simulated hills. The green army encountered the white. There were small yellow blocks representing cavalry, the red ones indicated artillery, and the blue infantry units. The students and their dates were divided into opposing teams.

Steffi compared it to a chess game. When they faced the white army, she advised Alex on tactical moves, and within half an hour the green troops had outflanked and struck the rear echelons of the opponent with an unchecked cavalry sweep that advanced through a forest and side roads.

"Ausgezeichnet, Generalfeldmarschall Stephanie Durhing Pfeiffer." Alex clicked his heels, saluted, and shook hands in mock congratulations.

Osborne spoke to Alex. "Dunham, I don't believe you introduced me to your charming young lady, who seems to have military skills."

"Sir, may I present Stephanie Pfeiffer. As you see, she's also the commanding general of the green army."

The Colonel smiled. "It's a pleasure to have you here, Miss Pfeiffer. I hope you have enjoyed your short stay at the Armory today."

"Yes, all of us visitors have learned from this afternoon's experience. Alex tells me you are a West Point graduate. Your future officers admire your knowledge and respect your discipline, Colonel."

"Thank you, Miss Pfeiffer, and I enjoy training these young men."

After the exercises at the Armory, dinner at the club was followed by a dance. By midnight, Doug climbed on a table, where he skidded on some scattered magazines. He waved a half-empty beer bottle and, with a gauzy southern drawl, demanded that Russ play his infamous recently composed "Upside-Down Piano Concerto." The small orchestra announced his presence with a trumpet fanfare, but the distracted soloist was sitting on the floor in a corner of the living room conversing seriously with several friends.

"Russ, on your feet. Find his glasses, somebody, then lead

him to the piano." Doug finished his beer, then collapsed on a sofa.

Alex and Steffi joined the singing crowd as they gathered around the piano. Russ was an accomplished modern and classical pianist and, after playing a number of popular tunes, yawned mindlessly. The long-anticipated "neo-classic" concerto polarized the guests.

Stephanie put her arm around Alex. "What in the world is he doing?"

"Wait and see. An unbelievable character."

Continuing a melody with one hand, he adroitly slipped under the piano, proceeding to play a complicated variation of "Chopsticks," applauded by rousing cheers. The uncontrolled adulation overwhelmed Russell Hawkins, who entertained the guests late into the evening. Alex and Steffi led their "tipsy" ladies to a weekend boardinghouse, because the Trinity insisted on the questionable honor of being the party's last survivors.

"Good night, General Pfeiffer."

She stood on a step above him, resting her face in his hair, as he kissed her neck. She trembled and moved closer.

"Alex, maybe we should stop. I can't seem to help myself when you do that." She tried to distract him. "Breakfast about nine. It's late; we need some rest."

"Can you handle these three 'zombies'? Need any help?"

Steffi guided her friends up the stairs. "Alex, I'll play house-mother and tuck them in."

It was not unreasonable that Alex thought the Harvard band should be more considerate. At their mediocre best, they simply weren't gentlemen. The clamorous noise of tubas, cymbals, and trombones was painful. Most annoying were the large kettle drums being struck with deafening regularity. The metallic rattle of several snare drums rolled in unison through the stillness of early morning. Alex turned over. It was six-thirty and he could hear Doug roaring with anger. Alex thought Harding must have the cumulative hangover of a lifetime.

"Dammit all, who the hell is sitting on my head?"

Dunsmore, still fully clothed except for his club tie draped over an ice bucket, had slept on the bar. "What's that sharp noise disturbing the sanctity of the premises? If it has human origin, who would have the affront to disturb our early-morning rest? Could it possibly be those despicable chaps from the Harvard band?"

Alex pulled on a warm-up suit and tennis shoes and dashed down to their room, stumbling over Doug's barbells. "On your feet, Red Dog; off the bar, Dunsmore; somebody find the Hawk's glasses. It's that damned Harvard band down at the station tuning up for the game, and we've only been bagged out four hours. Gentlemen, here is the plan of battle."

They followed Alex to the Armory, where the four picked up two dozen painted wooden rifles, fitted with straps, that were used during the first year of training.

Alex was chuckling. "Doug, they'll look real to those clowns."

The rifles were quickly passed to the laughing crowd of half-dressed, jeering students who had encircled the "invading" band. Alex sat on Red Dog's shoulders.

"All right, let's move out this bunch of musical illiterates. Drummers over here, start the marching cadence, and I mean now." Alex waved his wooden rifle in a threatening gesture, as the band at first failed to recognize the intended fun.

The leader was dressed in crimson tails, trousers, tall boots, and a giant hat with a pom-pom and wielded an impressive baton. He shouted with trepidation, "What on earth are these mad fools doing to us? For heaven's sake, someone call the police, and at once."

"Relax. No harm intended," Alex yelled. "We're having a march through the campus, and at your expense. Get the band organized and we'll stir up a little of that old school spirit. We're the ones in trouble. If Dean Sommerville gets wind of this, we've got one-way tickets home. There's probably no one quite like him up at Harvard."

The early-morning parade began, as Alex and Doug commanded the crowd, "Come on, Tigers, get these jerks moving in their regular formation, and remember, only Princeton songs."

A small group of loyal sons of the orange and black surrounded the band. They passed Steffi's boardinghouse, where the girls appeared in crew sweaters and pants. She climbed on Alex's shoulders at Blair Arch, which was the rallying point. A large group of students gathered to march with the band and began singing "Going Back." Steffi snatched a plumed crimson hat and wore it triumphantly as they proceeded across the campus.

Alex found Doug in the middle of the band. "They've been at it an hour now; the whole town's probably awake. Let's hope Smiley is away for the weekend. We'll march them to Nassau Hall."

When the band halted, the two shouted more instructions. "All right, you bunch of misplaced pieces of Harvard humanity, play 'Old Nassau,' and play it loud and clear."

The mosaic of students and their girls sang with unparalleled fervor. Dunsmore, perfectly attired for the occasion in pressed white flannels, blazer, and orange-and-black tie, addressed the throng of students with gentlemanly bravura. He turned authoritatively to the two cheerleaders, one standing on each verdigris ornamental tiger in front of Nassau Hall. "Now, chaps, it would behoove you to give three long locomotives for our visitors from Harvard after such a strenuous, tiresome morning."

"See that our good friends from Cambridge get fed," Alex called out. "Send some to Commons, the others to Tower. Doug, take fifteen of them, and I'll get the 'weapons' back to the Armory."

After breakfast, the club members and guests enjoyed a jazz session by some of the Harvard band members. Steffi and Alex sat on the floor with the rest of the weekend crowd listening to Dixieland music. With the last sounds of a lively tune, they found a private corner.

"Alex, I can't remember when I've had as much fun. Wouldn't it be great to be this carefree every weekend? If our parents could only see us now. I wonder if they had such good times when they were college students?"

There hadn't been mail from home for several weeks.

From the desk of Dr. Brian Dunham:

Dear Alex,

There was something in the sports page the other morning about Princeton students marching the Harvard band across the campus and through town with loaded guns. They must have been a group of irresponsible rowdies who had no place being in college. I'm certain you had no part in this immature spectacle. If you had, I would have heard from Dean Sommerville by now. As you know, the draft has been passed, and you should start seriously thinking about graduate, medical, or law school. There will be openings in the medical school when you finish back there.

Yours,
D3

Alex slammed the door to his room. "It hasn't changed," he grumbled to himself. "He's still trying to direct traffic, never can leave me alone although I'm a thousand miles away."

"You guys, it's so hot this afternoon that the sun might melt the bottom of Lake Carnegie...you know, the only rubber-bottomed lake in the world."

The crew joined in the laughter, relieving some tension, as they carefully lowered their shell for the last regatta of the season. Stephanie decided to stay several more days after Alex graduated and came to the boat house each morning to watch practice. She sat along the grassy shoreline among the spectators seeking shade under large weeping willows, refreshed by an occasional breeze off the lake.

She saw the two crews maneuver into position when the starting gun sounded and heard the diminutive coxswain call through his megaphone, "Three-four." They decided to start with a cadence of thirty-four strokes a minute over the mile-and-a-quarter course. The Princeton crew's strategy was successful, as they gained an early lead, and when the boats passed, Steffi followed the excited spectators along a stone path.

Nicholas Dunsmore took her arm. He wore his boater with an orange-and-black band. "It's looking awfully good, Steffi. Alex is quite the stroke, my dear."

"Nick, look at the perfect timing he's setting for the other oarsmen. It's hot enough right here; think what it must be like in the shell. They're covered with perspiration. See the exertion on their faces, and strain in their arm and leg muscles. I've never quite understood how anyone could enjoy a sport demanding such physical punishment."

The shell moved effortlessly over the lake as the oars were rhythmically lifted out of the water, leaving a pattern of enlarging circles. She decided this would be a scene to sketch, one of many unforgettable visual imprints. The perfect synchrony of their bodies and oars seemed to make time stand still. Suddenly she was among a cheering group as the red-and-blue shirts of the opposing crew were passed off to the winning boat.

Dunsmore flattered his classmate. "Steffi, keep your eyes on Alex. See, he dipped the losing stroke's shirt in the water, wrang it out, and threw it back to him like a ball. He was entitled to keep that shirt, doesn't rub their nose in it. He's a decent fellow. Now it's time for them to toss the coxswain. What a sight. Look at the little bugger hit the water. How could a small fellow make such a big splash?"

Steffi had draped Alex's white sweater over her arm while walking back to his room. "Although you have received your officer's commission, there is still an opportunity to serve as a civilian, to attend graduate school or work for the government in some capacity that our family and Professor Connor have recommended. These choices could fulfill your sense of gratitude and give you satisfaction. We have discussed your plans after graduation many times during the last several years, but I continue to have more questions about your decision to follow a military career."

Alex listened as they climbed the stairs to his room. "Sometimes I have disturbing dreams and there are worries, fears for you that I haven't reconciled. Is your decision final? Your father says that there is an opening at the medical or law . . . ”

“I can understand your doubts, Steffi, but you have known that I am determined to serve in the military during the days and months ahead. You must also realize that action, rather than a scholarly career, is my choice for now. There will be time for graduate school, the foreign service, or some other profession in the future. Will you try and understand? You approve, don’t you?”

“Alex Dunham, I shall always stand by you in whatever choice you make.” After several minutes, her mood changed to elfish confidence. “You know, sir, it will take time to learn how to salute you.” Steffi brought her hand awkwardly to her forehead, then smiled. “Am I doing it correctly?”

His exhaustion from the regatta was complete. As they lay next to each other, she could feel the deep, regular movements of his chest. She was captivated by his serene handsomeness as she kissed his moist forehead and touched beads of perspiration running off his sideburns.

She knew unmistakably he was the man she wanted to marry. As he drifted off to sleep, she happily reminisced about the last several days of graduation festivities. Tomorrow he would take the first step on a long journey to become a soldier.

Five
The Elite

Dearest Steffi,

Remember after graduation when the Officers' Basic Training here at Benning was billed as a "refresher course"? With a month left, some of us have named it the "Crusher Course." Reveille at four-thirty, then off to calisthenics. You should see the company do twenty-five push-ups in unison every two minutes. Just like the Radio City Rockettes. I almost forgot those gourmet powdered eggs, creamed chipped beef on toast (fondly known as who-who on a stick). We do close-order drill almost blindfolded, and the firing range is a second home. The heat and dust down here make it even more of a Sunday picnic. Sometimes, I think of the Trinity. Those guys would be wiped out in twenty-four hours, and to make life more miserable, they would get nothing stronger than 3.2 beer.

Each day, one of us has a chance to command the company during field exercises and we are graded by officers who are any-

133

thing but generous referees. Twenty-five-mile hikes are routine along with night maneuvers, and you thought crew was tough. I must have been born a mechanic, breaking down and assembling weapons. Sometime I will show you how to get home in the dark with only a compass and map.

By the way, please tell your father that we march past the four parachute towers each morning and they're looking for volunteers. Next Sunday I will call about dinnertime. If he's available, perhaps we can speak a moment.

All of your letters have kept me going, and you can't imagine what they mean to me. I write my letters from the small post library, and some nights I manage to read. The latest Hemingway novel you sent is my favorite. It looks like a ten-day leave is almost a sure thing, so get out your tango pumps for Christmas.

I love you more every day, and we will be together soon.

See you before long. With all my love,
Alex

Alex saw the large announcement tacked to the company bulletin board: "Officers and Enlisted Men interested in volunteering for Parachute Infantry Training should report to Lieutenant Colonel Robert Gray, Barracks 'D,' between 1000 and 1500 hours, Monday through Friday."

Gray looked older than his age, his face furrowed and tanned from long hours in the field. The questions were brief and precise.

"Be seated, Dunham. You seem to be ranked first in about everything you put your mind to. Your fitness report and academic standing in the infantry refresher course rank you as one of the top men, and you are the first volunteer. The announcement said ten hundred hours, and you have been outside my office for two hours."

"Yes, sir, Colonel, I want to be on the ground floor of this new service branch."

"Your 201 file states that your IQ is better than average. You are a Princeton graduate with honors and were captain of the varsity crew. I don't think someone with your background would volunteer for anything, let alone parachute training."

"Sir, I believe there are new and challenging opportunities in the Airborne."

Gray remained silent, carefully reviewing the remainder of Alex's personnel file. "So you are fluent in French and German? Not many officers I happen to know have these qualifications. Do you have any idea what will be expected of you in the Airborne?"

"Yes, sir. I've spoken with some of the noncommissioned officers over at the towers. They have outlined the training and discipline."

"Dunham, you will be required to meet every possible physical and intellectual demand we make of you. During training, the second Lieutenant bars mean nothing. If you do not perform every small command to perfection, there is a 'reward' of pushups on the spot and other devilish physical and mental harassment. You will be taught the rigors of parachuting, which will progress to five successful jumps. You shall be aggressive, innovative, and if you succeed in winning your wings, you will be challenged to demonstrate these qualities in battle. That's when your composure, leadership, and ability to think and act independently under pressure will be ultimately tested. Any comments?"

"When does the next rotation begin, sir?"

"Report to Parachute Training Headquarters at 0600 hours 2 January. Good luck; we are counting on men like you. Dismissed."

"Thank you, Colonel."

Dr. Brian Dunham glanced at Lucky's fragrant pine Advent wreath set with candles, whose flickering light surrounded the dining table. His instructions were explicit. "Enjoy yourselves at the party, but be in my library about ten-thirty. Take my car if you wish. Be careful; it's a bad night. You know the paper says we'll have gas rationing soon, now that we're at war."

Alex helped Steffi pull on her boots and they walked several blocks along Lake Front Drive to the Browning apartment. Shoo-Shoo was entertaining old Academy schoolmates. Most men were in uniform.

Alex shook his friend's hand. "Tombo, it's been an age. You're an air force pilot?"

"Alex, to be absolutely correct, it's *aviator,* and training in Texas was like a long vacation. Ideal weather, and all of my bombing runs were close to perfect. It looks like England. They say things will heat up over there in several months when daylight bombing missions begin. No fighter cover at this time, so there should be some excitement. I pity you 'dog faces' down there living like moles, digging foxholes and trenches in the mud."

All of the guests laughed.

"Tombo." Steffi spoke with gentle sarcasm. "You've got all that fresh air and the gentleman's life. Alex has always loved dust and mud, and now to make matters worse, he plans to jump out of airplanes. Can you imagine all of this?"

After holiday toasts, greetings, and good-byes, Steffi held Alex's arm as they walked back through the snow. Large wet flakes dropped on the white-carpeted sidewalk.

"Alex, why does your father want to chat, especially at this time of night?"

"He's been trying for years to convince me I should be a doctor or lawyer and is emphatic I shouldn't have volunteered for Airborne service with all of its risks and uncertainties. He wants you to be there to support his argument and convince me I have made the wrong decision."

She was skeptical. "In a way, I agree. Sometimes I worry that you have chosen the most hazardous branch of service and there's a chance you might not, you know . . . come home, no matter where you are or what you do."

"I know it bothers you and Dad. You're trying to protect me, but I must be part of an elite organization and strive for the best. Please understand."

"You really haven't changed over the years. Alex, succeeding and winning are important to you. In a way, it's unfortunate that the war has given you this chance to prove the point. Although I have doubts, you can count on my support."

They walked into Brian Dunham's partially darkened library and could see his silhouette behind the desk. They held hands. Alex felt the moisture in her palms as she squeezed his fingers. He noticed the monogrammed smoking jacket and red glow of his father's cigarette each time he inhaled.

"You are a newly minted second Lieutenant and have volunteered," Brian emphasized. "Volunteered for the paratroops. What exactly do you have in mind? You could have gone to medical school and made something of yourself. You wasted those valuable years at the Academy and Princeton that gave you an opportunity to prepare for a profession and help others. Alex, you haven't discussed your plans with Lucky or me. Have you given any thought to what Steffi might think of this decision? You've chosen the most dangerous, foolhardy branch of service and never had the judgment to discuss it with me. Where's your common sense? Do you really know what you're getting into?"

Between each sentence Alex became more preoccupied by the intense glow of the cigarette, which seemed like a burning eye searching his conscience.

"Alex, I'm waiting for some answers, and so is Steffi."

He tried to distinguish his father's features, partly obscured by the semidarkness.

"Dr. Brian," Alex replied, "over the last eight or nine years you and Lucky have given me opportunity and privilege I didn't know existed. Both of you have shown me a world where I have been able to learn, gain some experience, and meet accomplished teachers and successful friends. With this in mind, I am in a position to make decisions without your well-intentioned advice and shall accept the consequences. If military service doesn't meet with your approval, then you should try to accept the idea. Steffi and I have discussed the dangers of this choice, and as a surgeon, you live with uncertainty each day and should understand. This is final and I would hope you could send me off with good cheer."

"Dr. Dunham, Alex has given careful thought to his commitments and I know it will lead him to the future he has planned."

Steffi ended the conversation, "Thank you and now we must leave."

There was a silence they would always remember, then the ominous caveat: "Don't forget what I've said. I have offered you a better way, if only you would listen. You have ignored my wise counsel, and as your father, I strongly disagree with you. Think a minute, Son. It may cost you. . . . Now that's enough, Alex. Good night."

Alex and Stephanie sat on a large sofa in the Pfeiffer living room watching the snow whirl about the windows, driven by the lake wind. He put his arm around her shoulders, touched her nose, eyes, and cheeks.

She kissed his lips; their tongues caressed. She held the lapels of his deep olive-colored jacket. "Alex, I will be here for you. Come home to me, no matter what happens. Life without you . . ."

He shifted slightly away from her, removed his seal ring, and slipped it on her finger. He folded his hands around hers. "Please keep this. When there are times of doubt and fear, read the words engraved inside the band: 'Our love is timeless'."

She reached for two pillows, put on his jacket, and pulled his winter coat over them. Her voice was barely audible. "I will always wear this ring, because it holds our memories, our plans for the future."

They fell asleep on the sofa for several hours until Lottie called them to early breakfast. Before he reached Atlanta he sent a telegram:

Dearest Steffi,

When this is over, I'll be a real live jumping bean like the ones we saw at the Academy carnivals each spring. Seems so long ago. Talk to you soon. Write often.

Love you,
Alex

Sergeant Mike O'Donnell was the platoon's jump instructor,

or despised "gorilla," who never spoke, only growled or barked. Three weeks of intense infantry training had passed. It was time for the first jump. Alex stood at attention in the rear rank of the platoon facing the thirty-four-foot tower and tried to think of nothing except his instructions: "Look at the horizon, tuck in your chin, try to relax, and after a tap on the boot, jump."

"This here tower is gonna separate the ladies from the men. Just because you're ninety-day wonders, you're still miserable pieces of shit. Do you hear me?"

"Yes, Airborne Sergeant," the platoon responded in unison.

"That wasn't loud enough, and wasn't what I called you. Again, so they can hear you up in Washington."

"Sergeant, yes, Sergeant. We are miserable pieces of shit, Sergeant."

O'Donnell sneered. "Now the little lady from Princeton in her ballet skirt will dance for us."

Alex double-timed forward. "Dunham, sir."

His face was close. Alex felt saliva droplets while the Sergeant shouted, "Dunham, you're slow this morning. Give me ten and get that pretty face of yours in the dirt."

He did five push-ups; then O'Donnell put his foot on his back and pushed down. "Come on, Miss Princeton, show me some real double-time. Go."

Alex sprinted around the four thirty-foot towers, then saluted.

"Five more, schoolboy, then get back in formation."

O'Donnell gave final instructions before Alex jumped from the tower. The shoulder straps were attached to a pulley and a wheel that would break the fall at about twenty feet with a ten-foot glide to the ground. O'Donnell climbed the straight ladder to the top.

D3's intimidation had its merits. Alex would not be provoked.

"The Princeton lady will get his platinum ass up here to show the rest of you poor underprivileged citizens how it's done." O'Donnell shouted. "Haul your stinking butt up the tower, Dunham."

Alex felt the parachute harness being strapped on. He remembered sitting on the fire escape at home looking down, feeling free. At first he felt a stab of fear. Now there was no hesitation; he must go, go.

O'Donnell didn't tap but kicked Alex's boot. "All right, college boy, this should wash you out if anything does. Now don't piss in your pink panties."

It was a free fall that lasted several seconds before he was suddenly jerked to a soft landing. He took one faltering step forward, had a brief feeling of blackness, quickly unharnessed himself, and jogged back to the platoon.

At mail call there was a letter from Steffi and the familiar blue typewritten envelope:

From the desk of Dr. Brian Dunham:

Dear Alex,

By the time you receive this note you will be ready for your final two weeks of training and the five live parachute jumps that you wrote about. The 250-foot tower jumps sound like the old rigs they had at Overhill Amusement Park. Remember when we used to go out there during your visits with Lucky and me? We thought you were a daredevil then. I spoke to the freshman class at the medical school the other day, and they seem like a good group. When the war is over, you must settle down because we can arrange a place for you in the first year class. The Pfeiffers had dinner with us the other night, and Steffi is doing volunteer work at the hospital as well as the Red Cross. Glad you are in on the ground floor, and the next step should be a staff position, where you do some thinking rather than push-ups. Lucky sends her best.

Yours,
D3

O'Donnell stood in front of the platoon. "You've come through the last eight weeks. It's graduation time. Be on the ball, because we have some Washington VIPs and brass down here to size things up. Not one single fuck-up from any one of you I've trained. And if there is, you've got to face me, and may the good Lord help you poor bastards. This is the fifth and final jump for your parachute wings. Thomas, take one-third, Johnson, the second third, and Dunham, the last stick of my platoon. Move out to the DC-3s."

Alex watched O'Donnell's sharp features. He stood with hands behind his back, raising his voice and moving his head from side to side. There was no doubt about his orders. His voice and bearing translated into absolute authority. Alex respected O'Donnell's toughness and precision and the confidence he inspired. He decided he would use the best of his military traits when he was in a position to lead. Perhaps his language was another matter. Not Fowler's English Usage.

As the three planes approached the landing area, the jump-master checked each man's equipment again. They jumped with weapons and the platoon would attack and seize a simulated enemy position. Alex thought the exercise was carried out flawlessly, almost flawlessly. As he spilled air from his canopy and gathered in his chute, one unfortunate trooper had been blown by a crosswind and landed squarely on top of a gasoline truck near the hangar. The three sections of the platoon overran their objective within a short time, and later O'Donnell announced it was a success. Immediately after the final jump, parachute wings were pinned on a blue circle of his dress uniform by the commanding officer of the Parachute Infantry School before the attending VIPs. That afternoon Alex was promoted to first Lieutenant. He knew the Pfeiffers and Steffi would have enjoyed the impressive ceremony.

Rather than stand in line behind other officers with the same message for their families, Alex commandeered the post library telephone from the pleasant elderly lady who was a Red Cross volunteer. His fatigue from the long day could not mask his enthusiasm. His sense of accomplishing the first step in the strenuous program gave him a splendid feeling of satisfaction.

"Steffi, Steffi, it's Alex. I made it through the eight weeks, got my wings and promotion this afternoon. I can't wait for you to see them. If there's an elite in the army, we're it. Airborne patch on our left shoulder, overseas cap and bloused trousers with special paratrooper boots. The training has been tougher than you can imagine. A lot has been asked of us. It's the goal I worked for. Some great guys here; have a couple of good friends. Things are moving fast now. Next week they'll form up a new regiment, and I'm pulling some strings to get assigned."

"We're proud of you, Alex. None of us, except Tina, believes anyone can jump from an airplane and actually walk away. I guess it's not that hard, according to your letters. I love you. When can you come home for a while? Even Maxie looks for you every day."

"During the next three months training will be more difficult, but there's a chance for a week in July. It won't be long, Steffi; then I'll have a surprise for you."

"A surprise, what do you mean?"

"You know, sweetheart, first a question, then a surprise."

"I'll give you the answer right now; it's yes, yes, yes, a thousand times yes."

"Keep writing, Steffi, and wish me luck. See you soon, and all my love to you and the family. Good night."

"Be seated, Dunham."

Colonel John Conroy sat behind a gray metal desk in a meagerly furnished office whose only comforts were venetian blinds and a fan. His ruddy complexion, muscled neck, and broad shoulders gave him a pugnacious appearance. He spoke with a gravelly voice in clipped phrases that exacted respect. Alex imagined he was in his early to midthirties. His military presence made D3 seem charitable. The commander of the newly formed 504 Parachute Infantry Regiment had the reputation of an intelligent, motivated officer.

"So, you speak several languages and are quite an athlete. Supposed to have a good head on your shoulders, but you'll have to prove it. You have recently finished parachute school and will be one of three acting company commanders training the men who completed the course with you. I want aggressive, hard-nosed soldiers who have been taught Airborne infantry tactics and are combat-ready. Is that clear, Dunham?"

"Yes, sir."

"This is only the third authorized parachute regiment. I'll watch your every movement each minute of your life. Depending on your performance, I may want you for a staff position at the end of the training cycle. Any questions?"

"No, sir."

As spring became late May and early June, Alex thought the heat and dust became more unbearable, but he drove himself and his company. He led them in parachute jumps three times a week, calisthenics, crawling under live ammunition fire, compass exercises, and hand-to-hand combat, and forced marches increased from five to fifteen miles. Each night he reviewed the day's exercises with his platoon leaders, who in turn briefed noncommissioned officers to prevent repetition of errors. He worried about judgmental mistakes and his responsibility for the morale, discipline, and physical toughness of his men. With this punishing routine, he developed a quiet and rigid firmness in speech and bearing. He was highly visible to his company, respected and demanding.

The three privates stood in front of Alex's desk with a Sergeant posted at his office door.

"Sergeant, what is the charge?"

"Sir, Combs, Kilburg, and Murphy are six hours late from pass."

Alex waited.

Combs' mouth was dry and his speech was garbled. "It was my wife, sir. There was no one to take her home from the hospital."

"All right. Kilburg, you were due in yesterday morning."

"Sir, my car broke down. I missed the train and ran a couple of miles to the station."

Alex stared through each man. "Well, Murphy, what's your excuse? Where did that black eye come from?"

"Lieutenant, sir . . . there was a fight, you know, in a bar; it wasn't my fault. The boys from the 505 called us a bunch of 'fucking homos,' and I couldn't let that go, now could I, sir? We're special, the very best, not regular infantry, sir."

Alex stood. "You are three of my troopers, and we only have a month before this company is to be fully trained. If you were in combat you would have either been killed or caused the death of a buddy. Do you know what's going on right now in one of the other companies? No, dammit, you don't. There are five men who are having their Airborne patches torn off their shirts and caps, their boots have been taken, and they're out into the regular infantry. They have been disgraced in front of their company for being only thirty minutes late in reporting back from pass, like you three."

Alex saw their sweaty faces; Murphy was trembling.

"Another chance, sir," the other two pleaded.

Both Alex and Sergeant Caspar knew these soldiers as the "three blind mice." They were the demolition team of the First Platoon and had a reputation for the efficiency and expertise that his company required. Alex thought it was a question of punishment and enforcing discipline, but he could not afford to lose their skills.

Alex looked at Caspar. "We'll have none of this chicken shit punishment. Do you hear me?"

"Yes, sir."

"All right." Alex spoke with crispness. "Company punishment for these three is confinement to barracks until the end of training, daily latrine duty, and they will do an extra hour of calisthenics each day. If we run fifteen miles, they go five more, whatever the damn number is. If I ever see or hear of you three again, you're out of Airborne; walk to the gates of Benning in your damn bare feet and straight pants. Sergeant, you are personally responsible for carrying out my orders. Dismissed."

Later, Sergeant Johnny Caspar knocked on Alex's office door.

"Sir, don't you think that punishment was too easy on the men?"

"Dammit all, Caspar, you let me be the best judge of that. Pass the word. The company must know I have chewed their butts raw, and announce their restrictions to barracks at company formation. Sergeant, I know these men are called the three blind mice, and for good reason."

"Thank you, Lieutenant. The noncoms have told me morale is rock bottom over at Carmichael's company and the Colonel is really pissed off. If I may say so, sir, I believe you have been more than fair. Their lives won't be worth living when I get through with them. No chicken shit, sir, work 'em to death, right, sir?"

"Right, Sergeant, and everybody on the ball for the final exercise in four days."

Alex sat in the Officers' Club talking to other company commanders and some of the bright and not so bright rising stars in the Airborne and regular infantry. He had always been reticent and reserved during glib conversation, social backslapping, and inane chatter. Fellow officers never thought of him as one of the boys. Now he listened to tales circulating through the Benning community while he nursed a bottle of beer. He was preoccupied by plans for the final exercise and briefings in the coming four days as he forced some inconsequential small talk and restrained camaraderie.

"How are things going, Bob?" Alex offered his hand.

Bob Brewster was another provisional company commander and would be one of Alex's competitors in the final maneuvers. His company referred to him as "Bozo."

"Have a seat, Charlie." Brewster was openly contemptuous of Dunham, and "Princeton Charlie" was his expression of what he thought was clever deprecation.

Alex asked, "Tell me about that '39 game with Notre Dame, Bob. You guys had a thirteen-point lead until the last quarter. What happened anyway?"

"Shit, it was all that flea-flicker stuff. We ran over the little bastards, outweighed them fifteen pounds a man; I guess they were too quick."

He judged Brewster was all power, most of it below his neck.

Danny Carmichael slowly walked over from the bar, joined by his infantry friends. "Well, well, what's Albert Einstein doing here? Not really the original, but we call him Princeton Charlie.

You know good-time Charlie, never lifted a fucking finger in his life. Everything handed out on a silver platter. Eastern playboy type, you know the kind. What are you doing here tonight, slumming with us peons?"

Alex introduced Brewster, then the heavy drinking, braggadocio, and apocryphal anecdotes continued as each officer tried to upstage the other. With affected interest, Alex finished his beer, briefly mingled with another group, then inconspicuously moved to the back of the club and left.

"They may call me 'Chicken Shit' Carmichael, yet I have the best damned Airborne company the 504 will ever see. You know those five poor bastards who reported in late from pass last week? Well, I personally drummed them out of my company. Sent them out in disgrace. You know a little discipline is good for the men." His account was followed by loud approval and laughter.

Another officer joined the humor. "Great job, Danny. I guess we got too noisy for Charlie boy; it must be past his bedtime."

Alex was apprehensive. He wondered if he had given the upcoming exercises enough thought and planning. He told himself he must win these maneuvers if he were to succeed in the fierce contest of promotion. That night he and Sergeant Caspar met with his three platoon leaders.

Alex spoke to his men encouragingly.

"All right, gents, we have four days to figure out Colonel Conroy's graduation problem. Once we have decided, the 'where' is critical, and then come the 'how' and 'what' objectives he might select. Roy, give us some ideas."

Lieutenant Roy Fleming explained, "Right now Airborne thinking requires a drop away from the target area of at least five or six miles. We have about seven hours at the most to capture the objective. Takeoff time is fourteen hundred hours. My guess is there will be at least three tanks to block the advance of each company. Parachute infantry has problems with the tankers. We need more bazookas."

"Good, Roy. Let's get those 'requisitioned' any way we can, in addition to our allotment. Good thinking."

Alex spoke to another officer. "Jim, we've been together awhile; what's on your mind?"

"Well, sir, if I read the Colonel's mind correctly, the 'what' will be a bridge, because it is a favorite target of Airborne forces. I've listened to the Colonel during his weekly briefings, and the old fart always brings up the subject. I'll put some heavy money on a bridge as the primary objective. We can't forget it may be rigged for detonation."

Alex agreed. "The Colonel's weekly briefings for platoon leaders has been valuable for each of you, and as Jim says, a bridge is the probable target where regimental headquarters and the referees will be stationed. We'll send several squads on reconnaissance. Keep communications open with me." He turned to Sergeant Al Cunicello. "All right, Sergeant, sound off."

"Sir, I believe, there'll be minefields. We must scout and not get trapped. It would be fatal."

Alex felt more secure now. "We have four days left, and if you have more ideas, let's discuss them. We'll meet here at 2000 hours the night before jumpoff. Get advice from your Sergeants, but no—repeat, no—discussion with other companies. Remember, it's our game to win or lose."

Alex knew he had three reliable and conscientious platoon leaders and a group of experienced noncommissioned officers. They were serious and dedicated, no bravado, only smart and aggressive. He thought about these men and their loyalty. When the chance came, he would choose these types for his command.

His head gradually dropped. He drowsed with no idea of time or place. Later he stirred, half-awake. The bare wood of his stark office became a burst of soft colors from the sky, water, and countryside. Military duties and demands momentarily vanished. He closed his eyes to make the beauty last. He opened a pocket-sized book of poetry Steffi had given him. "Ode on a Grecian Urn" was relief from gripping reality. There was time to reread some lines they often enjoyed together. . . . He was sitting close to her. Both were enthralled by a Monet. Then he was listening to Pete Starke recite the first lines of Chaucer. Finally the memory of James Hodges. Alex was beginning to learn the true meaning of "I sing of arms and the man." They smiled serenely. The tranquil interlude passed. "Steffi, don't you think the poetry of Keats has more descriptive clarity than that of Shelley or Byron?" She nodded.

The six DC-3s with Alex's company circled while the transports with the other two companies joined; then the three groups flew toward different landing zones.

Brewster's company parachuted near a sprawling woods, causing "tree casualties," slowing his advance. At the time, he was unaware he had been dropped closest to the target. Earlier, Carmichael's men had landed on a river's edge, and if they were to advance, a shallow crossing or bridge had to be found. After assembling his dispersed troopers, Carmichael decided to cross the river directly to save time. Dunham's company hit an open wheat field and quickly assembled its equipment, ready to move out within minutes.

"Goddammit," Carmichael was screaming at two Sergeants. "Get those men together and ford the river. It can't be more than three feet deep."

The first six troopers started down the bank and sank in knee-deep mud, and three of them were carried downstream. Ten other parachutists jumped in, swimming frantically to recover the struggling men. Two were dragged to the river's edge. One drowned. Carmichael's advance was stalled and while shouting orders he was hit in the back by three thuds of flour. His own men had thrown simulated hand grenades, killing their company commander.

"That'll take care of that son of a bitch for good." One of the grenades had come from a buddy of the men who had been drummed out of the company. Carmichael was never a factor in the final exercise.

As Alex and Brewster converged on the target, which was, indeed, a railroad bridge, scouts reported two tanks that could slow his advance. Several minutes later, Jim Travis radioed that his men had surprised the confident tankers and infantry, some of whom were either casually chowing down, urinating, or having a smoke. Within several minutes, Travis reported in:

"Infantry captured, tanks destroyed. Now, we'll go for the target." This tactical success was recorded by the maneuver umpire.

Alex radioed back: "The scouts report Brewster converging on us. Travis, watch your left flank. There's got to be a minefield somewhere in front of either our company or his. Move to the right, east of the mines; draw their troops into the minefield."

Brewster led his company. "God almighty, I can almost smell that fucking bridge. I'll be a Captain in two weeks if we can make it for another mile. We'll ram through this field like the Notre Dame line." His company was at half-strength because they had failed to capture three tanks blocking their advance. Jim Travis confirmed that Brewster was on his flank. Another platoon leader reported the minefield at the same time Brewster arrived at the ominous stakes with yellow flags, armed with bells alerting the referees.

Brewster was stymied, attempting to avoid the minefield; however, his tactical decision was impulsive. It sounded like pealing church bells as he forged ahead with eighty men. Another maneuver evaluator indicated that Brewster and his advancing force were virtually destroyed.

It was late dusk as Alex led twenty men toward the bridge, rising out of the mist several hundred yards down the road. He knew it was time for both caution and aggressive action. No one knew of Carmichael's debacle.

Alex sent Travis's platoon forward, but a maneuver umpire judged they were ambushed, killed by a squad of headquarters infantry protecting the bridge. Later Dunham led his group and cleared the road of resistance.

"Where's Sergeant Caspar?" Alex ordered. "Tell him to get his ass up here on the double with his men."

Within minutes Caspar appeared with his three blind mice.

"Dammit, Sergeant, move them forward. Show me how good they are—"

"Lieutenant, sir," Caspar interrupted. "Watch us disarm that bridge. Combs, Kilburg, and Murphy haven't forgotten, sir."

"Get on with it, Caspar."

Alex was within one hundred yards of the bridge when someone in headquarters doused the kerosene lamps. Alex raised his field glasses and saw Caspar and his men move over the girders cutting ropes to the simulated detonators. Now the bridge was secure from explosion.

His squad approached regimental headquarters with its staff and referees. Alex carried his carbine at his side as they surrounded the large camouflaged tent.

"All of you bastards get your hands up, and make it pronto." Alex shouted. "Don't reach for a weapon, or it's a sack of flour in your face. You over there in the corner, you've got your back to me. Move out here where I can see you. What are you waiting for? Get your hands up." Alex rammed a rifle butt into the man's back. "Those riding boots must be cavalry."

The imposing figure turned to face Alex. He was a Brigadier General commanding the opposing force, an older, pretentious cavalryman. His regimental staff and remaining umpires in the tent had been grenaded with flour.

Conroy had observed the final attack on the bridge and enemy headquarters "All right, Dunham, you've captured this bridge and headquarters. Your company has performed well."

"Yes, Colonel Conroy, sir, that was our plan, but we had no idea that we could capture the bridge and headquarters company so quickly."

The Brigadier turned to the flour-covered referees. "Gentlemen, I believe this exercise is concluded. From the time of touchdown, how long did it take Lieutenant Dunham and his company to capture the objective?"

A referee from the Airborne announced, "Exactly five hours and thirty-five minutes, sir."

"Not bad, not bad at all, Dunham." Conroy spoke with measured approval. "Now we'll bring those trucks up for your company. You deserve a ride back to Benning. It's about ten miles."

Sergeant Caspar looked at Alex and slowly shook his head.

"Good of you, Colonel. Sergeant Caspar and I will assemble the company and form up in the morning, usual time, sir." Alex turned and saluted. "A pleasant evening to all of you prisoners of war."

Alex marched his company back to the "Frying Pan," a sobriquet that paratroopers had given their designated barracks area. It was well after midnight when he briefly addressed his men.

"Each one of you has done one hell of a fine job. Noncoms, platoon leaders, everyone performed as if you were combat-ready. You won this final training exercise hands down."

He walked through the ranks and spoke to most of the men individually.

"Good job, Jones. Keep at it, Wilcox. Someday in battle you will remember today, won't you, Murphy?"

"Reveille in four hours, calisthenics, then chow down," the First Sergeant announced with genuine glee.

"What are you?" Alex shouted.

There was a resounding, "The best."

"Who are you?"

"Airborne, sir."

He led calisthenics at daybreak, knowing the men were drained. They followed him and shouted cadence during certain of the more demanding exercises.

Conroy watched from his office. "Sergeant Major, have Lieutenant Dunham report to me in an hour."

Alex stood before Conroy in fresh fatigues.

"The final exercise yesterday was executed well, Dunham. But part of a platoon was ambushed one hundred yards from the objective."

"It won't happen a second time, sir."

"I've watched you for the last three months. Yesterday was satisfactory; better yet, you turned down the trucks. It seems to me that you're tough, persistent, and can think logically in difficult situations. That sort of aggressiveness will make the whole difference one of these days."

"I understand, sir."

"All right, enough of this palaver. You're a Captain now and have two weeks' leave; then we'll find out how smart you are. You will be on my staff after July first. Dismissed, Dunham."

Conroy sat back in his chair as the young officer left. He thought Captain Dunham had met the physical and tactical demands of a promising Airborne officer who would be prepared for more responsibility in the future. Conroy considered him brave, not foolish, but wondered if he was innovative, with original ideas. The Colonel turned in his chair, recalling the rifle butt his "promising" officer had rammed into the backside of his senior, Brigadier General Clarence Browne. Conroy expected that Alex probably had a certain capacity for violence. He knew the Airborne needed this aggressiveness and no one in his command would succeed without it.

The Pfeiffers met Alex at the University Club, where he was staying during his leave. They drove through the suburbs to the spacious grounds of the Arrowmink Club and were greeted with gay laughter and fragments of congratulatory conversation drifting through the colorful green-and-white tent. The sloping lawns of the club stretched to the edge of the golf course, where friends chatted as they enjoyed light hors d'oeuvres and cocktails. The engaged couple stood with their parents, receiving guests, and Stephanie would occasionally scurry joyously, flourishing her ring.

"Oh, Steffi, what a beautiful band. It's been a delight to watch you grow up together, and Austen and I wish you happiness."

"You're sweet, Auntie Helen. It's another day Alex and I will remember. Weren't we fortunate to have a lovely June afternoon?"

Anne Scott, a classmate from the Academy, dashed up the lawn, pulling a young Lieutenant with her.

Steffi ran toward her old friend. "Annie bananie, it's been so long. How kind of you to come."

"Steffi, you're beautiful, and I love your *trés, trés* elegant blue dress. May I introduce Stephen Gilmore? He's stationed near San Antonio and is in Tombo's squadron. What a coincidence. Someday soon I hope we can celebrate like this."

"Both of you come with me and we'll talk to Alex. You know, I can't stand to be away from him more than several minutes. We've done everything together for the last two weeks."

Brian and Lucky stood with Erich Pfeiffer, apart from the crowd's gaiety, near the eighteenth hole where Brian had finished with the same foursome for the last twenty years.

"Lucky," Brian remarked, "don't you think it's unusual Alex is staying at the University Club after you invited him to visit with us? He's a stranger now."

"Remember, dear, you two have had differences. You should be proud he's making his own choices and decisions. Brian, it will never be the same."

Erich nodded with approval. He thought Dunham was concerned and uneasy and lacked his customary composure, and Pfeiffer knew there was more on his friend's mind than golf.

Brian commented on the severe break and undulating surface of the eighteenth green. "You can see the fairway from here, Erich. It's the most demanding hole on the course. I can't tell you how many times I've three-putted this green and there goes a good score."

"Erich," Brian continued, "you know Alex doesn't write often since he's been away. Sometimes we hear about his training and whatever they do down there at Benning, and the few letters we receive have a certain remoteness. I probably should expect it. His military life is completely different, one I can't comprehend. Of course, we're pleased he's been promoted. I would imagine it's tough and dangerous duty. Regardless of our differences about his future, Lucky and I are concerned about him. And then there's his responsibility for Steffi."

"Brian, you surprise me." Pfeiffer's tone was understanding. "You're a surgeon, one of the best, and should realize there's risk in everything you do. Think of it the same way as Alex moves ahead. He's becoming a hard professional who knows his job and limitations. He is part of an elite force that will conduct dangerous missions and can handle the situation."

Dr. Brian Dunham agreed, and Lucky seemed satisfied.

As the guests began to leave, Teddy Rosenthal congratulated the couple. "Steffi, as always, you're radiant today, and little wonder. Where does time go? This fine young man of yours has been our friend since he started school many years ago. Rosie and I love you both." He drew Alex aside. "I know you have a room at the club. This afternoon we are going away for the weekend. Why don't you and Steffi 'house-sit' our apartment tonight? You leave tomorrow, don't you?"

"Dr. Teddy, you are a gem. As you might imagine, it's been impossible for us to be alone."

"Rosie and I hope and pray for you. May this nightmare soon be over."

"Dr. Rosenthal, it may well be a nightmare. Remember our conversation at Christmas before I entered the Academy? In a small way, I might be able to make a difference now. Some trying times, sacrifice, ahead." He smiled. "Don't forget, the Airborne makes Marines jealous."

Alex settled in a coach seat, opened his briefcase, and was surprised to find a tattered copy of *From Bull Run to Appomattox,* complete with detailed battle maps. War had changed, but not Jeb Stuart's visionary tactics.

From the desk of Dr. Brian Dunham:

Dear Captain,

Hope you enjoy this, and as we discussed many years ago, if Jeb Stuart hadn't been off on a wild goose chase at Gettysburg, the outcome might have been different. Again, congratulations to you and Steffi on your engagement and for many happy years ahead.

Yours,
D3

He used it as a bookmarker.

After completion of his first assignment on Colonel Conroy's staff, Alex stood in dress uniform before a large group of officers and selected noncommissioned officers in a hangar at Fort Benning. His voice carried; there was no mistaking his confidence. The 150-page translation and evaluation of captured German documents on the Airborne operation in Crete had required four days during which his other duties had been temporarily suspended. Conroy and the rest of his staff sat on an elevated platform as he began a report that was not to exceed twenty-five minutes.

A new Lieutenant spoke to his friend. "The great Captain Dunham is supposed to be a real smartass, thinks he can speak all these foreign languages, brainy type, you know. Wonder if he knows his right foot from his left? How good is he when it comes to the practical side of things? I've met these intellectual characters before. He's all hot air and bullshit."

"I understand he'd slit your throat with a smile; don't sell him short. He's deceptive; they say he's quiet and pretty much keeps to himself. You'd better cover your ass around this guy; get the idea? Don't forget, his company ran circles around Carmichael and Brewster. And where are they now? Picking shit with the chickens."

Alex pointed to a large map of Crete. As he turned, he realized that Crete resembled a large sausage, the kind he and Steffi used to order with pancakes at B and G's. "Gentlemen, we have used many of the German Airborne guidelines for our training, including the two-hundred-and-fifty-foot and thirty-four-foot towers and their 'static lines.' German student paratroopers also jumped from the tops of moving trucks to perfect the roll and somersault on firm ground that simulated a hard landing. They were taught to act quickly, and twelve jumpers in a stick had to leave the plane within eight seconds. This training information was obtained from captured documents, but today we are interested in their own evaluation of the Airborne invasion of Crete. This is a critique of the '*Schlussbericht und Bewertung der Operation Merkur, Luftwehrmacht und Fallschirmjäger Landungen, von General der Luftwaffe Kurt Student an das Oberkommando des Heeres. Die Zeitspanne war 20. Mai bis 30 Mai 1941'.*"

" 'Operation Merkur' was the first Airborne invasion in history, and in addition to *Fallschirmjäger*, other innovations included glider-borne infantry and artillery dropped by three large canopies. Finally the island was captured after ten days of fierce combat in which fifty percent of the attacking German force was killed or wounded. Obviously, not an acceptable operation. It is essential that we learn from their mistakes and miscalculations."

There was a series of questions and answers. Alex was not aware that Major General William Bedford had listened, unnoticed, from a rear corner of the hangar.

That evening, the Conroys entertained Bedford at dinner. The two reminisced about West Point, their bleak opportunities for advancement in prewar days, and Washington rumors. Bedford was pleasant but reserved and seldom revealed his concerns.

"John, you know we have one hell of a responsibility, because the brass wants two combat-ready Airborne divisions within six months. We need the highest-caliber officer we can possibly select and train. This must be a new, superior force. By the way, what was the name of that young Captain who spoke on the Crete operation?"

"His name is Dunham, and don't worry; I've got my eye on him. He's a comer. Believe me, he's got what we need." Conroy quickly related some details of Alex's last exercise. "Damn, I bet that old cavalryman's backside still aches from the rifle butt."

"Have him work up a summary on the possibility of using gliders to land Airborne troops and equipment. I want this report next week; then send him up to me in D.C. Go over it first; make any appropriate changes. You said he spoke several languages, including German?"

"We'll give it our best, General."

Each night when Alex translated and incorporated ideas from the German documents of glider operations he gave a word or two of thanks to Herr Professor Hans Neumann for his insistence on perfection. Alex's report, "The Feasibility of Glider Transportation of Airborne Troops and Equipment," was submitted to Conroy several days before the scheduled briefing by Bedford. Alex had learned to anticipate orders and directives from his senior, and the two had developed a businesslike, efficient command structure. It was like staying two steps ahead of D3. Alex thought Conroy was conscientious, fair, and not hesitant to encourage and approve new ideas.

"Alex, when you attend this briefing with General Bedford," Conroy stressed, "be positive and enthusiastic. The Airborne is growing day by day, and the General must have two full divisions ready for overseas assignment and possible combat within several months."

"Sir, I am convinced a glider force operating with parachute infantry units has great promise, yet we are not producing this type of 'dead flight aircraft' at the present and I would suggest this be of top priority," Alex replied.

"I have appended several thoughts and changed some of the language of the report. But be upbeat during the presentation. I'll be interested to know how your ideas are accepted, Dunham."

"Thank you for your suggestions, Colonel. My flight should return late on Friday. Your instructions will be followed to the letter, sir."

Alex was surprised that Bedford's Airborne Planning Section occupied a relatively small corner of one floor of the War Department. He saw several secretaries and officers seated in the General's sparse office. Bedford's staff was completing a meeting when he arrived.

The General stood in the back of his office with Major Robert "Pebble" Stone, his chief of staff.

"Pebble, you have a meanness that I like, and that's exactly why you're my 'hatchet man.' Challenge everything Dunham has to say. I want to hear his ideas and see how he handles himself with some old-fashioned 'needling'."

"Sir, as always, it will be my pleasure."

Alex introduced himself to General Bedford's secretary, whose name plate was on the front of her desk. "Good afternoon. I am Captain Alex Dunham and have an appointment. . . ."

She was appealing and personable. "Ah, bonjour, Capitaine Dunham, je m'appelle Madame Gisele Seulles, et quel plaisir de faire votre connaissance. I know that you have arrived shortly from Fort Benning and hope you had a pleasant flight." Madame Seulles was happy to meet him.

He greeted the middle-aged woman, whose graying hair was pulled back in an attractive chignon, "Enchanté, Madame. Le vol était très calme, et je suis heureux d'être à la capitale. I am surprised that you speak French. I haven't spoken your language in several months. Again, it is my pleasure to meet you."

She motioned him closer to her desk. "Captain, I have your 201 file here, and your home is Chicago, isn't it?"

He was charmed by her pronunciation of *Chicago*. "Yes, madame, it is."

"I would imagine your father is Dr. Brian Dunham?"

"Yes, indeed, you are quite correct."

"You know, Captain, he operated upon my brother several years ago and our family is grateful because he leads a perfectly normal life. We can speak again before you leave. One quick word of advice: Major Stone is a difficult officer; act accordingly. Bon courage, mon ami, à bientôt."

"Merci mille fois, madame, et je vous remerci."

"Je vous en prie, Alex Dunham."

General Bedford was cordial as he introduced his staff of four officers. "Have one of the girls bring us some coffee."

Stone stood, motioned for the pot and cups, then placed his chair at the General's side.

As they shook hands, Alex noticed Stone had a slightly flabby face and reddish complexion, which probably meant he was a drinker. He lacked the smart appearance of Airborne officers and had a paunch, and having been warned, Alex judged his physical slackness might mirror his thinking and command of facts. He sipped coffee and hastily thumbed through the report as Alex spoke.

Stone interrupted with a certain belligerence. "Hold the phone, Captain. Your name, oh, yes, Dunbar. You write here German paratroopers blew the fortifications at Fort Eben Emael in Belgium, 1940. Isn't that impressive enough? Why do we need gliders?"

"Major Stone, the operation was carried out at dawn and required only fifty-five men and eleven gliders that landed accurately on the roofs of the fort. The German paratroopers were concentrated in force directly on their objective, and the gliders carried specifically designed explosive charges to blow downward. Their weight was too heavy for the individual trooper. This glider-paratroop combination easily captured one of the Allies' most strongly defended positions, held by approximately a thousand troops."

Alex looked at Bedford. "I would also suggest, General, that in the immediate future our Airborne should have its own artillery regiments carried into battle by gliders. There are no plans for this support at present—"

"Dunbar," Stone interrupted again. "You must realize artillery for rapidly moving Airborne forces is impractical and there is no military technique for dropping this type of support."

Alex spoke more firmly. "Airborne troops are helpless against tanks, and presently we have nothing in the category of rocket launchers or bazookas that will penetrate German armor. One can visualize a time when seventy-five-millimeter packs or even 105 howitzers with modified barrels can be landed accurately by gliders behind enemy lines. This would be in addition to glider-borne infantry and medical and other essential supplies, such as food and ammunition."

Stone asked with sarcasm, "Who will fly these Airborne coffins, Dunbar? We can't waste trained parachutists to do the job."

"The Waco Company in Ohio is working on a glider prototype," Alex explained. "The air force could train pilots who also must have the basic infantry course and fight with paratroopers after landing. Finally, as the report indicates, I believe we should push this project of glider support for parachute infantry, and time is short. General Bedford, gentlemen, thank you for your attention. Are there further questions?"

There was silence.

Bedford pushed back his chair. "Captain Dunham, your report is innovative and has given us new insights. Well done, spoken with conviction. My regards to Johnny Conroy. Good luck with the 504."

After a brief conversation with the staff, Alex passed Gisele Seulles's desk. Her kindness and *gentillesse* were attractive. Honesty and gracious bearing were at a premium during the war. "Madame, votre conseil était sage. Je voudrais vous remercier beaucoup, and perhaps we shall meet again."

"Au revoir, Capitaine, et que Dieu vous benisse."

He found the nearest lavatory, removed his tie, unbuttoned his shirt, and splashed his face and head with cold water. He needed Steffi now. He could swim with her naked, hold her tall, slim body next to his, and smell the sun on her skin. They would be free together. He could hear her voice.

Steffi, dammit all, where are you this moment? he thought. *What are you doing? I must be with you. What would it be like, for God knows how long, without you? Screw this damn war. Maybe D3 was right after all.*

He quickly walked to a telephone at the airport and hesitated, staring at the dial. *Alex, you are mentally and emotionally toughened and disciplined,* he brooded. *You mustn't want what you can't have now. Control the yearning, be patient, and wait; wait for her. Steady; write a long letter this evening.*

He spoke with the florist. "Please send this gardenia to Madame Gisele Seulles, and her address is—"

"All right, Mr. General, spell it all out nice and clear like. I've never heard an American name like that before." A pristine flower, a pristine package, arranged by the skeleton-like florist, with small cuts on her soil-covered hands.

Alex passed the final draft across his desk. "Colonel Conroy, the Airborne Glider Manual AA-J 702 is complete, and it should contain all contingencies from A to Z in their combined operations."

He realized John Conroy was busy, harassed by numerous directives and official orders stuffed in the "In" and "Out" boxes on his desk.

"Good work, Alex. I'll read your final report tonight and then submit it to Ground and Air Force Commands in Washington. I know it will be the 'Bible' for this war and should be circulated in every army post within a month. Anything else, Captain?"

"Sir, there's something in the air, isn't there? Everyone seems to be moving faster, shorter tempers, a quicker pace, all of that sort of thing."

Conroy was cautious. "Perhaps, and with the completion of your manual I'll need your help more than ever. I want you fresh and ready to go. Out of my sight for five or six days. It's your last chance for leave. I don't want to see you until next week; then you can act as my deputy when I'm up in Charleston. Haven't seen the family for several months, have to be sure things are 'copacetic.' We're regular army, good times and bad."

Stephanie held his hand. "Alex, when I started the Academy, I never could say bumpy; it was always 'bumpily.' This has to be the bumpliest bus ride I've ever had, but who cares? We're together, and what gorgeous fall weather. Can't you come closer?"

They sat in the backseat of a local bus that completed the fifty-mile journey from Chicago to Galena in almost two hours. Alex thought it was a chariot compared to some of his rides in jeeps and army trucks. His men firmly believed the United States government issued its vehicles with square wheels.

The bus stopped abruptly as the driver announced, "All right, folks, we made it in record time, one hour and fifty-eight minutes. . . . All out for Galena. Let me tell you, it's been better than driving the Indy Five Hundred. I never get tired of my job."

Galena had the expected gas station, grocery and hardware stores, and a small restaurant-bar with a jukebox. The sign at the edge of town read: "Pop. 275." Alex threw his duffel bag over one shoulder, carrying Steffi's small suitcase in his free hand. He thought it weighed about the same as an ammunition case. They walked down a dusty road to the Pfeiffers' small farm, shaded by majestic elms and sycamores. She had never seen him in khaki fatigues with open collar, insignia, and parachute boots. His overseas cap was tucked under his belt.

"Steffi, your bag is heavier than a steamer trunk. You must

be serious about going overseas with us."

She stopped, pushed the duffel from his shoulder, pulled her bag away, then reached for him. Lithe, with firm arms and hands, she only had to lift her head slightly to reach his mouth. They stood in the middle of the isolated road gently moving against one another. She bit the tip of his tongue.

He held her at arm's length, and she bent her head back. The afternoon sun pinpointed their pupils. Their eyes became immovable, fixed on one another. Words raced through his mind. *Oh, God, how I love you, Steffi,* he thought. *I don't want to leave you. I'm not afraid, only sometimes for my men. Most of them are so young.*

"You must never, ever be afraid, do you understand, Stephanie D. Pfeiffer?"

"I'll try, Captain Alexander C. Dunham, honestly, sweetheart."

They rubbed noses. He grinned, then smacked her firm bottom. "Trying isn't good enough; you're playing on the first team now."

"Yes, sir. I have my orders and will always obey, cherish, and love you."

They ran the last fifty yards to the front door, where she fumbled through her purse for the key, then nudged the door open with her foot.

He carried her inside. "Steffi, what a perfect, quiet place. Absolutely no one to disturb us." He held her reaching hands. She had put his seal ring with her engagement diamond on her left ring finger. The seal ring was turned around. It was her wedding band.

A full-length oval tilt mirror stood in one corner of her bedroom. Alex carried it toward the large brass bed. They stood in front of it as he took off her linen jacket and slowly slipped her white button-down-collared shirt over her head. He had given it to her, as well as a pair of pajamas, before he left college. She thought he was maddeningly clumsy as he started to unhook her brassiere. After a pause they looked into the mirror as he cupped her breasts, tenderly kissing each one.

Her hands were trembling as she opened his shirt, pulled off his dog tags, and softly touched the blond hair of his chest.

"I've dreamed of this so long, Alex. It's unbelievable, because you are patient with me...I like that." She kicked off her shoes and dropped her skirt. Alex's brass belt buckle baffled her. After guiding her hands, she was able to remove his belt and unzip his pants. As they fell, coins and keys scattered over the wooden floor. He noticed a quarter rolling under an armoire at the opposite end of the room. Both smiled.

"Let me see you again." He was on his knees. "I want to kiss you here, there, here, everywhere."

Steffi quivered, then reached for his head. "Please stand up. I can't stand this anymore. We're torturing each other."

He held her in the coolness of the sheets, and as they embraced he sensuously lifted her over his body. "Steffi, slowly at first, angel, make it last for both of us."

She arched her back, her hips moving back and forth slowly, then faster and faster. Her strong thighs rhythmically squeezed him, and she began to moan. "Now, Alex, please now," she screamed with each thrust. "I love you; I love you; there are two of us, but right now only one."

He clenched and pulled at the bars of the headboard as they both felt ecstasy at the same time. She collapsed and fell forward, pushing her hips into him several more times, then wrapped her arms around his chest and sank her fingernails in his back. "Hold me tight; never let me go."

She lay on her side pressing against him. They relaxed, then slept. The room's shadows had shifted as he looked at beams in the ceiling and an antique rocker that faced two full-length glass doors opening in the center. Victorian curtains, which changed the rustic character of the house, rustled in the autumn breeze. There was a smell of cut alfalfa, corn, and wheat. He was startled by the sounds of scampering squirrels and nuts falling on the roof. The house itself creaked from time to time. Steffi breathed softly and her body would occasionally jerk from fatigue. His thoughts were drifting. He was overjoyed with her exceptional beauty and the keenness of her intellect. *Please,*

Lord, make me strong. I have to leave; how many months or perhaps years will it be? Do I have the inner courage to be away for who knows how long?

He was unable to struggle with the concept of time, because at this moment he held in his arms everything loving and beautiful he could imagine. He prayed that he might be spared to come home to her. *Don't be selfish,* he thought. *You should pray for the lives of the men you will command.* There were footsteps on the gravel walk.

"Wake up, Steffi; we have a visitor."

"For heaven's sake, who is it? Oh, yes, it must be Werner, our caretaker."

Stephanie lazily slipped on her skirt and pulled his shirt over her head, while Alex rummaged through a closet for a pair of Erich Pfeiffer's pants and an old sweater. They stood in their bare feet.

"Onkel Werner, wie nett Dich nach so langer Zeit wieder zu sehen.... Please do come in; I would like you to meet my fiancé, Alex Dunham."

"Steffale, Du warst gerade erst ein kleines Mädel... and now you have grown into a beautiful young woman. It is a pleasure to see you again and meet Mr. Dunham. Your parents announced you. I have brought some food and supplies for the next few days."

"Vielen Dank, Onkel Werner; we'll see you again before Monday."

Alex and Steffi washed and stacked the dishes.

"Steffi, you are une cuisinière extraordinaire; where did you acquire such expertise? With these delicious meals, I'll have to wear two harnesses, because a paratrooper can't weigh over a hundred eight-five pounds. Regulations go out the window this week. Madam, it's impossible to resist you or your cooking."

"Lottie has been a patient teacher, and I reach new heights of perfection when it's for you." She put down a wet plate and drew him toward her, looking at him sensuously. "Heights of perfection in cooking and other delicious things we do."

He watched. He knew he must remember every feature, smile, her unique voice. It had a boyish deep tonality. Not nasal, with emphasis on phrases, the last dropping in volume. It was youthful, vibrant, with a cheerful buoyancy and enthusiasm. He always knew she spoke German because of unusual word choice. The engaging accent, the time before place construction: "Alex, first we are going of course to the concert."

They walked with their arms around each other's waists. He could feel her rounded hips with each step. Her fingers were wrapped in the back of his webbed belt. The muscles of her arm ached, holding him closer with each step. At first the full moon was a soft, rich orange, becoming starkly brighter as it rose through the autumn mist and haze. For Alex, the evening blended the past into the present, the hayrides, their favorite walks along the lakefront at home, and the moonlit trails at Running Springs. They stopped at intervals, gazing across open wheat fields, enamored by the night's quiet, interrupted only by the flapping sound of an unseen bird.

They fell asleep before the fire, wrapped in a blanket smelling of mothballs. "We seem to fit each other perfectly," she whispered. "You feel wonderful exactly this way."

Later, he carried her to bed. It was almost light when they made love in a different way. Afterward, she rested on an elbow, studying his face. It was fuller and tanned, his fine blond hair cut shorter. She looked into his green eyes, which seemed to have more specks of brown, with the same or perhaps more intensity and awareness.

"It must be different for me, Alex, because after we make love, the fulfillment lasts. I can't let go of you. It's a deep feeling that has grown stronger, drawing me closer to you. Wherever you are, you're really with me."

They rode Erich Pfeiffer's grays, which Werner groomed and exercised. The day had an autumnal brightness with changing leaves, some falling, and the pervasive smell of plowed fields and the musty odor of burning leaves.

Alex watched her. "Steffi, you ride as you do everything else: perfectly. Look at those elbows tucked in, heels down, hands squarely over the pommel."

After a long canter through woods and harvested fields, they reached an abandoned barn, where he tethered the horses and loosened their cinch straps. She began to unwrap their small picnic.

He trifled, "Do you actually prefer chewing on that long piece of straw rather than having one of your appetizing turkey sandwiches?"

"Funny habit I have; must make me think clearly."

He touched her hair, brushing back ungainly strands, damp from an early shower.

"I suppose I should worry more about us, yet I always have had strong faith you will come home to me and we'll be married and have those blond, blue-eyed children we've talked about for a long time. I'll adore them; suppose it's having that imp Tina run after me for many years."

Occasionally he stood and looked at the horses, which were cooling down, munching alfalfa. "The last year hasn't been that bad, Steffi. Unfortunately, my father made my choice seem fatalistic. I've made some good, solid friends, and Colonel Conroy is a gem. You know he's fair, tough, gives me responsibility, backs me up. The best West Point turns out."

"Have you given any thought to what—?"

He smiled and touched her lips with a finger. "After the war, when we've settled down, the State Department is my goal. I'll be able to save money over the next several years. Law school should have first priority to give me a background in international affairs. How's that sound for starters?"

"Anything you want, but make certain you come home to me. Daddy has told me all about you, 'Jocko'." Steffi had become familiar with Airborne lingo. "And you are 'up and coming.' I know you and your parachute friends take chances bordering on insanity."

"Insanity, Miss Pfeiffer?" He pulled the straw from her mouth and held her head between his hands, winked, and kissed her. "I thought most sane people parachuted in and out of four-poster beds. Which reminds me, I have definite plans for you this afternoon. Are you willing after last night?"

He pulled her up and put his hand on her buttocks, pushing

her hips into his. "Nothing but sunshine, no wind, clear weather ahead for us at the drop zone. I love you, Steffi, Don't worry; impossible to get rid of me."

She adjusted her jodhpur in the stirrup; then he boosted her into the saddle. The horse's soft, wet muzzle snatched sugar cubes from his palm.

They could hear the blare of a jukebox, riotous laughter, and conversation when they entered Cavanaugh's bar and grille. Saturday night was the week's apogee in Galena. They settled in a corner booth next to each other. A sign read: "Smile, it's the second best thing you can do with your lips."

A talkative waitress stopped at the table. "OK, folks, let's make it quick. We got a whole gang of eager beavers here tonight. Hamburgers is the specialty of the house. How about fries and onions? Beer for the two lovebirds? Boy, you two look like you're 'ga-ga' over each other. You better have the works, right, Captain? By the way, what's your outfit?"

Alex pushed his thigh against Steffi. "Paratrooper."

Stella Koslowski's banter became one of disbelief. "Jesus, you mean you jump out of them airplanes and are sittin' there to tell me about it?"

Steffi cringed. He squeezed her hand.

"I'm not only here, but hungry and waiting for chow. On the ball, Sarge, we're starved."

"The works with suds, comin' up, sir. You know, it's same-day service here." The waitress left.

The crowd thinned out and Alex and Steffi were still dancing slowly, moving imperceptively. His supply of nickels had dwindled when a raucous voice interrupted, "Hey, ain't we heard Sinatra sing 'The Nearness of You' enough for tonight? Enough's enough. How 'bout something lively? Come on; let's jitter."

Alex led her to their table. At times her eyes were happy, then melancholy. "Alex, it's time for bed. We can walk home in the moonlight, and when you kiss me, as the lady said, we both can have another taste of the onions and suds. Please, let's leave now."

He stopped at a clearing in the trees along the road and pointed toward the moon. "Before this is over, you'll be a military wizard. While I'm away, look at the moon, because as it becomes fuller, it's called a bomber's moon and our missions will be scheduled at that time. The moon will make me think of you."

She laughed half-heartedly. "Alex, tonight I'll leave the curtains open and we can figure out whether that cow really jumped over the moon. Lottie always said it was so."

Later, they watched it slide beyond the trees. Shafts of moonlight were still reaching across the lane and fences in front of the farm. Sleep was impossible. They reminisced, discovering what each had done when they were apart and the joy of being together. The last several days had been wondrous, intoxicating.

They lay motionless. Everything had been said. Suddenly she shook his head and snatched his dog tags, draping them around her neck, then put on his shirt and grasped his shoulders.

"You don't think I know, do you?" She pushed the dog tags in his mouth. "This is what they'll do when you're killed. I know; I know. I'm not stupid."

He tried to calm her.

"Don't leave me. There's no one left; I'm terrified, Alex. God help us both."

He held her arms firmly behind her back. "Please, listen to me. Steffi, settle down, right now, do you hear me? Right now." He picked her up and carried her to the bathroom. "Sit here on my lap and steady yourself."

He wiped dripping perspiration from her face and hair as she sucked cold water from a towel. He rhythmically rocked her back and forth, stroking her hair, and softly hummed a tune that Nanna sang years ago: "Pony boy, pony boy, won't you be my pony boy? Carry me, marry me, never leave . . ."

When she became calmer, he led her back to bed. He had never seen such intensity in her face and deep blue eyes, darker in the dimness of the night. He caressed her neck, cheeks, and forehead and touched her closed eyelids.

"Remember the little kisses—we called them *Vöglein küssen,* you know, Steffi, the birdie kisses after dances? They were the ones we gave each other at your door before Pfeiffer midnight curfew. Everything, and listen to me carefully, everything will work out for us, and when all of this is over, we'll have our little Steffies and Alexes."

"Alex, please forgive me. Only a moment of fear and weakness; you know I'm strong and believe in you." She opened his tan shirt. "This is my shirt to keep, and wherever you go, I'm always in it with you." She lowered her head, her hair touching his face, as she kissed him, murmuring, "It's time, right now, Alex. I need you, want you; now give me our baby. I must, absolutely must, have a part of you with me. Do it now; please do it now."

He seized her passionately and, after he moved into her deeply, soon both felt a sudden, ecstatic release. Her smile was perfection, he thought angelic.

"Alex, now nothing can frighten me anymore or take you away from me."

She slept quietly with her head against his shoulder, still holding his hand, her legs curled around his body. For several minutes he stroked her hair and face, then pulled up a coverlet as a gentle night breeze cooled them. He buried his face in the pillow next to her head and, when he looked into the blackness, streaked with yellow flashes, asked himself, had he made the correct choice? Did he really believe in gratitude, repaying a nebulous debt, serving and being a leader? Was it all worth losing her? He felt her closeness and warmth calming his fear that this could be their last night together.

There were hundreds of white-steepled churches like the one near Galena and that autumn morning many congregations were singing "Onward Christian Soldiers." A prolonged sermon, more hymns, the offertory, and after the benediction worshipers slowly filed out. Steffi held his arm. "Let's stay a while longer, Alex, I want you to have my prayer book. I hope it will guide you when I can't be at your side. I have read it since I was a small girl. It might help you reach out for God's comfort, not only when life is good, but during the worst of times."

He opened the cracked leather book held together by a rubber band. They read the first prayer together. "God, heavenly Father, stand by me with your blessing and help me to complete my duties as I promised to do. Give me strength in all temptations and protect me in danger. Into your hands I give my body and my soul, my life and my death. Amen."

They sat in silence holding hands. No one would take it from him. He would try to memorize some of the prayers, and it would be in his left breast pocket, except in combat. He knew wars hadn't changed. A dead soldier's valuables were always picked by the enemy. Alex would only surrender his standard-issue wristwatch and boots to looters.

"Thank you, Stephanie. This will bring us together every day, not only while I'm away, but the rest of our lives."

They walked to the bus station and sat together in the same seat, the same bus, with the same driver, during their return to the city.

"Steffi, look; there's one of our favorite signs. It's a Burma Shave jingle." He pointed out the window.

"At Ease," she said.
"Maneuvers Begin
When You Get
Those Whiskers
Off Your Chin."
Use Burma Shave.

"That reminds me; you were going to buy your defender of democracy a gross of those shaving tubes. Well, Steffi?"

"Now, Captain, how could you possibly think I would forget such an important item in a man's daily ablutions? By the way, Alex, how many whatevers are in a gross?"

Alex stood in front of the observation car door, looking at his parents and the Pfeiffers. He could reach and touch Steffi's hand and feel her rings. Never say good-bye. A bientôt. Ich sehe Dich bald.

"You have the APO number, plenty of stationery, pens, and bottles of ink. Please don't forget, Steffi, keep the letters coming. Sometimes you may not hear from me for a while. Don't worry; you know it's only routine army mail. Remember the censors work overtime. You'll have to read between the lines to understand where we are and what we're doing."

She forced a wistful smile. "There'll be one for you every day, sweetheart. Everything I do and think, as though we were together."

He tapped his left breast pocket. "Always there with you, Steffi dear."

Brian, Lucky, and Katzie waved and Erich Pfeiffer saluted as the train gave a lurch. Steffi held out her hand and waved. She ran down the platform as it gained speed. He held onto the brass rail, listening to the monotonous, increasingly rapid sound as the wheels rolled over the tracks.

Alex watched the skyline gradually diminish. Now distance would hold his beloved girl, parents, friends, and memories. He must force himself to feel cold, assume the efficient malevolence of military duty and command. Now he must put on, then wear, his war face. A face he had chosen. He closed the door to the coach and sat erect in his seat, looking at the razorlike crease in his bloused trousers and highly polished boots.

The ceiling fan rotated at full speed, yet its rapid whir failed to relieve the stifling humidity and midday heat in the small dockside office of Colonel John Conroy, who sat in a sweat-drenched uniform before his three battalion commanders.

"Well, gentlemen, how do you like clean, sunny, friendly Casablanca? It's got to be the asshole of North Africa. At least the men are out of those stinking ships and our convoy made it without a scratch."

One of the other officers, Major John Hunt, smiled. "It's not a garden spot, Colonel. The men are billeted in tents and stone huts, and the two-mile march with full packs was a snap compared to training—"

Alex interrupted. "Colonel, without passes to the city, we

must have some entertainment for the men. I'll find a USO troop, movies every night. Usual morning inspections, evening marches, but the ghibli will keep us hunkered down. These sandstorms are almost a daily or nightly ritual. I've issued strict orders for the men to keep their rifles and other weapons cleaned, free of sand. It's everywhere, gets into the food and water."

"Dunham, leave those details to Captain Harris; it's your job to arrange transportation for the regiment into eastern Algeria within four or five days. Get hopping with those French railway officials, and don't take any shit. We move out on time, understand?"

"Sir," Alex replied, "we're set to go in rail cars from the first war, you know, the forty and eights. Not the Twentieth Century Limited. It's an eight-day haul northeast to Oujda. Some of the heavy equipment has to be trucked. Most of it will be shipped by train. The French have been cooperative, sometimes friendly. I'm certain we can trust them."

Several days before departure, Alex got his first mail from home. He sensed Steffi was trying to be happy and unconcerned. She had enclosed a small picture of her sitting with him in front of their favorite dolphin fountain near the lake. No flies, no grit or dust, no blinding desert heat, only the cool lake breeze as they sat together, carefree and happy, looking out over the whitecaps. He tucked the picture and letter in his prayer book.

Then:

From the desk of Dr. Brian Dunham:

Dear Alex,

None of us knows where you are. We hope you are safe and sound. As you remember, Lucky and I visited_____several years ago and our bet is you're there for_____Beautiful spot. You should learn about the history of the place. The weather has been hot and muggy, but I've been playing golf every Wednesday afternoon and over the weekends. We had dinner at_____with the Pfeiffers and Steffi the other night and she looked lovely. Aren't you glad we went ice-skating that day many years ago? Lucky has put together a CARE package that should reach you one of these days. Things at the____and medical school are fine, and I wish you were learning to take care of soldiers rather than being one.

Yours,
D3

After reaching Oujda, training intensified with night exercises, forced marches, practicing camouflage techniques, jumps, reviews, and parades for Allied commanders. The final move was to Tunisia, the departure point for what Alex and his men knew would be their first combat.

Six
Strike and Hold

There was a momentary pause, then the sudden jolt against his shoulders. He knew the main chute had opened. A cool blast of air cut into his face, and he heard its high pitch swirling around his helmet. Floating downward while the wind buffeted him laterally, he looked up where the full moon seemed to be within arm's reach. Its brightness was friendly and illuminated the rapidly approaching earth. Immediately to his left, he saw four falling paratroopers, the first with a fully opened billowing chute and the remaining three unfolding in rapid sequence.

Alex hit rocky ground, disengaged his harness, and quickly pulled out his Tommy gun. His battalion had jumped in a thirty-mile-an-hour wind. He was the last to parachute from his twenty-four-man stick, landing in front of them, prepared to lead. He fired a flare that looped in a brilliant arc, and within minutes fifteen men had assembled in an olive grove. The force

174

of the wind had lessened. The air was thin and dry. He read his maps and compass by clear moonlight.

"Where the hell are we, Major Dunham? Are we in Sicily or will I be visiting my relatives in Naples? I betcha the outfit has been blown all over, wherever we are." Sergeant Al Cunicello and his father had a delicatessen on the Lower East Side of Manhattan.

Alex had followed the meandering western coastline of Sicily with the pilots, but sharp gusts scattered his paratroopers several miles from their designated drop zone. He called for a quick muster.

"Nine men unaccounted for, sir," Cunicello answered.

Then they heard a distant shout.

"Let's go, Airborne. Cut my fucking chute out of this olive tree."

Two men ran to the far end of the grove and pulled Lieutenant Pete Drake from the harness of his entangled parachute. To their rear, they heard an agonizing call for a medic. One of the men was dragged over a jagged rock wall after he landed.

"Corporal, it's my leg, right here. God, help me. Make me strong . . . the pain."

Kopczek took out his knife, cut the jump pants, and saw two ends of bone protruding through the skin. "All right, Graham, take it easy. Here's a shot of morphine. We'll get help before daylight."

One by one and in small groups, more troopers joined Major Alex Dunham's small force during the first hour. Now, over 150 men, whose objective was to capture the German-Italian airfield at Piano Lupo, were advancing rapidly.

Alex gave a series of terse orders. "All right, Carlson, Drake, each of you take some men. We advance north and west on either side of this road. Be alert for an ambush. There must be Krauts or Italians around here someplace. Move toward gunfire; that's where we'll find the enemy. Cut telephone wires; we know they go to German command posts. Grenade bunkers; blow up bridges, railroad tracks; lay mines, and guard the roads. Destroy everything in sight, create havoc, and raise holy hell. There aren't supposed to be any Kraut tanks according to intelligence, but I don't believe it. Now follow me; get a move on."

The quickly organized combat team was divided into three sections, each roughly five hundred yards apart. Because of the wind, they had no idea if the rest of the battalion had dropped on its landing zone. Alex saw rolling, inhospitable terrain divided by low walls that surrounded farms. The arid landscape was punctuated by olive groves. Another forty-five minutes had passed when a lead scout collared a nonchalant Sicilian, strolling along the road in their line of advance, seemingly oblivious to the danger.

Alex looked for Cunicello. "Get over here and interrogate this man. Find out where Piano Lupo is. Make it pronto."

Cunicello grabbed his coat. "Puotete darni la direzione per l'aeroporto di Piano Lupo? Where's the airport at Piano Lupo?"

"Non so di che cusa state parlando." He didn't know.

Now Cunicello was shouting. "Dobbiamo avere questa direzione immediatament, voi dovete sapere dove e perche abitate qui." He thought the Sicilian should know because he lived nearby.

The peasant arrogantly threw back his head and told the sergeant to go fly a kite: "Andate a perdervi."

Cunicello warned again, "Encora una volta altrimente vi uccidiamo."

"Baciami il mio culo, Americano." He told Cunicello to kiss his ass.

"Major, this fucking little asshole says he don't know anything."

Alex reached down and pulled out his trench knife from its leg strap. "Sergeant, ask him once more how we get to the airfield at Piano Lupo. Tell him if we don't have an answer in ten seconds, I'll cut off his prick piece by piece."

There was no answer.

"Two of you hold him." Alex slit open the Sicilian's shirt and cut his belt, and his pants fell to the ground. As Alex ran the tip of his trench knife down both thighs, drawing blood, the man's screams were muffled by Cunicello's hand. There was no answer.

"Sergeant, put his cock on your rifle butt and tell this little bastard I'll start chopping it like a piece of sausage." Alex saw urine and feces run down his legs.

"Prendi questa strada per sei miglie, segui la strada a sinistra per un altre tre miglie."

Cunicello crossed himself. "Major Dunham, sir, sir, hold on a second. Sir, he says take this road about six miles until it splits. Follow the road to the left for another three miles. That's home plate, but he's seen German tanks at the fork in the road. There are a group of Italian pillboxes guarding the 'Y' and airfield." The Sicilian was covered with dirt and fecal matter, a terrified animal, when Alex took him by the hair and booted him in a ditch.

In the widespread confusion of the drop, fifty more paratroopers pulling a 75mm gun, by chance found their way to Dunham's column. They had broken down another artillery piece into several loads carried by mules. The Germans and Italians had become aware of the Airborne landings, and Alex could hear and see continuous flashes of fire within several thousand yards. He thought the enemy was being attacked by another group of Americans. Several minutes later, Lieutenant Tom Hamilton and Alex heard the unmistakable metallic grinding of tank treads whose steady sound meant they were on a road. A heavy weapons squad with bazookas was sent forward, and after their attack they watched with horror as shots were deflected by thick frontal armor. The troopers were cut down by German infantry who had not been detected, then were crushed by tank treads.

Alex turned to Hamilton. "Set up an ambush. Get your men in that irrigation ditch, and we'll dig in at the olive grove."

Hamilton and his small detachment eliminated enemy infantry protecting the unscathed Tiger tank; then its menacing turret and gun swung in a sweeping arc, firing into the olive grove. The high-velocity shell tore a gaping hole in the small rise above the road and shredded a group of trees.

Alex saw about a dozen of his men killed or badly wounded. Several troopers jumped on the rear of the tank, dropped grenades in the two large exhaust mufflers, then scrambled for cover. They heard the deafening explosion as the Tiger tank spewed streaks of ignited fuel and burst into a large fireball. Casualties crawled or were dragged back.

He reached for his walkie-talkie. "Battalion, this is Major Dunham. Christ, we've been hit pretty hard. Get the medics up here with stretchers on the double. How far to the road junction, Sergeant Brennan?"

"About another three or four miles, Major. My guess is we'll run into some heavy resistance. We'll have to hit them hard before daylight."

As the moon gradually faded into approaching dawn, Alex looked through his field glasses. "Brennan, get word to Drake and Carlson; we're moving across this godforsaken desert to the 'Y' down the road. It must be cleared of enemy infantry." As he gave the order, they came under a heavy mortar attack, wounding Brennan and killing several other men near him.

"Goddammit, Carlson," Alex shouted. "Get your butt over here. We'll nail those bastards with the mortars. They're on our right flank just over the top of the rise."

Carlson and Alex led part of a platoon, first crawling up the short incline to the ridge, then charging and firing into Italian infantry who defended shallow trenches. The paratroopers shouted and roared in a frenzy as they attacked the mortar positions protected by several machine guns. Alex fired, dropped to the ground, and ran forward among and over the shattered bodies of his men and the enemy. The attack was over in minutes.

Rapidly moving trucks with German reinforcements arrived, but their attempt to renew the battle failed. Before they could engage the paratroopers, several bazooka rounds created flaming traps from which few escaped. Burning men were shot.

Alex stood at the edge of the road holding his Tommy gun as prisoners were disarmed and led past destroyed equipment, abandoned weapons, and the dead. A tall, aristocratic-looking German officer saluted as he walked into captivity. Alex acknowledged him with a nod and saw the black, silver-scripted "Gross Deutschland" insignia on his *Manschettenband* as he lowered his arm. After Alex looked at the cuff, he realized his battalion had engaged one of the Wehrmacht's outstanding armored divisions.

The scorching sun was up. Alex paused near an abandoned railroad crossing and took a swallow from his canteen. Although warmed by the intense heat, its wetness was welcome. He watched the main column of his combat group move on, and as they passed, a man in fatigues and helmet stepped forward. A weary Alex thought he looked familiar.

"What in the devil are you doing out here?" Alex managed a smile. "Isn't this one damn excuse for a Mediterranean cruise? You've got to be Ralph Bagshaw, the war correspondent for the *Daily News*, right?"

"Yes, I am, and thoroughly enjoying a peaceful voyage on Mare Nostrum, and you're let's see, Major Alex Dunham. I've come up by jeep from the main invasion headquarters back in Gela." He focused his Leica and took a picture of Alex leaning against a low wall separating the road from a railroad station. It was a portrait of an unshaven, dust-covered officer during the turbulence of battle.

Bagshaw looked at the shelled train station. "What's up, Major?"

Alex quickly explained the situation. "My battalion was blown off course by strong winds last night preventing precise drops on our landing zones. Their advance was going well, but German panzers were unexpected. Intelligence was slack. Our objective is about four to five miles northwest along this road that parallels the coast. We're protecting the left flank of the main invasion force near Gela. I can't say much more now, except the men are fighting well and morale is high."

They stopped speaking. There was a low-pitched thumping sound, then a whine. Alex jumped on Bagshaw, slamming him into the ground, as mortar and small-arms fire struck, tearing holes in the wall and showering fragments of rock and dirt where they had been standing.

Later Alex lay prone on a small knoll. "Sergeant, find Captain Harris and Lieutenant Carlson. I want them to scout the terrain toward the 'Y.' It's a little after 1200 hours and we need cover until sunset. The men have been fighting for more than twelve hours."

As the three officers scanned the flat, parched countryside, they saw a series of intertwining irrigation ditches near the "Y" in the road.

"Carlson," Alex called to one of his platoon leaders, "let's get on the ball. Set up an aid station in this olive grove and get the medics looking after our casualties before they're evacuated. Disperse the men; deploy them in ditches; have water, K rations, ammunition brought up from regiment. We go for the fork in the road, then the airfield. Get the seventy-fives camouflaged. Organize the perimeter patrols, no unnecessary firing."

In early afternoon, Alex, his battalion Sergeant, his communication tech, and Harris lay in an irrigation ditch. There were shimmering waves of heat and a choking pall of dust over the battlefield as Dunham spoke. "One of us stays awake until dusk. That means you, Fitts. Your walkie-talkie keeps us in touch with regiment and the destroyers offshore."

The three drowsed from heat and fatigue, occasionally awakened by static from the backpack of the communication equipment. Suddenly it was silenced by a nearby thundering explosion that threw them against the sides of the ditch.

Dunham crawled to the edge of the trench and could see a *Schwere Abteilung* of six Tiger tanks approaching the "Y." They were outlined in frightening silhouettes against the lengthening afternoon shadows. He could not allow them to block the road to the airfield.

Alex wiped the dust from his eyes. "Everyone accounted for? Fitts, is the walkie-talkie working?" Another groaning 88mm shell ripped through the trees of a nearby grove.

"My God, that was a close one," Harris yelled. "Hope they haven't pinpointed our position."

"Let's not wait to find out." Alex pulled Harris to his feet. "Jake, hotfoot it over to that seventy-five and have them aim for the belly of the tank as it climbs the ridge."

They watched anxiously as the crew fired twice, destroying the tank treads. It burned as the magazine exploded. The paratroopers had mined the eastern side of the road making up the

"Y," where another tank was disabled.

"Fitts," Alex shouted above the din, "get on the navy's frequency and have the offshore destroyers fire on these coordinates."

When the remaining panzers turned and tried to retreat, the "Y" became an inferno of bursting metal and gray-black clouds of dense smoke. Now it was almost a training march, but Alex suspected the airfield would be heavily defended. Looking over his maps, he planned a careful assault to surprise the enemy and minimize his casualties. He knew this was the ultimate game of his life.

Dunham's group moved through the destruction and mayhem at the "Y." Part of another battalion secured the small, critical intersection and protected the right flank of Alex's unit as it veered north and west. At first he thought the airfield at Piano Lupo was probably like a gasoline station on Route 30 in the middle of Wyoming, but now he made out five or six hangars and cross-shaped runways that had not been destroyed. Alex was able to count a dozen closely parked Italian aircraft with bright yellow-and-red-striped wings and recognized them as advanced fighters. He thought they could be destroyed with several bazooka rounds.

Alex spread out his map. "Hamilton, you and Carlson lead our flanks while we draw their fire on the road. The old end run play. We must—repeat, must—have Piano Lupo by midnight. That should give us almost three hours."

The paratroopers struck the airfield perimeter shortly after nine in full moonlight. Although his men were outnumbered by a battalion of Italians reinforced by Panzer Grenadiers, they charged the well-placed machine guns and a system of trenches and towers guarding the airstrip. After less than an hour of close combat, the defensive force was overwhelmed by a surprise attack from the rear.

Captain Jake Harris listened to a confident Alex. "Have the bazookas take out those fighters. The Wops had to be expecting us. God damn if they aren't surrendering in droves. The Krauts couldn't make those little bastards lift a fucking finger; they didn't even blow up the airstrip."

Harris was contemptuous. "They barely put up a fight, sir. Let's get these prisoners back to Gela, where the army can feed them spaghetti and some *vino*."

Alex slapped Jake on the back. "Round up Drake, Hamilton, and Carlson. Fitts, contact Regiment and send the word: 'Piano Lupo secured. Expect German panzers at daybreak. Losses acceptable. Further orders. Dunham'."

They saw burning aircraft and an abandoned Tiger tank that had run out of fuel. The troopers had spiked its lethal 88mm gun with grenades. The airfield was littered with the remains of trucks, mortars, and piles of small arms that had never been fired.

As they walked toward the first hangar, each man cautiously advanced between stacks of crates until they were startled by a sudden movement and scratching sounds. Cunicello had disappeared behind a row of large boxes.

"What the hell are you up to, Sergeant?" Jake Harris yelled.

There was a troublesome pause. A grinning Cunicello appeared holding his helmet, filled with kittens peering over the edge as their mother clawed at his boots. Troopers crowded around, petting their fluffy striped coats.

The brief interlude of repressed laughter was interrupted by a "let's get going" motion from Alex. "Sergeant, we'll come back one of these days. Send them to the deli at home, where they can feast on fresh calamari. Now, I want the men to dig in, foxholes to the north, east, and west. The Krauts have armor, but we can call in air strikes. If only we had something more effective than bazookas. I never thought they were worth a damn anyway."

Lieutenants Pete Drake and Danny Naughton found them in the second hangar, stacks of wooden crates marked in German: *Panzerfaust*.

"Major, *Panzerfaust*?" Drake was puzzled.

Alex's voice reverberated in the hangar. "Men, damned if we haven't hit a gold mine."

Three Sergeants, Captain Harris, and Lieutenant Jackson rested on the wing of a *Macchi-Castoldi 200* whose landing gear, tail, and a section of fuselage had been punctured by shell fire. They jumped down and walked toward Alex to inspect the wooden boxes.

Alex pulled a lid that had been forced open and removed a large paper folded between two of the four crated weapons. With a flashlight in one hand, he translated in a crisp voice: " '*Anweisung zum Gebrauch der Panzerfaust 30. Mit Befehl des Wehrmachtsamtes, Wa. Prw 7.*' All right, listen up, men; here are the instructions for use of the *Panzerfausts*. This is a recoilless, one-shot, throwaway, hand-held antitank weapon like our bazooka. It's quite simple in design, with a three-foot exhaust barrel, a warhead with a hollow charge of TNT, and a mixture of Hexogene—that's a jelly which holds the TNT in shape. You flip up the simple sighting arm and push down on the trigger right here."

He continued to read the instructions, occasionally looking at his men. "The projectile travels twenty-seven yards a second and will pierce five-inch armor at thirty to forty yards. Don't stand within ten yards of the end of the barrel because of the heat and exhaust when it's fired. Hold it at the shoulder or under the armpit, whether you're on your belly or standing behind protection. Don't forget, the enemy tank is approaching at about a hundred fifty yards a minute. We have the advantage now, because this weapon can penetrate the frontal armor of their Tiger tanks. Fire directly at the heavy armor, then the hull or turret. Any questions?"

Cunicello was mischievous. "Major, sir, you mean to tell me we have to fight the fucking Krauts with these shitty little toilet plungers? I sure as hell hope they work."

The hangar was momentarily filled with laughter. "At ease, Connie." Alex was thinking about the coming tank assault. "We learned about the *Panzerfausts* in Tunisia and are lucky bastards to give them some of their own crap. All right then, the six of us will carry two weapons for the tank attack in several hours. Fire from a ditch or foxhole and have two men with you to hold off the Kraut grenadiers who will be riding or walking near the tanks. Dismissed."

Alex motioned for Cunicello. "Set up a detail to guard the hangar. We move out for the minefields at 0600 hours."

"Fitts, get off this message to Colonel Conroy and Division: 'Have captured supply of *Panzerfausts*. Send in a DC-3 by dawn to Piano Lupo. Remove captured equipment to division headquarters. Verify and confirm. Dunham'."

"Major, is that all, sir?"

Alex rested against a crate as Fitts transmitted Dunham's orders on the walkie-talkie. "That's it, Fitts." Then Alex spoke to Lieutenant Drake. "It's some kind of miracle the crates didn't burn or explode during the firefight. What were the Italians thinking? They must want us to win this goddamned war. We can't let the panzers or their infantry overrun us tomorrow. This equipment must be flown back to Gela, and now."

By three that morning, Alex and Jake Harris had reconnoitered the airfield perimeter, finding the men dug in, no easy task in the baked, dry earth.

Harris pointed to the eastern end of the airfield. "Sir, we need some mines out there at least one to two hundred yards to protect the holes and slit trenches."

Alex assembled and loaded ten *Panzerfausts*, then lay against an empty crate. He looked up at the sky, the quiet of the night broken only by distant gunfire and sharp taps of shovels as the troopers laid a thin minefield around the airfield.

He remembered how he had waited and trained for this day. *Piano Lupo is ours, and I'll stay here, hang on, if it means . . . you know what I mean, God. It hasn't been a bad day for the men. With the German* Wunder Waffen, *we can beat them with their own weapons. My mind is drifting now. Concentrate; concentrate, I can't. Must stay awake. Where's my girl tonight? Thousands of miles. Looking at the same moon? Ever see her again?* His head dropped. He fell into a dark sleep.

Two DC-3s cut their engines in the early, clear dawn. Alex ate some K rations, tilted his canteen, then greeted the pilots.

"You must be some of those fly boys who tried to drop us in the Balkans, Italy, or the drink, right? Welcome to Camp Piano Lupo."

One of the pilots looked at a deep crater in the runway. "Morning, sir, looks like your boys have raised a little hell around here. There's a line of Italian prisoners strung out on the road from here to Gela."

Alex chuckled. "Wars are won on the ground, gentlemen; now let's get these *Panzerfausts* back to Division. It'll be a nice surprise for General Harper. We knew they had them. As of now, they are the official property of parachute infantry, made in Germany. We'll eat the Krauts alive with their '*Spezial Waffen*'."

Carlson seemed puzzled, "What's all this talk about waffles, Major?"

"Forget the waffles, Hank; get the men busy loading these crates before the Tigers wake up."

Alex turned to the air force officers, casual, clean-shaven, wearing sunglasses and hats wrinkled by headsets. They probably had ham and eggs and real coffee for breakfast, perhaps some of Carlson's waffles. "I've translated the instructions for assembling and firing these antitank weapons. Deliver them to General Harper back at Division. Have this confirmed by radio communication. Oh, yes, gentlemen of the wild blue yonder, with these explosives aboard, don't let the navy shoot you down. We have plenty of pilots, but these weapons are rare Sicilian birds."

"Harris, have the men load up the crates in thirty minutes." Alex called for Cunicello, "Where the hell are you?"

Sergeant Cunicello hurriedly appeared pulling up his pants. "The usual morning crap that I hope is never permanent, Major. Never have gotten used to performing in public, sir. I know the Germans mine certain places because they know we like our privacy. Clever bastards, aren't they?"

"Enough of that shit, Cunicello. You've been lucky again. Get a squad; we're going out for target practice this morning. Haul ass, Sergeant."

Cunicello was insistent. "Now Major, Christ, sir, the battalion commander doesn't belong in a foxhole out there in front of those panzers."

Before sunrise, Captain Harris and Alex were on their bellies in the cool Sicilian earth waiting for the sixty-ton dinosaurs. They could destroy the hangars now that the weapons had been removed. Alex thought the *Luftwaffe* had flown in the *Panzer-fausts*, but the Grenadiers had no idea they had been delivered because the Germans were communicating with Italian commanders by telephone. The first night, his paratroopers had cut the wires and created confusion that had paralyzed the enemy. For Alex it was a vivid memory from training. Airborne infantry is ineffective against tanks.

He saw Jake Harris knock out the lead tank with a well-aimed shot from fifty yards and watched the column pause on the small ridge behind the airfield to the east. To his dismay, Cunicello ran toward the second tank as the brittle ground at his feet was grazed by machine-gun fire. Alex lifted his binoculars and saw Connie dive in a drainage ditch and fire. The turret was blown off and the explosion was felt several hundred yards away. German infantry was trapped in a minefield and was eliminated by machine-gun fire. The remaining tanks retreated toward the "Y." Alex could hear the men shouting, "Let's go, Airborne. They're on the run."

Alex crawled back toward the airfield. "Fitts, call in an air strike at the 'Y.' Tell them five Tigers are prowling on the army's left flank."

In the afternoon, Major Dunham made his way by jeep eastward to the "Y." He saw impressive bunkers that had been obliterated by naval gunfire and parachute artillery. Some of his paratroopers were strewn among the burning tanks, destroyed trucks, and artillery pieces. The sickening sweet smell of bloated bodies swollen by the summer heat hung in the dusty air. His men mangled, covered with crawling flies. Several skeletons of burned troopers still sat grotesquely behind a machine gun mounted on a jeep. Piano Lupo was captured, the left flank of the main invasion force secured, and a thousand *Panzerfausts* were an unexpected bonus of the battle. His division would use them during the remainder of the war.

He shouldered his Tommy gun while the jeep bumped along the narrow Sicilian road to Regimental Command Post. The whole operation was as close to a cake-walk as he could imagine, but he turned away, revulsed by the sight of his paratroopers crushed by tanks, some burned and decomposed beyond recognition. He surveyed the dreadful ravage, knowing victory was foremost, paramount.

The regiment was flown back to North Africa after ten days of grueling combat. The heat of the Tunisian desert was more searing than Sicily, and the unpredictable ghibli interfered with routine training and exercises. The blowing clouds of sand were blinding and suffocating, but each night a welcome coolness brought some relief to the weary parachute infantry.

Alex eagerly slit open the thin blue V-mail letter.

My dearest Alex,

How I miss you and pray for you each day and night. The papers have been full of news about landings in ——— and ———Several nights ago we had dinner with Lucky, Brian and ——— His ——— in the ——— were censored. It was incredible he saw you briefly. He told us the complete story of the ——— You know, that part of the Peloponnesian Wars, and there was a small picture of you in the ——— No name, and your shoulder patch had been blacked out. He said the whole ———went ——— without any ——— but there were ———due to high winds. I watched the moon each night as you told me. My thoughts and prayers are with you and your men. We are going west for several weeks and I'll write more tomorrow. I love you, Alex.

Steffi

He tucked it in his breast pocket with his prayer book. Then he read the blue typewritten one:

From the desk of Dr. Brian Dunham:

Dear Alex,

It must have been quite ——— Great fireworks according to ——— We have your letters, and Lucky and I are so relieved to know that you are ——— You will have some interesting stories and we hope all of this is over soon. We have sent you a CARE package with instant coffee, chocolate, and some other items you might need. It's been a hot summer and all of us miss you. The men at the hospital send their best regards. Sometime you'll have to tell me how the ———

Yours,
D3

Alex moved a pointer over a large map. "They haven't told us yet, but it has to be Italy and a drop behind the Germans, along the west coast." He reviewed logistics with Harris, Naughton, Drake, Hamilton, and Carlson, his battalion officers. They had been decorated for the Sicilian campaign and called themselves the first team.

Carlson had anticipated future operations. "Major, they had better stop the train on the drop zone this time. We were slowed down by that thirty-mile-an-hour wind back in Sicily. Seems like years ago chasing the Wops around the countryside. Thank God for those *Panzerfausts*. We'll sure as hell need them if we take off for Italy. The Krauts are giving the Second Army one hell of a time."

"I have a feeling we'll know in several days, Hank," Alex said. "I would imagine a flight to Naples and then a jump north. The full regiment engaged."

Harris was complaining again, "They give us the shitty end of the stick each time, don't they, Major?"

"Come on, Jake, it'll be another walk-on." Alex rolled the map. "Cheer up. You're Airborne; we always look for a good fight, remember? They didn't give you that Bronze Star for picking your nose in Sicily."

Two weeks later, Alex stood against the railing of a landing craft and could see the Alban Hills through his field glasses. Their off-white color dominated the skyline twenty miles inland from Anzio, a seaside resort dating back to Roman emperors. He kicked at a loose piece of rope hanging from the bulkhead. Orders for the 504 had been changed at the last minute. It would not be an Airborne drop, but a regimental beach assault.

The February morning was bright, and the disembarkment proceeded without incident. It was all too perfect. Suddenly there was the terrifying sound of sirens from German dive-bombers attacking out of the sun. He saw huge, boiling circles of water among the landing craft. Only one was hit, flinging equipment and men in the greenish, shallow water. After he reached shore, Alex watched the remaining craft quickly drop their ramps. Within several hours the regiment had moved out along the flat, barren countryside. The *Luftwaffe's Stukas* had been driven off by naval gunfire.

"Harris, you were right about the brown end of the stick." Alex was speaking to his staff. "Here we are, right out in front of regiment patrolling this canal, trying to protect the army's flank again. Airborne troops used as infantry, probably for several months. We've got to make the most of a crappy situation. This will be old-fashioned trench warfare, plenty of patrolling, close combat, and night operations. Have the men dig bunkers, deep trenches, and set up the barbed wire and minefields. This is no damn job for our outfit."

Alex and his battalion officers slogged through ankle-deep mud to a building which had been a modest seaside resort hotel, but now only portions of its walls were standing. Closely spaced logs covered with camouflage netting served as the roof of Colonel John Conroy's well-protected regimental command post. A small iron stove radiated sufficient heat to warm the dreary vault that had been a wine cellar. It had the musty odor of aged vats. A kerosene lamp hanging from a hook in the ceiling cast a dim light over maps and aerial photographs spread out over several oak barrels.

"We've been here four goddamned days," Conroy bristled. "No armor, no heavy artillery, and the Germans up in those hills are pounding the living hell out of us all day and most of the night. Even the hospital tents are fair game. We should have been on the move the first twenty-four hours, no digging in, no hesitation, and on the way to Rome. Christ, gentlemen, it's only twenty miles from here. No imaginative leadership, no leadership at all, and now they want us to go after the artillery positions in the foothills above the canal. I don't have to tell you that they're firing on anything moving in daylight. Dunham, it's a night operation for your battalion."

Alex shook his head. "A night operation to knock out eighty-eight-millimeter artillery. A tall order, sir."

"Gentlemen, you heard me loud and clear," Conroy explained precisely. "You go for those guns. They have our range, are hidden about a thousand feet up in the hills, and unless we destroy them, this beachhead is dead. Here are the aerial photos of their positions." He pointed to the photographs. "If you hadn't made Piano Lupo look easy last summer, you'd be sitting in those comfortable, muddy trenches patrolling the canal. All of you gentlemen should be sharper after Sicily and six months of training in Tunisia."

Lieutenant Hank Carlson and his fifty men moved slowly through semidarkness under a drenching rain. Their first objective was a gun emplacement almost five miles forward of battalion headquarters. Alex had given Carlson the plan of attack and watched the last of his troopers move single file through the wintry terrain. By midnight, Carlson's paratroopers had reached the barbed wire guarding the first of six guns.

Carlson signaled to Martinez and Preston to kill the sentries. He watched as the two moved silently behind the weary guards who dropped without a cry, their throats slit. The men cautiously crawled through underbrush, cutting the wire. They could hear conversation and occasional laughter of the enemy, who seemed unconcerned. Carlson and a squad advanced within twenty yards of the huge artillery piece and then charged, firing automatic weapons and tossing hand grenades at the sandbagged position. Screams of the dying pierced the night as four troopers jammed a satchel charge into the breech. The explosion rocked the ground, forcing paratroopers to seek cover behind boulders and trees.

Private Norris reported to Carlson, "Sir, we've lost about twenty-five men, but the heavy-weapons squad is in good shape."

Carlson's voice wavered. He had doubts about pressing the

attack. "Norris, repeat, how many men? For Christ's sake, have the medics stay with the wounded. We must move on and try to knock out the next eighty-eight. They'll sure as hell be ready for us. Norris, get the hell on the walkie-talkie and raise Major Dunham. Tell him we've taken out the first gun but need reinforcements, and now. It's urgent, do you hear me, urgent." The rain had changed to wet snow, and the penetrating cold was slowing the advance.

At first light, Carlson could see the second gun. His men were spread out, expecting a raid from an alerted enemy, and then suddenly were attacked by a platoon-sized force. The brutal combat was at close quarters, men being gouged and stabbed by trench knives and bayonets, armless, legless, and decapitated by automatic weapons. The snow was covered with bloodied bodies. Wounded were crying for help. During the brief, violent struggle, the company had lost over half of its strength.

Carlson and his Sergeant crouched behind a tree trunk, yelling and motioning their men to pull back to the first sandbagged gun emplacement, where they could find cover. "Give me those field glasses, Sergeant. Thank God, I can see a column moving toward us. We must hold on for now. Get the men spread out in the bunker for some chow and rest. Send out scouts to contact the reinforcements."

Alex and Lieutenant Tom Hamilton deployed two platoons around the first gun emplacement and then found Carlson scouting the high ground behind the second gun.

"What's the situation here, Lieutenant?" Alex questioned.

"Major Dunham, we almost got the second gun, then were pushed around by a platoon of Krauts. Sir, I decided to pull back until we got reinforcements. It's damned good to see you. We've lost over half of our team, but we're ready to go."

Alex took his field glasses. "Hank, send out a platoon to draw fire from their flanks, then infiltrate the high ground behind the eighty-eight and overrun them from the rear. You and Hamilton take one hundred men, and I'll lead what's left of your force for a frontal assault. Let's move. Good hunting."

Cloaked in falling snow, Alex and his team crawled

through a shallow trench. He called out, "Wilensky, get your goddammed ass over here and set up the mortar. We know the Krauts are dug in around the gun up on that rise waiting for our attack."

There was no answer. Wilensky and his mortar squad were crouched in a shell hole whose bottom was a thin layer of ice. "God almighty, Major Dunham, look what's left of my men, arms, legs; there's one Kraut still looking at me. Do you think he's dead, sir? We have to move over this pile of bodies to get set up. I don't think our men—"

"Corporal Wilensky." Alex jerked his field jacket. "Do it now. If the Airborne has taught you any fucking lesson, it's to attack, and you shall obey my order. Now, goddammit, start firing."

Wilensky turned to his mortar man. "Brownie, what in hell is the Major doing? Look at him, leading a squad toward machine-gun fire. All right, start lobbing those babies right on target about fifty yards ahead of him."

Alex ran forward over the wet ground, firing his weapon, dropping to throw grenades. "Stay with me, Stanton; we've almost reached the sandbags in front of the gun. The mortar squad did its job. Christ, look at those Germans scattered across the bunkers. What the hell was that? My God, Wilensky and the heavy-weapons squad stopped firing. Where are they? Shit, all I can see is muddy snow."

Stanton looked at the small hill. "Sir, sir, over here, Major. Lieutenant Carlson and Hamilton have secured the high ground and knocked out the second gun, but Carlson has been wounded."

After the formidable 88mm artillery piece exploded, Alex led his men forward over open ground. Bodies of Germans and paratroopers were scattered about the sandbags; the destruction of the giant gun had killed soldiers yards from its pit. He could see grenadiers retreating through brush toward the hills near the third gun but knew he was unable to continue the attack. Static from a walkie-talkie intruded on the sudden silence that hung over the battle area. Several prisoners were disarmed. The wounded were carried or managed to make the freezing march back to battalion headquarters.

The file of battered paratroopers trudged over the snow-covered hills. Alex gave his last order to a medic. "I want the burial team sent out tomorrow morning to recover the dead. All of the wounded accounted for?"

"Yes, Major, including Lieutenant Carlson."

Conroy leaned forward and took out his silver flask, engraved with the regimental seal. "Major Dunham, have a little hair off the dog that just bit you." He couldn't refuse and then took a long drink of scotch from John Conroy's special supply, which he suspected was brought in every week to headquarters. He was both warmed and sickened by its woody taste.

"Major, can you get the rest of those guns?" Conroy's tone was truculent.

"Sir, once the Krauts have dug in the eighty-eights with only the muzzles exposed, the air force can't spot them. The time for air strikes is now. We lost seventy-five men knocking out those guns last night and early this morning. I don't think these casualties are acceptable, sir."

"All right, all right, our mission is to guard the canal and kick the shit out of their patrols. Those bastards at headquarters have given us more than we can chew. You've made your point, Dunham. Carry on."

The rain and snow during the next several weeks turned the plain at Anzio into a quagmire. The nightly patrols and savage firefights continued. After one of many briefings, Alex stretched out on his cot, hands behind his head. Water slowly trickled from a leak in his bunker's roof. He thought the monotonous rhythm matched the cadence of marching soldiers, who had vanished like the steady flow of drops disappearing in the pail beyond the heels of his boots.

Alex heard footsteps on the hard ridges of frozen mud. His thoughts were interrupted by the strained voice of Sergeant Cunicello.

"Major, Lieutenant Drake and his patrol have been trapped by the Krauts near the 'factory' for the last two hours. We already sent out a couple of squads to rescue them. They've been driven back by a Tiger tank and infantry. The Lieutenant is badly wounded, and some of his men have been hit. We can't leave them out there overnight."

Alex tried to move his fingers numbed by cold, put on his gloves, then picked up his Browning automatic rifle. "Sergeant, get your men; we'll move out now and bring them into the field hospital before they freeze to death. Harris, where's your BAR? Plenty of grenades, a *Panzerfaust*, and three bazookas. We need a machine gunner."

Dunham led the men through a series of trenches approaching the Tiger from the rear, where they ambushed the Panzer Grenadiers with automatic rifle and machine-gun fire that allowed Harris to crawl within thirty yards of the mammoth tank. He steadied the *Panzerfaust*. The missile blew off the treads and penetrated the soft rear armament, smashing the engine. The snow-filled night sky was illuminated by the explosion. The crew was shot as they frantically crawled from the turret hatch. A squad of German infantry cautiously moved toward the firing, where a dozen or more were killed and several prisoners taken.

Alex questioned a Panzer Grenadier officer. "Sie und Ihre Soldaten haben diesen Panzer verteidigt. Wo sind die verwundeten amerikanischen Soldaten?" Where were the Lieutenant and his wounded men?

"Folgen Sie mir, major."

Alex and his men followed the German officer and several prisoners to Drake and his team, who lay splayed out in a ditch near the canal.

"Cunicello, have your men and the Krauts carry the wounded back to our lines."

One of Pete Drake's men had wrapped a belt around his leg. Alex could see his gaunt, pallid face in the light of the burning tank.

"Pete, how goes it, paratrooper? Are you with me?"

He managed a feeble grin, but his voice was barely a squeak. "God, Major, get me the hell out of here. It's my leg, it's on fire, and the rest of me is half-frozen. Let's go." He tried to stand but fell.

Alex picked him up and carried him over his shoulder back through the wire and trenches to Regimental CP. "Hamilton, bring the medics up here. Take the prisoners back to Regiment and see that they're fed and, then and only then, interrogated."

He lowered Drake onto a stretcher. Muscle and bone were mixed with fragments of his pants and boots, and then the blood. Alex's tunic was soaked. Sticky congealed blood covered his gloves and had seeped through his shirt. He felt its warmth on his chest. He knew Lieutenant Peter Drake was dying, by the ghastly paleness of his face and his limp body. Alex thought Drake probably had never been to bed with a girl. As he carried one end of the stretcher, he felt waves of nausea and remorse. Drake was one of the team. He was slipping away.

"Medic, cover him with blankets and get the doctor on the double."

Alex rested his BAR against an instrument table in the operating room of the tent hospital. Drake was given more plasma and blood as his uniform and boots were cut off with swift efficiency. The nurses had done it, and done it before. Pete and his squad hadn't been rescued in time. It was the bleeding, the cold, the snow, and frozen mud. Goddammit, someone should have sent the word sooner. Alex's attention was diverted by humming generators producing beams of bright, then dim light. The surgeon's mask was pulled down. He was young but had experience.

"Doctor, I'm counting on you to bring this young officer through." Alex followed him into the tent which was a makeshift operating room. "He's one of my staff. We've been taking too many casualties along this shitty canal that some other outfit should be patrolling."

The surgeon was brusque. "Wait outside, Major; we'll do our best."

Alex sat against a large box of medical supplies, head between his knees. He didn't know how much time had elapsed, but when he felt a nudge against his arm he reflexively snatched his BAR.

Alex looked up wearily. "Well, Doctor, how did things go with my Lieutenant?"

"I'm sorry, Major Dunham, the fractures, blood loss, and injury itself—"

"Don't explain, Doctor. I want his personal effects collected by your medics and sent home with the rest of his gear. Thank you for what you have done for Drake. My father..." Alex walked away. D3 would have saved Drake. Alex knew it.

He returned through the winding trenches back to his bunker. That night, as usual, the Germans began on schedule. The heavy artillery was concealed by day up in Caesar's Alban Hills, and each night they pounded every square inch near the canal. It always lasted an hour.

Conroy was livid. "Who the hell do you think you are, Dunham, some kind of fucking Tarzan? What in God's name were you doing out there last night knocking out German armor and rescuing that squad? Most of them were dead when you got there anyway. After all of these years together, you're on your stupid belly with your pretty little ass up in the air trying to get it shot off. Now listen once more; my battalion commanders don't crawl through frozen shit to drag back wounded and dead men. It's not one of your duties in my, do you hear, *my* regiment. Have I made myself clear?"

Alex stared beyond his commanding officer. The entire operation at Anzio had been a failure. He wondered what Airborne infantry was doing in foxholes. "Yes, Colonel," he answered flatly.

"Dammit, Dunham, I need you alive, not a dead hero. We've been in this litter box for three months now and have lost twenty percent of our regimental strength. You undoubtedly will be overjoyed to learn we're being taken out of the line next week. Sent back to England for R and R and to rebuild what's left of our outfit. More training. Once more, keep your stupid head down."

Conroy stood and turned his back. "Alex, why the hell are you always doing things like this? Now I have to waste my time writing up some ridiculous report, a recommendation, what have you, for a tin medal... 'bravery under fire,' all that crap. Christ only knows why you're still alive. You're dismissed, Lieutenant Colonel."

After the Anzio operation, the Regiment had been restructuring its cohesion for several months. Alex wondered what this vague, meaningless military term meant. *That's right,* he thought. *It's training replacements for the casualties at the canal in Italy, again sharpening the edge for more destruction and killing.* The English countryside seemed an improbable place for the constant, endless military exercises. The night jumps into pastoral settings perfected the battalion's fighting efficiency for quick strikes in future combat. He ruminated over the folly at Anzio.

Alex knelt, resting his head on the pew in front of him, fingers clenched and white. It was evensong and the choir chanted the last phrases of the Apostle's Creed. There was stillness except for the rustle of ecclesiastic robes and the soft sound of slowly shuffling feet. He felt the tranquillity of the small cathedral with its glow of candles and pervasive odor of incense.

He was unaware his friend Father Bruce Critchley stood beside him. They hadn't spoken for a week.

"Colonel Dunham." Critchley touched his shoulder. "I've only come up from London. It's been several days, and I've missed our conversations."

It had grown darker and Alex was barely able to see the priest's figure in black-and-purple vestments.

"Do join me for tea in the rectory."

Father Critchley was tall and slightly stooped, and Alex judged he was in his late forties. His face had the celibate pallor and deep lines of a scholar and aesthete who had suffered without complaint. His speech had a deep British accent, measured and reassuring.

Alex stood quickly. Their greeting was one of friendly constraint.

"It seems a while, Father. Was your journey pleasant?"

The rectory housekeeper served tea in the comfortable library, warmed by a bright fire.

"Yes, milk, thank you very much." Alex relaxed.

After an inconsequential chat, Critchley subtly turned their conversation to his friend's doubts. He was holding a precisely balanced pencil between his index fingers.

Alex thought the sharp end must have been particularly uncomfortable.

Critchley was hesitant, sensitive to Alex's intelligence and insight, which he thought were several multiples beyond most military officers he had known. He searched for a reasonable approach.

"Colonel, you mentioned several weeks ago you were concerned. Actually, you know it's a far stronger word, perhaps some guilt about your casualties in Sicily and Italy. Apparently the cost was acceptable in the first operation, however, not in the Italian campaign."

Alex struggled with logic and emotions. "Father, it seems long ago now, but I made the decision to serve. I thought it was my sense of gratitude for a privileged life, education, a duty to friends and people I had come to know. My father encouraged, strongly advised, a career in medicine. However, my choice was a life of action rather than study. I was convinced there was a debt to be repaid. Doing, you see, leading men to right the wrongs, wrongs I never personally experienced but vividly imagined and thought I understood. In the beginning I saw the war as a burning commitment. Father, there's been a price for that commitment."

Father Critchley walked toward a window. "Although I have never known the horror and terror of battle, you have served with honor and distinction and must prevail in your present duties. Remember, God accepts remorse. Embrace His goodness; accept His forgiveness."

"Father, it seems to me God doesn't take sides in war. He doesn't decide who is morally right or wrong; however, with or without God, anything is possible." He shrugged his shoulders. "Logic can't solve this dilemma for me. My conscience, the guilt of it all....I have been tested by combat and the violence of killing. Can I expect forgiveness for what I have done in the name of duty?" Alex lowered his voice. "I am not afraid of death. Where can I turn? What can I do?"

"My dear friend, perhaps you have lost faith in divine guidance. Your compulsion, your drive, the necessity for victory is understandable. Duty to lead without fear in these dim days. But, and I have said this before, the issue . . ." He looked down, fumbling with the crucifix on his vestments. "Search; reach for God; believe in His infinite compassion and love." Their eyes met. "If faith is in your daily prayers, you will again know the goodness of the world God created, the unshakable belief in everything you have ever hoped and dreamed. Believe that God's hand guides those things you are unable to see or touch. Faith is waiting; faith is patience. I pray you accept what He so gladly offers."

Alex stood, walked to the fire, reached under his tight collar, adjusted his tie, then straightened his battle jacket. The fire consumed their bodies; he cringed at their screams. *Look, Dunham . . . almighty God is letting them be burned alive, only charred skeletons, strangely deformed caricatures of another life.* He turned from the white embers.

"Father, I know you are correct in all of your beliefs that are so difficult for me to accept. Thank you for your patience, understanding, and friendship. All of us will be moving out soon, and I shall never see you again. For now my faith is in the number of grenades I carry, my Browning automatic rifle, the mortars, machine guns, and a knife that protect me. Regardless of being held prisoner by this war, please believe me, Father, I shall continue my search for faith and God's goodness. His forgiveness."

Critchley buoyantly chatted about early unfolding daffodils as he led Alex through the rectory garden, then to the gate. "Good-bye for now, Colonel, and may God be with you."

The day began with the resonance of gritty sand and dirt on the soles of his boots as Alex climbed the metal stairs to the top floor of an abandoned Dutch power plant. After reaching a blown-out window facing the Draas River, he turned to his adjutant, Jake Harris, and three company commanders. Two pair of field glasses were passed among the battalion officers. After surveying the width of the river and heavily defended opposite embankment, he felt a numbing despair for his men and realized his mission was tactically compromised before it had begun.

"Jake, all of you have seen the terrain and know the objective." Alex spoke with composure. "We'll make the crossing several hundred yards down there to the right. The exact location and time depend on when they deliver the boats. There should be a couple of dozen. The river is about four hundred yards wide at that point, the current almost ten miles an hour. There's a plateau at the takeoff point that drops about twenty-five feet to that narrow beach. See it? Division has given us orders to capture the railroad and main auto bridge upstream, intact, and I repeat intact."

Lieutenant Tom Hamilton looked through the window. "Colonel, there's still some haze. I would guess the auto bridge is about two miles east of where we hit the shore. Sound about right?"

"Those are close to the numbers. Now, Dan, Hank, take a look at the Kraut defenses. After crossing the river, we have to secure that flat, grassy plain. It stretches about three hundred yards, no concealment until the embankment that is actually a dike. There's a road running along its top. You can see German trucks with reinforcements and supplies moving along it now. This will be our first chance for cover, and then we can regroup."

Lieutenant Dan Naughton and Hank Carlson zipped up their field jackets in the chill air, and Hamilton snapped his parachute harness that resembled suspenders. "Colonel Dunham." Jake Harris turned away from the window. "This is no goddamn job for parachute infantry."

Naughton put down his carbine. "God almighty, sir, what the hell are we running into? Take the field glasses. Look at those fucking slit trenches, machine gun emplacements, and pillboxes. Christ, there are two wicked-looking old forts before we get to the railroad bridge. Probably manned with ten or twelve Krauts with twenty-millimeter guns, and Battalion is supposed to knock out all of that crap before we get the bridges? Damned if some twenty-millimeter flak isn't firing at us right now."

Of the company commanders, Alex thought Hank Carlson was steady; he got his share of close combat at Anzio where he was wounded and now was fit again. "Colonel, I don't think we have any definite tactical plan here. It's every man for himself at least until we get to the opposite embankment; then we go for the bridges. I take it that the southern approaches are held by our other two battalions?"

"Hank, you've got the picture." Alex repeated, "This is critical. All the Krauts have to be dug out before dark. The whole mission of securing the bridges is on our shoulders. All of you carry BARs, grenades. The men use fixed bayonets. Remember, it's always: 'Follow me.' Tell your Sergeants if you're hit, they take over." He looked at the defenses again, then spoke deliberately to each officer. "The men are to be told only—I repeat, only—they shouldn't be surprised if there's heavy fire during the crossing. That's about it. We'll have one hell of a party when it's over. Good luck and remember, it's always the mission first. You can't think about the men and casualties. Each of us is expendable."

Alex led his officers down the stairs. He knew each had the same fears. At best, probably 50 percent of the men would be killed and the wounded would be carried downstream in riddled boats. The bridges must be captured and the road to northern Holland secured for waiting armor and infantry.

A stiff breeze blew from the west as Alex looked at the choppy brown water where they would launch their assault craft. From time to time small-arms fire dropped among the men.

A Private passed Alex. "By the time it gets here, it's sort of like peanuts falling from a bag at the county fair, right, Colonel?"

Dunham thought morale and readiness were high; nevertheless, the men were edgy. The boats had not arrived. He cursed supply, engineers, transport, anyone responsible for delivering them. He thought if they had attacked in early morning, a haze would have covered the river and the Germans might have been caught by surprise. He looked back. A dozen tanks were shelling the opposite shore, while low-level fighters strafed the pillboxes and forts. He was reassured when a convoy of trucks finally arrived in midafternoon. Relief turned to dismay when he saw twenty-foot-long boats with plywood bottoms. They were made of canvas, and each had only six oars.

"All right." Alex stood among his troopers. "Let's load ammunition and weapons on the double. They have better lifeboats on the *Queen Mary,* but let's do our best. It's a snap; row like hell straight at the Krauts. They've had us do everything but play sailor boys. We're up to that, too."

One of the men shouted, "Colonel, we'll get across this damned river even if we have to swim."

Dunham watched Major Jake Harris organize their lead boat with twenty men and for a brief moment remembered his rowing days on Lake Carnegie. They could sprint 400 yards in three or four minutes. No records today. He moved quickly through the line of waiting boats as the men scrambled to load equipment and drag them down the embankment, although he realized small-arms fire could puncture the canvas.

Alex knew it was time and signaled tank commanders for a smokescreen. Several minutes later he saw it had vanished into a feeble white cloud, blown downstream before the last boats reached the water. The air strikes were ineffective, but the tanks gave covering fire for his fragile armada.

"OK, Jake, blow the whistle," Alex yelled. "Let's go; move out." He watched the men struggle to lift the boats loaded with rifles, ammunition, machine guns, and mortars that doubled their weight. His lead boat slid down the embankment, but each man was mired in soft sand before he could hoist himself aboard. Boats took on water, tilted, overturned, or circled out of control before they could head for the opposite shore. Men fell overboard, then were dragged back in by another trooper, before the crossing had begun. Half of the small flotilla had moved offshore before any heavy rounds from the enemy were fired. Suddenly the boats were engulfed by flying metal and phosphorus bombs. Alex saw his men being hit, some afire, others drowning before they could be pulled aboard.

He thought with 400 yards to the opposite shore and the intensity of enemy fire, the only essential movement was to paddle like hell. As he rowed in the bow of the boat, he glanced to the right and rear where Danny Naughton had been before a dull, whining thud. The boat was hit by a 20mm shell and disintegrated.

Alex was covered by a pink mist, pelted by fragments of boat, flesh, and bone. It ran down his face. There was the bitter taste of blood. It clung to his uniform and hands and briefly clouded his vision.

Within ten minutes, the broad surface of the river was covered by the small canvas crafts, all jammed with frantically rowing men, some using oars and others rifle butts.

Through the concussion and blasts of gunfire, men in each boat were screaming, "For God's sake row, row, row, harder, faster, faster; we've got to make the shore." Some men were shouting prayers, entreating for a chance to reach solid ground: "Our Father, Our Father, Hail Mary full . . . Give us a break to get the bastards. Come on, Ski; let's go, Jonesey; only a few more yards, Frankie. Row, you crazy son of a bitch. How the hell can I row with this rifle butt? . . ." One paratrooper was blown out of his boat shrouded in a fog of red khaki; another was hit by shrapnel and toppled over the side. The last anyone saw of him were his boots disappearing beneath the surface of the water.

Alex looked back at the engineer who had been steering his boat. He had been shot and was hanging over the stern, arms dangling ludicrously in the water. The boat began to turn uncontrollably in a wide circle.

"For God's sake, Ryan," Alex shouted frantically. "Pull him in. Take his paddle and use it. Now get this fucking dinghy headed for the shore." As he cried out, he heard himself ridiculously repeating the cadence of the Princeton coxswain: "Stroke, one, two, three, catch-two." Alex was furiously rowing through the hideous sights and sounds of the river churned by a steady wave of a pounding enemy barrage. He thought if he should survive, he would always remember this indelible scene of slaughter, a scene beyond his imagination.

"Oh, my God, Alex." Jake Harris's arm had been completely severed. "Take out your forty-five and do it, for Christ's sake Alex. Kill me now. The pain, I can't breathe."

Alex dragged him into the bottom of the boat, where he could see the shattered bones of Jake's shoulder and spongy material. He thought it was lung. Spray and geysers shot up around them caused by every type of enemy fire. There were overturned boats, boats floating downstream loaded with dead and wounded. Nearing exhaustion, he shouted for Sergeant Cunicello.

"Connie, how are things back there? Answer me, Sergeant. Goddammit, how are things at the rear of the boat? The men, ammunition?" Alex looked back. Cunicello's helmet had been blown off, and Alex saw the staggering sight of a half-filled skull. Gray-white brain matter was running down the side and front of Cunicello's blood-soaked uniform. Now there were five men alive in his boat with only fifty more yards to the beach.

Oh, God, Alex prayed, *spare me for a few more minutes. Then I can start to kill. Yes, God help me, I'm not only going to kill these bastards, but murder them. Spare me to avenge my men, to settle their score. Please, please, I'm begging you for just a few more minutes; then I'll have my chance.*

Alex felt the plywood bottom scrape the sand where they became lodged. "Everybody out, and follow me. Get the weapons, all the ammunition you can lay your hands on. Stay with me."

After climbing over the dead and wounded, Dunham and his men collapsed, physically unstrung, seeking shelter behind a small unexpected sandbar. After several minutes, Alex got up on one knee and, looking to both sides, saw more boats had reached the beach. Within a short distance there was another group of paratroopers. He moved among them ordering, "No prisoners, not one goddamned prisoner."

"Where's the bazooka team?" Alex ran across the marshy ground, partially hidden by tall reeds.

"Here, sir. I have two *Panzerfausts* we captured in Sicily."

"That's more like it; have a trooper with you if you're hit. We want those two pillboxes and the small forts knocked out. Is there a machine gunner here?"

"Over here, Colonel." He was a small, jaunty soldier with bandoliers dangling from his neck.

"Hamilton, where the hell are you?" Alex's voice was strangely calm.

"Up here on the rise, Colonel."

Alex was on his hands and knees in the rocky sand. "Now listen up. It's every man for himself until we reach that embankment in front of us. It's rough going, about three hundred yards of open ground. Set the machine gun up behind the sandbar; give us covering fire to the right. The rest of you move; now follow me."

At first there were men at Alex's side, some dropping, others breaking away to grenade a trench, bayonetting the enemy. No quarter was shown to the foe who surrendered, and those who ran were shot. The relentless fire from German emplacements, which had so unmercifully decimated the small flotilla, was diminishing minute by minute.

Alex couldn't think, only react. He felt a strange change, a metamorphosis, as he was drawn out of himself, running, falling, firing, then momentarily dropping from fatigue. He felt foreign, a primal man. His anger, rage, and lust to kill were consuming. The tanks from the opposite shore were still laying down a barrage that passed over the attack and gave him some temporary relief. Mortars and machine guns supported the thinly advancing line of his paratroopers. As they attacked the embankment, enemy fire was methodically silenced and Alex and his group saw they had retreated toward their next line of defense, now disorganized, concealed in orchards, barns, and small houses.

Hamilton followed Dunham's orders. "Take fifteen men and clean out these slit trenches over there. I don't want any Krauts behind us or on our flanks. Use grenades and bayonets."

The crossing and attack had begun an hour ago, and now additional boats had returned with reinforcements and heavy weapons. Alex judged there were 150 men moving toward the railroad span, but the main bridge still was almost one-quarter of a mile east. By now the paratroopers were operating in smaller groups, clearing all resistance before the bridge. The bazooka man knocked out the first pillbox and Hamilton shot the escaping defenders. Beyond the demolished pillbox, twenty-five Waffen SS surrendered to a Corporal in Alex's combat group.

Alex ran forward. "Decker, for God's sake watch your—"

An enemy soldier no older than seventeen, who had raised his arms in surrender, lobbed a grenade. Decker was blown backward, an unrecognizable mass of uniform, blood, and torn flesh.

"Komm vorwärts, you miserable piece of shit." Alex leveled his automatic weapon at close range and shot the German through the neck. He fell in a shower of blood, his head sagging, puppetlike, to one side. The remainder of the black uniforms slumped from bursts of fire or were bayonetted. Separated groups of paratroopers were rapidly moving forward, now that the second pillbox had been destroyed by grenades. Alex knew that enemy resistance was breaking.

He stood in the midst of small-arms fire directing the aim of the *Panzerfaust*: "Patterson, aim that baby at the slit in the fort where you can see the barrel of the twenty-millimeter gun. If you miss, miss high and take off the roof. Steady at fifty yards."

The roof flew upward in scattered pieces of cement and brick while Alex led a charge killing the enemy, whose hands were raised in surrender. Then he yelled for his radioman carrying an eighty-pound pack of equipment who had lagged behind.

"Anderson, it's 1630; raise Regiment. Tell them we are attacking the north end of the main railroad bridge. Confirm if the south end is secure."

The south approaches to the railroad and main auto routes had been captured in desperate fighting, and the assault on the main bridge began. Small squads of men roamed through orchards as a furious firefight began for control of the north end. The remainder of Alex's battalion advanced with difficulty but within an hour held the northern approach. Over two hundred Germans were trapped in the middle of the bridge as Alex moved forward with a Sergeant.

Alex pointed his BAR at an approaching enemy officer, who waved a white handkerchief. Then he ordered a large group of soldiers to lay down their weapons and surrender, shouting, "Befehle Deinen Soldaten sofort alle Waffen nieder zulegen und Euch zu ergeben. Schnell machen, Schnell machen."

Looking up at the girders of the huge bridge, Alex saw a number of German soldiers sniping at troopers, jeeps, and tanks below. "Hamilton, take ten men and clean them out." As he spoke, Hamilton dropped at his side. He had been shot through the head at close range.

Alex turned to a paratrooper carrying an ammunition box. "Give me clips for the BAR and get some men over here. I want every one of those bastards in the next five minutes. Do you hear me, soldier?"

He fired with his small group of troopers, and bodies began to fall from the top of the highway bridge onto the road or in the river.

"Colonel, watch yourself; you can't see all of them," a Private yelled.

Within several minutes, the firing and sniping stopped.

"Get a medic for the Lieutenant." Alex took Hamilton's helmet off and saw that his face and forehead were a mass of torn tissue and shattered skull. In the approaching dusk Alex saw bodies dangling from the girders and catwalks like grotesque gargoyles. Arms, legs, and torsos with field gray-green uniforms were strewn about the steel supports, creating an eerie scene of unforgettable horror. It was a sudden, innocent flash when Steffi asked, "Alex, aren't those stone creatures around your dormitory windows horrible? Why are they there, anyway?" He had long since forgotten his answer, but it was banal, had something to do with medieval rainspouts. That time and place were far away. Now the rainspouts were twisted and mangled, dripping blood and scattered viscera.

By six-thirty, military traffic of all types moved over the great auto bridge and Colonel Conroy had contacted division headquarters confirming the bridge had been secured. Later, Captain Hank Carlson set up a forward command post several hundred yards beyond the regimental headquarters.

Alex sat on an ammunition crate in the corner of a camouflaged tent. His uniform was covered with the gruesome remnants of battle, bloodstains and dirt on his soaked tunic, wet boots, and torn pants.

Conroy was relentless. "They're going to try and hit us in the morning, so I've brought up our other two battalions. Your casualties aren't known yet, probably close to three hundred men killed, wounded, others missing. I want a full battle report within forty-eight hours. Pull the rest of your battalion back through the lines to the southeast of town toward Beek. Look at me, Lieutenant Colonel Dunham."

Alex leaned against a tent pole, legs stretched out; his head had dropped forward. His helmet lay next to him on the ground, BAR beneath his legs. Four days of beard, hair wet from sweat, a face covered with grime, his eyes were focused on Conroy's feet.

"I said look at me, Dunham."

"Yes, sir." Then he looked up.

"Your mission—and, I repeat, your mission—has succeeded. Without the bridge the whole operation would have been a failure. I've talked to General Harper, and both of us think capturing the bridge intact was probably one of the finest small infantry unit actions in the war. You stuck your neck out when you could have dogged it. You're damn lucky to be alive tonight. I'm putting you in for the—"

"No, nothing, nothing," Alex interrupted. "It's the men out there in the river, on the embankment, in the bottom of the boats. I'm a lucky bastard, should have gone down with them."

Conroy stood, hands behind his back. "Now let's get this straight, Dunham. You were in the first boat and somehow survived. It was your duty; you were an officer leading his men. Now have a quick one for the best goddamned battalion and regimental commanders in the Airborne." They drank brandy from his well-used dented silver flask.

"Thanks, sir. I'll be up at Battalion C.P., northern end of the bridge. Got to get the tanks moving. Dismissed, sir?" Alex picked up his weapon and helmet, saluted, and left Conroy's headquarters.

"Colonel Dunham, we've set up the C.P. here in this farmhouse. It's about a thousand yards in front of the bridge." The driver braked the jeep in front of a small stone building. Alex saw the roof had been torn off, and only part of the walls remained.

He walked through the skeleton of an entrance. "Carlson, you've been promoted to assistant battalion commander, so handle operations and intelligence. Part of your company is all we have left after this afternoon's battle. Like Pickett at Gettysburg, wasn't it?"

The young Captain was calling in artillery fire but looked up for a moment. "Sir, it wasn't Gettysburg, but none of us has ever seen anything like it and probably never will."

"Tell the tech to keep alert with the walkie-talkie. I'm lying down a minute." Alex rolled a damp, musty-smelling blanket under his head. Closing his eyes instantly brought back the clamor of bursting shells, sporadic machine-gun fire, the dull thud of men being killed, screams of the wounded, and grunts and cries of his men attacking, throwing grenades, bayonetting the enemy. He still tasted, felt, the spray of water, pink with blood, on his face.

Hours of battle and Conroy's well-intended brandy produced a deadening sleep lasting several hours. Carlson's constant chatter and the intermittent clatter of the walkie-talkie finally woke him. He splashed his head with cold water.

He put on his helmet and walked to Carlson. "Captain, call for my jeep. I'm off to the forward positions around the bridge, then back to the river. Before dark, we expect panzers with their infantry. The Krauts are good at that type of attack. Some may have already been concealed in the woods or dug in beyond the bridge. You know, only the muzzle showing."

He saw a tent with a large red cross several hundred yards up from the shore. Trucks were stacked with bodies, parts of what had been his men. Father Dillworth, who had volunteered to cross in his boat, was giving last rites while the regimental surgeon and medics were removing pieces of metal from a paratrooper's leg.

Alex waited. "Doctor, tell me about things. There are still dead men in the bottom of six or seven boats. Is there anyone alive down here? What happened to Major Jake Harris? Did they find Naughton's boat?"

The answer was distant, factual. "Colonel, Harris had his shoulder and arm blown off. Was dead when we got here. Naughton's boat disappeared."

"Thank you for what you have done for my boys, these men. They fought like hell. You know, Doctor, we rowed through a flying curtain of steel. We had to get the bridge. Those were my orders."

"Yes, Colonel, it took great courage. All of us watched from the power plant. You were right out in front all the way."

Alex shifted and regripped his BAR. The continuous firing caused the *Cosmoline* in its stock to melt. It stuck to his hands.

"I want to see Major Harris, and now." He clenched the stock for strength, the self-control to confront his friend, a fearless officer.

There was a deepening darkness as Alex approached the trucks. Two medics picked up Harris's crumpled body. Here was Alex's bright, handsome assistant commander, not unlike a piece of butchered beef. He leaned down, held the coldness of Harris's hand. The crest, the motto, the dull, lifeless ruby of his West Point ring.

"Father, you were in my boat." Alex turned to Dillworth. "It was far too dangerous a mission for a noncombatant. You volunteered. Didn't have to, did you? The men will never forget you."

"Colonel Dunham, I wanted to be there when they needed me. You led them without hesitation and with courage."

Alex held the priest's arms. "Listen to me: you, you alone made the difference, Father Dillworth, and I thank you for your devotion to the men. We've lost the better part of my battalion and its officers. I have seen some of them stacked up, mutilated, only bits and pieces of humanity."

"Colonel, let's sit down a few minutes. You performed your duty, followed orders, and accomplished the mission with extraordinary bravery. Your men fought through the dark valley to give the rest of us a better chance. God has spared the two of us for another time and place."

Alex felt the priest's kindness, the calmness of his benevo-lence.

"I'll talk to you some more in several days," Dillworth sug-gested. "You have been staring at the face of death so long, and today was a lifetime of that face. It would be a good idea to get back to the C.P. It's darker now, and your driver is waiting."

"Thank you, Father. In several days, then." He turned to leave, then glanced back. Dillworth's salute wasn't regulation; it wasn't military; it wasn't an Airborne salute. Alex hoped it was a sign he understood his grief.

He walked along the bank of the river. Alex thought they would have done better with his college shell, rowed faster. Five or six canvas boats were gently rocked from side to side by small lapping waves. When he started, they were a light green, but now they were stained a deep red. Scattered helmets bobbing in the water, upright rifles with bayonets jammed in the sand, and remains of soiled red uniforms all met his gaze. A distended piece of intestine floated near a partially sunken gunnel. It entered and left through a hole in the canvas, like a serpent coil-ing in and out of the boat's bottom.

The medical team slept under sagging tents. The river reflected distant, leaping flames with the approach of dawn. Deep, rumbling explosions sounded in the city. The trucks with his men had disappeared.

He felt the catastrophic horror, intensified by his physical exhaustion. He wondered why they hadn't crossed at daybreak in the fog and surprised the enemy. He should have disputed the time and circumstances of an attack in full daylight. The boats were late. They weren't boats but canvas toys. Logic, training, tactics, it was an Airborne unit, not paddling sailors.

He could hear their haunting, jovial requests as his men car-ried the clumsy boats, filled with weapons and explosives. "Hey, Colonel Dunham, be sure the folks get my Purple Heart, and don't forget my Good Conduct Medal, sir." They had fought and died with incomparable fury. The carnage was overwhelming.

"Colonel, Colonel Dunham, sir, your jeep was stuck in the sand. We've dug it out for you, sir."

Corpsmen, helmets with red crosses, loomed before him.

"As you were." Alex acknowledged them. "You've done your duty today. Get some rest."

The two looked at each other with astonishment, then left.

"Good Lord, Colonel Dunham is so tough he gives killing a bad name and now he's down here on the river worrying about the battalion," one of the corpsmen said. "I pity those poor Kraut bastards. What he did along this embankment here and at the bridge. You know what I mean; it was a fucking massacre."

The gears ground as the jeep spun out of the sandy landing area, away from the small boats and what had been their cargo.

Alex could see the Norman church at Nonant through splattering raindrops driven erratically down the restaurant window by the blustery autumn wind. He put on his coat, pulled up the collar, and walked toward the portal. There was a small cemetery with tilted crosses, religious figures, and stone markers with names that were partially obliterated by time and weather. The north wall was straight and a short, sharply slanted roof extended to the south wall. The tower was an extension of the same architecture. There were no windows in the north wall and several arched ones on the south side. He thought it was large for a village church. It was dusk and Alex was comforted by the odor of wooden pews and candles. He returned late every Friday afternoon and rented a sparsely furnished room in a small hotel, spared from the Allied advance through Normandy.

His knees and legs ached as he knelt, eyes fixed on a maize-colored crucifix. He looked at the stations of the cross. Peeling stone and streaks of water had muted their once-bright colors. He could hear Colonel Conroy's biting southern accent. "Now, Dunham, you shall be sent to train and rebuild the battalion. Get them combat-ready, another first team. Go through the training routines you perfected at Benning. You have four months. Plenty of time after being moved out of the line in Holland. Organize the one hundred men who survived into a spit-and-polish training cadre. Use those deserted French barracks northwest of Paris. At least there's a roof over their heads, food, and some warmth during the rainy season and early snowfalls. I have provided and commandeered everything available from supply headquarters. I expect the usual attention to detail your reputation enjoys."

Alex rubbed his eyes and face with rough hands, then tightened a wool scarf. He needed warmth. His body, his mind. He continued to ask why he was spared, remembering the lines: "Under the wide and starry sky, dig my grave and let me die." Was God listening? Did He know the incessant regret? Did He understand the denigration of killing, the gnawing sorrow? Alex wondered if he could give himself to the woman he loved. Would he see and know the beauty of seasons, feel the salty, pure ocean spray? He desperately wanted to find the way. He had restless sleep along a pew and later returned through the rain to his room. It was 0215 hours.

He was shaving one morning and began to laugh uproariously. D3 had once told him if one could eat, sleep, and have regular bowel movements, one could perform his work. He looked at a lean face with dark blotches beneath the eyes; sleep had escaped every mental trick and scheme. Reciting poetry, trying to remember music, then there was the chronological sequence of English monarchs. Eventually he recalled the title "Reign by Reign." *With better weather, you shall run longer and farther each morning, follow the five-mile trail through the woods, shave, cold shower before reveille. Punish yourself, absolve yourself; where's redemption? How do I find it? Now stand by with a different company each morning for report, then calisthenics and chow. Dunham, keep occupied, busy every waking hour. Supervise weapon instruction, drills, then afternoon classes in tactics and strategy for the new officers.* He thought it was Benning again, but Benning would be a relief.

Alex stood before maps and aerial photographs of Sicily, Anzio, and the Draas River.

"Although the winds were gale-force and the regiment was scattered over a six-mile area, our battalion was more fortunate. We held the road block, drew the German armor and infantry toward a weak center, then destroyed their flanks. The capture of the airfield at Piano Lupo to the northwest was a victory that denied *Luftwaffe* operations. The bonus at the airfield was bagging one thousand *Panzerfausts* with instructions. It was fortunate because the Krauts had a rocket-fired weapon, the only one that could penetrate frontal armor of Panther and Tiger tanks. Highly effective at Anzio and Normandy."

He continued, "You must remember Airborne units and tanks are a bad mix. The bazooka has never been effective except to destroy tank tracks at close range. The captured *Panzerfausts* will be of enormous advantage in future battles. Remember this lesson, gentlemen. In Sicily there were brave men in this regiment who followed bazooka routine waiting until enemy tanks were at two hundred yards. That was too late. The men were run over. Don't forget these combat errors. Use the captured *Panzerfausts*."

"But, sir, the instructions were in German. Who in the regiment—?" one of the officers asked.

"Wir haben die Waffen aus den Kisten genommen, dann zusammen gesetzt. We fired several for practice and then destroyed a *Schwere Abteilung* of six panzers. That's enough brain work today. Monday, be prepared to discuss innovative and future use of Airborne forces. Imagine, for instance, landing techniques and transportation of troops ten years in the future."

As he paused, Alex looked at the twenty or so young officers and remembered how "Buzzer" O'Brien would ask a question as class ended.

"One of our resourceful Sergeants has requisitioned a bottle of nineteen thirty-eight Beaujolais. It's for the man who identifies the author of this prescient quote: 'Where is the Prince who can afford so to cover his country with troops for its defense, as that ten thousand men, descending from the clouds, might not, in many places, do an infinite amount of mischief before a force could be brought to repel them?' Dismissed, but don't become a jeep casualty; save yourself to destroy the enemy."

The class stood, saluted, and then came forward. Alex was trapped against the maps and photos. He knew what to expect, then looked down, hands placed behind his back.

"Colonel, a word or two about the bridge. We understand that you..."

The new officers glanced at his battle jacket and ribbons, a two-inch-wide orange-and-green band on each epaulet that they knew was a presidential unit citation and one from the Dutch government. He adjusted his overseas cap, returned their salutes, and left.

Alex brooded. *You can't have it done in Nonant; they'll recognize you. Go to Bayeux; it's larger and you can buy the woman you want.* On a balmy April evening, he drove along a poplar-lined road, northwest toward the Channel. It was a Roman road, paved, repaired, traveled for centuries...perfectly straight for miles. He thought the hotel was decent, a clean bed with hard mattress, rough wool blanket, basin with cold water, but no soap.

There she is, Colonel, speak to her, not too commanding. Be firm, persuasive. She was of medium height, dark-eyed, with brown hair gathered in back with a smudged white bow. She wore an old, tight-fitting cotton sweater with a cross on a gold chain. Her skirt emphasized a good middle-aged figure. *Dunham, she is at least forty and knows what she's doing.*

"Madame prenez le dîner avec moi, s'il vous plaît." He held her hand, closed her fingers over ten dollars, and ordered pot-au-feu, wine, bread, and cheese. She sipped her wine. He drank his. Two brandies. *It's almost ten o'clock, still light. Bleu foncée sky, quiet night, hold her arm, walk along the canal, then take her to the room.* She leaned against his shoulder and held his hand. It was *épatant* to be with a handsome American officer. He opened the door and spoke.

"Ces sont vos instructions. Aujourd'hui est le sixième mois d'anniversaire quand trois cent de mes hommes étaient... slaughtered."

He held her arms. "You do exactly as I say." He gave her more money. "First, remove my jacket, tie, and shirt." She obeyed. He took off a thin leather belt. Fifty lashes tonight and the same next week. He lay facedown on the bed and held the wooden frame. He thought, *Each blow is for your dead men. After all, you were their commander.* After several minutes, he mumbled, "Madame, the next are for my friends and officers. Make them especially hard."

He tried to move. He squeezed the frame and turned his head. She was sitting on the floor next to him, and he felt cold on his back. There were two small bloodstained towels hanging over the edge of the basin. Then she wiped his sweat-soaked hair and face and stroked his cheek.

"Le même temps au restaurant, semaine prochaine." Dunham told her that there would be a good wine with dinner next week.

"Oui, mon Colonel, mais la prochaine fois, plus d'argent." She agreed but asked for more money and wanted a bottle of Calvados.

Alex sat before Colonel Conroy, grimaced, and silently complained, *Dammit, I can't lean back. It's taken a month for my back to heal. Sit up straight.*

"Dunham, you've done a first-rate job training replacements, and the regiment is at full strength with your new battalion. Snipers, pathfinders, heavy weapons, artillery, all combat-ready. Incidentally, I missed you at the celebration. Thank the Lord, this European war is over; they'll need a full Allied Airborne Army for the Pacific. No one knows now."

"I understand, John." He flinched at the description "new battalion."

"I have selected you and about one hundred other officers and men from the regiment for detached duty in Germany. The details of our occupation command will be decided before the end of summer. You'll be assigned to Bavaria. You shall command these officers and men who will direct aid to the local population, food, medical supplies, probably some military police work. Your temporary duty orders have been cut. First a full written and verbal report to General Bedford in Washington, then a six-week leave, including travel time. Report back to Frankfurt no later than September first."

"This means I'm being detached from the 504 after almost three years?"

Conroy stood and walked to a window of his headquarters. Colonel John Conroy, West Point 1930, was not a sentimental man. Alex knew the army would always be Conroy's life. He looked out over the parade grounds, barracks, and garages, scanning marching troops and assembled equipment.

"Alex, you and I are only two of several original officers who have come through this. Here's the question I asked myself when you stuck that rifle butt into the old general's ass, I can't remember how long ago anymore. I wondered if you were really as combative and tough as you acted that night when you rushed into maneuver headquarters. Now I know, Alex. You'll never be able to forget. You'll have a good life; brave men always do."

Alex would not give anything away to Conroy; it was D3's style.

"Thank you, sir. You'll have my full report to General Bedford before I leave. As usual, make appropriate changes." *Now, Dunham,* he thought, *wait before you say any more, nothing to embarrass your regimental commander or yourself.* He tried to recall a correct way to say good-bye, then the regimental motto: "Sir, it will always be 'Strike and Hold.' It has been an honor and pleasure to serve in your command."

They shook hands. "Always the best to you." Conroy hesitated, then smiled. "By the way, where the hell did you ever learn to paddle a canoe? Damn, never have seen anything like it, Dunham. Carry on, and good luck in whatever you do. Someday we'll meet again."

His driver looked in the rearview mirror. "It's not much farther, Colonel Dunham. Chipping Camden is the next village."

Alex had telephoned Sir Reginald and Lady Converse-Jones, friends of Brian and Lucky.

Lady Margaret's invitation was cordial: "Do come along and spend the night with us, Alex. We're looking forward to meeting you. Not much in the pot; however, we can have a long chat, a brisk walk. You're flying home on Saturday, isn't that correct?"

Alex was greeted in the library by Sir Reginald. "Jolly good to see you, Dunham. Your parents visited us several years before the war. I imagined you would have been a surgeon, like your distinguished father."

"It's a pleasure to be your guest, sir. To answer your question, it wasn't a difficult decision and medicine was an interest at one time, but I couldn't be a slacker while others served, could I?"

"Righto, good man. You're young, plenty of time. Not an old buzzard of a retired surgeon out to pasture like myself."

They rose as Lady Margaret brought the tea service. Her cultured voice conveyed kindness. She had a pale complexion and thin, birdlike face, and Alex judged she was in her late sixties.

Sir Reginald was more outgoing, with a probing intellect. "By the way, you were in on the Draas party, weren't you, Alex? Your regiment got plenty of splash in the press. Actually, quite a show. You winkled out the Jerries magnificently."

Lady Margaret gently intervened. "Perhaps Alex would rather not, Reggie."

Alex's answer was oblique. "Sir Reginald, I was satisfied that my men had superb battlefield care and, later on, the best hospital treatment. When I return to Washington, I have to report to Airborne headquarters."

Their brief conversation was interrupted by barking dogs and a car rolling up the driveway.

Sir Reginald walked to the hallway. "That must be Sheila; she usually pops out from London on Friday nights. You know she's a Wren officer, Alex."

Lieutenant Sheila Converse-Jones was as extroverted as her mother was restrained.

"Heavens, Daddy, we have been invaded by the Americans right here in our library. They seem to be everywhere."

Sir Reginald introduced his daughter as he took her coat and blue-and-white piped naval hat. Her father looked admiringly at a young woman in her twenties with black hair, dark eyes, and naturally pink cheeks.

Alex seated Sheila at the small dining room table and, after grace, complimented his hostess. "It's an unexpected luxury enjoying your company and dinner tonight, Lady Margaret. Many of my officers and friends, well, they no longer have—"

"You know, Alex, we lost our Duncan over Germany." There were deep lines of sadness in her drawn face. "He was such a fine young man."

Alex helped her clear the table and carried the plates to the kitchen. They washed the dishes together, and he held her hand under the cold water.

"I'm sorry about your son. I hope you realize, I understand irreplaceable losses in one's life. Lady Margaret, there were many; sometimes I see them all."

During coffee, the group admired an original lithograph of Banbury Cross above an ornately carved chest.

Sheila continued gaily. "We've finally won this European war after six years. It's about time, wouldn't you agree? You're rather young for that rank, aren't you, Colonel Dunham?"

"Please, Sheila, it's Alex, and my rank is Lieutenant Colonel. I've been fortunate because I began service in the Airborne at basement level and happened to have a run of good luck."

"Where are you from in the States, Colonel . . . Alex?"

"Chicago. I've been away several years. Sometimes I wonder if there have been changes. Of course, change has a far different meaning in England. The sketch of Banbury Cross and your history here in the Cotswold country are obvious reminders."

"Oh, yes, Chicago, that's where those dreadful gangsters are, Capone, mobsters, machine guns, and all that rot."

Alex smiled. "Well, Sheila, machine guns have been rather useful these days, you know."

"Quite so." She had a bright curiosity about the enormous distances in America, its huge cities, mountains, and deserts, and the vastness of the plains.

"We are early risers. Why don't you two defenders of the empire discuss the glorious victory? Give our best regards to your mother and father, Alex. We've been close friends and colleagues, and Margaret and dear Lucky have corresponded over the years. After the war we plan to have Brian speak at the College of Surgeons down in London. Good night all."

Alex had always been a "sloucher," hands behind his head, legs crossed. He had probably drunk too much. His face was flushed; he was relaxed, at ease for the first time in months. He thought the kidney pie, brussels sprouts, coffee, and sherry had been a luxurious meal. As he listened to and watched Sheila, it was difficult to believe he was in friendly surroundings. Her tone softened as she spoke of the death of her brother two years previously, graduation from the Priory, service in the Wrens, and the various personalities she served at the Admiralty.

"You know, I can never sort out the American ribbons. Your army and navy ones are quite different." She moved closer, touching his jacket.

"European theater with four battle stars, Bronze Star, Silver Star, Mediterranean theater one battle star, and the one above the others?"

"Not really much, Lieutenant Sheila Converse-Jones. I happened to be there. It belongs to my men."

Alex sat up slowly, looking into the whiteness of the fireplace. The young paratrooper had been hit by a phosphorous bomb and was being incinerated. His face melted like wax as he screamed. Alex saw only a flash of his red-and-blue insignia, then shot him. He stood abruptly, spilling some wine as he moved away from the heat of the fireplace. He wondered how he could manage at home—old places, friends—and cope with Steffi. *Please, God, make it all go away.*

"It's been a charming evening. This is my first visit to a home in many months. Sheila, I can sleep here on the sofa."

"Mother has made up Duncan's room for you. It's upstairs, then go left; it's the one with the squeaky door."

Alex entered a room not unlike his at home. More books, a desk with mementos, and a framed picture of a Royal Air Force crew standing in dress uniform before a bomber. Flight Lieutenant Duncan Converse-Jones stood in the center of the eight men. Alex looked at their faces, an earthly life beyond reach. Sitting in the dark, he gazed over a rolling landscape outlined by a full moon. There it was, the same moon over the farm in Galena, Sicily, and Holland. It was the bomber's moon in Chipping Camden. *Oh, God,* he thought, *I hope you took them quickly, one flash, not falling forty thousand feet with time to think and fear.*

The door slowly opened and he recognized Sheila in a white turtleneck sweater, pants, and her naval jacket.

"Do come with me, Alex; it won't be long." Her light, carefree voice was low and had a cheerless quality.

They drove several miles through the countryside on a one-way road, then turned toward a small village church surrounded by trees silhouetted against the night sky.

"Alex, it's not quite light enough. We shall find an altar candle. Well, here we are. Do you have a match or lighter?"

"Yes, a reliable old Zippo given to me by some of my officers." He flipped back the lid, which made a clicking, metallic sound, then struck the flint wheel. The flame seemed enormous compared to the size of the lighter.

"Over here, Alex."

He lit the wick of a large white candle. Their faces were illuminated by a pale orange glow.

She held the candle over her head with both hands and moved toward a stained-glass window. It depicted the crucifixion. Her expression was happily serene. "Many of our young men have given themselves and are with Him now."

As they slowly moved, the lambent light spread a warm hue across the stark walls. Only their faces and her hands were visible. Alex felt the rest of his body but seemed to be separated from it by the darkness. He was curious if it would be the same after death.

"You see, we keep our regimental flags here in the transept. There is one from 1918, the present war, and the Union Jack hangs between them. An old tradition." The candle shone on a list of names. There was "Flight Lieutenant Duncan F. P. Converse-Jones, 1919–43."

As the candle flickered low, Alex touched the cold stone. It was a subtle, cruel reality not unlike the death he had seen. But different. It was a civilized finality.

Now they were in subdued light. "Mother will never understand, Alex. He was her love; she lived for him. I've tried to be gay and happy, but she is unable to forget. This war has been frightfully terrible for everyone, especially for us British, such a proud people. What is there left to say to my dear mother?"

Alex searched. "Perhaps your mother believes God has been cruel or suspects there is no God because her prayers have been unanswered. Possibly she has asked too much and feels cheated in this unfair life. She needs time. It must be unbearable loneliness for her. I can't give you a wise answer, Sheila, because I have felt the same loss in different ways. Keep helping in the confusion of her despair."

He took her arm as they walked down the nave. There was the moonlight so lovely, so deadly, so wicked. Somehow he felt wondrously young again, the innocent, believing choir boy learning his psalms:

> The Lord watches over you—
> the Lord is the shade at your right hand;
> the sun will not harm you by day,
> nor the moon by night.

Alex asked himself if he ever believed in these words, or was it the harsh world of reality that had conditioned his thoughts and beliefs?

When he closed the small front door, he put his arm around her and kissed her forehead. She felt a sudden loneliness, a longing for him, then stepped back. It was a composed good-bye.

The next morning, Alex was driven to Liverpool through fog and a fine rain and began the first part of the eighteen-hour flight to New York.

Seven
Return

"M adam has been expecting you, Colonel Dunham. I'm Rivington, sir."

The butler was immaculately dressed in a gray morning coat with a narrow band of white handkerchief in his left breast pocket, stiffly starched pleated shirt, striped trousers, and polished shoes. He was dignified and formal without pomposity. Alex was ushered to a sunroom of the Drakes' Long Island estate that overlooked spacious gardens, a kaleidoscope of rich colors accented by a checkerboard of brick and neatly clipped shrubs.

The question had an appealing British inflection. "Would you care for anything to drink, Colonel? It's terribly close today."

"Thank you, Rivington; lemonade would be fine." He sat on a flower-patterned love seat admiring the well-chosen low glass table set with a fresh arrangement of summer flowers. There were bright draperies and superbly appointed furniture that set

223

off an ecru carpet with a wide shrimp-colored border.

The doors to an elaborately sculpted terrace with white tables and striped umbrellas were open, allowing a fresh ocean breeze to circulate. The lemonade was served on a circular silver tray with a selection of fresh fruit garnished with mint leaves and a variety of cheeses. Alex thought it was an ideal refreshment for a humid mid-June day.

Light footsteps interrupted his preoccupation with the elegant surroundings. Mrs. Antonia Drake was in her late forties and rather tall, with delicate features, fair skin, and dark hair. She wore a flowing, diaphanous pink batiste gown that gave the impression she was gliding, rather than walking.

"Alex Dunham, Colonel Dunham, I am delighted that my Peter's commanding officer rang me up and has come for a short visit. Please sit down. You must have just returned from overseas, and how delightful of you to think of me."

"Yes, Mrs. Drake, transatlantic air travel has become almost routine during the course of the war. New York and London seem closer now, not the seven-day passage that was more civilized and enjoyable."

"For years Peter's father and I made a glorious Cunarder every summer. You know he left us before Peter went overseas. It was a shock, but things do change, don't they?"

She had been drinking and was struggling with each thought, slurred word, and sentence. There were pauses, some embarrassingly long. He sensed a doll-like vulnerability as she chatted. Rivington appeared with a gin and quinine that she balanced perilously in a cocktail napkin.

Alex sat next to her. "I hope my visit is not intrusive. Your son and I were close friends and spoke of you often. Peter invited me to sail with you on the Sound after the war."

She put down her glass. Lipstick smudged the rim. "I seldom saw him during prep school and college years. Then we became closer after he volunteered. I visited several times at Fort Benning when he first served with you, and here are his letters. You are mentioned in many of them." She reached for a packet of tattered V-mail. "He was my dearest boy."

"Mrs. Drake, you mustn't. He was one of our finest officers; never complained. I remember his courage in battle."

"I wanted him to come home to me, Colonel. My life is, you know, perfectly ghastly without him."

She took Alex's hand and he put his arm around her waist to steady her. There were streaks of tears mixed with mascara running down her cheeks. He was transfixed by her gaze.

"Before you leave, Alex Dunham, please, once, kiss me good-bye, kiss me good-bye the way my Peter did."

Alex felt her slim, fragile body, the deep sigh, and held her, firmly kissing her cheek. He tasted her tears, the gin on her lips.

"God knows and keeps your dear son, Mrs. Drake," he whispered softly.

As Alex turned to leave, he bumped the coffee table and the red flowers on the table reeled before him. The nurses had thrown blankets over his naked blood-splattered body with blotches of blue; there was his boyish, sallow face, lids forever closed.

Rivington held the door. "Sir, Madam deeply appreciates that you came. If I may, do write now and then. How can she carry on without him? There's no family with Mr. Peter gone."

"Rely on me, Mr. Rivington. I shall never forget her son, a brave officer. She must keep occupied, enjoy her friends, and perhaps soon her loss will become more bearable."

He looked squarely at the butler, shook his hand, and left in a waiting taxi.

First Avenue was bustling with traffic, the repeated sounds of shifting gears, reeking exhaust of buses, and bumping, shoving crowds returning from work. Connie's young sister, Gabriella, gave him directions to the delicatessen. It was in the middle of the block, on the east side of the street toward the river, not far from Beekman Hill. *Look for baskets of fresh fruit displayed on the sidewalk.* Her accented voice had said, "Sa facile trovare."

He stood opposite the storefront with a large sign: "Cunicello's Italian Deli." He wondered how often his right-hand man had opened the store in the morning before going to school, arranged the boxes, and then made afternoon bicycle deliveries to special customers. Alex thought he probably swept the wooden floors each evening and set out the trash after hosing down the sidewalk. He smelled the citrus aroma of a variety of fruits, then walked through a screen door with a small brass bell that announced each customer. A myriad of trays with fresh meat, sausages, and cheeses were neatly arranged over blocks of ice behind large glass cases. Several ceiling fans with strings of fly paper spun in the summer heat.

"Hey ya, Dunham, *buon giorno*, come on over here, eh?" The senior Cunicello sat in a back corner at a small round table with a red-checkered cloth. "Gaby, pour some Asti for both of us. Sit down here with me. Tell me how youz two won this *maledizione* war. The two boys and Gaby take care of the customers. Look at 'em all, nice business, eh? Came to the city when I was a kid, and look what working hard done for my family."

"Mr. Cunicello, I'm honored to meet you. Gaby's instructions were right on the mark. You've got a first-class store here; Connie told me about the family many times. He was reliable, the very best of my men." Alex lifted his cold glass to his host. There was a friendly ringing sound when they met.

"Gabriella *innamorata,* come here and meet Alberto's friend."

She wore a black dress and white apron. Alex looked at her black hair tied in a soft knot, dark eyes, and full youthful face. She greeted him with a warm smile. He judged she was a happy young woman who managed the store with her father's unqualified approval.

"Colonel Dunham, please follow me." Gabriella led him to an adjoining room. "I want you to see our picture. Our Connie is with all of us each day. He knows we're laughing, happy, and working hard."

Alex looked at a sepia, color-tinted, oversize picture of Sergeant Alberto Cunicello. He wore his Airborne overseas cap, metal regimental badges of the 504 on each epaulet, and his infectious smile made Alex think he was ready to speak. At the bottom of the frame he saw miniature crossed American and

Italian flags and several burning candles.

"Gaby," Alex said, "your brother was with me from the start until our last mission. He was loyal, never faltered in his duty, and I shall remember his bravery and cheerful sense of humor. The night we dropped in Sicily a few years ago, he had good reason to ask me exactly where we were and thought we could have had a good meal with your relatives in Naples. It was a welcome laugh all of us needed at that time. Believe me, he had a knack for speaking to stubborn Sicilians."

Neither realized Alberto's father stood behind them. "Now there's my son, Colonel Dunham; he's a great man. He's always my real nice boy, does what I say, fights for his country, and lighting candles each morning tells us he's here with us, even right now, smiling just like in the picture."

Alex raised the Venetian goblet, finishing the Asti. Signor Cunicello and Gaby kissed his cheeks. There was the lingering fragrance of fresh fruit, the scent of candles, and sweet taste of wine when he left. The small bell on the door rang again as he adjusted his overseas cap and stepped into the afternoon sun.

Alex was satisfied when the after-battle report on the Draas River crossing had been officially approved by the Airborne chief of staff at the Pentagon. The regiment had been dropped precisely on three separate landing zones in full moonlight. The next morning, his battalion was selected to make the river crossing because of its battle-worthiness in Sicily and Anzio. He had been uncompromisingly honest that casualties were excessive, equipment was unacceptable, the mission been hastily organized, and, finally, Airborne units should be engaged in combat no longer than forty-eight hours.

He felt relieved to be standing in the paddock near the stables of retired cavalry Colonel Walter Harris. Alex rested his dusty boot on a wooden fence, enjoying the morning freshness in Virginia hunt country. The stable hands told him Mrs. Harris was visiting in Washington and the Colonel would return shortly from cross-country eventing. He felt Jake's ring in his pocket and fingered its smooth and rough surfaces.

"Finally, I have the questionable honor of meeting the Airborne battalion commander who dodged enough bullets so that my son was killed." The Colonel was outfitted informally for trial runs and rode a large gelding. His horse was black, with four white stockings and a handsome blaze. He was lathered, breathing heavily, as Alex reached for his muzzle.

"Goddammit, keep away from him, whatever your name is." The Colonel pulled his horse's reins.

"Colonel, I'm Dunham of the 504, tried to ring you up this morning, but there was no answer. I took a bus out from Washington to Middleburg."

"Well now, isn't that kind of the Lieutenant Colonel," with unmistakable emphasis on "Lieutenant." "And exactly what do you think your little ass-kissing trip will accomplish?"

"Sir, your son, Jake, was my assistant battalion commander—"

"Dunham, stop the horse crap; you came out here to see what I could do for you. You must know I have friends in Washington. Jake was a West Point graduate and should have commanded your battalion in Holland. If he had, there wouldn't have been the heavy losses and near-catastrophe. He would have been out in front of his men, not sitting on his butt in some headquarters the way you probably were. Where did the Airborne find a civilian like you?" He struck a boot with his riding crop.

A desultory stare before he spoke. "Sir, as I mentioned, Jake was my close friend from our days at Fort Benning and we were together through all of our training and wartime operations. I have come to give you and—"

"Junior, you can't give me anything; my son is dead. He had a great future, killed in a ridiculous mission that you led."

Alex reached in his pocket. "Sir, this is for you and Mrs. Harris. I thank you for your time." He turned and had walked several hundred yards down the long, grassed driveway when be heard hoofbeats.

"Now just a minute, Dunham; where did this ring come from?" the Colonel asked.

Alex walked up to the car he had borrowed from a garage mechanic in Middleburg.

"As one soldier to another, how did you come to have my son's West Point ring?" The Colonel's tone had become imploring.

Alex felt the father's masked grief, the despair of his loss, experienced his angry sorrow.

Harris dismounted, stepping up behind Alex. There was only the jangling sound of his horse's bridle and bit.

Alex turned and faced the older man. "Colonel Harris, Jake and I were in the lead boat. The river was wide. Enemy fire was intense. Less than fifty yards to the shoreline. Jake was hit by a mortar fragment. He died almost instantly. Nothing to do for him. After we took the bridge, I found him with my other men at the field hospital near the river. I took the ring for you and his mother." Alex paused. "There's no more to say. Sir, you would have been proud of his conduct and deportment under fire."

The gauge of the 1939 Dodge read empty when he returned it to the mechanic. Alex gave him two dollars.

The three-day sit-up journey by train to Los Angeles was delayed and Alex was annoyed, weary. Visiting his old home was wrenching. He had no idea where his mother might be and was unconcerned. It was a relief to check into an old hotel along the beach, where he rested, swam, and walked. He needed to be alone. The following day he had an appointment with Charles J. Naughton, the president of a West Coast hotel chain. His secretary said he could see the Colonel before a business luncheon.

After identifying himself at the reception desk in the art-deco lobby, Alex was accompanied by "C.J.'s" secretary to his elaborate office. She was a fair-complected brunette whose voice and refined manner reflected tactful efficiency.

"It's been dreadfully long since I've been home, and I should imagine London is in a terrible state, Colonel Dunham. You have made a tiring journey for a brief visit with my employer."

"Miss," Alex looked at her desk, "Raleigh, isn't it? You probably know his son, Daniel, who was one of my Airborne officers. We went through the war together, including our last mission on the Draas River in Holland. I wanted to speak with his father about Lieutenant Naughton."

Madeline Raleigh switched on the intercom. "Colonel Alex Dunham to see you, Mr. Naughton."

Alex sat on a low, luxurious leather couch in front of C.J.'s desk. The successful hotelier could always look down on his clients or business associates. Two eight-foot mounted fans in each far corner of the office provided relief from the sultry California heat.

"Madeline." C.J. flicked the ash from his cigar. "Stay on and take notes if there are any calls. Well, Dunham, you were my son's commanding officer. You have made a long trip. Oh, yes, Madeline, get Rupert in ten minutes. I need an architectural consultant for the 'Navajo'—you know, the new one in San Francisco. The ballroom and lobby don't have an authentic western decor."

Alex listened while C.J. drummed a pencil. "Yes, young Dan was quite a kid, always looking for adventure, something different, you know, a thrill-seeker. Used to like the parachute rides down at, where was that damn place anyway, Madeline?"

Madeline reminded him, "Near your Long Beach Terrace Hotel, Mr. Naughton."

"Madeline, get Andrews for me, after I speak with Rupert. It's the advertising for the lodge under construction in Denver. It's got to be ready for the ski season. The sports crowd has to love it."

Then C.J. gave Alex a harried look. "You say you knew my boy; how come you're here then? Anything you want, need money, best restaurant in town, a girl for the night, whatever it is, name it, soldier."

Alex glanced at the office walls, covered with an array of autographed pictures including celebrities, politicians, and important friends in the business world. He turned to C.J., who was short and comically small for his large desk and chair. "Your son, as you recall, Mr. Naughton—"

"Madeline, don't forget the luncheon appointment at twelve-thirty. What was it? Yes, Dunham."

Alex continued, "Your son was in my Airborne battalion in Sicily, Italy, and Holland. He was a courageous officer, good leader, and his ingenuity would have pleased you."

"It probably would have, Dunham, but he made his choice."

Alex looked at the Oriental rug. It had mixed shades of red. He felt the fans blowing wetness on his face and neck. Pink spray. Lieutenant Naughton and his twenty men suddenly disappeared in a vapor of blood and dirty water. It happened about ten feet away.

C.J. inhaled deeply on his cigar, blowing a cloud of bluish smoke toward Alex. "Well, Colonel, I guess that's it, pal. He has a younger brother, full of pee and vinegar, who can take over from me when the time comes. Thanks for showing up. Madeline, what about my other afternoon appointments? You know how important they are."

Alex walked across the office, turned, and faced C.J. "By the way, sir, I'll send you a picture of Danny being decorated by our division commander. It's a knockout—for real, you know—better than anything here in your gallery. Good-bye, Mr. Naughton."

Madeline and Alex strolled through the office lobby. "Colonel, I have some time now. Are you free for lunch?"

They sat in a corner of a formal dining room.

"Daniel and I had plans to marry when he came home." Madeline's loneliness. "A family and home would have been divine. It was a childhood dream. He must have been a good officer, smart, clever, and unusual athleticism. He thrived in the outdoors. Completely different from his father. Summertime, we sailed along the coast of the Baja peninsula, and we skied in the high Sierras during winter holidays. It was all quite lovely, Colonel."

Alex leaned back in his velvet-covered chair. "Miss Raleigh, he was one of the first team, a name we gave our battalion officers. Danny was a fine man."

Madeline pulled back her chair. "Do keep yourself busy for a while, Colonel Dunham. May I drive you over to San Bernadino after work? It's easier than taking the bus; then we can chat more before you leave."

Alex threw his duffel on the overhead luggage rack and tilted his seat back. He was disgusted, alone and disillusioned, and hungry. Later, a brassy-voiced vendor came through the coach and Alex ordered a ham sandwich with mustard, then finished a warm soda. He folded his summer uniform jacket across his lap and fell asleep. It was several hours later when he was awakened by a sensation of pins and needles in his toes, squeezed by the foot rest.

The coach lights were dimmed, and as he turned he saw a young woman with a small suitcase between her feet standing at the end of the aisle opposite his seat. He stretched, yawned, then noticed she wore a forest green skirt, jacket, and dress cap with a short visor. She was a Marine Lieutenant.

Alex pushed himself up from his seat, straightened his tie. "Good evening, Lieutenant. Please take my seat; the train is packed tonight. I should move about a little. Stiff from sitting, need to limber up."

She stepped toward Alex. "Thank you, sir. I appreciate your kindness, especially since I wasn't able to get a reservation."

He picked up her bag and put it on the overhead rack next to his. As she took off her cap, he looked down on her auburn hair neatly rolled above the collar. Brown eyes glanced at him with amazement: a senior officer had relinquished his seat.

"I'm Lieutenant Erin Kelly and am stationed near Los Angeles. I work for General Sheldon Tennant, Air Wing Five."

Alex smiled. "I knew we had a Women's Marine Corps, although I've never had the occasion to meet one of you. I'm Lieutenant Colonel Alex Dunham, 504 Airborne. Get some sleep and rest. Perhaps in the morning we can have breakfast."

They shook hands. She had a firm, friendly grip.

Alex walked back to the observation car, switched on a light, and read some current magazines with familiar covers he hadn't seen for several years. He was awakened by the porter who bumped his feet with a small broom and silent butler. It was almost daylight and Erin Kelly sat opposite him.

Alex had a quizzical look. "Do I snore, Lieutenant? Rank has its privilege, you know. If I do, no one has had the nerve to tell me."

She scanned his three rows of ribbons. "Have you had a good war, Colonel?" It was a common question in the military.

Alex sat up straighter, no longer smiled, and hesitated. "If you want an honest answer, come over and sit next to me. I practically have to telegraph my conversation from here. Eighteen months of routine training, sixty jumps, fortunately without injury, then two years of combat in Sicily, Italy, and Holland. It's good to be home on leave."

"Those three rows of ribbons tell a different story. You're too modest, Colonel."

"Not really, Kelly; it was a job to be done. It's over now. And yourself, you're a well-turned-out Marine; tell me more, if you wish."

The "a" was broad when she said "Milwaukee"; it was an educated, midwestern, probably Catholic, accent. "I enlisted after my fiancé, Jim, was wounded on Guadalcanal. He was with the First Marine Division and fought in several more of the island campaigns. We wrote often and he told me what he could. It seems long ago. Many changes in those years. You know, the small-town college football hero, thousands like him, who wanted to serve."

Alex nodded. "I know those types. They stand out, take chances, and are leaders."

"The routine and discipline of the Corps were really quite easy for me, Colonel. You probably wouldn't guess that I was a novitiate but decided to leave. I'm too worldly and believe God wanted me to follow a different path. I didn't have the calling. After my confirmation, I was saintly and would fabricate sins, then the following week confess I had told a lie."

Alex was delighted by her refreshing Irishness.

Kelly continued to speak of her fiancé. "In Jim's latest letters, I could sense he had too much time to think about his life. The combat, losses, and death took their toll. He was wounded badly again, recuperated at the naval hospital down in Diego, where I could visit almost every evening and on weekends. He changed, you know. The strict indoctrination, 'obey any and every order,' was part of him at first, yet he knew that killing, even in war, was a mortal sin. His conscience dictated there was no absolution for what he thought were crimes committed in the name of duty. Gradually he began to believe heaven was beyond his reach. I have tried to understand what he suffered, but how could anyone know, unless he went through war day by day, month after month? The First Marines are the best. Only a few of his friends are left. He rationalized that killing, although in battle, was a deliberate and calculated crime, too much for him to bear."

Alex stood, looking at her buffed brown shoes. They were like the Bryn Mawr walkers that he had joked about at college. *What can I say to her?* he wondered. *At least he's alive; both are young and can find a future someday.* "Lieutenant, I have a sense of Jim's suffering. You see, I've been through it myself. One never really forgets." He held her hands, her dark eyes glistening. "All right now, Kelly, it's another day. Let's get some breakfast and show me that Marine pride."

Later in the morning, the train made an unscheduled stop. Alex stood in the vestibule between cars, looking toward the station platform as the train began to move again. He saw Lieutenant Erin Kelly standing next to a flag-draped coffin, head bowed, gloved hands at her sides.

"You know, Captain, Lieutenant, whatever you are, think of it." The stranger's voice had a malicious timbre. "I pay good money for my ticket to ride this train and be on time for work, but they stop to cater to you people in the service. All the special treatment should end, and now. Be like the rest of us and come back to the real world."

Alex moved toward the man dressed in an oyster white linen suit with panama hat and put a hand over his mouth, then twisted his nose until blood ran down his white shirt and silk tie. He slowly slid to the floor of the moving train, whimpering and sputtering red saliva into the hat that had fallen over his face.

Countless times Stephanie had imagined being with Alex again and if it would ever happen. She had wondered if reality was censored letters, hope, fear, a dreaded telegram, or the possibility of a future together. Sometimes she thought her life might be a shadow of past happiness.

After Alex saw her through the station glass doors, crisscrossed with wire mesh, they walked to each other slowly at first, then with quickening steps. Nothing was said. He folded his arms around her, his face in her hair as she quietly wept. Between muffled sobs she repeated his name as if she were learning, saying it for the first time. They moved toward a station bench, arms about one another.

He felt her wet cheek on his face. "Steffi, it's been forever. Now, at last, I thought I would—"

"God brought you home to me. Alex, you're my life; please never leave me again."

They stared at each other in disbelief and the happiness neither had known for a seemingly endless time. He wiped her face. They smiled and laughed as if they knew God had cheated death for them.

"How many times, how many ways, can I say and show my love for you, Steffi?"

"Be mine, Alex; please keep holding me. Kiss me again. You are in my heart and mind; we are part of one another."

She thought his tanned face looked older, dark circles gave his green eyes a melancholy quality, and the etched furrows at the corners of his lids were from bright sun, wind, and the strain of battle. They slowly crossed the station's arched foyer, stopping now and then to embrace.

Steffi became more talkative. "Alex, it's finally over, and from now on, we shall treasure each day."

He dropped his duffel bag. "Please, Stephanie, please take me home. Home with you, no noise, no fear of death."

"No more death, Alex."

"Yes, help me understand why I survived. The others . . . , how can you want me, a living reminder?" His gaze was penetrating, cold, one she had never seen. But she hadn't been siphoned through the debris of the Draas River. She kissed his eyes, his dry mouth.

Their lips were still touching when she whispered, "We'll go now; the calmness you need is waiting. Tranquillity will be our refuge."

He walked into her studio on the top floor of an apartment building overlooking the lake. A large window, extending into a skylight, added a cheerful brightness to the entire living area. Her easel sat by the window. There was a bedroom with a large, comfortable-looking pencil post bed, modest bath and kitchen, a small living room, and a dining area. He was instantly drawn to its warmth and intimacy.

She removed his tie. "Now, give me your coat."

He took her hand and led her to the bedroom. They lay down, clinging, fearful they might be separated again. They kissed, their eyes fixed, lingering, knowing time had deepened their love. She caressed his face and hair; they dared not let go. As afternoon became early evening, they fell asleep, her head on his chest. Later she was awakened by his deep breathing, interrupted by fitful movements, and felt the closeness of his body. She lightly touched his face and neck. He stirred, aroused by her presence. Her warm tears wet his face when she kissed him fervently.

"God," she quietly beseeched, "guide us with your wisdom, comfort us with your compassion, and protect us with your love. I thank you with all of my heart for bringing Alex home."

"Steffi, now I know God really does answer prayers." He closed his eyes, wondering about the prayers of families who had lost their men. Alex hoped God would guide, comfort, and protect them in their grief.

"Alex, it's time for a warm shower before dinner." Steffi was smiling, excited. "I bought a new spray nozzle at Fields and had the shower retiled last spring. It's large enough for both of us." They threw off their clothes and dashed for the bathroom.

"Steffi, I haven't had a shower like this for three years."

They washed each other in a cascade of water. There were fine lines at the edges of her eyes, whose blueness was deeper, and faint dimples enhanced the charm of her smile. A high forehead was marked by a faint wrinkle between her eyebrows, which had darkened with her hair. Her parted lips showed the striking whiteness of her teeth.

Alex stepped back. "Let me look at you. I can see the outline of your bathing suit." His finger made a line in the soap over her back and between her thighs as she pulled him closer.

"I hope you like my tan. It's for you, Alex." He felt the slippery texture of her bronzed skin.

"Alex, let me wash your hair."

He put his arms around her waist while she reached for a milky bar of soap and lathered his closely cropped hair. With each motion her breasts touched his chest. He gripped, then squeezed the porcelain faucets. The aching need, longing. "Now it's your turn, Steffi." When he held her head under the warm water, she closed her eyes as he mounded soap suds.

He blew puffs of soap off her face and neck and kissed her nipples, following the curvature of her neck where he felt rapidly pulsating arteries against his cheek. Warm, soapy water ran down their faces when they kissed. At first it was tender, then quickly became a frantic embrace. She clutched his shoulders and chest and pulled his hair, moving his head from side to side in splashing water. She bit his lips and neck.

"Alex, keep doing"—her words sprayed streams of water in his face—"keep doing it. Don't ever stop, I have missed, love you so, yes, hard, that way, deep inside me, keep moving, now all of you."

She held his neck and he lifted her up and pushed between her smooth tanned legs, which were wrapped around his hips. Their movements became more chaotically rhythmic, as they slid back and forth against the tile wall.

He pulled her ear and hair into his mouth, then leaned back. "It's been as close to eternity as I can imagine, missing, wanting you."

They gradually relaxed, then sank to their knees, sitting with their arms and legs around one another, kissing and licking each other's lips. They stared, entranced.

Both dried off with large terry towels and then relaxed on her bed.

"Never leave me, Alex." She kissed his hand, then pulled his fingers in her mouth.

He lay on top of her. "Never, I'll never leave again. I thought about it countless times. If I were killed, you would be with me." They held, pressed against one another, and yielded to deep sleep.

"Stephanie Pfeiffer, you're so bloody organized." "Bloody" didn't seem natural but was a familiar expression, mimicking his British Airborne friends. "I can't believe it. Salad, baked potatoes with margarine, sour cream, and chives. You must have saved food stamps at least a month for this steak. I have promoted you to battalion cook, because every part of your meal is ready and hot at the same time. The army fed us well, but it's hard to remember when I've had a dinner like this. You know every possible version of Spam was the fanciest dish we had." He had set the table, remembering that knife edges faced the plate, salad dish left, goblet right. The warm flicker of two candles brightened the room, and a small flower arrangement decorated the table.

Steffi briefly bowed her head and reached for his hand. "Thank you, Lord, for this day, and we ask your blessing for this food and our first meal together. Amen."

He walked around the small table and kissed the back of her head.

"Homecoming surprise, Alex. A split of champagne. Compliments of the house."

They touched glasses.

"Happy days are here, Steffi, happy days, sweetheart."

They watched the winding lanes of traffic and city lights reflected off the surface of the lake calmed by the summer evening. He had his arm around her hips, then slowly ran his hand over brown, perfectly shaped thighs.

"I looked at your picture whenever we weren't in combat, and you are more beautiful than I remember." His thoughts were muddled, moving across time and distance. It wasn't the champagne; it was being alone with her. The darkness was the peace of home, not the deep blackness of Anzio. No patrols out tonight. Alex felt uneasy. Where was his BAR? Where was the enemy tonight? Where were his men? He felt the surge of expectation, the excitement of battle. *Harris, Drake, Naughton, are your men hooked up? Thank God we're through the flak, three minutes to the drop zone; wait, now wait. Check the terrain, Dunham. It's your responsibility; don't fuck up. Yes, now I see the canals through the dim light, the small woods to the right. Green light's on; go, go.* He wondered if he missed the old thrill, or perhaps it had all been a furious, vivid dream.

Later, he carried her through the early evening darkness and lowered her on their bed. She held her arms over her head as he pulled off her blouse and skirt. They sat together the next morning, leisurely finishing coffee.

"Steffi, you can guess this is not my usual Airborne routine, sleeping late with a charming young lady." He put his arm around her. There was the magnetic closeness, the sensitive questioning.

"Over the weeks and months I wondered, imagined what you did, because the censors enjoyed removing some of the most interesting parts of your letters. Steffi, tell me about your everyday life, your work, and did you find time to sketch and paint?"

"My life was always with you, Alex, yet I realized that busying myself was the answer to loneliness. Yes, my watercolors improved and I had a small showing in a gallery near the Art Institute. Can you believe that some collectors actually bought several of my paintings? After you left, I worked at St. Mark's helping the deacons and taught Sunday school. The children were playful, trusting, and I pretended they were ours."

Her enthusiasm intrigued him. "Please tell me more."

"After you left, Eileen O'Keefe, the mayor's wife, and our mothers organized the Servicemen's Centers in the Loop and North Side. Thousands of soldiers and sailors came to these clubs for meals, movies, dances, and a place to sleep. At first, I felt awkward socializing, but friendships, listening to their problems and stories, made it clear how families and wives suffered,

waiting for their men to return. I knew many would not be fortunate, but we made them feel at home. Some days I visited hospitals with the Red Cross and wrote letters for the men who had
been wounded. The time passed quickly in some ways, but not
when I worried about you. God has been good to us, Alex; we're
together again."

In the afternoon, they ran along the edge of the lake, splashing water mixed with small bursts of sand until they reached
their favorite fountain. The dolphins hadn't changed. Steffi sat
next to him on the edge of the pool as they rinsed their feet. He
wet her thighs with cold water. She pulled his hands tightly
between her legs. The afternoon sun was bright and hot on their
faces. An onshore breeze recalled past summers when they sat
together talking, laughing. At that time, only the present
seemed important. He had given her the gardenia here and wondered if she had the same poignant memories.

For the moment they were alone, although the beach was
usually teeming with bathers at this time of year. Steffi reached
for him. "Alex, I still have your gardenia to remind me of that
special day when we knew we were in love."

"Our separation has been long and difficult, Steffi, and it's
amazing we were thinking of the same day, the same flower, the
same memory."

They wandered lazily to the partially shaded pool, where
there was relief from sun and humidity.

Alex picked up a small stick and began drawing in the sand.
She saw lines protruding from squares, an uneven rectangle
with a series of Xs and circles around a large Y.

"Alex, with all of your other talents, you could be one of the
world's greatest contemporary artists. Your sand drawings look
like sophisticated cubism to me."

He laughed. "I could never match those delightful sketches
in your letters. I've saved all of them."

Then she showered him with cold water. "You're in for it
now, Little Red Rover; take that and that." He let her spray
him unmercifully, walking through sheets of water holding

onto her, kissing her dripping face. They cavorted in reckless circles around the dolphins.

Alex wiped her face. "It's getting late, Steff; we're doing the town tonight. Time to move out, soldier."

They ran home. He stayed several yards behind watching her long legs, contracting thigh muscles, stretched arms, and breasts skimming under her wet shirt. She turned. "Come on, slowpoke, let's sprint together."

He gave her shoulder a friendly bump. "You may be good, champ, but I'll be out of the shower before you get home."

She dangled her keys. "Sorry, Alex; you can't get in without me."

Steffi knotted and straightened his khaki tie. "I could have been your driver, valet, and cook. Now it's my chance. What should I wear tonight?" She stood in front of him posing as a sensuous model, with a tempting bare leg.

"Your blue linen suit would be perfect for the Camelia House, but you look wonderful in anything." He took her hands. They knelt on the edge of the bed, holding one another.

"I love you, Alex. I want you now."

"We'll have all night, Miss Pfeiffer; now let's get these troops out of the hot sun."

They were greeted by the maître d'. "Madam, it's a great pleasure having both of you here this evening after several years. Is it Colonel or Lieutenant Colonel Dunham?"

"Juan, it's the way it used to be when we were younger, always Alex for you."

He seated them at a secluded table and removed a bottle of Chardonnay from a dripping ice bucket next to their table. Juan passed the cork by his nose with a practiced gesture. "Colonel, I knew you would return someday. Nineteen thirty-four was a good year. Once again, welcome home. May you enjoy celebrating this evening together."

She sipped, enjoying her wine. "Alex, we can order later. Listen to the romantic music; let's dance now. We've waited years; it will be as if we were in another world."

They were strikingly handsome, moving among the small

dinner crowd, occasionally murmuring a word or two as they danced slowly among other couples.

"There were many nights I worried about you, Alex, looked at the moon, wondering, waiting, praying. At times I thought we would never have each other again." She softly touched his lips.

"You feel so wonderful when you're close to me." He stroked the back of her neck, then took her arm and led her to their table. Both heard a friendly, resonant voice greet them.

"General Gibson, sir, it is a pleasure to see you and Mrs. Gibson again," Alex said with formality. "May I present my fiancée, Stephanie Pfeiffer?"

"It's a pleasant surprise to see both of you," General Gibson replied. "We have known your parents over the years, and I have followed your tour of duty overseas. All of us are also proud of Miss Pfeiffer for her commendable work with the Red Cross, organizing the Servicemen's Centers and volunteer work in our hospitals. You've been a busy young lady."

Gibson introduced the couple to several other guests and then turned to Alex. "I would gather you have just returned from Europe and you're both celebrating the occasion. Stephanie, you have good reason to celebrate; your fiancé has been through some of the most difficult combat of the war. Our Airborne forces have been magnificent. Alex, how long have you been home?"

"Sir, ten days ago I reported to the Pentagon and your friend General William Bedford and submitted some of our regimental battle reports."

Steffi stepped away and looked beyond Alex. The room, elegantly appointed with burgundy drapes and carpet, suddenly became a microcosm of distorted colors to her, blended with dissonant conversation and music.

"We have organized the eighth war bond rally in Sherman Park on Saturday night." Gibson continued. "There will be men who have returned from the Pacific; however, I want you to speak about parachute operations in Europe, but not at great length. Agreed?"

"General, I would be pleased to attend and say a few words if you wish," Alex answered as if it had been a command.

The General asked the waiter for a piece of paper and pencil. "Give me your telephone number and my adjutant, Major Mike Johnson, will give you the details. We begin at six with fireworks, bands, lots of spirit. The theme is bring the war to a quick end. We need a decorated officer, a man with your record, to generate enthusiam."

Alex stepped forward and shook the General's hand. "Yes, sir, I'll do my best."

Steffi chatted abstractedly with other guests. "It's been a pleasure for Alex and me to meet all of you. Good evening, General and Mrs. Gibson."

Steffi was quiet and pushed away Alex's hand as they walked back to their table. "I don't become upset often, Alex, but where have you been for the last week? I expected you to come home to me as soon as you returned to the States. Sometimes I really don't understand you."

Alex paused. "Look at me, Steffi. I had to visit the families of the men who were closest to me. They weren't as fortunate. It's difficult to forget how they died. It was in a world apart from tonight's luxury."

She left the table. He sat alone among the mirthful crowd waiting. . . . He was uncertain if she could imagine his dilemma. When she returned, he saw a thin film of tears. After he kissed her, she held his hand and touched his seal ring, "Facta Non Verba," knowing action was his way.

"I'll try to understand, but you could have telephoned. Alex, sometimes you're selfish, and you ignored me." Her expression gradually changed. There was a fragile smile. "Now let's ask Juan to spoil us with dinner; then we can finish our wine and make plans for tomorrow."

They danced several more times, humming melodies, trying to remember some lyrics from their favorite songs.

"May we go home now?" Steffi asked. "It's bedtime."

That night, they sat cross-legged in bed, faces touching. Steffi's lips moved slowly. "Because we belong to each other, I hope you will trust me with those days still haunting you. Believe me, I know I can help. First you must give me the chance.

I imagine part of your anguish comes from concealing your secrets, an unwillingness to expose your fears. Bring them out in the daylight for me to share."

He thought she was more compelling than he remembered. "Yes, Stephanie, I promise. I know I must, but time, time...At first I revelled in the images, sounds, smell, and challenge of battle, because we were winning without many casualties. But it all began to change with the deaths of most of my men. The responsibility, the guilt. I'm no longer certain, no longer positive, that I chose the correct course several years ago. If this is true, then who am I? Should I have listened to D3? Tell me, Stephanie, who am I? The civilized, educated man you once knew or a trained killer, who celebrates savagery? Deep inside, do I really love war, the rage and excitement it brings me?"

"Alex, I've known you all these years. You followed your conscience, strong beliefs, acted on honorable principles. We love each other; let me help you through this turmoil. I truly believe God made you a good, kind, loving man, but war has changed you. It has deepened your guilt, eroded your beliefs, and you doubt your choices. Now you question the strong sense of gratitude that drove you. Please look at me. We're both exhausted and need rest. Each day we'll talk, and before long, the memories will be less painful." She turned off the light.

Both Steffi and Alex were awakened by the flat, clopping sound of horse hooves under their window. The morning milk was being delivered.

They paused on the steps of the Art Institute the following afternoon. Alex reached dramatically for the railing with a conspiratorial expression. He feigned collapse. "Steffi, you know I'm still a growing boy." With the skill of an accomplished actor he muttered, "Hunger, Hunger, oder ich fall um. If you don't feed me soon, I'll fall down."

They were still laughing, finishing an enormous lunch at the museum's garden café, then pushed back their empty dishes and glasses.

"Now that my little boy's tummy is full," she teased, "let's look for Monet's houseboat on the Seine. Alex, it's in the same place and gallery, and because we both enjoy it, why don't I try to copy it for us someday?"

"Good idea, Steffi. And whenever we wish, we could pretend to be on holiday. Now, let's find the Dufys; I think they're in the next wing.

"After the liberation of Paris," he recalled, "we were sent back to France. Over a spring weekend, when the weather was good, I decided to take several of my officers to Monet's gardens at Giverny. Later we spent the afternoon at Clichy. Perhaps they thought the excursion was an order for cultural and humanitarian rehabilitation."

Steffi visualized a Spartan Alex guiding his rough Airborne friends through a garden of lilies and visiting racetracks. "Did it improve their appreciation of the finer things in life, Alex?"

He laughed. "It gave my men an excuse to get thoroughly drunk in Paris. Of course, their commanding officer had to drive them back to the barracks."

Steffi pointed to a Dufy. "We appreciate Monet and his unique use of color more than Dufy's style. I've always thought there was depth and meaning to Monet's themes. Dufy's paintings of the racetrack crowd and Mediterranean scenes appear to be less sophisticated."

"He's not only a painter," Alex added, "but also designed decorative textiles and ceramics. Really a later impressionist. Am I correct?"

"Yes, Alex, but I think we've seen enough art today. The train takes almost half an hour, and we shouldn't be late for the orchestra's program at Woodland. I have some snacks for now; then we can have 'goodies' when we get home."

They lay on a blanket near the edge of the audience. Alex ran his hand down her back. "Too hot for a brassiere?"

She playfully cuffed his chin. "Don't stop now; I like it when you rub me that way." Both sat up with the crescendo of the opening drumroll. The first movement was energizing; then the music became delightfully melodic and pleasing. The setting was ideal, the orchestra superb, when she leaned toward him with a mischievous look. "I can hear and feel it now, Alex."

"Hear and feel what, Maestro Pfeiffer?"

Woodland was near the lake. The huge tent was impressive, and its ambience was enhanced by large trees and fragrant bushes. Five hundred yards from the podium was the main line of the Northwest Railroad. Steffi barely had finished her cryptic remark when a freight train, with an endless number of cars, began its journey past the orchestra shell, muting the final movement of the Clock symphony. It was a known, expected interruption to the regular members, who thought the location was an unlikely choice for the long-anticipated summer concert season.

"Steffi, this is a new, modern version with a train whistle, the roar of wheels pounding the tracks, and the locomotive's hissing steam. What would Haydn think? It's a good time to leave. We've heard most of the program." They gathered their picnic basket and strolled toward the station. Alex stopped and put his arms around her as they approached a poorly lighted area before reaching the platform. "What an enjoyable day. We're so fortunate. Now I need to hold and kiss you. After all, it's been an age since this morning."

After Alex telephoned, Lucky invited friends for a homecoming dinner. She thought the Rosenthals, Ralph Bagshaw, and his new wife would be friendly, entertaining guests. Alex and Steffi arrived early for a brief reunion. Both hoped it would be without intrusive questions or solutions for his future. Steffi wore a pink silk dress with white piping around the collar and sleeves, and Alex stood next to her in his summer tans.

"Steffi, you're always beautiful, especially tonight. Please stay close; sit next to me during dinner. Mention it to Lucky; she'll understand."

When Colleen opened the door, she rolled down her sleeves, then gave Alex a hug. "It's good, so good to see you." She wiped away tears. "God has brought my laddie home safe and sound."

"Thank you, Colleen." He kissed her and smiled. "I've missed you, too, your cheerfulness and those spectacular brownies and ice cream."

Lucky was happily talkative, putting her arms around him.

"Alex, my dear man."

He thought she tried to say "son."

"It's delightful to see you home again." Lucky admired his uniform. "You look the same, you handsome devil."

He was reserved. She had no idea. No bombed or leveled buildings. No hunger. No death. "Yes, Lucky, it's pleasant to be here."

Brian Dunham was late from golf and hurried into the living room. "Son, I can't believe it; you're actually walking through the door into your home."

Alex was skeptical about the "walking" and "home," then put his hand on his father's shoulder. "It's good to see you, Dad. It was a long trip."

Steffi stood in the background. Alex reached for her hand, rubbing his thumb over her rings.

"We both made it, Colonel," Ralph Bagshaw greeted Alex facetiously. "The Krauts really had us locked in that morning, but a miss, is a miss, is a miss," Bagshaw punned, then introduced his wife.

The Rosenthals embraced him. "Peace be with you both and no more of this war, already." Tears fogged Teddy's thick glasses. "Alex, I remember your youthful optimism. You have helped right things, yet our relatives and friends in Poland are gone."

"I am dreadfully sorry, Dr. Teddy, but now it's time for justice and reconciliation. After the savagery and horror, we should hope that forgiveness may be possible."

Bagshaw drew Alex and Steffi aside. "A word or two before dinner. This Wednesday the Press Club meets, and would you and Steffi join Marge and me for luncheon? You know we are brothers in arms, so to speak. You rascal, you. You almost broke my back when you jumped on me during the mortar attack. I want you to speak for about thirty minutes. Strictly off the cuff, Colonel."

"We would be delighted," Alex said. "Although you must have General Gibson's permission and follow his ground rules for this type of interview. Obviously, I can't be identified or quoted because I'm still in uniform."

"Absolutely, Alex, strictly off the cuff," Bagshaw reassured him. "We'll expect you at twelve-thirty. Steffi, I never told you when all of us had dinner that night several years ago how this man of yours threw me down and literally covered my derriere during an enemy shelling at a godforsaken railroad crossing in Sicily. He has a good ear for mortar fire."

Steffi put her arm around Alex's waist. "Alex, you haven't begun to tell me anything, have you?"

"Steff, Ralph is like all reporters. Never tells the truth, only makes up good bedtime tales. He's a literary genius, exceptional with exaggerated war stories."

"He's too modest for his own good, Stephanie," Bagshaw said seriously.

As dinner began, Alex thought his father was directing a medical conference. He had forgotten how Brian controlled and dominated conversations. He couldn't restrain his desire to be heard first and last. Alex remembered the same anecdotes told in different ways, political opinions, often extreme, everyone's shortcomings exposed; then there was a final diatribe on lost chances and egregious errors made by the armed forces in Europe.

Alex dropped Steffi's hand, then would reach. What comfort to touch, wrap his fingers in hers, hold her wrist. He would gently push under her fingernails.

Brian Dunham sat at the head of the table. "Well, Alex, tell us all about it. The conquering commander has returned. You must have been in the thick of things."

"As I recall, Dad, most everything was said in my letters. Mr. Bagshaw has a fuller, more comprehensive view of the war. Mine is actually rather narrow, isn't it, Ralph?" Alex looked toward Bagshaw.

"Brian, the broad front strategy was sound, as opposed to the single corridor concept. You know the push through Holland was an unfortunate decision," Bagshaw explained.

Alex looked at the two fish, his old radiant friends swimming in opposite directions. He thought they were silently graceful, still reflecting the same filtered candlelight. Teddy Rosenthal watched Alex reach out, touch . . . searching fingers on cool glass while conversation swirled about him.

"Yes, Dad, our regiment was in Holland, part of the single, full-blooded thrust, as the British described it. As Mr. Bagshaw mentioned, a successful operation and tactical victory, but a strategic failure."

"You wrote something or other about—what was it, Lucky?—the Draas River crossing; tell us more. You were there and are some sort of hero, aren't you?" Brian questioned. "Ralph and General Gibson have given us a few details."

Bagshaw intervened. "Brian, Alex has agreed to speak to the Press Club on Wednesday. Perhaps after the luncheon he could fill in some of the specifics you were asking about. The Chicago Club is an ideal place for these discussions." He looked at Steffi. "By the way, have you and Alex planned a trip to the West?"

Brian interrupted. "Ralph, my son apparently saw it first-hand, not from a reporters' pool."

Alex remained silent, folding his hands after adjusting the cuffs of his shirt.

"By the way, Son, how long have you been back in the States? Was it a long flight? Probably stops in Ireland and New-foundland. My friend Reggie Converse-Jones wrote and said they had a pleasant visit with you. Shame about their son."

"I reported to the Pentagon ten days ago," Alex said. "Final combat evaluations, that sort of thing."

Dr. Dunham held the edge of the table. For the first time, Alex thought the handsome face he remembered was unattrac-tive, accentuated by a deep scowl and set jaws. "Ten days ago. What the devil have you been doing before you called Lucky?"

"Dad, my duties took me elsewhere in the country. For the last several days Steffi and I have had our own private time, things we enjoy, being together. I hope you understand."

Brian's tone was sharp. "Frankly, Alex, I don't believe I do. How could you spend almost three years overseas and not tele-phone your parents or fiancée when you returned? You should have tried to contact us. We deserve to know your reasons as well as an apology, wouldn't you agree?"

Ralph Bagshaw suggested. "Tread lightly, Brian. You are

speaking to an Airborne Colonel, even though he may be your son."

"Airborne Colonel...he should be more considerate of his family. We've given him everything," Brian snapped.

Teddy Rosenthal cleared his throat and moved uneasily in his chair. "Brian, perhaps Alex had specific military duties that preempted his personal wishes."

Alex squeezed Steffi's fingers and tried to force a smile that she thought was more of a grimace. His gaze was unwavering, fixed on his father.

"Again, Son, you owe Lucky, Steffi, and me an apology and explanation."

It had been shouted, explained, taught; it was doctrine. An officer stands to explain, emphasize his position. And then Alex did stand, after folding his napkin and placing it precisely parallel to the Delft dinner and salad plates. He stood erect, no movement, expressionless, lips tightly drawn. His face was gaunt, cheeks slightly sunken, and his voice caustic. He touched the silk of Steffi's dress, the warm, inviting skin of her arms. Or was he standing in the windblown, freezing rain before the raiding party at Anzio, cradling his BAR? The mud sucked at his boots as he finished explaining the plan of attack. Then he jammed the clip in his weapon. It was time to move, strike hard. It would be deadly and exacting.

"I have no apologies for inconsiderate conduct, but there were matters that required my attention before coming home. I have explained them to Steffi. She has tried to understand. I would imagine if she respects my judgment, you would also, without further discussion."

"I thought you had learned something from me." Brian put down his napkin. "You simply don't face the facts; you have never listened, never taken my advice."

"Very well, Dr. Brian." Alex's intonation was forceful. "It was imperative for me to visit the relatives of close friends and officers. I traveled to various parts of the country, which postponed my arrival. Next week, Steffi and I have planned to see the parents of another officer. Your sense of humility should suggest that my delay in returning was like a doctor speaking with the family of a patient who has died." Alex paused. "Thank you and Lucky for taking me into your home, for my education and opportunity to make something of myself. You have said over the years that I have failed to follow your good advice. I have made my decisions, my choices, and went where duty led me. There have been months of combat, most of my men and friends are dead; however, I have no regrets for any unhappiness or disappointment I have caused you now, or in the past. It has occurred to me on many occasions that every day I live is one I don't deserve, a day that my men deserve. Good-bye."

Brian Dunham could see Alex reach for the two sparkling fish, slowly turning them face to face. There was the black band of his multidialed wristwatch. His strong, graceful hands smashed their heads together, shattering the crystal.

Alex turned to the Rosenthals and Bagshaws with composure that belied his seething turmoil. "Good evening, and until Wednesday, Roger. Another time, Rosie and Teddy. One evening we'll have some of your special ravioli again, like the good old days, and Steffi doesn't expect a formal invitation." He drew Stephanie's chair back slowly. "We must leave now; please do come with me."

She looked at him. "Wait for me downstairs, Alex."

He left. Never returned.

Colleen stood at the door; her hands covered her face. "My precious lad, never forget that God loves you. Take Him into your heart, your mind; accept the faith He offers you."

"Good night, my dear Colleen, and thank you," Alex said. "You always have been my good, kind friend."

Steffi moved into Alex's empty chair, closer to Brian Dunham. "You're a doctor and have professed to make people feel better, to help them get well. What have you done to your son tonight? You have tried to destroy him. None of us here can know what suffering he has inflicted or endured. Can you begin to imagine his guilt, his bravery, his anger, his deep sorrow? You have misjudged my *man*." She gave "man" a German inflection. "He is stronger, kinder, and has experienced more in his young life than you can comprehend. You have mocked him as a 'conquering hero.' Alex has always been self-effacing, loving, and has given of himself. I forgive you, but how can I forget your petty, crass behavior? Now you may have lost him. Search your conscience; ask yourself why you have been so frightfully thoughtless and cruel."

Ralph Bagshaw was dumbfounded. "Christ, Brian," he said contemptuously. "Why have you demeaned your son? He put his life on the line over the last three years in situations beyond your puny imagination. I'll never forget Sicily. The stench, the bloated bodies covered with flies, the dead turning purple in summer heat. The inhumane suffering and endless rain, snow in Italy. The river crossing in Holland was just a goddamned shooting gallery for the Germans. He was plain lucky but says, 'Every day I live is one I don't deserve.' Don't forget those words. Actually, Brian, I'm charitable—you're a pretentious buffoon. Lucky, thanks for dinner. By the way, Brian, if we should ever meet again, reconsider what you said to Alex."

Colleen pushed the silver coffee service across an antique table with studied carelessness. The spoons, cups, and saucers rattled and shook furiously. She returned to the kitchen as the dining room door swung back and forth, creating a vacuumlike sound. She sat at a small oilcloth-covered table, hands resting on her knees, staring despondently through the window screen. It was an unusually hot night with little relief, although her face was cooled by an occasional southwest breeze carrying the fetid odor of the stockyards. She clenched her fists.

Teddy broke the uncomfortable silence. "Brian and Lucky, it's been difficult for you both. Try to understand Alex. He is a courageous soldier who chose to fight in the most hazardous situations at crucial times. His kind, gentle nature has another, quite different, aggressive and angry quality. He has suppressed his fear, commanded and led men to their death. His guilt of being spared their pain makes him ask why a benevolent God would not only protect him but also sanction him to kill. The beautiful crystal fish smashed with a sudden, detached coolness, their touch, sight gone...something he treasured, quite remarkable, you know. Brian, you have, unfortunately, provoked his anger, not unlike rage in battle. He struggles for control and understanding, uncertain of the course he has pursued. He will follow the long, often endless path of seeking redemption but must, above all, find an encompassing reason for his life. Give him your unconditional love and help."

Brian Dunham made a concession. "Well, Teddy, you know Lucky and I really do love the boy and I have always tried to understand him. He is intelligent and hardworking but had too many ideas of his own, never listened to my advice. If only he had taken the exemption from military service and become a physician, we wouldn't have this uncomfortable situation tonight. He's always been too idealistic. All of this philosophical nonsense about gratitude, service, and being privileged is ridiculous. He should have kept his nose to the grindstone in medical school over the last three years, rather than proving he's a 'hotshot' paratrooper. Why didn't he let me solve the problems of the world for him? Does he think he's some kind of a messiah? He's too damn sensitive for his own good; don't you agree, Lucky?"

She placed her cup back on the coffee table, twisting her napkin. Her tone was plaintive. "Brian, he's our son, isn't he? We should be able to solve our problems. He's been thoughtful and loving, always courteous, and oh, so very handsome."

Teddy entreated, "The only hope of bringing him back is for both of you to understand his troubled feelings. Simply tell, show him how much you love him."

Steffi and Alex sat in a small café after the confrontation with D3. They finished two mugs of coffee and doughnuts without speaking. He left a quarter, then took her hand. They walked to St. Mark's and sat in a back pew.

"Alex," Stephanie said. "Take me with you into the last three years."

"The blinding sun, dust, mud, the sharp wind, floating downward forever, the killing, the spray of red water. Don't ask now, Steffi."

She watched him kneel, holding his head in his hands. They

were alone in the quiet, shadowy light. He breathed deeply, wiping tears on his sleeve. He had never surrendered and wondered if he should burden her with his guilt, the horror of violent death, his desperate need for consolation. He asked himself if Stephanie Pfeiffer was the enemy. The enemy who would mock and torment him. He was uncertain if she could ever respect him if he revealed his weaknesses.

He felt her arm around his shoulders drawing him closer, closer.

"Alex, trust, do trust me," Stephanie was pleading. "You can tell me as much or as little as you wish about things troubling you. Speak to me about the early days first; then the rest will slowly follow. Remember, confidence and friendship are the strength of our love."

He put his head in her lap, and she caressed his head and face. He felt the gentleness of her hands.

"That's good, Alex. When you are ready, I will listen."

"I have never cried, Steffi. I am deeply ashamed. Perhaps it's self-pity unbecoming a soldier. Can I permit that? Will you ever respect me again?"

"Tears will help and relieve you," she answered. "How could those tears lessen my love and esteem for you? They show me your intense feelings for the friends and the men you have lost. They are tears of your compassion, your fear."

"Those men were my responsibility. Combat was a game at first. It became worse with time. The river crossing was the ultimate folly. A battle that should never have been fought. How can I escape the primal frenzy of that afternoon? Why was I spared? I only prayed to avenge the deaths of my men in their toy boats. Those for revenge were answered, but not the ones to save them. It's the unforgettable, gnawing guilt. Can you understand? What can I do to redeem myself for their terrible, unthinkable ways of dying?"

His eyes were reddened and swollen. "Steffi, my first visit after I returned was to the mother of one of my officers, Peter Drake, who bled to death as we carried him to a field hospital one night. Then an Italian family whose son was decapitated. Later the father of a West Pointer who was my assistant battalion commander struck by mortar fire. Another friend from California and his twenty paratroopers were vaporized by twenty-millimeter shells. Next week you and I are going to visit the parents of a young Lieutenant who was standing next to me when he was shot. It was my duty and absolute obligation, my *need*, to visit their families."

She pushed her legs into the hard wooden kneeler and clenched the pew. After an imperceptible shudder, she gradually recovered her composure. "Alex, remember your training and discipline during the last four years. You knew there would be hazard and danger and you would lose your men and friends, perhaps be killed yourself. Suffering and death were to be expected. If you had faltered or failed and not been a courageous leader during those dreadful nights and days, *then* you should feel guilty. In Holland you obeyed unrealistic orders, led what you thought was an impossible attack, and succeeded. You are deeply saddened and haunted by the brutality of war, but you fought and God spared you for good reasons. I also know He returned you to me for the love we can give each other. Do think about this, pray for His help, and trust He will offer you His hand. Try to surrender yourself and accept the faith He offers."

The "Victory" cab door was opened with a flourish by the doorman at the Chicago Club. His grandiose formality was punctuated by a silk black top hat, green riding breeches, red coat, and Wellington boots. He strolled imperiously toward his desk at the end of a red carpet, then returned with an envelope on a small tray.

"Colonel Dunham, I believe. An important message, sir." He passed the envelope with a gloved hand. Alex recognized the familiar blue type. "Steffi, we have several busy hours; would you put this in your purse?"

They were greeted warmly by Ralph Bagshaw and his wife, who accompanied them to Cathedral Hall, where the Midwest press corps lunched for its monthly meeting. Both were relieved that Bagshaw seemed to have forgotten the unsavory evening with D3.

"Alex and Steffi, welcome to the den of truth seekers. You should have worn your parachute boots to kick them for apocryphal and outrageous tales."

"You were good to invite us," Alex said. "I hope I won't disappoint you."

Bagshaw seated them on either side of General Paul Gibson at the guest table. The hum of conversation was friendly and welcome to Alex, who spoke with the General about future Airborne operations in the Pacific.

Bagshaw juggled a cup of coffee as he walked to the podium.

"Gentlemen and guests. It is my particular pleasure to introduce Lieutenant Colonel Alex Dunham, commander of 3rd battalion, 504 Airborne Infantry Regiment. I have known him a number of years. In recognition of my outstanding combat record under fire in Sicily, he graciously placed himself between a German mortar attack and my oversize butt." Bagshaw's good-natured humor endeared him to his fellow reporters, who responded with hilarity and tapped their glasses. "More seriously, though, gentlemen, Colonel Dunham has been decorated with the Bronze and Silver Stars as well as the Distinguished Service Cross for unusual bravery. He will briefly discuss the Draas River crossing in Holland, then answer questions. This entire session is off the record—I repeat, off the record."

Alex pushed back his chair and stood at attention before General Gibson.

"Proceed, Lieutenant Colonel." Gibson saw the small light on the podium cast a pale shadow over Alex's face that exaggerated his weariness and fatigue.

"Good afternoon, General Gibson, Mr. Bagshaw, members of the press." Alex surveyed the audience. "As usual, your distinguished colleague has grossly misrepresented the facts. In Sicily we used donkeys to carry heavy weapons. Actually, gentlemen, it was the donkey and his pack I was trying to protect. After nothing more than a firecracker or two, the donkey was safe, but it was necessary to send an orderly back to headquarters because your Pulitzer Prize-winning reporter needed a clean pair of shorts."

The audience clapped and bellowed with laughter as Bagshaw gave Steffi an affectionate hug. "He's a remarkable fellow and both of you are incredibly fortunate."

Occasionally Alex turned toward General Gibson as he spoke of the river crossing. "We were ordered to capture the second of several bridges critical to the narrow corridor leading to the vital Ruhr industrial complex. Success of the entire operation might well have ended the war within a short time. Because of the urgency, we had to attack in a small number of poorly constructed canvas boats over a distance of four hundred yards. Air strikes were inadequate, and a smokescreen was dissipated by an afternoon wind. We were subjected to heavy fire, then proceeded across open ground, eliminated enemy infantry, pillboxes, and two well-defended forts. The entire operation required almost four hours." Alex continued to add more specific military details, personal anecdotes and comments praising the actions of individuals and small groups of paratroopers.

The first question was asked by the senior reporter sitting at a large center table. "Colonel Dunham, you said there was considerable urgency to the operation. How much planning and time were given to the final attack on the Draas bridges?"

"Sir," Alex explained, "our other two battalions held off enemy attacks from the north and east while we captured the waterways around the Draas. We had expected stiff resistance downstream from the jump-off point; therefore, the only option was a frontal assault. There were delays in delivery of the boats, the time of day was not optimal, and we had to improvise rather than plan."

"Colonel," another reporter asked, "wasn't it an unusual order for Airborne troops to cross a river, four hundred yards wide, then capture two bridges? Sounds like an infantry operation, sir."

"Agreed," Alex replied. "We reached our designated drop zones with precision several nights before and at this juncture had the advantage of surprise. The general plan for Airborne units to secure the town of Beek, smaller bridges, and canals surrounding the Draas, was successful. Although the mission was accomplished, the critical element of surprise was lost by the midday attack. Our Airborne forces should not have been committed to battle longer than three or four days."

A younger reporter asked the obvious question: "If the Germans held the bridge, why wasn't it blown before you captured it?"

"That was a problem of major concern. The Germans waited until the last minute before making the decision to destroy it. Large numbers of our troops and tanks were on the bridge and the casualties would have been greater, but fortunately, the Dutch underground had sabotaged the detonating devices."

"Colonel Dunham, given the immediacy and high priority of capturing the Draas bridges intact, were the casualties sustained by your battalion reasonable?"

He peered over the podium at General Gibson, who sat with folded arms, expressionless, and then Alex looked up at the high, vaulted ceiling, richly ornamented stone embossed with colorful university seals outlined by indirect lighting. He thought everyone in Cathedral Hall would have been killed.

"Yes. . . ." He briefly closed his eyes and held the bridge of his nose. "The casualties were acceptable for this mission. General Gibson reminds you these remarks are not to be quoted."

That night after dinner they washed and dried dishes. "After my daily press conferences, there's nothing like a long run, then dip in the lake to cool off, right, Stephanie Pfeiffer?"

"Right, Alexander the Great. You were the epitome of the perfect, discreet officer." She draped the dish towel around his neck and pulled his face toward her. "It's wonderful, Alex. I love you more every day. Mr. Bagshaw told me how lucky we are."

He kissed her, then smiled lasciviously. "You must know how much I like it when you don't wear a brassiere."

When she spoke, her lips moved against his cheek, "Colonel Dunham, where's that sharp eye of yours? Did I have one on this afternoon at your monumental press conference? Incidentally, I've always liked your sense of humor. Good line about protecting the donkey. You're a real antihero, aren't you?"

Steffi moved away slightly. "The envelope in my purse. I completely forgot about it. I'm curious. The blue type means only one person, correct?"

"Only one person, Steffi, but there's nothing more to say or do."

"Give him a chance, Alex."

They read it together.

From the desk of Dr. Brian Dunham:

Dear Alex,

It was good to see you home after many months. Lucky was delighted and Colleen even baked a week's supply of brownies for you. Try and overlook our little tiff; all of us have a difference of opinion now and then. It's taken a long time, and now I realize you must follow a different course. I know you will work hard and succeed in whatever you do. Lucky and I hope to see you and Steffi, although we may be off on a vacation soon. Good luck.

Yours,
D3

P.S. My surgical schedule has been hectic. One of my assistants graciously delivered this to the Chicago Club. Hope it reached you.

He tore it up, dropping it in a wicker letter holder on her desk.

"Nothing has changed; he's really a stranger," Alex said. "Probably always has been. Once in a while, a pat on the back, same old D3, distant, cold, never satisfied. Frankly, Steff, he was insulting the other night. I always hoped he would support my decisions. No more unpleasant chatter; what's on the schedule tomorrow?"

It was like an enormous state fair. A huge crowd had gathered in Sherman Park, children with ice cream and hot dogs, adults in line for refreshments, and bands playing patriotic music. The pleasant late afternoon was ideal for the eighth war bond rally. A towering billboard stood draped with flags and resembled an oversize thermometer. The wide red line was bordered by graduated figures that reached several million dollars. The goal would be reached this evening. A myriad of seats began to fill when Alex and Steffi entered the large concert shell. Later they were joined by the Pfeiffers, General Gibson, and the mayor's staff, who had organized the program. A fledgling soloist would sing the national anthem. There were choral groups, dancers, and several popular jazz bands.

Bob Nelson, a loquacious radio announcer, was the master of ceremonies and directed the performance with consummate, if not dramatic, skill.

"All right, get those Sousa marches started." He swung his arm forward, pointing to the military band. "Where's Doris? She's on for the anthem in ten minutes. Christ, Charles, see that she's sober and remembers the frigging words." He turned to Alex with an intimidating grin. "Colonel, if there's anything that screws up a show, it's some dumb broad who freezes during 'The Star-Spangled Banner,' don't you agree?"

"Absolutely, Mr. Nelson, absolutely."

There were cheers, enthusiastic clapping, and whistling with each succeeding performer and band. Alex and Steffi sat in the back of the shell shouting to one another over the clamor of the crowd.

"Exactly what does Mr. Nelson expect me to do?" Alex asked.

She was caught up in the excitement. "Play the harmonica, sing 'Old Man River,' the way you always do in front of twenty thousand people. Seriously, though, tell them you've been there, there'll be more fighting, and the troops need their support on the home front. Everything you've probably said one way or another in the past. It's second nature to you now. Your confidence; be positive and upbeat."

"Where's 'Superman'?" Nelson was becoming more jocular,

more waggish. "Now, Colonel Dunham, you are the 'heavy' in this act. You gotta give 'em patriotism out of your eyes, ears, nose, and mouth. Baby, you tell 'em we've knocked out the Krauts and so it's time to do some 'Nip' bashing. Got the idea? No shouting; keep it clean, good old apple pie stuff. It's win the war, bring the boys back home, and reach deep in your pockets."

Alex stood by Nelson, who recited a list of decorations which many GIs had been awarded. "Ladies and gentlemen," he announced, "now I give you Colonel Alex Dunham, one of our armed forces' youngest and most courageous officers."

Alex stepped forward and looked down from the platform. The crowd could not see six soldiers in wheelchairs, four amputees, and two other men on crutches. He brushed by Nelson, walked down several steps, and carried the first wheelchair to the stage, then the second, when several members of the band lifted up the others. He directed the rest of the servicemen to the center of the stage. There had been a note, probably a chord, even a short passage he heard during the evening ceremonies. He walked among the flimsy boats being loaded for the Draas crossing and could hear some of his battalion singing one of their macabre tunes:

> *The fires burn for you, but not for me.*
> *Old Saint Pete comes for you, not for me.*
> *Oh, Mister death, where's your sword? It's for you, not me.*
> *There's no damn chance for you; there is for me.*
> *Trooper, the Grim Reaper wants you, not me.*

Nelson was frantic. "What the hell is he doing? The whole show is off schedule. The bands have already played 'God Bless America' five times, while he's fooling around."

Alex saluted each man. "Lieutenant Colonel Dunham, 504 Parachute Infantry. Your name, where are you from, soldier, wounded in Italy? You were with the Eighth Air Force, right, Captain?" Greeting each one, he jotted down his name and unit, then stood behind them. It was the first time, but the words and sentiment were spontaneous. There was a hush over the sprawling crowd, interrupted only by a baby's cry and occasional laughter.

"My name is Lieutenant Colonel Alex Dunham, Parachute Infantry, and my home is Chicago." He was encouraged by shouts of: "Three cheers for Chicago's own," "Welcome home for our hero," and "The Airborne."

"God willing, this is our final war bond rally, so send it over the top for Uncle Sam and let's end this war. Victory is ours, but we want your fathers, sons, and brothers back home safe and sound. Let's make it soon. All branches of the armed services have fought with bravery, and I know how proud you are of them. Each and every one of you knows that sometimes heroes don't make it home, but here are twelve, sitting and standing in front of you this evening." He moved behind the first wheelchair. "Private First Class Wood, 5th Marines, wounded on Iwo Jima. Captain Green, United States Eighth Air Force, shot down on his twenty-fourth mission over Germany. . . ." Alex proceeded to introduce each man.

"Let me finish. Your generosity for these men and the millions of others who are giving the enemy a bloody nose, will win the war, and bring us peace. Good night, and may God bless all of you."

The rally concluded as the gathering sang "America the Beautiful." The familiar, the different faces. Haunting faces seen before. Alex remained behind, speaking to each man, down on one knee before the wheelchairs. "You have fought with bravery; congratulations, and I wish you well."

Steffi watched and could hear fragments of their conversation. She held her father's hand. "Dad, every one of these wounded men seems to be a part of him. He reaches out, knows their problems and sacrifice. How long will it take him to give them up, forget their sorrow and grief? How did he manage to do the things he did, feeling the way he does?"

Her father reminded her, "Stephanie, at this time Alex is a complex of anger, anger that can become rage, then crushing sorrow. Remorse follows. You both must be patient, especially you, my angel. Step by each slow step, he will forget and redeem himself for what he thought was wrong. Always love him, encourage him."

Erich Pfeiffer kissed his daughter. Alex joined them and they walked to the car. Katzie was waiting in the backseat. She folded her handkerchief and quickly slipped it in her purse.

The senior Thomas Hamilton stood in front of his four-door simonized 1935 DeSoto parked in the small, dusty lot of the Abington railroad station in Wisconsin. Hamilton was a large man with sparse black hair and a leathered, reddened face, in contrast to the white skin of his forehead, which had been shielded by a visored work cap. His square hands seemed disproportionately larger than the rest of his body because the sleeves of his three-buttoned coat were short and showed the cuffs of his denim shirt. A black tie was knotted loosely. His bib overalls barely reached his black high-topped, button hook shoes.

"Mr. Dunham? You must be Tommy's commanding officer. I'm Tom Senior. Pleased to have you here in Abington."

"Mr. Hamilton, my name is Alex Dunham and this is my fiancée, Stephanie Pfeiffer."

He greeted Steffi with a grip that made her wince. "Ma'am, sit in the backseat. Mr. Dunham up front with me."

Alex judged they drove almost ten miles over a narrow unpaved road through rolling countryside with scattered farms surrounded by large shade trees. The searing sun shone off tall corn stalks.

"Looks like a good season, Mr. Hamilton," Alex said.

He nodded. "That's right, it is. Lots of work to do."

Steffi wondered if they had cows.

Mr. Hamilton turned toward the backseat. "That's right, Missus Dunham, dairy farm on our place, too."

They climbed the steps of the front porch, where Mrs. Hamilton sat in a cushioned swing that made an easy, creaking sound as it slowly moved back and forth. She fanned herself, managing to stay cool in her plain cotton dress. A gold star flag hung in the window behind the swing.

Mrs. Hamilton greeted the visitors with a, "Good day to you," then spoke to a young boy. "Robby, fetch Mr. and Mrs. Dunham some tea; chip off plenty of ice."

Alex and Steffi were refreshed by the minted drink. The shaded porch eased the heat. She sat with Mrs. Hamilton on the old swing while Alex and her husband relaxed in wooden rockers. Occasionally they could hear a haunting train whistle, a train that might have brought Lieutenant Thomas Hamilton Jr. home.

"So you two are from down Chicago way. Good ride up?" Mr. Hamilton wondered.

"Stephanie and I enjoyed the trip, Mr. Hamilton. The Northwest railroad has a fine roadbed; you can really tell on the curves."

"Any farmers in your family, Mrs. Dunham?"

"No, Mrs. Hamilton, my father has a business and we have a small place in the country. We call it a farm, but we don't raise much in the way of crops."

"Well, if you call it a farm, what sort of work do people do there?"

"It's a small house with stables, Mrs. Hamilton. We go there to get away from the city."

"Good idea. Have no use for cities. Robby, does Martha need me in the kitchen?"

"Yes, Mother." He held the screen door open.

Mr. Hamilton would occasionally sit forward and violently swat at elusive flies. They had finished their iced tea when his wife appeared. "Dinner's ready."

Alex followed Steffi and Mr. Hamilton into the front parlor. It wasn't used often, and everything was neatly in place. The top of a tall Zenith radio, with a wooden grated front speaker, was covered by a linen doily with a picture of Lieutenant Thomas Hamilton Jr. in front of battalion headquarters. The first team stood as a group of seven and their mascot, "Striker," an English bull terrier, lay at Tommy's feet. Alex had forgotten how tall Hamilton was. It was logical, as he had been an All-American end at the University of Wisconsin.

"Lord, bless our daily bread and grant us a plentiful harvest. We welcome our friends to this table and remember our loving son, Tommy." Mr. Hamilton unfolded his napkin.

Steffi spoke to Mrs. Hamilton. "Your cherry pie is absolutely wonderful."

"Martha, bring Mr. and Mrs. Dunham another piece, then clear the table." Mrs. Hamilton reached for a toothpick. Pork was a nightmare.

Hamilton pushed back his chair and lit his pipe. Aromatic smoke filled the room. His voice had a steady calmness. "What happened to our Tommy, Mr. Dunham?"

Alex used the silverware, salt and pepper shakers, and sugar bowl to explain the river crossing. The Hamiltons watched and listened while the two children stood next to Steffi's chair, absorbed, holding her hands. Alex methodically moved the table-ware.

"Mr. and Mrs. Hamilton, Tommy and I managed to get across the river with the battalion, defeat the enemy infantry, and reach the bridge about six that evening. There were German snipers on the girders and the two of us took several men to clean them out. He was standing beside me when he was hit in the head at close range. He died instantly. Of the seven men in the picture on top of your radio, there were only two of us left after Tommy was killed. All of us fought together through Sicily and Italy. He was respected by his men, was the best in the tradition of Airborne officers. He was my good friend. A brave soldier. I miss him."

Mrs. Hamilton's voice wavered. "He didn't suffer any, did he, Mr. Dunham?"

"No, Mrs. Hamilton, it all happened with the blink of an eye."

"Children, clear the table; clean the dishes. Poppa and I have to take our friends down to the station."

He was captivated by his bride's radiance, enhanced by a pale blue suit and pillbox hat with a delicate face-length veil. He could feel her tremble, then firmly steadied her hand and looked into her innocent eyes; they were azure blue today. Once again Alex luxuriated in his old happiness. He felt buoyant and content. Stephanie Pfeiffer and Alexander Dunham stood before Bishop Evans in a chapel at St. Mark's, where sunlight streamed through its leaded windows that imparted a warm cheerfulness to the occasion.

"Friends," the Bishop began, "we are gathered in the sight of God to bless the joining of Stephanie and Alexander in Christian marriage. . . . "

Steffi turned to Alex. "In the name of God, I, Stephanie, take you, Alexander, to be my husband. . . . This is my solemn vow."

Alex repeated the same commitment, and they exchanged rings. "I give you this ring as a sign of my vow. With all that I am and all that I have, I honor you in the name of the Father, the Son . . . "

"And now, Alex," Bishop Evans solemnly whispered, "you may kiss your bride."

Without waiting, Alex impetuously put his arms around her waist, kissing her through the veil that spread lipstick over his face in an intriguing netlike pattern. She tried to lift it but willingly succumbed to his spontaneity. The small congregation and Bishop Evans joined in contained laughter and smiles.

A larger group of friends enjoyed champagne and wedding cake at a private reception at the Worcester, joking with the excited couple about smeared lipstick and their flushed cheeks.

Katzie and Erich beamed. "We're delighted for them, Lucky. It's ideal. They have grown up together and, God willing, will have many blissful years ahead. We thought a small reception—"

"Yes, both of us are also pleased," Brian agreed. "But this young husband must give serious consideration to the future, raising and supporting a family. *Responsibility*, yes, that's the word I was searching for."

Katzie spoke with unaccustomed firmness. "Brian, if any young man has known responsibility, it's Alex. All of us are proud of him. He's always been a son for Erich and me."

Steffi and Alex shook hands with Brian and kissed Lucky.

His father was reticent. "Steffi, have you made some plans for a honeymoon?" "Honeymoon" seemed awkward for him.

"Yes Dr. Brian, we've planned a ten-day camping trip in the north woods and are anxious to leave. It's the most exciting thing in our lives now." Steffi took Alex's hand and they drifted toward Tombo and Shoo-Shoo.

Alex greeted his old friend, "Welcome home, *pilote extraordinaire.* Tombo, we're delighted both of you were able to join us. There hasn't been a reasonable excuse for a party since those Christmas dances before the war. Weren't those the days? And are T.O. and your mother well?"

The two couples stood together laughing, exchanging stories of Academy days, until Alex and Tombo moved away from the group.

"Tombo, you must have had some *interesting* times during those twenty-five missions over the Continent. We had our bad days." Alex looked at his schoolmate's Eighth Air Force shoulder patch. "The remembering is difficult.... Incidentally, I only have nine months left. It's occupation duty. You should have decided on a wedding date before I'm discharged."

Tombo put down his champagne and began to reminisce about his crew and squadron. "We named our B-17 *Shoo-Shoo,* and it brought us good luck, but there were missions that are impossible to forget. I'm thankful to have brought most of the men back to base, but the deep raids over Germany during nineteen forty-three were suicidal. The brass must have been crazy." His laugh was strange, with deep sarcasm. "Absolutely crazy. But, Alex, we shouldn't complain; we're home and will wait so you and Steff can be best man and bridesmaid."

Later the newlyweds waved to the guests, then dashed across the lobby to the desk for their key. They had a suite overlooking the lake.

The sign was made from roughly cut pieces of a log and read: "Amos Twitchell's—The Great Outdoors, Inc.," and, painted in smaller letters: "We Have Everything But The Campfire." They dropped their bags on the dusty plank floor.

The proprietor stood at the front counter beneath a giant mounted moose head. Steffi and Alex had slept erratically during the eight-hour train ride from Chicago and decided to rent their camping gear after a country-style breakfast—real eggs, hash brown potatoes, ham, all the food Alex had thought about over the last several years. There were no powdered eggs in northern Minnesota.

"Looks like you two mighta just got yourselves hitched." Twitchell grinned. "Want to get some camping gear for the honeymoon?"

Amos Twitchell, tall and muscular, wore a suede leather Indian jacket and faded corduroy pants.

Alex thought he was probably conceived, raised, and lived in the woods and on lakes most of his life. He was surrounded by shotguns, knives, fishing tackle, and clothing for all seasons.

"So, you're in the service, Lieutenant Colonel. From the boots and shoulder patch, it's Airborne, right?"

Alex answered. "'Right with Eversharp,' Mr. Twitchell. My wife and I want to rent some of your gear for about ten days."

"What weapons did you carry, Colonel?"

"Standard-issue Colt forty-five, six-inch knife with brass knuckles, demolition kit, grenades, and a BAR. Sometimes even a toothbrush."

The blasé answer made Twitchell smile. He had admitted Alex into his secret fraternity.

Alex looked at his new acquaintance. "Twitchell, you could have been my point man. The Airborne would have been perfect for you."

"It'll take a few minutes," Twitchell said. "I'll get a pup tent, a couple of down sleeping bags, tin ware, and a small hatchet for campfires."

Steffi leaned on the counter. "Have you got a cast-iron pan, Mr. Twitchell? I'm planning on some fish fries and pancakes for the General."

Twitchell made a list. "Then you need poles, lures, and a trout net. The fishing has been great this summer. You've got to have backpacks, compass, and a map. But you know all of that,

Colonel. By the way, we don't carry parachutes here, sorry."

"Mr. Twitchell, is it possible to arrange a ride to the nearest lodge, preferably at a lake where we can get a canoe, then take off?"

"Well," Twitchell said. "It seems to me you want adventure, no easy trails or shortcuts. Let me suggest Shakoka Lodge on Lake Coquihalla. It's about twenty miles from here, and I'll have everything loaded in the Ford in an hour. Make yourself to home, have some freshly brewed country coffee, and if you see anything you want to buy, let me know."

"I would like to pay you now, Mr. Twitchell."

"That's fine with me, Colonel, but it's all half-price for you." He looked with approval at the battle stars on Alex's ribbons. "You've been away a long while. I want both of you to have a good time, you know, a real good honeymoon."

"Thanks so much, Mr. Twitchell. I really can't, you know. . . ."

"It's an order, Colonel," followed by several hard, amiable pats on his back.

As they sipped coffee and strolled through the store, the two saw wool blankets, shawls, knitted caps, cable knit sweaters, and gloves hanging from long wooden poles suspended from the high ceiling.

"Steffi, look around to your heart's content. I'll meet you by the stove in several minutes." Alex walked toward the back of the store and admired some charcoal sketches and watercolors of woodland scenes. He wondered which one she would like. After placing several on the tops of barrels, he selected a bright watercolor of a canoe with two anglers on a calm lake. One of the fishermen was a woman. He carefully rolled it, placing it in a cardboard tube.

"What have you been doing? It seems like you have been gone a century." She reached for his hands.

"Something for you, Steff. Wait and see. Hope you like it."

"Can't you tell me? Come on, Alex; you're such a tease. I like the suspense of waiting, too." She reached for the tube, which he quickly pulled away.

"Wait until tonight, sweetheart."

It was a cool evening. Glowing logs with popping flames spread a welcome warmth through the sitting room of Shakoka Lodge, where Steffi and Alex lounged in a deep-seated leather sofa, whose cushions had been indented by innumerable summer guests. They both became drowsier, sleepily hypnotized by the fire.

Her voice was intimate. "It's difficult to believe we're together again after all of these years. It's a new beginning for us."

They got up, slowly moving to the stairs. Sometimes her expressions and mood changed quickly, and now she was the impish girl of years ago. "Isn't it time for my surprise?"

"Yes, only with one condition."

She barely touched her upper lip with the tip of her tongue. "I know what that is; let's go, and right now."

They sat on the bed, each in a pair of Alex's olive drab longjohns, as she tediously removed the rolled watercolor from its tube. They held the corners of the painting while she critiqued the details. "Alex, it's beautiful, the bright greens and blues. It tells a story, both of us fishing in peace and solitude, only sounds of the wilderness. This is a cheerful addition to my sketches and prints that we can share." She released her ends of the painting as it rolled into his hands. He carefully replaced it in the container.

"You haven't forgotten the ice-skating doll you brought at Christmas years ago, have you?" she wondered. "It is still one of my treasures. I looked at it many times while you were away, imagining if you would come home. When I was ill that Christmas, I kept the ice-skater on my bedside table, anxious to be with you. Later I wore your outrageously expensive Cartier Cracker-jack ring to bed every night. Remember how you would draw me toward you when we did a *courbez* at the end of a dance?"

"What wonderful times of growing up together, lighthearted days when we learned about each other, likes, dislikes. Interesting, Steffi, we never argued, did we?"

She could see his fluorescent watch in the darkness of their small room.

He pulled a wool blanket up to their chins and touched her hair and face. "I've thought about it many times. God had to have made us for each other in some miraculous way. In looking back, I know I fell in love with you from the beginning. Whether at school, college, or overseas, you were inescapably part of me. At night and whenever there was time, I read from your prayer book and managed to overcome my fears."

"Alex, let's get some rest now. We can have an early start and load the canoe."

Later they became restless and tried to move. They had been sleeping face to face. "Are you awake?" she asked.

"Sure, now I am, and it's time to jettison these longjohns." He reached for her top button, then opened the rest as far as her waist.

She pulled off her shirt, and he slipped down the tight-fitting pants that were caught at her ankles. She struggled to kick them off and lay on top of him, beginning to unfasten the long row of buttons. She pressed her breasts over his chest and abdomen. "It's my turn to tease tonight. Besides, you couldn't escape if you tried; we're trapped in the trough of this old mattress." She pulled down his bottoms, kissing his thighs, stroking his pelvis. They made love, then lay exhausted in each other's arms.

A shaft of early sunlight streamed under the shutters when she looked at him with a playful expression. "Imagine being together in the sleeping bags and pup tent. By the way, did you happen to hear how this old bed squeaked last night? Hope we didn't wake up the other guests."

They slept longer and swam before breakfast.

"Not that I'm the greatest trout fisherman in the world, Steff, but casting really isn't that difficult. Just watch a couple of times."

He sat in front of the canoe, rhythmically drawing back,

casting the line and lure. *Was it a grenade?* he thought. *No dammit, it's the football I used to throw. Yes, get it out of your mind, your memory; remember, only a football. Wait a minute, Dunham; wasn't it satisfying? Didn't it make you feel good to flush out the enemy? Revenge, oh God, give me revenge for the slaughter in my boats. The sight of those bodies thrown into the air.* He trolled a while longer.

"Okay, Steffi, I'll paddle slowly, hardly any disturbance of the water; now throw out your line." He watched her. The sun was coming up and cleared the mist hovering over the surface of the lake. The silence around them was interrupted only by the muffled sounds of their paddles.

"Steady, you've got a strike; look at the bowed rod. Let it run a little, give a little, but each time slowly reel in some." She turned her head as Alex pulled out the hook, then let the three-pounder trail in the water to keep fresh.

He leaned back and kissed her, pushing his tongue into her open mouth. Her arms were limp, but she managed to hold the fishing rod.

"How many more, Alex?"

He smiled. "How many more what?"

"Fishes, fishes, kisses, kisses, you know trout, how many more should we catch? Kiss me again."

Alex pitched their tent near the lake, dug a small hole, lined the edges with stone, and placed a grill over pieces of chopped wood. It was early evening, and Steffi cooked pan-fried fish and potatoes.

After their first dinner in Twitchell's great outdoors, they sat near the water's edge sipping coffee and gazed over the motionless expanse of water, broken by intermittent ripples. They listened to the silence.

"Take my field jacket, Steffi; roll up the sleeves. Remember the captain's baggy sweater from the Academy? Stay warm; please come closer, angel. I'm sure you had summer nights like this in Colorado, and when I worked in Wyoming I hiked at night, then I'd find a rocky butte, look at the stars, and imagine what we would be doing together."

Alex's thoughts shifted. "You know, Steffi, we carried out jumps and field exercises in Tunisia almost every night before the Sicilian operation. There were sudden drops in temperature, almost a sixty-degree difference from daytime. The moon and stars usually filled a deep blue night sky."

She looked at his angular features, softened by moonlight. "Tell me more about those times, Alex."

"Later, it was different. We trained in England during summer weather with occasional rain. It was easier than coping with the unpredictable desert winds. In Holland, our battalion made a perfect strike on the landing zone five miles from the Draas. My men thought it was a joke, because the only enemy was a herd of grazing cows. We cleared the canals, but there was some nasty fighting for farmhouses. About thirty-six hours later Colonel Conroy called me back to Regiment and we planned a river crossing. We should have attacked during early morning fog, but the boats were late and we lost the advantage of surprise. Everything seemed to move in slow motion. The men were ready, confident, but had no idea of the strong resistance they would meet along the river. Unbelievable that the boats were made of canvas. Several weeks ago at Roger Bagshaw's press conference I lied about the casualties. Sometimes I believe I can forget, but the sights and sounds were . . . "

Alex picked up a stick and broke it over his knee and threw the pieces toward the lake. They floated along the surface momentarily, then quietly disappeared. He tried to believe his men had never existed.

Later, Alex and Steffi strolled barefoot along the shore, skimming pebbles across the water, laughing and relishing the freshness of the outdoors. They slid nude into his sleeping bag, contentedly holding each other, unable to sleep.

"Alex, you're such a busy beaver, nibbling on my ears, kissing my neck, tickling my toes. What's it take to make you sleepy?"

He pinned down her arms, pressing into her. "You should know what it takes, and it's not a fifteen-mile march."

A pelting rain and breeze hit the small tent in the morning. Steffi crawled out of their sleeping bag. "Can two of us dress in here without going outside?"

"Just watch." He knelt and slipped a wool sweater over her head while she pulled on a pair of heavy pants and laced her hiking boots. "Now it's your turn, madam, but be careful with your hands, or we'll be in here all day."

"Yes, sir, as you say, sir, I shall keep my hands to myself." They threw on rain jackets, ate oranges and dry cereal, then packed a small lunch.

Alex pretended to give a command. "A long hike today, soldier, with full field pack."

"Please only a few miles, Alex. It's my legs; I can barely walk." Steffi groaned. "You've worn me out."

By noon, they had tramped several miles down the shoreline, then rested on a log and dried off in the midday sun.

"Let's eat some of those sticky peanut butter and jelly sandwiches. Maybe they'll give your legs some strength," Alex said.

She gave him a tempting look. "In that case, let me have two and I'll be ready for tonight."

He grinned, trying to move his tongue, caught by sweet paste. After several swallows of fresh, cold water he managed to make himself understood. "They're like one of Colleen's afterschool treats. She's always been a gem. Anyway, let's stay here. I'll spread out the ponchos, and we can look and listen. Why don't you take the field glasses?"

They lay next to each other scanning wildlife in the isolated woodlands. She looked intently at her new husband, although nothing was said for a while.

"Alex, being with you, camping, doing anything, is thrilling for me. Nothing fancy, you know, simply you and I. God made this beauty all around us. Please keep these peaceful images in mind when unexpected sounds, sights, and figures of the past suddenly jostle your balance. Try and remember good days and the promise of years ahead for us."

She continued to speak as he looked into the sunlight that danced off the lake. It was the old ache, strain around his eyes, and pinched forehead, waiting, watching for any movement. Gradually he relaxed. "You know I will. Every day is better, not the confusion of combat." He put his head in her lap. "Not the bitterness of killing, the fear of being killed, constantly worrying about the men, boys. No one can conceive of it."

Alex covered the entrance to their small tent with mosquito netting while Steffi fried trout, heated corn, and brewed coffee.

"As usual, your meal is sensational, Mrs. Dunham."

She beamed. "It's not the cooking, Alex, it's the fresh air and hiking that make you hungry."

They watched the flames of the campfire and warmed their chilled hands as the northern dusk deepened. He moved next to her. "Now that you're rested, let's go canoeing."

"Yes. It's still light, Alex. Why don't we paddle along the shore and devour the rest of this gorgeous day?"

They moved across the still water for a short distance. "Listen," she said. "Listen to those haunting sounds. What could they be?"

"Come back here and sit in front of me. Be still now; you'll see. It will be an unforgettable sight."

She watched expectantly when Alex pointed to a tongue of land covered with tall grass and long-stemmed reeds. Her voice was a whisper. "I've never seen birds like these." She had a surprised expression that delighted him.

"Look, look, Alex; one is nesting and a larger one seems to be keeping watch. Could we move closer? Then I can see more clearly."

Drifting silently, they only heard the sound of water droplets from the canoe's edge. She was intrigued by the black-and-white pattern of their feathers and stared in innocent wonder at the dark red eyes that seemed to warn, "You have come close enough, stranger." Steffi looked up with an enchanted smile as several more loons made an awkward landing in a spray of water. She covered her mouth, trying to contain pure joy, as a loon dropped its head, diving gracefully beneath the surface.

"Look, Alex; one is struggling to take off. How can he get in the air? He's actually running on the water, flapping his wings, before he flies."

She rested against Alex's knees, bewitched by the plaintive, fragile call barely audible above a slight breeze. "Alex, please, can't we stay longer?"

"We mustn't disturb their haven, Steffi. We'll come back."

The canoe slowly glided away from their solitary friends.

Later, he drew her closer, felt her warm body and breasts through her sweater. They looked across the wide, tree-lined lake whose tranquillity was occasionally disturbed by ducks or geese landing on its smooth surface. The marshy smell of the water. Lieutenant Colonel Alexander Dunham was trying to forget he had crossed the Draas River.

She raised herself on one arm, and he felt her breath on his face. "God created this beautiful world with the hope of life full of joy and peace. You know Alex, from the beginning we were imperfect. God could only show the way, not make our decisions. He loves us regardless of our weaknesses and sins, if we ask forgiveness. It is there for the taking. He is our faith, and faith is the certainty our sins and guilt will be forgiven. You probably have put your faith in things you can hear, touch, see; you know, the realities. Faith is a belief in the unseen, belief beyond logic. It is within your power, and redemption is there for your acceptance. Look at the stars, the lake; listen to the loons. Believe that God made everything. He knows the goodness and love in you."

It was dark. She felt his tears on her cheeks. The battalion commander, the disciplined, unyielding soldier who had prayed for revenge, stared at his death, gave himself to his wife. Now he had trusted her with his second, hidden world of fearful secrets and memories.

"Thank you, Stephanie. I understand and will try to believe. Please forgive my stumbling now, but you're guiding me in the dark with a compass I am just learning to read."

She felt the scars on his back as they turned in his sleeping bag. It wasn't the burn of a belt that expurgated his guilt; it was the gentle movements of her hands that caressed his demonizing wounds. Soon he heard her quiet breathing, followed by sleep. He closed his eyes.

"God, I truly ask your forgiveness. Embrace my men in everlasting peace. Give me the strength to redeem myself in your eyes."

Amos Twitchell welcomed them. "Well, you two survived ten days and you're smiling like it was the first time you ever met. A good sign. See you both next year. They were good days except for a quick downpour now and then. But you liked those nights together, too. Ground pretty hard? Oh, I almost forgot; here is something to remind you of your time up north." He gave Steffi a carved likeness of a common loon.

The train left after lunch.

The crystal calyx bowl filled with striking red freesia embellished the center of the dining room table. Long tapered candles gave the room a soft hue. The flower petals, dotted with drops of water, seemed to alleviate the warmth of a late September evening. Alex held Steffi's hand as the small party entered the intimate dining room. He drew back her chair. She wore a pale green sleeveless dress with pearls.

When Alex touched her shoulders, he was reminded they had anticipated an evening alone but acquiesced to her parents. He was delighted by her beauty and the decor of the refined setting.

"Mr. and Mrs. Pfeiffer." Alex looked toward Katzie. "It's a pleasure to be with you, Steffi, and your guests this evening. Over the years, I've never forgotten the beauty of this room."

Mrs. Pfeiffer reached for his hand. "Alex, remember the night of the bouncing hard roll? Tonight Lottie has baked one of your favorites: popovers."

"What an unexpected surprise. Believe me, Mrs. Pfeiffer, these special rations are not served by the United States Army."

T. Harrington Clarke and his youngish wife sat across from Alex and Steffi, joining in the brief informal toast by Erich Pfeiffer.

"Alex, I feel you are truly our son. All of us rejoice in your safe return from the war. Your speech at the bond rally several weeks ago was superb. There have been many trying days, but God has brought you home to us. May He bless both of your young lives."

"Thank you. It has always been an honor to be your guest." He glanced at Stephanie. "And now I am a member of your family. Steffi has been understanding and patient with me. A long separation, a long war, Mr. Pfeiffer."

In the midst of this formality, Alex felt awkward and reserved in his conversation. He sat erect, a veneer of ease, a forced smile. His eyes drifted down to the grayness of the dining room carpet, and for a moment he thought the mud had frozen. He periodically shook from the penetrating, wet cold in his bunker at Anzio. The K rations stuck to his lips and tongue. Now it was dark. He would take Cunicello and several men and crawl through trenches, under the wire, and knock out the Tiger tank with its Panzer Grenadiers. Their mission was to rescue Peter Drake and his squad.

Erich said congenially, "Well, Harry, I guess you and Helen will be up at the lake for Labor Day, swimming, boating with the children. As I remember, young Harry is almost eighteen now, and he must be a joy for you two and his sisters."

Alex moved back slightly as Lottie served a magnificent shrimp cocktail and, when she passed behind him, bumped his shoulder with her free hand. He looked up and smiled.

Clarke had the confidence of wealth and family name. With this privilege he enjoyed a spacious North Shore home and country-club life of golf, tennis, and skeet shooting. His wit and humor were engaging for Erich Pfeiffer, who knew that sobriety was not one of his virtues. He sipped, then chewed his wine before dinner.

"Hmm, Château Lafite Rothschild, probably 1920." Clarke's speech was slushy. "Can't you bring the shrimp a little closer, miss? You're making it extraordinarily difficult for me." He watched, then scrutinized Alex. "You know, Erich," Clarke continued to chatter, "I would never let any son of mine fight in a damn war; he's too smart for that sort of thing. I haven't raised him to be gun fodder. I'll make certain of that. Anyway, he's too young."

"Harry, old chap," Erich said. "You may not have much to say when Uncle Sam sends his greetings someday. It's a fact of life."

"Wait and see," Clarke answered. "He'll join his grandfather's and my business, and we'll arrange that 'essential classification.' By the way, Dunham, your father is some big surgeon here in town; why didn't he do something for you? Think about it. You've basically wasted the last four years of your life."

Alex looked at Clarke but spoke to Erich. "Mr. Pfeiffer, several years ago I rode your gelding, Shannon. Could be a champion jumper, sir. Tell me, have you been trotting him on the inside diagonals as we discussed?"

"You and Steffi must spend time at the farm when you return from Germany next year," Erich suggested. "It would be a perfect vacation and good rest. Shannon and a handsome chestnut mare are waiting for you. She's new to the barn. They need to be exercised every day."

Clarke turned to Alex. "You'll never get anywhere in this life spending more time in the service. How do you expect to make a living in a competitive world?"

Katzie intervened. "Now Harry, you know from your own experience that with hard work and patience everything eventually falls into place."

Alex released Steffi's hand and his strained features relaxed, with a renewed brightness in his eyes. He speared a shrimp, then dipped it into Lottie's lamaize sauce. He waited, stalking Clarke.

"None of you actually listened to me and seemed to have missed my point. Those rows of ribbons on Dunham's jacket don't mean 'diddly-squat.' They won't get him a job. What does that flashy red-and-blue one stand for, anyway? Just a bunch of fruit salad." Clarke picked up his wineglass.

There it was, the herbal smell of a nearby olive grove, the dust kicked up by the fucking lying little Sicilian. Then he reached intuitively for his trench knife and slit the prisoner's belt and trousers. He ran the tip of the blade down the front of both thighs, and Piano Lupo was his for the asking.

Alex moved imperceptibly forward and picked up his steak knife, slowly stroking its sharpened blade across each palm as he had done hundreds of times in training and combat. A befuddled Clarke was unnerved, dazzled by the speed and deadly accuracy of the next movements, as the knife cut through the first tall candle wick and then the other, leaving two small puffs of smoke and a sizzling sound as they fell into the hot wax. Alex reached across the table and placed the knife on Clarke's Manhattan blue Tiffany dinner plate in a room whose light was suddenly more subdued. He had an expression of devilish glee as he watched T. Harrington Clarke slump in his chair, wipe the sweat from his forehead, and retch in a linen napkin embroidered with a scripted "P."

The dining room door swung open, and Lottie stepped forward announcing that ambrosia fruit salad was being served. "Would Madam prefer whipped cream with maraschino cherries or a brandy flambé?"

Lottie was serving coffee while Erich Pfeiffer lifted the lid from a leather humidor and clipped the end of a gold-banded cigar. The flare of a match illuminated his sharp, dark-complected features and thinning gray hair.

Erich brushed her soft cheeks. "Steffi, *mein Mädel*, remember when you were my little girl and sat on the floor watching me ceremoniously light my cigar?"

"Of course, Dad. You always slipped the colored cigar band on my finger, and I pretended to be the wife of a handsome prince."

"Steffi, the evening doesn't seem complete without your handsome prince. Where is he, dear?"

She stood with her back to her parents, tall, slightly broad, athletic shoulders, with well-figured thighs and legs. She turned; her blond hair swung around the back of her neck.

"He's making arrangements for his flight to Washington and then Frankfurt. He leaves at the end of the week for his new assignment. You know how much I'll miss him. His feelings about the war lessen each day. Imagine Mr. Clarke's predicament the other night."

"Dear, your husband is a soldier, an officer trained to command, lead, and, for all the reasons you know, won't tolerate disrespect, particularly contemptuous remarks about the military." Erich put down his cigar. "Harry Clarke is a spoiled little boy who likes his schnapps and has too much money. How could he grasp what your husband has experienced?"

"When it's over, Dad, Alex has planned to take a law degree and work for the State Department. He'll probably want to serve, you know, his idealism and that attitude, 'I'm going to change the world'."

"Good." It was more of a *"gut."* "He'll make you a happy wife, accomplish great things, with his disciplined intellect, firmness, and ambition. I'll always remember the night he stood in the snow. It was years ago. Lord knows how long he waited for me, that serious, concerned look and voice. 'How is Stephanie, sir? Please remember me to her, sir. Thank you, Mr. Pfeiffer, sir.' He loves you deeply, my dear. He's protective of others. Don't forget—you always come first. His anger is to be expected on occasions; he'll become more tolerant with his new assignment. Steffi, in another year or less he's yours for a lifetime."

She sat down on the floor in front of her father. "Thank you. I know he's fine, but I occasionally become anxious. I can't help myself; I love him so. It's an obsession. I think you know how I feel. You're right; a year passes quickly."

Erich put his arms around her. "Steffi, alles wird gut werden."

Several days later, Steffi and Alex walked out of the Midway terminal into a gusting wind that blew particles of dirt into their faces and eyes. Alex propped his briefcase against the worn duffel bag. He pulled her closer. There were a series of whispered, abbreviated sentences.

"I love you, Stephanie. . . . Home at least by June . . . Will try to help in small ways. . . . Aid to the people, military justice system. . . . Make up for the destruction. . . . Home with you, law school, State Department. . . . Our love, our children, a family together for a lifetime. . . . Please be patient a few more months." He cradled the back of her head as they kissed. She held him, unwilling to let go.

"I'll write every day, Alex. Be careful; I want you so. You're my darling husband; come home to me soon. I'm weak now, my thoughts, my feelings, please forgive me, but I can't; I want to share your love. It hurts, Alex, because we're part of each other."

He squeezed her arms, drew away, and tried to smile. "It's now, Steffi, easier when it's fast. The future is what is important. We must keep planning."

Their eyes met, happy and sad. She dropped her head, turned, and slowly walked away. He approached the metal ladder to the open door, looked back, and saw her exquisite face with a faint smile as she waved. He watched a moment, saluted, then climbed aboard. The gray camouflaged transport taxied, engines accelerating with blasts of exhaust as it rolled down the runway. She remained until it became a vanishing point, lost in a huge autumn cloud.

Eight

If Only . . .

C olonel Dunham, sir, I've never really been able to understand how those fly boys could drop a pickle in a frog's asshole from eight miles up but couldn't put us down on a cow
pasture from a thousand feet. Just look at that; they were able to
blow the station to smithereens, but the church wasn't
scratched."

Alex slapped his Sergeant's knee as Jackson maneuvered
the jeep around the rubble of tangled steel girders, railway
tracks scattered in grotesque patterns, and huge, water-filled
bomb craters that were once the railroad station, the *Bahnhof*, at
Oberburg. "Jaybird" Jackson's rough language, disregard of danger, and unmanageable courage were the credentials of a flam-
boyant soldier, married to the Airborne.

Alex turned to his driver. "Jackson, you remember Holland?
The pilots weren't that bad. Only got nervous in the service when
the flak became thick. Speaking of staying on target, keep us out

283

of those craters. They'd never find us in the mud down there; then what would every Fräulein in Bavaria do without First Sergeant Jay Jackson, who has spread the word he's the regiment's greatest Airborne hero?"

The early November air was penetratingly cold as Alex made his daily inspection of the rail yards. It was the responsibility of the commander of the regional United States Military Occupation Force to organize crews that would reopen the rail line to Nuremberg before winter prevented further work. The jeep carommed over pockmarked ground toward a group of men wearing visor caps and worn, dirt-covered field gray jackets and pants. Others wore khaki with torn sweaters and cut-off jackboots. There were no gloves to protect them from the cold, abrasive wooden ties, and long segments of rail that numbed their hands. The *Arbeitsleiter* stepped forward as Alex and Jackson climbed the stone and gravel of the steep incline to the rail bed.

The foreman came to attention. "Guten Morgen, Herr Kommandant. Wie Sie sehen, die Arbeit geht gut voran." The work was proceeding well.

Alex stood in mud-splattered paratroop boots, bloused trousers, and battle jacket, a .45 Colt in his holster. "Gut gemacht, Herr Proeschel, Sie und Ihre Arbeiter haben viel geschafft." Alex complimented the leader and his men on their progress. "Ich sehe an Ihrer alten Uniform, dass Sie sicherlich mit dem Afrika Korps gekämpft haben." Alex knew he had fought with the Afrika Korps.

The foreman spoke with pride. "Jawohl, Herr Kommandant, mit Generalfeldmarschall Rommel." He reached in his pocket and showed him the brassard of the Korps. Alex admired the bronze medallion with its palm tree and *Ritterkreuz*. The other workers crowded around.

"Wir müssen die Bahnlinie nach Nürnberg vor dem Winter fertig haben. We need food, medical supplies, clothing, and some heavy construction equipment for your town's people. I'll be here every day," Alex said.

"Übrigens, Herr Kommandant Dunham, wo haben Sie denn

so gut Deutsch gelernt?" He was surprised by Alex's fluency in German.

The Colonel smiled. "Es kommt ganz natürlich."

At headquarters, Alex sat at an old water-stained, worm-eaten table that a Corporal commandeered as a desk. The only redeeming quality was a set of questionably sturdy legs decorated with ornamental claw feet. Its disreputable state was not unlike that of the broken crystal chandelier that barely illuminated neatly stacked army requests and reports, arranged in a standard-issue "in" and "out" tiered metal tray. He sat in an armchair with a faded, partly shredded damask cushion, then looked up at the flaking, water-spotted ceiling hoping pieces of plaster would spare his desk:

My dearest Steffi,

Before finishing countless forms and answering letters, this is a chance to chat with you and say again how I miss you. In the midst of this destruction and misery, I long to be with you every day. I always wonder about the little things you are doing and how I could brighten your life if you were here. By the way, have you adopted Maxie to take my place? I'm sure he's a good chap. Maxie has orders from Lieutenant Colonel Dunham to sleep at the foot of our bed. I need plenty of room with you, sweetheart.

We seem to be making progress with shelters and have stored food for the coming winter, although clothing and medical supplies are in critical demand. The destruction is hard to comprehend. Our Bavarian occupation force is quite fortunate, because we live in old German army barracks with large wood-burning stoves. I mentioned that the Orangerie was an ideal headquarters and was built over two hundred years ago for the local earl to entertain in style. My office is a bit drafty because I gave the staff orders for some of the roof tiles to be removed for home repairs in the city. It was badly bombed, including the surrounding area. Can't believe it, two months have passed, only eight more until my tour ends. I think about you and miss you more every day. Will write tomorrow.

My love always,
Alex

Sergeant Jackson and Corporal Dunne arranged chairs in a large circle of an adjoining room at headquarters. The Corporal served mugs of brewed American coffee as the group of newly appointed city officials, several doctors, school directors, the clergy, and their *Bürgermeister* gathered for the weekly meeting with Alex.

Pastor Friedrich Örtel spoke in halting English. *"Herr Oberst, der* coffee here *mit* milk *und* sugar, it goes so *gut. Und der Duft*, it makes you give me more, *ja?"* They all agreed the taste and smell of genuine coffee was an unexpected luxury, lending congeniality to the meeting.

Alex spoke in German and was flanked by a Lieutenant who took notes. "Good morning, gentlemen. I am pleased you are all in attendance as I ordered. The influx of refugees from eastern Germany has dramatically increased during the last several months, and overcrowding, sanitation, and health problems are reaching alarming proportions. I want each of you to accommodate these desperate people in any type of housing facility available, whether it is the hospital, schools, church rectories, or nearby farms and families in Oberburg who can offer them shelter. This is of the highest priority, and our headquarters will offer needed assistance. Essential medicines, food, and surplus army clothing should arrive from Nuremberg. Do you appreciate the urgency of this situation?"

Several civilian leaders indicated they wished to speak, but *Bürgermeister* Gunther Lang responded first. "Colonel Dunham, I shall organize those present to provide and share necessary shelter and we will set up a station to collect extra clothing and blankets that might be available. Young people will be sent to the nearby forests to cut trees and distribute wood for the coming winter. As you may imagine, *mein Herr*, adequate food and medicine are the most critical needs."

"Herr Lang, my staff and I have inspected the rail line to Nuremberg each day, and it should be operational before the first snowfall. Army doctors and nurses will visit your hospital every week for immunization and care for the more serious medical and surgical cases. I have good news. Food staples have been

flown into Nuremberg and, fortunately, are sufficient for the next four months. My thanks for your cooperation, gentlemen, and until next week."

Alex began a friendly conversation with the haggard senior assembly who warmed themselves near the tile stove. As the group was ready to leave, Pastor Örtel suggested to his colleagues that the church and rectory were available as a collecting headquarters and distribution center.

"May I remind you, our churches can also provide refuge for two hundred people during the coming winter. We must organize all of our collective resources to help one another. You realize, success is possible with Colonel Dunham's assistance, because we have already survived this terrible war."

As the group dispersed, Alex continued the conversation. "You have been most generous, Pastor, and I had planned to attend your services. However, pressing responsibilities have consumed my days and off-duty hours. It would be a pleasure to speak with you when you have free time."

"Son, I will see you some evening, if you wish," Örtel offered. "Would next week be convenient?"

"I shall come to your rectory. Major Carlson will make arrangements Pastor, ich werde Kaffee und etwas Brot bringen."

"Until next week, *auf Wiedersehn, Herr Oberst.*"

Alex watched the pastor pour the coffee into a kettle. It was heating on a small wood stove in the kitchen, which was the only warm room in the rectory. He cut a loaf of dark bread into thick slices spread with cooked goose fat, ate a salted potato, and sipped the black coffee. A sumptuous dinner for Örtel.

Alex sat near the stove. "I understand you were stationed in Russia and managed to escape to the west. You were fortunate and now you are serving your parish trying to cope with the devastation."

"Yes, Colonel, I was born and lived in Oberburg during the years before the war. I know the people and their spiritual and physical needs."

As Örtel rose to stoke the fire, Alex noticed his drawn, prematurely aged face. His white collar was slightly soiled, visible above the edge of his overcoat, held together by a tattered leather army belt.

"How long were you on the Eastern Front, Pastor?"

"I was an army chaplain for two years during the last great battles and long retreat. We made our way through Hungary and Czechoslovakia to the American lines only kilometers ahead of the Russians. Colonel, those were bad days. The fighting and loss of life were frightening. God has spared me to help my people. I give thanks each day. Enough of that. You're a *Fallschirm-jäger*; that's a paratrooper, isn't it? Where's your home?"

"Quite correct, an Airborne Infantry officer, and my home and new wife are in Chicago. Have you ever heard of it?"

"Oh, yes, that's the city in the middle of America on a big lake. Must be like Hamburg and Bremerhaven used to be. I imagine you also have beautiful churches, art galleries, and an orchestra."

Alex grinned—no mention of gangsters—then finished his coffee and another slice of dark bread spread with *Ersatz* paté. "You know Pastor, I've never eaten this, not foie gras, but it's surprisingly appetizing. These past three months have been a good lesson for me. I have seen the destruction in Oberburg and the rest of Bavaria, and while it will take years to rebuild, the people are energetic, industrious in many different ways. Perhaps my help will be a compensation for the suffering I have caused during this ugly war. You understand, Pastor, at times I worry, often become despondent over the sacrifice and death of my men."

As they walked to the door, Örtel shook hands. "Yes, son, every good deed is known by the Lord, and He has already forgiven you. I am your friend and sincerely hope you come to our services. Speak with me whenever you wish. It would be my honor to listen, offer you advice."

Alex heard the pastor bolt the rectory door, then walked up the hill to the officers' quarters. There were distant songs and casual laughter from an unseen *Bierstube*. He occasionally stubbed his boots on the uneven wet cobblestones, sparkling under dim street lamps, whose light was filtered through falling snow.

A humdrum of conversation surrounded Alex as he made his morning tour on the ground floor of the Orangerie, where refugees were being interviewed by a small group of civilians and several of his German-speaking staff. The large area was formerly a ballroom, whose elaborate parquet floors were stained by footprints from a multitude of refugees and displaced persons. Alex thought orderliness dictated that the flooring be repaired and waxed to promote confidence and dignity at head-quarters. He was pleased with the temporary wooden partitions separating the enormous room into small cubicles that provided a semblance of privacy.

The voice of the young Lieutenant was intimidating. "*Familie von Ravenstein*, you must understand that the hospital is overcrowded now. There are absolutely no beds today. The medical staff can only see patients who are urgently ill."

"Herr Leutnant." A young woman spoke. "My father has a high fever, and there is terrible-smelling yellow pus coming out of his leg. He is in great pain; please understand."

"Fräulein von Ravenstein, rules are rules in the army, as your father knows. I am not authorized to make exceptions."

Alex moved toward the desk and stood behind a tall, thin figure waiting between a seated elderly couple.

"Good morning, Colonel Dunham." The Lieutenant rose. "We have a problem here, sir."

My entire command is aware of that fact, Lieutenant. Perhaps a chair for Fräulein?"

The officer answered, "von Ravenstein."

"Carry on, Lieutenant. There is a situation in the motor pool that requires your attention."

He thumbed through the family's *Ausweise* and the General's *Wehrpass*. General Walter von Ravenstein, age fifty-four, commander 10th Panzer Armee, *Kriegschulen* Potsdam and Dresden, decorated with the Pour Le Merite, World War I. Wounded in Russia 10-5-194_, compound fracture of left femur, chronic infection. Hilda (*Gattin*) age fifty-two and Elisa (*Tochter*) age twenty-two.

Softened light from the green glass of the desk lamp

reflected on their faces, a composite of anxiety, despair, and fear. He noticed the young woman's callused hands and gray wool dress with sleeves hanging over her wrists. Dark, wavy hair accentuated high cheekbones, a fair complexion, and full lips. He put down his pen. Here were the Pfeiffers, he thought. A different time, a different place, but the Pfeiffers, displaced, forlorn, sick, and hungry. They needed help. A doctor with the expertise of D3.

"General von Ravenstein, arrangements have been made for you to be examined by our army surgeon this afternoon. He comes to the hospital today, and I will personally speak with him about your medical problem. Transportation will be arranged, and while you are waiting keep warm near the large stove at the south entrance. *Alles Gute* and perhaps someday we can discuss your armored operations on the Eastern Front."

The General had a military bearing and bowed his head slightly. Frau von Ravenstein held her husband's arm, smiled, and reached for Alex's hand.

Elisa von Ravenstein was formal as her deep voice expressed relief. "Your kindness is greatly appreciated by my mother and father, and may God bless your good work. Again, Colonel, thank you."

Their eyes met briefly with warm, almost sensual understanding. Her youthful beauty and serenity distracted him.

"Es ist gern geschehn, Fräulein." Alex answered that it was his pleasure.

Several weeks later, Sergeant Jackson stood at attention before Alex's desk. He put down his pen. "At ease, Jackson. Any problems with the rail line?"

Jackson smirked. "Well, sir, as they used to say on the radio at home, 'There's good news tonight'."

"And, Sergeant, exactly what does that mean?"

"In my refined judgment, sir, the best-looking Fräulein in Germany is waiting to speak with you."

"With me, Jackson? What's this all about?"

"It shall be my pleasure to introduce Fräulein Elisa von Ravenstein to the Colonel."

Alex flushed. "Yes, we have already met and discussed her father's problems. Did you know he was a General who was wounded in Russia?"

"Sir, and I thought I could arrange a pleasant evening for you with the Fräulein. It must get pretty dull up there at officers' quarters. Follow me, sir?"

"Very well, Sergeant, you have made your point. Show her in. Jackson, check each of my file cabinets in the corner. I need these records this afternoon."

When she entered, Alex drew a chair in front of his desk. "It is a pleasure to see you again, Fräulein. Please be seated." He thought the war had not affected her youthful, refreshing approach. Her smile was cheerful as she sat holding a fishnet bag filled with a paper-wrapped package.

"Guten Tag, Herr Oberst. Please excuse the interruption. My mother thought you would enjoy this home-cooked soup and a loaf of bread. We're grateful for your generosity, and *mein Papa* improves with each day." She spoke without dialect. "The doctors have treated him with great skill and consideration."

"I'm delighted the General is recovering, and perhaps one of these days we could discuss life before the war."

"Thank you again, Colonel Dunham. My parents would be pleased to entertain you at some time in the future."

She placed the package on the corner of his desk and then rolled the netted bag. "Auf Wiedersehn bis zum nächsten Mal." She hoped that they would meet again. Jackson opened the door and she left.

Alex remained standing and pushed his gold wedding band into the base of his finger until it ached. He knew the von Ravensteins were aristocracy from the east, enduring hardships with thousands of other unfortunate families. Again, then again, he would hear Stephanie speak of redemption, faith. Now she was near him. . . . *Alex, it is there for your acceptance and true belief.*

Jackson and Alex worked late into the evening. "Let's not forget the bread and soup that Fräulein von Ravenstein brought, Colonel; we're both starved."

Alex thought it was filling and unusually flavored. He wiped the crumbs on his handkerchief and thought of Steffi's cooking in the north woods, then opened a familiar letter:

From the desk of Dr. Brian Dunham:

Dear Alex,

Lucky and I had dinner with Steffi and the Pfeiffers and they spoke of the reopening of the rail line to Nuremberg. It must have been gratifying for you and your staff. General Gibson told us we are sending enormous amounts of food and supplies and now part of this help will reach your zone for distribution. It sounds as though you are doing a worthwhile job. Steffi mentioned your interest in law school. That's a first-rate idea, as law school provides a sound grounding for international affairs. We haven't heard from you for several months. Lucky has sent along a Christmas box. Take care of yourself.

> *Yours,*
> *D3*

St. Johannis was cold, dank. Alex felt snow from the collar and shoulders of his greatcoat drip down his sleeves onto his hands, an annoying diversion as he listened, absorbed in Pastor Örtel's sermon.

"God's forgiveness to us and our forgiveness of others are without condition. Remember when He forgives us, He accepts us for what we are, sometimes distorted, ugly, subject to violent, compulsive acts." There was a fullness to his voice. "Too often we are arrogant, selfish, and cruel. These transgressions are a struggle to preserve the image we have of ourselves. God understands our sins because He knows our weaknesses, and when we trespass we have failed to love Him and realize He loves each of us. For example, if we kill in rage, destroy our enemies for survival"—Örtel looked toward Alex—"He embraces those of us who are truly repentant and willing to accept Him." The pastor opened his arms. "May God guide and keep you during these trying days, and may you always seek His compassion and love."

As Alex walked to his pew after communion, he noticed the von Ravenstein family, who nodded at his tall, lean figure. They waited for him on the steps of the church.

Frau von Ravenstein spoke first. "I wish we could have sent more food, Herr Oberst Dunham. You realize times are hard."

"Good morning." Alex shook their thinly gloved hands. "Fräulein von Ravenstein was kind to bring your delicious home-cooked dinner. I appreciate your thoughtfulness. I shared it with my Sergeant." He looked at the three, feeling a stabbing longing for Steffi and the Pfeiffers. "The snow must be early this year. Perhaps a hard winter ahead."

"Colonel, I have improved beyond expectations after many months of discomfort from the infection, which interfered with my walking," the General said. "Would you join us for supper at your convenience? It would be our honor and pleasure."

Alex glanced at Elisa, who wore a black wool babushka dusted with snowflakes. They followed the congregation down the grooved stairs to the town square. He escorted them along a bombed-out street near the rectory. "Do let me drive the family home. It would be my pleasure, Frau von Ravenstein."

The General sat with him in the front seat of the snow-covered jeep. "Now, directions, Herr General." After a circuitous drive, they reached a faded yellow apartment building near the edge of town. The four stood briefly at the entrance.

As he opened the gate, he felt the cold metal through his gloves. "I accept your hospitality. Would the middle of the week be satisfactory?" Alex was aware Elisa had been watching him, smiling faintly when he spoke. She avoided his glance.

The General stepped out of the jeep. "Colonel, my wife is an excellent cook and, with Lisel, won't disappoint you. Until *Mittwoch*, then."

After Alex and Jackson supervised the unloading of food and medical supplies for distribution at the military depot near the station, they returned to headquarters, where Captain Hank Carlson was waiting with a metal cart stacked with reports and additional civilian requests. Alex felt it was his good fortune to work with a congenial aide, a feeling often tinged with sadness. He was the surviving officer of his battalion's first team. A Corporal brought a tray of sandwiches, soup, and tea.

"By the way, Alex, don't forget your mail. It arrived early this morning with some of the dispatches from Frankfurt." Carlson pointed to the sorted mail.

Alex recognized Steffi's distinctive script, then tore open the envelope.

My dearest Alex,

I have the most wonderful news for you, sweetheart. Alex, imagine, our baby will be born in about seven months. I have been to the doctor several times, and everything is fine. Sometimes I feel a little sick in the morning, but that goes away quickly because I'm so happy for us. I'm absolutely sure he will look like you, and please start thinking of a name for our son. One or two girls' names in case my intuition is wrong, but remember, aren't I always right?

Mother and I are planning a small nursery in our apartment, and it will be a delight to decorate it. Blue, of course. I know how happy you will be for us. Please hurry home; I'm overjoyed and excited. Having a child has always been our hope and dream.

With the excitement and good news, I haven't asked about your work. I know all goes well. More tomorrow.

P.S. I think "little Alex" would be perfect, don't you?

> *Your loving wife,*
> *Steffi*

Alex rose, waving his letter, and knocked over his chair.

"What is it, Alex? Must be tremendous news." Carlson was laughing.

"Hank, Hank, you won't believe it; we're having a baby in June. I wish you had met Steffi; she's the most marvelous wife in the world. Take my job. I want to be with her now. It's difficult to wait until then."

Carlson hugged his commanding officer. Both laughed and cavorted about the office.

"Alex, I have a great idea. Where's Jackson, that incomparable source of food and drink?"

Jackson stood at the door of Alex's office listening to the conversation and watching the two usually formal officers act like schoolboys.

"Sir, you don't have to ask; I have a bottle tucked away at the barracks. Brought it all the way from Paris. Best bottle of champagne in Germany. It's time for you to celebrate over the good news about the Colonel's son. Give me thirty minutes; then you can toast the young man and his mother. We go off duty about that time, anyway."

HEADQUARTERS UNITED STATES MILITARY OPERATION FORCE
A.P.O. 7599
121145– 1755– HUSMOF– BAVGER–

TO: MRS. STEPHANIE D. DUNHAM
FROM: LT. COLONEL ALEXANDER C. DUNHAM
RE: A. C. DUNHAM II

WHAT WONDERFUL NEWS STOP OUR FONDEST WISH COME TRUE STOP
ALEX EXCELLENT STOP IN EMERGENCY ELIZABETH STOP YOU MUST KEEP
HEALTHY STOP CONSTANTLY WITH BOTH OF YOU STOP LOVE TO MY DEAR
WIFE STOP LETTER FOLLOWS STOP ALEX

AMEMWAM: LT. COL. DUNHAM, C.O.
504 DET. COM.

Alex stomped the snow from his boots and brushed his coat before entering the apartment building. It had been spared from total destruction. Nearby bomb blasts had chipped large pieces of stucco and torn deep cracks in the walls. As he looked up in the early evening darkness, he saw machine-gun bullet tracks that had raked the wooden cornice.

After ringing the shrill doorbell, he was met by Frau von Ravenstein, who wore a long, dark gown with silk tassels that almost reached her ankles.

Her greeting was *herzlich*: "*Guten Abend*, Colonel. *Willkom-*

men zu unserem Haus." She took his coat and overseas cap, carefully hanging them in the hall alcove.

The General sat in a deep chair whose velveteen nap had faded over the years. He made an effort to rise, but Alex quickly approached, extending his hand.

"General von Ravenstein, it is a pleasure to be with you and your family. A bottle of red wine will warm us on this frigid winter evening. Your home is far more comfortable than some of our billets over the years, agreed?"

Elisa had come from the kitchen and stood behind her father's chair, hands on the shoulders of his worn, threadbare dinner jacket. His pants were from another suit, but his bow tie was centered neatly between his wing-tipped formal collar. She wore a dark green sweater over her long, form-fitting dinner dress, stylish before the war.

Alex sensed they were a proud, harmonious family.

"Quite correct, Colonel; the wine and our coal stove will cheer us tonight, along with good conversation." The General motioned to Alex. "Do be seated. Now, Lisel, help Mama in the kitchen." Alex was aware of his naturally abrupt but amiable manner.

"You have organized your staff well, Colonel Dunham. Within three months we have been supplied with food, more clothing, shelter, and the hospital has treated large numbers of patients. The people in Oberburg admire your hard work and discipline. But now, it's time for dinner. The women have a pleasant surprise: *Hasenpfeffer*, potato dumplings, and stewed red cabbage."

As they walked together into the small dining room, Alex noticed pictures of two young men in Wehrmacht uniforms on a table in the living room.

Alex seated Elisa. The General kissed his wife, then nodded to his daughter.

"Heavenly Father." Her voice was solemn. "We thank you for this food, our home and health, and ask that better days are coming for our people. Each day we pray for our beloved Otto and Kurt, their eternal peace and happiness. Amen."

Alex clenched his hands, slowly lifted his head, and looked

between two burnt-down candles in tarnished, dented brass holders. *Is T. Harrington Clarke here somewhere? Clarke, you miserable bastard. You always had the soft life, and tonight I'll make you suffer. Yes, I would cut off your fifty-dollar shoes and make you walk barefoot in the ice and snow until you begged to give the people of this city every last one of your fucking copper pennies. Now, Clarke, bleed for the suffering of these people, the deaths of my men.*

With a benign smile, Alex turned to his hostess. "It's a superb dish, Frau von Ravenstein. Please accept my compliments."

"Colonel, this is rabbit stew and I'm glad it suits you." Frau von Ravenstein passed a small serving dish of horseradish. "The General has been able to hunt lately, as he did on our estate before the war. You know, I think Lisel misses our old, spacious home more than Walter and I. She keeps occupied with her work at St. Johannis. This helps her forget those days, doesn't it, Lisel?"

"It helps, but I still remember our beautiful house, long walks and special places in the country with its peaceful surroundings. The fragrance of our springtime and summer flowers was everywhere. And then my two—"

"That's enough, Lisel, my dear." The General spoke firmly. "It's time for Colonel Dunham and me to discuss other matters. Would you and Mama bring our wine and pudding after you clear the table?"

Alex followed von Ravenstein to the living room, where he lit his pipe. "By the way, General, may I ask what tobacco you're using?" Dunham smiled. "It's not only making me cough, but now my eyes are burning."

"Interesting smoke." Von Ravenstein chuckled. "A friend gave me a pinch of tobacco and I mixed it with some dried oak leaves. Makes for an unusual aroma, wouldn't you agree?"

"Unusual, indeed, *Herr General*, but before the holidays I'll requisition some cartons of cigarettes and you can enjoy some real tobacco."

The General stroked his pipe, looking at it fondly. "You

know, Dunham, this friend of mine has seen the good and bad days with me. We were still riding the tide until the panzer battle at Viorsk. We had outstanding men and equipment, but rather than attacking their weak flanks, I was ordered to strike at the stronger center protected in depth by minefields, supported by heavy artillery. I discussed this grave situation with my officers, but our decisions were overruled by the army group commander. In thirty years as a soldier, it was the one time I was tempted to disobey to save my panzer army. It was promising at first. Then our front collapsed in three days. We never regained the initiative because of casualties among experienced tank crews, junior officers, and loss of our superior equipment." He slowly shook his head. "I have never seen such carnage. Charred bodies, mangled tanks, clouds of dark smoke billowing endlessly upward. I have overcome depression because I am convinced I could have prevented the disaster. From then on it was eighteen months of retreat, defeat after defeat. However, the important matter was that we managed to fight well to the end with limited resources. It was a question of discipline and dedication. The honorable, I tell you, sir, the honorable soldiers' code is to fight against any odds in his struggle to be victorious." He put down his shiny pipe.

Alex leaned forward, hands clasped between his knees. "You are a professional soldier, General von Ravenstein. All of your life you have been dedicated to the military, the esprit of the bayonet, the camaraderie of the soldier. You have fought in both great wars and possess a certain acquired detachment that has maintained your strength as a commander. I imagine there were situations in which death would have come as a relief. While you are the soldier's soldier, skilled in warfare, I am a civilian trained and indoctrinated in combat. My final battle was fought in Holland over a year ago. Although far smaller in scope than yours, there were similarities. The planning was shoddy, impulsive. Contrary to your debacle, we were successful and accomplished our mission because of the sacrifices made by our men."

"Yes, I've heard about the *Schwerpunkt* in Holland. Brilliant attack, Colonel Dunham."

"General, I have continued to ask myself: Were the losses acceptable for the victory? How could the operation have been executed without such unnecessary casualties? My men fought with valor and remarkable courage. You have reminded me again of the importance of honor and a soldier's duty. You have helped me understand." He sat back, contemplative, and realized the problems at the Draas were not singular to his experience.

After the four had conversed about European cuisine, threats from the East, and their countries' recovery, Alex stood. "May I thank you for a hospitable evening, Frau von Ravenstein? Your dinner was delicious and the General and I had a discussion that changed some of my views. Gute Nacht, Familie von Ravenstein."

Alex followed Elisa to the apartment entrance. She was correct but friendly. "Since the rail line is open, our family would be happy to have you attend the Christkindl Markt in Nuremberg several weeks from now. It would be a memorable holiday time, one quite different from any you have ever celebrated."

"Thank you, Fräulein Elisa; I am certain my schedule would allow me to join you. Again, accept my appreciation for a wonderful evening in your home." He held her hand, then forced open the frozen gate.

After inspecting the headquarters guard of the Orangerie, Hank Carlson had coffee and a cigarette in a room richly decorated with eighteenth-century ceramic tiles. The colorful chamber had been converted into a kitchen. He checked in his revolver, pulled on his coat, and walked toward the east end, where he noticed a wedge of light beneath the door marked: "Lieutenant Colonel A. Dunham, Commanding Officer." Carlson looked at his watch. Midnight. He knocked several times, but there was no answer.

The clicking sound of the handle being pushed down on the fragile wooden door made Alex raise his head.

Carlson shook his shoulder. "Colonel, sir. What are you doing here at this late hour?"

He rubbed his eyes. "Is that you, Hank? I might ask the same question. I was trying to complete these fitness reports, food and clothing requisitions, and a letter to my wife. Why don't you turn on that chandelier? After all, we're living here like the landed gentry of several hundred years ago."

"Some coffee, sir?"

"Stop that 'sir' nonsense, Hank. Cream and sugar would be fine."

"How's your wife, Alex? I want to meet her someday and, of course, Alex Junior."

"We have a small apartment overlooking the lake. It's ideal, quiet, with a skylight. You know she's an artist. We grew up together. It's never changed, Hank; we were always in love. Steffi will be a good mother, firm, kind, and patient. Loves children. She writes every day, only six months left. What about your family? I know you're from Denver, University of Colorado, a skier. By the way, you're up for promotion, Major Carlson."

"That sounds great, but do I really deserve it?"

"Deserve it?" Alex had a pensive look. "You held the north end of the bridge while Tom Hamilton and I were trying to knock down those snipers. During this tour of duty, we couldn't have opened the rail line without your help. You're doing outstanding work managing the food distribution and communications."

"I'll be glad to do more, Alex. I'm accustomed to long hours because our family had a rough time during the depression, when I earned my tuition for college. Managed to help my father with the lumber mill, and now Mom writes that my three younger brothers are good students. We had a happy, close family, although times were hard." He grinned. "I majored in skiing. Seriously, though, it was economics and I hope to establish myself in some branch of Denver's commerce after the war. Still a small town compared to Chicago."

Alex savored his coffee. "Major, may I make a suggestion? You should meet an intelligent, attractive girl, and I should take a day away from the desk. Agreed?"

"I understand, Alex. You know, I'm not a bar fly and none of us on the staff is particularly interested in some of the local street walkers."

"Hank, I've met a wonderful family here in Oberburg, who originally came from eastern Germany. General and Frau von Ravenstein have invited me over for dinner several times and are not what you would imagine an aristocratic German army officer and his wife might be. And I think their daughter, Elisa, would be of more than passing interest to you."

Hank warmed his hands on a second cup of coffee. "Tell me more, Alex; it gets better second by second. Is she my type?"

"Here's the plan. Join us for our train trip to celebrate pre-holiday festivities at the Christkindl Markt in Nuremberg. Nothing fancy, plenty of snow and good conversation. The date has been arranged, and you'll find Elisa charming. By the way, Major, get out your German books and learn more than *ja, nein,* and *schnell machen.* Although they speak some English, sometime you might learn to say, 'Wie nett Sie heute Abend aussehen, Fräulein.' Hank, tell Lisel how attractive she is, and who knows what might happen?"

Later, they walked up the snowy street to the officers' quarters and noticed the sign of *Der Graue Wolf* swinging on its flimsy hinges blown by heavy snow and wind. The large door of the *Gasthof* opened as Alex and Carlson passed. They were greeted by the deep voice of its proprietor, Fritz Wittmann.

"Ah, gentlemen, I needed the fresh air and I find you on my doorstep. Come in from the cruel weather for *Glühwein.* Herr Oberst Dunham, it warms the stomach and frees the mind. Do join me."

Alex paused. "It would be our pleasure. Please meet my adjutant, Major Carlson." The trio walked past the crowded bar, then upstairs to his apartment.

Alex took off his coat, shook the snow on the planks of the rough floor, and moved toward the fire sipping his hot drink. He was fatigued from the cold and late hour and sat across from his friends enjoying their conversation. He looked through his wine glass at the distorted flames of the fire, relaxed and content for the moment.

Wittmann had settled in his overstuffed chair, listening to Carlson, who became more talkative as they finished a second mug of warm red wine.

The *Glühwein* heightened Carlson's affability. "Herr Wittmann, your town and this area are fortunate to have a military commander of Colonel Dunham's concern and devotion to his work. We are damned happy this war is over. You have been generous with the railroad crews, and they have told us about your hospitality, the occasional free food and drink. It helped keep up morale, and now the Nuremburg line is open."

Wittmann nodded and lifted his glass to Alex. "Prosit. Thank you, sir, for your skillful efficiency, which will bring about our return to an ordinary life. Things are not so good with the Russians, *ja?*"

"You know, Wittmann"—Carlson rubbed his hands near the fire—"the Colonel and I have had incredible luck during the last several years, and now he's beginning to forget the bad times. Directing the administration and recovery of the local provinces, helping the people here in Oberburg, and understanding the difficulties have made him more tolerant and patient. Wittmann, I feel he's a happier man."

"As it should be, Major Carlson," Wittmann replied. "The people have great regard for both of you and your men. Again, my compliments to Colonel Dunham and his command."

Alex emptied his mug. "Well, gentlemen, your praise is generous. Everyone has done his share, and returning home will be a gratifying end to our tour of duty here." Then he spoke directly to Wittmann. "Thank you once more for your hospitality, sir. Major Carlson and I have had an unexpectedly pleasant evening with you. *Gute Nacht, mein Freund*; perhaps we shall meet again under better circumstances."

Wittmann watched the bootprints of the two officers quickly fill with snow as their animated conversation faded in the winter night. He dusted flakes from his closely cropped hair and square face and saw his friends become a blur in the rapidly falling snow. Herr Fritz Wittmann, formerly *Leutnant* Wittmann, had recovered from wounds as a *Fallschirmjäger* at Monte Cassino.

He had a shrewd understanding of the style and manner of Airborne officers and knew of the American river crossing in Holland and Dunham's bravery and ordeal. But now he had seen Alex's smile, sensed his grace.

A small group of civilians and soldiers waited in a cleared area beyond the station that had not been rebuilt. It was a bitterly cold mid-December afternoon as the five-car train stopped near the passengers who clambered aboard for choice seats next to the windows. The salvaged prewar wooden coaches were dimly lit and warmed by steam ducts running below the seats along the window side. Lisel was crowded between her parents on a hard wooden seat opposite Alex and Hank Carlson.

Carlson joked, "I'd say riding western saddle was more comfortable than this early-twentieth-century imitation of a train. Remember the Lionel engines at Christmas, Alex? Not much difference."

The von Ravensteins were puzzled, but Lisel joined in the laughter.

"Elisa," Carlson admitted, "Colonel Dunham gave me orders to learn a bit of German, but it seems to me that you understand more English than we thought."

"Major, my fluency improved after attending *Gymnasium* in Switzerland," Elisa answered.

"That's fortunate for us, Elisa, but tell us *amis* about the Christmas market."

"The celebration is an old one, and before the war many vendors gathered selling Christmas cookies, sausage, and children's toys," Elisa explained. "Unfortunately, there will only be a few carollers. However, we may be surprised. It's a wonderful holiday tradition. Do you have similar customs in your hometown, Major Carlson?"

He smiled. "Not exactly, Lisel. Our bazaars are in department stores, schools, and churches. At Christmas our family skied in the Rocky Mountains, outside of Denver, which are like your Alps." He winked. "By the way, Lisel, please call me Hank."

Alex was the interpreter as the five chatted until the train reached the ruins of the Nuremberg station. Beneath a shell of steel supports, people scurried along the concrete platforms avoiding the deep fissures left by bomb blasts. In this twisted mass, a huge clock kept accurate time. They walked together along cleared pathways surrounded by rubble, remaining walls, and crumbling chimneys.

Hank casually remarked to Alex, "Looks like our boys in the Eighth Air Force really did a number here. Snow actually softens the harshness."

Lisel stopped in front of her parents and the two officers. "The bells at St. Lorenz are pealing for vespers now, and we should go in."

They walked down the nave, but evening prayers were being held in an apse whose cobalt stained glass somehow had been spared from the air raids. Their implausible survival made the cold less intense. Without comment, Frau von Ravenstein passed her ragged fur muff among her family to warm their hands. As Alex sang the closing words of a hymn, he thought the jubilant voices of the small gathering were more powerful than the shattering sound of bombs that had devastated the cathedral.

They walked to St. Marienplatz after church.

"My friends, some Christmas huts, they are here for all of us." Elisa led Hank to one of the booths. "Look at the lanterns and candles, and there they are, some cookies, the wonderful smell of Christmas."

Hank was delighted by the scent of spices and bought two cinnamon hearts threaded with a red ribbon and hung one around Lisel's neck, then gave the other to her mother.

She turned. "I want to keep it as a memory, but I'm hungry; do you mind if I eat it? I'll save the ribbon."

Carlson bought several more for her and his friends.

Alex first heard carolling when they walked over the packed snow of the crowded square. They strolled toward the music and stood among a cheerful group gathered about the singers at the entrance of the cathedral. Alex and the von Ravensteins joined in the carol of "Ihr Kinderlein kommet; oh kommet doch all . . ." "Children come; please all gather to view the birth of Christ." It had been three years since he and Steffi had enjoyed Christmas together, and while he sang, the happiness of the words and melody were the promises of a family for him and his wife. When the choir finished several hymns, he saw Hank standing behind Elisa. She leaned against him.

"Lisel, it was fun to hum along, but the words escaped me." He was more intent. "You realize I need a teacher who can give me lessons each day."

She smiled temptingly. "As you say, Major, for you to be a good student in German I must, indeed, see you every day. Sie sehen heute Abend sehr nett aus. You look handsome this evening, Major."

He laughed. "But, Lisel, that's exactly what Alex taught me to say to you."

A cardboard sign advertising hot sausages attracted their attention as they trudged through the snow toward the station. The merchant was accommodating and sold Alex several more, perhaps because he spoke German. They hurried along the platform to the waiting train, which blew small clouds of steam into the raw night air. After huddling for warmth, they feasted on the sausage and rolls as the train lurched and bumped its way back to Oberburg. When they reached Alex's jeep, he gave the keys to Hank, who drove the von Ravensteins to their apartment through the snow and wind.

Frau von Ravenstein extended the invitation: "It's cold and icy; why don't you spent the night on our sofa, Major Carlson?" Hank needed no persuasion and slept contentedly, wrapped in a patched quilt. He congratulated himself. It was a luxury compared to the previous Christmas in the Ardennes forest.

After the holidays, Alex received a note from the General suggesting that February would be a good month to hunt rabbit and deer in the Fichtelgebirge, a forest northeast of Oberburg. They met later. "Colonel would you have the time for relaxation over the coming weekend? The weather promises to be bright and clear, without snowfall."

"General, I need exercise, more fresh air, and there might be several good meals in the offing. You know the country roads. Be

my navigator. Will pick you up at five o'clock Saturday morning."
That was agreeable to von Ravenstein.

They were perched on two large rocks overlooking a broad meadow where the General pointed to rabbit and deer tracks. Alex quietly attached a telescopic sight to his Garand M-1 rifle. The General had a .22 rifle for rabbits. It was boot-deep snow.

"Colonel, this is more like it. Good, bright Bavarian winter sun. No wind. Not Russia. Take the twenty-two; you have the first shot. We'll see how good you are."

After a chilling wait, two rabbits chased one another across the far end of the field, bounding along the surface of the snow. Alex fired, missed, then quickly passed the rifle to the General, who knocked one down.

Alex lifted up the prey. "*Gute Jagd*, General. I'll be your bird dog, and then we can move on."

They bagged four rabbits. "I've noticed the deer tracks lead across the valley to the next rise," the General said. "They are looking for berries or grass. You see those two newly felled trees about a kilometer on the left? We can have some cheese and bread while we wait for the deer. Sound like a good idea?"

They sat on one end of a log partially protected by scrub pine as the General unpacked lunch and leisurely began to eat. Without warning, their conversation was interrupted by a series of shots splintering the bark of a nearby tree. Both dived in the deep snow for cover between the tree trunks.

"There must be other hunters up here." The General looked cautiously over the snowbank. "But I don't understand; there are no deer close to us. They should be more careful; it's open country with good visibility. We must stay flat, no movement, and wait."

Alex removed the telescopic sight and carefully scanned the general direction of the firing when two more shots chipped branches off the logs.

"General," Alex spoke with assurance. "It's not deer they want; perhaps we're their game. Here, take a look at our hunters. They're bold, wearing black pants and coats, moving in the open on that hill above us. Their uniforms make a clear target against the snow."

Von Ravenstein took the telescopic sight. "*Ja, Herr Oberst,* we may have trouble here. Those are SS uniforms with the insignia removed, but they wear the scabbards with knives and one has a rifle. I see three of them. They look young, and I hope they are nervous. Who knows? They may have been hiding in these mountains for several months."

"Well, my good friend, anyone who fires at us must pay a price. Give me the telescopic sight for my rifle, and we'll shave some hair off their heads. Stay where you are. I'll move to the left and give them a little surprise. They won't suspect that I'm behind that boulder over there."

After steadying himself in the snow and bracing his Garand on the edge of the large rock, Alex fired, spraying snow around their feet. The one carrying the rifle, hit in the leg, screamed, "Nicht wieder schiessen." He wanted the firing to stop and dropped his weapon. The three SS men were unaware Alex had moved closer and slightly to their rear. He waved to the General to stand and approach them.

Von Ravenstein warily climbed the short ridge. "Dammit all, why did you shoot at us? You must know the war is over. What are you doing here wearing those uniforms? I want an answer now. You were SS, weren't you? From your age, Hitlerjugend. Was it the 12th SS Panzer Division?"

The General turned quickly, slipped on some ice, and fell to his knees as one of the black uniformed intruders threw his knife. Alex was surprised by the older man's agility as he rolled in the snow, then drew his Parabella service revolver, firing over the head of his would-be assassin. Alex felt the old rage, the exhilaration, as he ran toward the three, shouting. "Drop your weapons, and if you move again, you're dead. *Hände hoch.*" They slowly raised their arms.

After plodding through the heavy snow, von Ravenstein watched Alex tear off their belts and slash each renegade across the face. Blood streamed from their lips and noses. When he confiscated their weapons, he felt the old, pitiless rage. "Now, you little bastards, take off your boots and pants, *schnell, schnell.*" They defiantly threw their uniforms in a pile at his feet.

"Dunham, I know they're SS, but let me prove it to you." The General stepped forward, ripped open one of their jackets, and pointed to the tattoo in the left armpit. "There it is, Colonel. They must be arrested."

Alex tied their wrists. Their fingers became blue as he tightened the leather belts, then pushed them through the snow to the jeep, where they were stacked on top of each other against frozen metal. Von Ravenstein guarded them with his drawn revolver. The three had not spoken since their capture, then began to cry out like frostbitten animals before they were driven to the army brig near the outskirts of Oberburg.

It was late afternoon when the jeep drew up to the front of the von Ravensteins' apartment. Hank Carlson and Elisa, opening the gate, were talkative and jovial. "Well, it looks like a few rabbits, but where's the big game, General?"

"Quite so, Carlson." The General unbuttoned his leather coat. "Bigger game. We bagged some wild, talking animals seldom seen in our forests. I would guess they are being cared for in their cages at this very moment. Wouldn't you agree, Colonel Dunham?"

Alex climbed into the jeep. "Until next week, General, and I assure you our hunting will be more pleasant, perhaps not as challenging."

During mid-May, Alex and Lieutenant Grey reviewed and updated files, reports, and personnel records so the transition of command to Hank Carlson would be efficient. Their bureaucratic routine was interrupted by the otherwise militarily correct Carlson, who briskly opened the door.

At first he was more formal in the presence of the young officer. "Sir, I would like to have a word with you immediately." He grinned. "It's more a matter of life than death."

Alex nodded at Grey. "We'll finish up after lunch. The Major apparently has some pressing military matters to discuss."

"That's right, sir; it's one of the most important events a man can discuss with his brother officer."

"Well, well, Hank, try sitting down. You can think better

when you're not jumping around like a grasshopper. You haven't been as excited since I learned I was becoming a father."

"But, Alex, Lisel and I are going to be married. It's the greatest thing since the war ended, and I proposed to her in German; can you imagine that? Will you be my best man?"

"Marvelous news, Hank. Absolutely wonderful. You two are a perfect pair, and of course I'd be honored to be your best man. She's a fine young woman, and those weekend skiing trips down at the Zugspitze must have convinced her you are the one." Alex smiled. "The best of wishes to you and Lisel. When is the great day? Has to be within the month, before I return to the States."

"We've asked Pastor Örtel to perform the ceremony in early June. He's spoken to both of us, and although we've only known one another six or seven months, we're certain of what we want."

"I've watched both of you, and it's that sixth sense of mine, *Fingerspitzengefühl*, that says it will be a long and happy life. I'll be on time and won't lose the ring. Let's call in Sergeant Jackson and see if he can arrange another impromptu celebration."

After toasting and chatting: "I should be on my way now. A quick inspection, then Lisel and I have arranged a treat for the family. Jackson has put in another of his infamous requisitions. He's a damn genius. Somehow he found a ham and the trimmings for our dinner tonight. We expect you, Alex."

"I'll be there at seven. I can find a special wedding gift in the next several days. A trip to the new P.X. should do it." Alex joked, "How about cookware, you know, pots and pans, so you can help Lisel in the kitchen?"

While Jackson typed orders of the day, Alex opened his mail:

From the desk of Dr. Brian Dunham:

Dear Alex,

Lucky and I enjoyed your letter, and it won't be long before you're home for good. We both look forward to seeing you and getting news about what's happening in Germany and your command. Steffi is fine, and Harold Webster is looking after her. Her weight and blood pressure are normal, and the baby is kicking and has a good-sounding heart. I never actually thought of myself as a grandfather. The idea strikes me as being topnotch. I'll get busy and enroll him at the Academy and Princeton. How's that sound, Son? Lucky and I send our love. Take care of yourself.

Yours,
D3

Pastor Örtel welcomed Elisa, Hank, and their guests to the rectory. "In another year I am certain your wedding reception would have been more elaborate. For now, Sergeant Jackson and the Colonel have kindly brought all of us tea and this lovely cake, for which we are thankful."

Jackson smiled as he spoke to the small party. "Pastor, it's probably safer to toast with tea than some of the after-shave lotion that supply tells us is champagne. I feel honored to be here and wish the newlyweds happiness."

The small group applauded and General von Ravenstein kissed Elisa. "*Mein Liebchen,* Mother and I are delighted for you and Henry. Although we are saddened to lose you, we shall plan to visit when things are better. It is good you have married a fine American officer. This is a little step in bringing all of us together again in a happier world." The General lifted his delicate chipped teacup, "Prosit. And good times for the future."

Alex was amused. The incorrigible Jackson had "borrowed" a command passenger car for the morning and drove the von Ravensteins home, then took the married couple to the motor pool, where a jeep was waiting. It was packed with a small army tent and some provisions. Hank had planned a week of camping and fishing at the "General's lake," where he and Alex had fished during the spring. As they left the rectory, Alex felt the excitement of his own honeymoon. He remained behind with Örtel.

Over the months, they worked in a spirit of camaraderie. "Pastor, I am pleased that our understanding has allowed us to solve problems peculiar to the occupation. Your people and our command have cooperated with democratic energy. Again, my deep thanks for the splendid ceremony. It was as if Stephanie and I were being married again."

"I'm happy for the married couple and for you, because I believe you are beginning to accept forgiveness. Remember, you cannot be forever burdened with the guilt for obeying orders. Be proud you have served your country and guided us in our attempts to recover."

"Pastor Örtel, I feel better about myself each day; however, there are lapses when my anger is difficult to manage."

"Son, all of us have heard the story. Those SS men you treated harshly several weeks ago must learn from hard experience to become decent citizens. They tried to kill you and the General, and punishment must be their lot."

"Thank you for your help, Pastor. Next time I go fishing up at the General's lake, I'll bring back some trout for you."

"Good day, Alex. *Gott behüte Dich.*"

My dearest husband,

I saw Dr. Webster this morning, and he said the baby is due in the middle of July. You know sometimes they are wrong. When the baby is born, you will be home with me. I walk every day and sit at our favorite fountain talking to the baby about you, and I imagine he knows all about his father by now. I can only guess, but you will probably fly to New York, and then please call me. The arrival party will be waiting for you, my handsome soldier. Hope you won't mind, because I look as though there is a pumpkin in my dress. You can't possibly mistake me for someone else. I know you'll help me lose weight after I leave the hospital. By the way, Dr. Brian is quite overwhelmed with the idea of being a grandfather. Isn't that wonderful?

Not much more news for now. I'll write again before you leave Germany. Hank and Elisa sound like an adorable couple, and we can entertain them when they return on their way to Denver.

Little Alex and I send our love and kisses to you.

Always love you, my dear Alex,
Steffi

Alex sat in the back of a small fishing boat and was wrapped in the warmth of early morning sun that shone off the lake's surface, rippled by a soft breeze. He leaned against his folded sweater in the stern with his feet braced against one of the bottom ribs. His fishing rod bowed occasionally, which made him tighten his grip on the cork handle and reel. The forest was silent; nothing moved. He was entranced by the majesty of the Alpine conifers that reached into a blue, cloudless sky. The quiet and serenity lulled him into a dreamlike state as he leisurely gazed into the sky and the depth of the water.

His thoughts, scrambled with memories, were erratic.

It's difficult to imagine that I only have a week before I leave for home. I wonder how I was able to sleep last night knowing I will see Steffi and the baby soon. Never want to have another batch of those dried-up army pancakes; they hit your stomach like a brick. Looking forward to her fluffy stack, warm butter, maple syrup. Where are you this morning, Steffi? One of your letters said you feel the baby moving, and now I want to put my hand on your tummy and kiss you. It's almost been a year, and I can see the blueness of your eyes, and your blondness.

The motor pool washed down my jeep yesterday. They got the mud off the windshield. Thanks, Corporal Jones. He's a damn good soldier and made certain my BAR never jammed, and I mean never jammed. Who makes the jeep anyway? Suppose it's General Motors; no, that's not right. It's an outfit called Willys-Knight. The army's most used vehicle runs like a clock. This morning I remember coming up the unpaved road to General von Ravenstein's lake, like Grant took Richmond. Yes, it was Grant, not that shit Sherman. I had to stop a minute and take a leak, and I was careful not to spray the spring flowers or my boots. Getting warmer, so off with the field jacket. If I'm hot here, it must be sweltering at home.

Steffi, it's wonderful how this lake reminds me of the one at your ranch in Colorado, though it's much larger. All right, Dunham, let's get organized. It's about ten o'clock. Hank is bringing butter and potatoes. Lisel knows where the road ends. That's where we rent the rowboats from Herr Wehrmeyer. Looks like he was a Kraut soldier. Boats always clean and ready for the Colonel. Sometimes he's obsequious. Probably has to kiss his wife's ass. Fishing rods, lures, some live bait, net, and stringer. No question the Germans are organized, clever, and what equipment. Makes me laugh when it took Panzerfausts *to knock out their Tigers. They sure as hell did a job for us in Sicily. Now, listen,* Dunham, bridge *and* Draas *are words you never heard. Seems like the breeze is getting stronger. On with the field jacket again. Check the Garand and BAR. No more shit from the SS that's for sure. They're mean bastards. Deserved what I gave them. If it hadn't been for the General, I would have, well, you know; don't think about it. It was that old feeling again. Sometimes I can't help it.*

The sky is perfect, that Colorado, Wyoming blue, Steffi. Unbelievably peaceful. No loons in Deutschland. Sun is great, can start to troll. It's good the boys in the mess gave me a couple of doughnuts and coffee. Fresh air makes me hungry. Strange how the body works. Good, there's my fourth strike. Nice trout lunch. Should have plenty for Hank and Lisel. What a perfect couple. He's a quick learner. Not bad with German after a couple of months. Wonder how old Professor Neumann is? My favorite was Pete Starke. He always seemed to understand. I bet he got me into college. Great years with crew. Those four hundred yards across the Draas would have been easy in our shell.

Think I'll just slouch back and rest a couple of minutes. Let the trout strike if they want. Damn grateful we got the people enough food for the winter. They're working to put the pieces back together. Yes, the pieces are coming together like a huge puzzle. Hard to understand. Read too late last night. Permission to drift off a bit, Colonel Conroy. Permission granted, Dunham. . . .

How long has it been? Must have dozed off longer than I planned. How can the weather change so damn fast? Where's the sun? The water is choppy. That breeze on my face. It's more than a breeze; it's spray. Boat's rocking but not taking on water. My jacket's soaked. Oars secured. Where's the rifle and BAR? Good, right here under my legs.

What the hell's that noise? Who in his right might would be firing twenty-millimeter shells at this fucking little rowboat? Not the Draas again. Look at those shots hit the water around us. Jake, get your ass up here in the front of the boat. Shit, there's no cover. Connie, do you see what I see? It's Naughton and his men. They're in the water. They're swimming to us. Steady now, we've about reached them. I'll give you covering fire, plenty of ammo. I must keep firing. Where are my gloves? Barrel's hot. Go in after them; they're hurt. I'm emptying the BAR at the enemy on the shore. I want all of them back, do you hear me? Not one man lost. Now the Krauts are on the run. Shore is secured now. No, goddammit, you men are not listening. Bring them back. That's an order from your battalion commander. You and the rest in our boat can do it. We're safe from enemy fire. You're doing well, but I'm coming in to help you.

I'm in the water now. Start reaching for them. There, I've got Naughton, he's alive. Get the machine gunner; he's loaded down with ammo. See his head bobbing around. Jesus, where are his arms and legs? There's the Sergeant with the Panzerfaust. We need them both. I've got them. Everybody is getting to the shore. There's the little rise in the sand. That's where we'll set up shop. Kick the Krauts' asses up over their ears. Good, we've almost made it. What the hell hit me in the head? Where's the blood on my face coming from? Bad headache, spinning, all of a sudden dizzy. The water is freezing. Turn on your hot shower, Steffi. That's it, smile at me. Let me hold you. Can you believe it? All of my men are safe. Every last one made it. We're attacking now. Steffi, we'll always be together. We're on the move; we've got to hit them hard, capture the bridge.

It's all blue now; see those bubbles. They make strange noises. Probably they're mine. Where's the sun? The blue is going fast. I feel heavy. Hard to see any longer. It's more quiet, hardly a sound. Getting weaker. Letting . . . Who's reaching for me? Those gentle arms carry me now. It's been so long. Waiting all of my life. Feel the unimaginable timelessness. Now the dark is becoming brightness. Finally I know; take me, God. At last, I am yours.

The body of Lieutenant Colonel Alexander Clarke Dunham (A.U.S. Serial No. 040284. 3 Bn. 504 Regt. 82nd Abn. Div.) was recovered at 1545 hours 15 June 194__ identified by Major Henry Clay Carlson and a German civilian, Hans Wehrmeyer. Dunham was taken to Military Police Headquarters in Oberburg, then transported by rail to Frankfurt, West Germany, accompanied by a detail of five paratroopers commanded by Major Carlson. An autopsy was performed at the United States Military Hospital. The causes of death were:

1. Depressed skull fracture, left frontal bone.
2. Acute subdural hematoma, left frontal lobe.
3. Asphyxiation, secondary to drowning.

The Office of the Adjutant General sorted the personal items found on the body of Lieutenant Colonel Alexander Dunham:

1. One prayer book with smeared but legible printing: "Stephanie D. Pfeiffer."
2. One gold wedding ring with an inscription: "Stephanie– Alexander."
3. One wallet-sized photograph of a fair-haired woman, the signature illegible. The photograph's impression on its front was "DuBois" and, in smaller letters, "Chicago."
4. One wallet tied with a frayed dark velvet piece of ribbon. It contained ten American dollars. In a compartment was a small photograph of seven Airborne officers. The only legible word was "First." A dog lay at the feet of one officer. In addition, there was a crumpled picture of two young people, arms around one another. It appeared to have been taken in a small booth.
5. Fastened to a metal key chain a brass plate that read: "Everything the College Man Needs" 8691.
6. One Airborne-issue wristwatch.
7. Dog tags recording the blood type as AB; religion, Protestant. These belongings were packed with his clothing and were sent by ship to his wife.

Lieutenant Colonel Dunham's casket was flown by Military Air Transport Command to Washington, D.C., then taken by auto to the Arlington National Cemetery by order of the Commanding General of United States Occupation Forces, Berlin. The wife, Stephanie Pfeiffer Dunham, was notified of his death on 18 June.

The telegram read:

WESTERN
UNION

WA71 46 GOVT-WASHINGTON DC 27 22A   194__ 18 JUN AM 3 25
MRS STEPHANIE P. DUNHAM
1012 ASTOR COURT CHGO=

THE SECRETARY OF WAR ASKS THAT I ASSURE YOU OF HIS DEEP SYMPA-
THY IN THE LOSS OF YOUR HUSBAND LIEUTENANT COLONEL ALEXANDER
C. DUNHAM WHO DIED OF INJURIES SUSTAINED IN AN ACCIDENT IN GER-
MANY ON FIFTEEN JUNE. BURIAL AT ARLINGTON NATIONAL CEMETERY
TWENTY JUNE, 1100 HOURS. CONFIRMING LETTER FOLLOWS.
T. G. GORDON, ADJUTANT GENERAL

She read in fine print at the bottom of the telegram: "The company will appreciate suggestions from its patrons concerning its service."

It was a still, foggy morning above the Potomac. Moisture clung to the fresh leaves of scattered trees, and the grass was covered with droplets of water. Steffi saw wetness on the tips of his brown shoes and cuffless summer tans not covered by his black robe. She looked up at Father Edward Dillworth, who had made the river crossing with Alex.

The graveside ceremony was conducted with routine military precision. The Twenty-third Psalm, the sharp sound of a rifle volley, and lingering Taps. Steffi watched in disbelief as the honor guard held the taut flag over the casket. A series of white-gloved hands snapped it smartly in half, then folded it swiftly into rapidly moving, increasingly thick triangles.

An officer moved toward her with the flag and placed it in her outstretched arms. She pressed it against her protruding abdomen and breasts. *Hold him tightly now.*

"Mrs. Dunham, I am General William Bedford, Commander of United States Airborne Forces."

She dropped her head slightly in recognition.

"I have known your husband from the beginning of his army career, over four years ago. He was one of our most talented and courageous officers before, during, and after the war. His unstinting leadership in Sicily, Italy, and subsequently Holland was outstanding."

She stared into the distance, and listened to a voice without intonation.

"His single-minded and determined actions at the Draas River have become legendary in the annals of Airborne combat." He moved slightly, took her arm, and led her to the side of the small white tent, away from relatives and friends. "You know, Stephanie, there are strong, brave men among us who earn honor and serve the good of the people. Their memory and courage are examples for others to perform great deeds. The world is the home of these dedicated men, whose honor lives on, without visible sign, and who are always a part of our lives."

Bedford had inspected the site of the river crossing, agonized over the losses, and read Alex's after-battle reports. He stood erect, struggling to be a realistic, matter-of-fact officer. "I shall remember you, your husband, and the child who will be born soon. All of you will have a place in my heart and mind until..." He saluted, turned, and disappeared among the small gathering.

"I'm exhausted, Dad, but can't sit still. I have to move about, walk, run, anything, but please take me back to Alex right now, please, my dear papa. I must be near him; you understand, don't you?"

Erich and Steffi were taken to the grave and marker by the Officer of the Day.

"Now, leave us alone for a while." She couldn't kneel without her father's help, then felt the dampness of the newly laid sod on her legs and feet. She shook from nauseating anguish and the misting rain. Her thoughts were aimless, disconnected. Always the same why. *Why the three of us, especially Alex? What have we done? What sins have we committed? God, why have You been cruel? I know Alex is with You. Please welcome him to Your paradise. I am lost, confused. I need Your help.*

She came back with her father once more before dark, and smoothed the fresh grass. *Let me be with you once more, Alex.*

The Pfeiffers and their daughter returned home early the next morning. The train had blue coaches with white lettering and numbers.

Several days later, she jiggled a key in the small metal door of her apartment mailbox. It was stuck again—why bother? She knew there would be nothing from Alex. There was a blue typewritten envelope.

From the desk of Dr. Brian Dunham:

Dear Steffi,

I will be with you when the baby is delivered in several weeks and you shall be a brave mother. There was little time to speak at Arlington. This should suffice. All of us miss Alex, but life must go on and someday another person will replace him, which would be normal. I didn't know all of the details of his war record or service in Germany until I received a fine letter from General Bedford and our friend Paul Gibson. We are proud of him. I think you have come to realize that my advice would have been helpful. Please call on Lucky or me at any time. All of these things are difficult to say. Perhaps my note is some consolation. Actually, we loved Alex. Time will ease the loss. If only . . .

Yours,
D3

She sat back in a large rocker, swollen feet resting on an ottoman, looking at a sketch she had done of Alex at the Academy years before. Then she walked to the window, methodically tearing the letter into shreds. They fell in a small shower like fluttering confetti.

Her atelier had a skylight with southeast exposure that illuminated the studio with changing shades of light, which gave her sketches a range of pleasing tones. There were a number of unfinished canvases with palettes. A table in the center of the room, with jars of brushes, provided the essentials for her work. Smocks were splattered with faded colors and hung on pegs behind an oversize wicker chair, where she could rest, supported by a pillow, and look at the lake, with its changing moods.

Several months after little Alex was born, her commercial sketches had been accepted by one of the larger department stores, where she was promoted to an advertising consultant. She could work at home and be with her son, and Katzie would help.

Raise him with love, gentle firmness, and discipline. No prodding, criticism with encouragement. Although he would never see his father, he would know him. Pictures and sketches. Gradually she would tell him of his father's short life, gratitude, courage, accomplishments. Already she saw a resemblance. Blond hair, blue-green eyes, other features that had drawn her to Alex. Hopes that he would experience his father's active world. She would stand at his side. The Lord had fulfilled her wish, a wish that she cherished. A son in the image of his father.

It was a warm Indian summer afternoon with only an occasional passage of refreshing air from the lakefront. Steffi opened the door, tossed her handbag toward the dresser, and threw her wrinkled dress on the bed. She was exhausted. One shoe lay near the door, the other kicked under a night-table. A shower soaked her hair and drops trickled down her face as she mixed a salad and sipped iced tea.

She pulled on a white crew shirt with crossed oars over the left breast, a faded "P" on its back, short white rowing *trous*, and slipped on tennis shoes stained with paint. She put down the beaded glass of tea, ducked into a smock, then sat on the floor leaning against the wall and looked at her largest easel. It was an unfinished penciled drawing sketched from a photograph thumb-tacked to its side. It had been taken several years previously in Sicily. Each night she searched for any detail she might have overlooked, and sometimes she was surprised by an unexpected nuance.

It was a three-quarter view of Alex against a waist-high wall. His rank was designated by a maple leaf, discernible on the front of his helmet, covered with camouflage netting. The helmet straps were unfastened, hanging at the side of his face. She could see an edge of hair, although was always drawn to his face and hands. He had several days of beard, patches of charcoal on his cheeks further darkened by dirt. She wondered about but never solved a detail. The top of his combat tunic was buttoned. The Airborne insignia was on his left shoulder, and maple leaves were stitched to cloth epaulets. A holster band ran across his chest from left to right. A weapon was not visible. There was a strap, a remaining part of parachute harness over each shoulder attached to his wide belt in front and probably in back. A canteen hung from his left hip. The sleeves were buttoned and his right hand clasped his left below the waist. She could see his jump boots were covered with dirt. His expression was confident. She imagined he was speaking or listening to someone not shown in the photograph. It was a picture of an exhausted soldier after battle, framed in time.

He appeared older. She wondered what he was thinking and had suffered. Scenes began drifting. Her lids burned with fatigue and tears. She crawled to the sofa, briefly glancing over the stillness of the lake. The quiet of evening was interrupted by distant laughter of swimmers, now and then the rumble of a starting car. The tinkling sound of a falling spoon, placed absentmindedly in the pocket of her smock, suddenly awakened her. She went to the bed and carried their long pillow with a faint odor of his hair tonic. After it faded, she would sprinkle several drops on the pillow cover.

She lay on her side and folded the pillow into her face, breasts, and thighs. Now he was here. They were alone, and she whispered, "Alex, though you will be gone only several more months, we'll write every day, and come home soon. Please complete your duties. I'll be here waiting for you."

"It's only a short time. Quick tour to help clear up some of the problems. Situations gone wrong. I know you understand, Steffi."

"Tell me, what we will call our five blue-eyed blond babies? I want them for us. Can you imagine me as a mother of our children?"

"Well, we can eliminate Brian, Erich, Luckett, and Katrina, so let's begin with Christopher, Timothy, and Nicholas. But what about little Alex? Is that all right for a beginning?"

"Any name, any name, whatever you want, Alex."

"Now that we have settled that issue, I love you. I have loved you since the first day, Steffi. By the way, Miss Pfeiffer, may I please have the next dance?"

She stood, holding her pillow. A schoolboy, tie askew, with a bowl-shaped haircut put his arm around her waist and pressed her cheek. Then the tall, lean oarsman wrapped his arms around her and she felt his flushed face and blistered hands when they slowly danced to piano music in the early morning hours after a regatta . . . before he left for the war, when she rested her head on the shoulder of his uniform. *Come home, Alex.* Finally they danced in the small crowd before dinner. He was back after three years. Safe. At last they would be married.

She was moving slowly. He was close. She felt the strength of his arms and hands. He wore a starched summer uniform with orange-and-green epaulets. The collar insignia shone. She looked down at a row of ribbons and felt the length of his body, the movement of his legs. He was with her; the certainty was strong, undeniable. Then she could hear him say, "You are my wife, dearest friend, lover. Timeless, nothing can ever . . ."

Her voice was soft; she caressed the back of his head and neck.

"Alex, of all times, it had to be now. It's the telephone. One minute, sweetheart. Please wait for me. Mother said she would call. Probably wants to know when we're bringing the baby out west to the ranch. Dear, don't you think we should leave before the cold weather?"

Acknowledgments

Although a number of characters in this book are based on people known by the author and the book includes actual events before, during, and after World War II—including combat in Sicily, Italy, and Holland during 1943 and 1944—it is important to emphasize that the story is fiction, particularly in its character portrayals, the majority of events, and some of the descriptive battle scenes.

I wish to thank Lieutenant Colonel Jerry R. Bolzak, graduate of the United States Military Academy, Class of 1975, a veteran of the 101st Airborne Division, and director of the Army Officer Education Program, Princeton University, since 1995. His knowledge of the training, indoctrination, and combat readiness of Airborne Forces has been important to the story.

Henry Blair Keep (1918–83) former Major, 3rd Battalion, 504th Regiment, 82nd Airborne Division, gave me numerous verbal descriptions and a ten-page log of his battalion's unprecedented attack across the Waal River, Nijmegen, Holland on 20 September 1944. I have been honored by his friendship and kindness.

Brigadier General George D. Eggers, Jr. (retired), formerly Chief of Staff, 7th United States Army Corps, Stuttgart, was a source of encouragement while writing this book.

I am deeply grateful to Ms. Barbara Blaesing Santler for her accounts of life in postwar Germany, expertise in German, and other invaluable contributions to the manuscript.

Dr. Carol Stillman Hart reviewed the first draft of the book with patience and understanding.

I have drawn on several important books and papers for the re-creation of training, dispositions and battles of United States Airborne Forces during World War II. The splendid autobiography of Lieutenant General James M. Gavin, *On to Berlin* (New York, N.Y., Viking Press, 1978) was helpful for battle scenarios in Sicily and Anzio. The attack across the Waal River at Nijmegen, Holland has been described in *A Bridge Too Far* (New York, N.Y., Simon and Schuster, 1974) by Cornelius Ryan, who also interviewed Major Henry B. Keep. The 504 Regimental History, *The Devils in Baggy Pants* (Paris, Draeger Frères Press, 1945) and the *History of the 82nd Airborne Division* (Atlanta, GA, Albert Love Enterprises, 1946) provided information on their combat and casualties. *Paratrooper* (New York, N.Y., St. Martin's Press, 1979) by Gerard M. Devlin, was a factual source of the inception, training, and equipment of United States Airborne Forces in World War II. Details of the function and models of the German antitank weapon were described in *Panzerfaust* (Atglen, PA, Schiffer Military/Aviation History, 1994) by Wolfgang Fleischer. The maneuvers and exercises of the newly formed Airborne units were documented in *The U.S. Army GHQ Maneuvers of 1941* (Washington, D.C., Center of Military History, United States Army, 1992) by Christopher R. Gabel. *German Paratroops in World War II* (London, Ian Allan Ltd., 1978) by Volkmar Kuhn was especially useful in describing "Operation Mercury," the first major parachute and glider operation of World War II on Crete.

Book jacket by Sprecher Design House, Santa Barbara, California.

Photograph of author by H. Ross Watson, Jr.